The Silk Vendetta

By Victoria Holt:

THE SILK VENDETTA
SECRET FOR A NIGHTINGALE
THE ROAD TO PARADISE ISLAND
THE LANDOWER LEGACY
THE TIME OF THE HUNTER'S MOON
THE DEMON LOVER
THE JUDAS KISS
THE MASK OF THE ENCHANTRESS
THE SPRING OF THE TIGER
MY ENEMY THE QUEEN
THE DEVIL ON HORSEBACK
THE PRIDE OF THE PEACOCK
LORD OF THE FAR ISLAND
THE HOUSE OF A THOUSAND LANTERNS
THE CURSE OF THE KINGS
ON THE NIGHT OF THE SEVENTH MOON
THE SHADOW OF THE LYNX
THE SECRET WOMAN
THE SHIVERING SANDS
THE QUEEN'S CONFESSION
THE KING OF THE CASTLE
MENFREYA IN THE MORNING
THE LEGEND OF THE SEVENTH VIRGIN
BRIDE OF PENDORRIC
KIRKLAND REVELS
MISTRESS OF MELLYN

THE SILK VENDETTA

Victoria Holt

DOUBLEDAY & COMPANY, INC.
GARDEN CITY, NEW YORK

CONTENTS

The Silk House

As I grew out of childhood it began to dawn on me that there was something rather mysterious about my presence in The Silk House. I did not quite belong and yet I felt a passionate attachment to the place. To me it was a source of wonder; I used to dream about all the things which had happened there and all the people who had lived in it over the centuries.

Of course, it had changed somewhat since those days. The Sallongers had changed it when Sir Francis's ancestor bought it just over a hundred years before. He it was who had renamed it The Silk House —a most incongruous name, even though there was a reason for it. I had seen some old papers which Philip Sallonger had shown me—for he shared my interest in the house—and in these the house was named as the King's Hunting Lodge. Which King? I wondered. Perhaps the wicked Rufus had come riding this way. It might have been William the Conqueror himself. Normans had loved their forests and revelled in their hunting. But that was probably going back in time a little too far.

There it proudly stood as though the trees had retreated to make room for it. There were gardens which must have been made in Tudor days. The walled one was evidence of this with red bricks enclosing the beds of herbs round the pond with the statue of Hermes poised over it as though ready for flight.

But the forest surrounded it and from the top windows one could see the magnificent trees—oak, beech and horse chestnut—so beautiful in the spring, so splendid in the summer, magnificent in the au-

tumn with their variegated coloured leaves just before they fell making
a carpet for our feet through which we loved to shuffle noisily; but
none the less beautiful when the winter denuded them of their foliage
and they made intriguing patterns against the grey and often stormy
skies.

It was a big house and had been enlarged by the Sallongers when
they came. They used it as a country residence. They also had a town
house where Sir Francis spent most of his time and when he was not
there he would be travelling through the country, for besides his headquarters in Spitalfields there were factories in Macclesfield and other
parts of England. His grandfather had received his knighthood because he was one of the biggest silk manufacturers in the country and
therefore an asset to society.

The ladies of the household would have preferred not to be in trade,
but silk was more important to Sir Francis than anything else; and it
was hoped that Charles and Philip would be the same when the time
came for them to join their father in carrying on with the production
of that most beautiful of all materials. So because of the family's fer-
vour for the product which had enriched them, and with a complete
disregard for historical association, the words The Silk House had
been set up over the ancient gateway in big bronze letters.

I could not remember any place but The Silk House being my
home. It was a strange position in which I found myself, and it surprised me that I did not question this earlier. I suppose children take
most things for granted. They have to. They know of nothing else but
that by which they are surrounded.

I was there in the nursery with Charles, Philip, Julia and Cassandra
who was usually known as Cassie. It did not occur to me that I was
like a cuckoo in the nest. Sir Francis and Lady Sallonger were Papa
and Mama to them; to me they were Sir Francis and Lady Sallonger.
Then there was Nanny—the autocrat of the nursery—who would
often regard me with pursed lips from which would emerge a little
puffing sound which indicated a critical state of mind. I was called
simply Lenore—not Miss Lenore; the others were always Miss Julia
and Miss Cassie. It was apparent in the attitude of Amy the nursery
maid who always served me last at meals. I had the toys which Julia
and Cassie discarded although at Christmas there would be a doll or
something special of my own. Miss Everton, the governess, would
sometimes look at me with an expression bordering on disdain; and

she seemed to resent the fact that I could learn faster than Julia or Cassie. So I should have been warned.

Clarkson, the butler, ignored me; but then he ignored the other children, too. He was a very important gentleman who ruled below stairs with Mrs. Dillon, the cook. They were the aristocrats of the servants' hall where the observance of class distinction was more rigid than it was upstairs. Each of the servants was in a definite niche from which he or she could not emerge. Clarkson and Mrs. Dillon kept as stern a watch on protocol as I imagine would be in existence at the court of Queen Victoria. All the servants had their places at the table for meals—Clarkson at one end, Mrs. Dillon at the other. On the right hand side of Mrs. Dillon was Henry the footman. Miss Logan—Lady Sallonger's lady's maid, when she ate in the kitchen which she did not always do for she could have her meals taken up to her room—was on the other side of Clarkson. Grace, the parlourmaid, was next to Henry. Then there were May and Jenny, the housemaids, Amy the nursery maid and Carrie the tweeny. When Sir Francis came to The Silk House, Cobb, the coachman, joined them for meals, but he was mostly in London; and there he had his own Mews cottage attached to the London home. There were several grooms but they had their quarters over the stables, which were quite extensive, for besides horses to ride, there was a gig and a dog cart. And of course Sir Francis's carriage was housed there when he came to The Silk House.

That was below stairs; and in that no-man's land between the upper and lower echelons of society, as though floating in limbo, was the governess, Miss Everton. I often thought she must be very lonely. She had her meals in her room—taken up grudgingly by one of the maids. Nanny, of course, ate in her own room adjoining the nursery; there she had a spirit stove on which she cooked a little, if she did not fancy the food served in the kitchen; and there always seemed to be a fire burning in the grate which had a hob for her kettle from which she brewed her many cups of tea.

I often thought about Miss Everton, particularly when I realized that I was in a similar position.

Julia was over a year older than I; the boys were several years our senior, the elder being Charles. They seemed very grand and grown up. Philip chiefly ignored us but Charles would bully us when the mood took him. Julia was inclined to be imperious; she was hot-tempered and now and then flew into uncontrollable rages. She and I quarrelled a good deal. Nanny would say: "Now Miss Julia. Now Lenore. Stop that. It's jangling on my nerves." Nanny was rather proud of her nerves. They always had to be considered.

Cassie was different. She was younger than either of us. I heard it said that she had given Lady Sallonger 'a hard time when she came along' and that there could be no more. It was the reason for Cassie's affliction. I had heard the servants whispering about "instruments" when they eyed her in a manner which made me think of the rack and thumbscrews of the Inquisition. They were referring to Cassie's right leg, which had not grown as long as the left and as a result she limped. She was small and pale and pronounced "delicate." But she was of a gentle, loving disposition and her disability had not soured her in the least. She and I loved each other dearly. We used to read and sew together. We were both adept with the needle. I think my proficiency was due to Grand'mère.

Grand'mère was the most important person in my life. She was mine—the only one in the household to whom I really belonged. She and I were apart from the rest of the household. She liked me to have meals with the other children although I should have loved to have them with her; she liked me to go with them on their riding lessons; and particularly she wanted me to study with them. Grand'mère was a part of the mystery. She was my Grand'mère and not theirs.

She lived at the very top of the house in the big room which had been built by one of the Sallongers. It had big windows and the roof even was of glass to let the light in. Grand'mère needed the light. In that room she had her loom and sewing machine and there she worked through the days. Beside the machine were the dressmaker's dummies —like effigies of real people . . . three shapely ladies of various sizes, often clothed in exquisite garments. I had names for them: Emmeline was the small one, Lady Ingleby the middle size and the Duchess of Malfi was the largest. Bales of material came to the house from Spital-fields. Grand'mère used to draw the gowns first and then set about making them. I shall never forget the smell of those bales of materials. They had strange exotic names which I learned. As well as fine silks, satins and brocades there were lustrings, alamodes, paduasoys, velvets and ducapes. I would often sit listening to the whir of the machine and watching Grand'mère's little black slipper working at the treadle.

"Hand me those scissors, *ma petite,*" she would say. "Bring me the pins. Ah, what should I do without my little helper." Then I felt happy.

"You work very hard, Grand'mère," I said to her one day.

"I am this lucky lady," she replied. She spoke a mixture of French and English which was different from the speech of anyone else. In the school room we did a kind of laboured French, announcing our possession of a pen or a dog or a cat and asking the way to the post office. Julia and Cassie had to struggle with it far more earnestly than I, who, because I lived so close to Grand'mère, could deliver the words with ease and a different accent from that of Miss Everton, which did not please her.

Grand'mère went on: "I am here in this beautiful house with my little one. I am happy. She is happy. She is growing into a talented lady. Oh yes you are. It is here that you will get that which will make you get on in the world. This is the good life here, *mon amour.*"

I loved the way she said *mon amour.* It reminded me that she loved me very dearly—more than anyone else did.

She never joined the rest of the household. It was only when she was making dresses for the family that she came down to the drawing room to see Lady Sallonger, which was because Lady Sallonger was too delicate to mount the stairs to be fitted.

Each afternoon Grand'mère took a walk in the gardens. I often joined her then and we would sit in the pond garden and talk. There was always plenty to talk about with Grand'mère. A great deal of it was about the materials and how they were woven and what sort of dresses would be most suitable for them. Grand'mère was at The Silk House to design dresses and to show how materials should be made up in the way most suitable for them. A kind of brake would arrive, drawn by two horses which had come the sixteen miles from Spitalfields to Epping Forest, and the bales would be carried up to the top of the house. I would dash up to examine them with Grand'mère.

She would grow ecstatic. She was very excitable. She would hold the materials to her cheek and sigh. Then she would drape them round me and clasp her hands in ecstasy, her bright brown eyes shining with enthusiasm. We looked forward to the arrival of the bales.

Grand'mère was quite an important person in the household. She made her own rules. I supposed she could have taken her meals with the family had she wished. But she was as autocratic in her way as Clarkson and Mrs. Dillon were in theirs.

Her meals were carried up to the top of the house and none of the housemaids dared show the slightest resentment, for Grand'mère had an air of great dignity and authority. Oh yes, she was certainly an important person in the household. She accepted these services in a different way from Miss Everton, who always felt she had to make sure that she received the deference due to her. Grand'mère just behaved as though there was no need to stress *her* importance for they all must be aware of it.

When I began to discover that I was different from the other children it was a great relief to remember that Grand'mère and I belonged together. On the rare occasions when Sir Francis came to The Silk House, he always visited Grand'mère. They talked about the materials, of course, and he discussed all sorts of things with her.

It was because of this that she was regarded with some awe by the rest of the household. The top rooms of the house were ours. There were four of them: the big light workroom; our bedrooms—two small rooms with narrow slits of windows and a communicating door between them; and a small sitting room. The small rooms were part of the old house—the workroom, of course, having been added by a Sallonger.

"This is our domain," said Grand'mère. "Here we are in our little kingdom. This is yours and mine . . . and here we are kings in our little castle . . . but perhaps I say queens, eh?"

She was a small woman with masses of hair which had once been black and now had streaks of white in it. She wore it piled high on her head with a Spanish comb sparkling in it. She was very proud of her hair.

"The hair must always be . . . *elegant,*" she said. "Even the finest satin and best silk in the whole world will give you little . . . if there is no style in the hair." Her eyes were large; they sparkled with joy or blazed with indignation, or could go cold with contempt or light up with love. They betrayed each and every one of Grand'mère's moods. They were her great beauty, of course—they and her hair. She had long slender fingers, and I shall always remember their darting movements over patterns she had made as she cut out the dress materials on the big table in the workroom. She was so slight that sometimes I feared she would float away. I told her this and added: "What should I do if you did?"

Usually she laughed at my fancies but she did not laugh at that one. She was very serious.

"All will be well with you . . . always . . . as it was with me. I could stand on these two feet . . . from the time I was a young girl. It is because there is something I can do well. That is what there must be. Something . . . anything . . . better than others . . . and there will always be a place for you in the world. You see, I fashion a work of art with a bale of cloth, a sewing machine and a pair of scissors . . . Oh, but it is more than that. Anyone can work the treadle, anyone can cut . . . cut . . . cut. No, it is a little something . . . the inspiration . . . the little bit of genius which you bring to your trade. That is what counts. And if you have that . . . there will always be a place for you. You, my little one, will walk in my footsteps. I will show you the way. And then . . . whatever happens, you have nothing to fear. Always I will watch over you."

I knew she would.

It was no hardship for me to learn from her. When the bales came in, she would make sketches and ask my opinion. When I drew a design myself she was delighted. She showed me where I had gone wrong and then put in a few deft touches; it was a design which was used in the end. "Lenore's gown," she called it. I always remembered it because it was made of a lovely shade of lavender. Afterwards Grand'mère told me that Sir Francis was very pleased. It was the right gown for the material.

When the dresses had been seen by Sir Francis and some of his managers, they were packed up and taken away. Then fresh bales arrived. There was a very exclusive salon in London where they were sold. This was another branch of the Sallonger silk empire.

I remember well the day when she talked to me and told me how we came to be living here at The Silk House.

I had gone to her perplexed. We had been riding for we had riding lessons every day. One of the grooms always took us. We had begun by riding round the paddock; there was a jump there, too.

Julia was a good horsewoman. I was quite good, too. Cassie could not get on with it. I think she was rather frightened of the horses although she had been given the mildest in the stables. I always kept my eyes on her when we cantered or galloped round the paddock and I think she took special comfort from this fact.

When we had finished riding, Julia said: "I smell something good cooking in the kitchen."

So we went there.

"You got mud on your boots?" demanded Mrs. Dillon.

"No we have not, Mrs. Dillon," retorted Julia.

"Well, I'm glad of that because I don't want none of that mud in my kitchen, Miss Julia."

"The cakes smell good," said Julia.

"And so they should . . . the goodness that's in them."

We all sat down at the table and looked at Mrs. Dillon appealingly and with something like adoration at the batch of cakes which had just come out of the oven.

"All right then," said Mrs. Dillon grudgingly. "But that Miss Everton wouldn't like it. Nor Nanny neither . . . eating between meals indeed. You should wait for your proper tea time."

"That's hours away," said Julia. "That one for me."

"Miss Greedy-Guts, that's what you are," said Mrs. Dillon. "That's the biggest."

"A compliment to you, Mrs. Dillon," I reminded her.

"I don't want no compliments thank you, Lenore. I know what my cakes is . . . and that is good. There. One for you, Miss Julia. One for you, Miss Cassie. And one for you, Lenore."

I noticed it then. *Miss* Julia. *Miss* Cassie . . . and Lenore.

I pondered on this for some time and chose the opportunity when I was sitting in the pond garden with Grand'mère. I asked why it was that I was never called Miss, but just plainly by my name like Grace or May or one of the servants.

Grand'mère was silent for a moment, then she said: "These servants are very . . . how is it . . . aware. That is it. They are very aware of little things . . . like who should be called this or that . . . who should have this place or that. You are my granddaughter. That is not like being the daughter of Sir Francis and Lady Sallonger. Therefore people like Mrs. Dillon . . . they will say . . . 'Oh, no Miss for her!' "

"You mean I am in the same group as Grace or May?"

She pursed her lips, lifted her hands and swayed from side to side. She used her hands and shoulders a great deal in conversations which was very expressive.

"We are not going to worry ourselves with the ways of such as Mrs.

Dillon. We smile. We say, Oh, so it is like that, is it? Very well. What is it going to mean to me not to be called Miss. What is Miss? It is just a nothing. You are as well without the Miss."

"Yes, but *why*, Grand'mère?"

"It is simple. You are not a daughter of the house, so you cannot have a Miss from Mrs. Dillon."

"When the Dallington girls come over to tea and to play with us, they are called Miss . . . and they are not daughters of the house. Are we servants here, Grand'mère?"

"We serve . . . if that is servants. Perhaps. But we are here together . . . you and I . . . we live well. We are at peace. Why do we worry about a little Miss?"

"I only want to know, Grand'mère. What are we doing in this house which we are not of?"

She hesitated for a moment, then seemed to come to a decision. "We came here when you were eight months old. Such a lovely baby you were. I thought it good for you to come here. Here we could be together . . . the Grand'mère and her little one. I thought we could be happy here and they promised that you should have the education . . . the upbringing of a daughter of the house. But we did not talk of 'Miss.' So that is why it is not given you. Who wants to be Miss? You do not. Come, little one. There is more to life than the little word Miss."

"Tell me about our coming here. Why is it that I have no father . . . no mother?"

She sighed. "This has to come," she said as though to herself. "Your mother was the most beautiful and lovely girl that ever lived. Her name was Marie Louise. She was my child, my little one, *mon amour*. We lived in the village of Villers-Mûre. It was beautiful. The sun shone often and it was warm. Summer is summer in Villers-Mûre. You wake up and you know the sun will be shining all through the day. Not as here . . . when it peeps out and goes away again and can't make up its mind."

"Do you want to be in Villers-Mûre?"

She shook her head vehemently. "I want to be here. Here is where I now belong . . . and so do you, *ma petite*. This is where you will be happy . . . and one day you will not care whether they call you Miss or not."

"I don't care now, Grand'mère. I only wanted to *know*."

"Villers-Mûre is far away from here. It is right across the land of France and you know, do you not—for the good Miss Everton will have told you—that France is one big country . . . bigger than this little island. There are mountains and little towns and villages . . . and just over the border is Italy. The mulberries grow well there and that means . . . silk. These little worms who spin the silk for us love the mulberry leaves and where these grow well, there will be the silk."

"So you have always known about silk?"

"Villers-Mûre is the home of the silk worm . . . and silk was our way of living. Without silk there would be no Villers-Mûre. The St. Allengères have always lived there and may it please the good God they always will. Let me tell you. The St. Allengères live in a beautiful place. It is rather like this house . . . only there is no forest . . . but mountains. It is a grand house . . . the home of the St. Allengères for centuries. There are lawns and flowers and trees and a river which runs through the grounds. All around are the little houses where the workmen live with their families. There is the big manufactory. It is beautiful . . . white with splashes of colour about the walls for the oleanders and the bougainvilleas grow well there. There are the *mûreraies*—the mulberry groves—and they have the best silk worms in the world. Theirs are the finest looms . . . better than anything they have in India or China . . . which perhaps are the homes of the silk. Some of the best silk in the world comes from Villers-Mûre."

"And you lived there and you worked for these St. Allengères?"

She nodded. "We had a pretty little house . . . the best of them all. Flowers covered the walls. It was beautiful; and my daughter, my Marie Louise, was very happy. She was a girl who was made for happiness. She found laughter everywhere. She was beautiful. You have her eyes. They dance; they laugh; but they were never stormy as yours can be, my little one. They were darkest blue . . . like yours and her hair was almost black . . . blacker than yours, soft and rippling. She was a beauty. She saw no evil in anything. She was unaware . . . and she died."

"How did she die?"

"She died when you were born. It happens sometimes. She should not have died. I would have cared for her as I have cared for you. I should have made the world a happy place for her. But she died . . . but she left me you . . . and that makes me happy."

"And my father?" I asked.

She was silent. Then she said: "Sometimes these things happen. You will understand later on. Sometimes children are born . . . and where is the father?"

"You mean . . . he left her?"

She took my hand and kissed it. "She was very beautiful," she said. "But whatever happened she left me you, my child, and that was the best gift she could have left me. In place of herself I had her child and all my joy has henceforth been in you."

"Oh Grand'mère," I said. "It is so sad."

"It was summer," she said. "She tarried too long in the sweet scented meadows. She was altogether innocent. Perhaps I should have warned her."

"And she was deserted by my father?"

"I cannot say. I was concerned with her. I did not know that you were to come until it was almost time for your arrival. Then it happened . . . and she died. I remember sitting by her bed and the desolation which swept over me . . . until the midwife came and put you into my arms. You were my salvation. I saw then that I had lost my daughter but I had her child. Since then you have been all in all to me."

"I wish I knew who my father was."

She shook her head and lifted her shoulders.

"And so you came here?" I prompted.

"Yes, I came here. It seemed best. It is always difficult when such things happen in a little community. You know how it is with Clarkson and Mrs. Dillon. They whisper . . . they chatter. I did not want you to grow up among that."

"You mean they would have despised me because my parents were not married?"

She nodded. "The St. Allengères are a rich family . . . a powerful family. They *are* Villers-Mûre. Everyone works for them. They are the big silk name in France and in Italy, too. So Monsieur St. Allengère who is the big man at the head . . . he is the father of us all . . . and the silk families throughout the world they are . . . how do you say it? . . . in . . . touch. They know each other. They compare. They are rivals. 'My silk is better than your silk.' You know, this sort of thing."

"Yes," I said, still thinking of my mother and the man who had betrayed her and the scandal that there would have been in Villers-Mûre.

"Sir Francis . . . he pays a visit now and then. There is a show of friendship between the two families . . . but is it friendship? Each wants to make the best silk. They have secrets . . . They show this little bit . . . and that . . . but no more . . . nothing of importance."

"I understand, Grand'mère, but I want to hear about my mother."

"She will be happy when she looks down from heaven and sees us together. She will know what we are to each other. Sir Francis came to Villers-Mûre. I remember it well. There is a family connection . . . you see. They say that years and years ago they were one family. Listen to their names. St. Allengère . . . and in English that has become Sallonger."

"Why yes," I cried excitedly. "So the family here is related to that one in France?"

Again that lift of the shoulders. "You will have heard from Miss Everton about something called the Edict of Nantes."

"Oh yes," I cried. "It was signed by Henri IV of France in the year . . . well, I think it was 1598."

"Yes, yes, but what did it do? It gave freedom to the Huguenots to worship as they wished."

"I remember that. The King was Huguenot at the time and the Parisians would not accept a Protestant King so he said that Paris was worth a Mass and he would become a Catholic."

She smiled, well pleased. "Ah, what it is to be educated! Well, they changed it all."

"It was called the Revocation and it was signed by Louis XIV many years later."

"Yes, and it drove many thousands of Huguenots out of France. One branch of the St. Allengères settled in England. They set up silk manufactories in various places. They brought with them their knowledge of how to weave these beautiful fabrics. They worked hard and prospered."

"How very interesting! And so Sir Francis visits his relatives in France?"

"Very rarely. The family connection is not remembered much. There is the rivalry between Sallongers of England and the St. Allengères of France. When Sir Francis comes to France they show him

a little . . . not much . . . and they try to find out what he is doing
. . . They are rivals. That is the way it is in business."

"Did you see Sir Francis when you were there?"

She nodded. "There I worked as I do here. I had my loom. I knew
a good many secrets . . . and I shall always have them. I was a good
weaver. All the people who lived there were engaged in the making of
silk . . . and so was I."

"And my mother?"

"She too. Monsieur St. Allengère sent for me and he asked me how
I would like to go to England. At first I did not know what to say. I
could not believe it but when I understood I saw that it was a good
thing. It was best for you and what was good for you must be for me
also. So I accepted his offer which is for me to come here . . . to live
in this house . . . to work the loom when something special is required . . . and to make the fashion dresses which help to sell our
silk."

"You mean Sir Francis offered us a home here?"

"It was arranged between him and Monsieur St. Allengère. I was to
have my loom and my sewing machine and I was to live here and do
for Sir Francis what I had been doing in France."

"And you left your home to do this . . . to come all this way to a
country of strangers?"

"Home is where your loved ones are. I had my baby and as long as
I was with you, I was content. Here, it is the good life. You are
educated with the daughters of the house . . . and I believe you do
well, eh? Miss Julia . . . is she not a little envious because you are
cleverer than she is? And you love Miss Cassie, do you not? She is a
sister to you. Sir Francis is a good man. He keeps his word and Lady
Sallonger . . . she is demanding shall we say . . . but she is not un-
kind. We have much and we must give a little in return. I never fail to
thank the good God for finding a way for me."

I threw my arms about her neck and clung to her.

"It doesn't matter, does it?" I said. "As long as we are together."

So that was how I learned something of my history; but I felt that
there was a great deal more to know.

* * *

Grand'mère was right. Life was pleasant. I was reconciled and the
slight difference with which I was treated did not worry me very

much. I was not one of them. I accepted that. They had been kind to us. They had allowed us to leave the little place where everyone would know that my mother had had me without being married. I was well aware of the stigma attached to that, for there was more than one girl in the surrounding villages who had had to face what they called "trouble." One of them had eventually married the one they called "the man" and had about six children now—but it was still remembered.

I wondered a great deal about my father. Sometimes I thought it was rather romantic not to know who one's father was. One could imagine someone who was more exciting and handsome than real people were. One day, I told myself, I will go and find him. That started me off on a new type of daydream. I had a good many imaginary fathers after that talk with Grand'mère. Naturally I could not expect to be treated like *Miss* Julia or *Miss* Cassie, but how dull their lives were compared with mine. They had not been born to the most beautiful girl in the world; they did not possess a mysterious, anonymous father.

I realized that we were, in a way, servants of the house. Grand'mère was of a higher grade—perhaps in the same category as Clarkson or at least Mrs. Dillon—but a servant none the less; she was highly prized because of her skills and I was there because of her. So . . . I accepted my lot.

It was true that Lady Sallonger was demanding. I was expected to be a maid to her. She was really beautiful—or had been in her youth and the signs remained. She would lie on the sofa in the drawing room every day, always beautifully dressed in a be-ribboned negligée and Miss Logan had to spend lots of time doing her hair and helping her dress. Then she would make her slow progress to the drawing room from her bedroom leaning heavily on Clarkson's arm while Henry carried her embroidery bag and prepared to give further assistance should it be needed. She often called on me to read to her. She seemed to like to keep me busy. She was always gentle and spoke in a tired voice which seemed to have a reproach in it—against fate, I supposed, which had given her a bad time with Cassie and made an invalid of her.

It would be: "Lenore, bring me a cushion. Oh, that's better. Sit there, will you, child? Please put the rug over my feet. They are getting chilly. Ring the bell. I want more coal on the fire. Bring me my embroidery. Oh dear, I think that is a wrong stitch. You can undo that. Perhaps you can put it right. I do hate going back over things. But do it later. Read to me now . . ."

She would keep me reading for what seemed like hours. She often dozed and thinking she was asleep I would stop reading, and then be reprimanded and told to go on. She liked the works of Mrs. Henry Wood. I remember *The Channings* and *Mrs. Halliburton's Troubles* as well as *East Lynne*. All these I read aloud to her. She said I had a more soothing voice than Miss Logan's.

And all the time I was doing these tasks I was thinking of how much we owed these Sallongers who had allowed us to come here and escape my mother's shame. It was really like something out of Mrs. Henry Wood's books, and I was naturally thrilled to be at the centre of such a drama.

Perhaps being in a humble position makes one more considerate of others. Cassie had always been my friend; Julia was too haughty, too condescending to be a real friend. Cassie was different. She looked to me for help and to one of my nature that was very endearing. I liked to have authority. I liked to look after people. I realized my feelings were not entirely altruistic. I liked the feeling of importance which came to me when I was assisting others, so I used to help Cassie with her lessons. When we went walking I made my pace fit hers while Julia and Miss Everton strode on. When we rode I kept my eye on her. She repaid me with a kind of silent adoration which gave me great satisfaction.

It was accepted in the household that I look after Cassie in the same way as I was expected to wait on Lady Sallonger.

There was one other who aroused pity in me. That was Willie. He was what Mrs. Dillon called "Minnie Wardle's left-over." Minnie Wardle had, by all accounts, been "a flighty piece," "no better than she ought to be," who had reaped her just reward and "got her come-uppance" in the form of Willie.

The child was the result of her friendship with a horse dealer who had hung round the place until Minnie was pregnant and then disappeared. Minnie Wardle thought she knew how to handle such a situation and visited the wise old woman who lived in a hut in the forest about a mile or so from The Silk House. But this time she was not clever enough, for it did not work; and when Willie was born—again quoting Mrs. Dillon—he was "tuppence short." Her ladyship had not wanted to turn the girl out and had let her stay on, Willie with her; but before the child was a year old, the horse dealer came back and Minnie disappeared with him, leaving behind the wages of her sin to be shouldered by someone else. The child was sent to the stables to be brought up by Mrs. Carter, wife of the head groom. She had been trying to have children for some time and not being able to get one was glad to take someone else's. But no sooner did she take in Willie than she started to breed and now had six of her own and was not very interested in Willie—particularly as he was "a screw loose."

Poor Willie—he belonged to no one really; no one cared about him. I often thought he was not so stupid as he seemed. He could not read or write, but then there were many of them who could not do that. He had a mongrel which followed him everywhere and was known by Mrs. Dillon as "that dratted dog." I was glad to see the boy with something which loved him and on whom he could shower affection. He seemed brighter after he acquired the dog. He liked to sit with the dog beside him looking into the lake, which was in the forest not very far from The Silk House. One came upon it unexpectedly. There was a clearing in the trees and then suddenly one saw this expanse of water. Children fished in it. One would see them with their little jars beside them and hear them shrieking with glee when they found a tadpole. Willows trailed in the water and loosestrife with its star-like blossoms grew side by side, with the flowers we called skull-caps, among the ubiquitous woundwort. I never failed to wonder at the marvels of the forest. It was full of surprises. One could ride through the trees and suddenly come upon a cluster of houses, a little hamlet or a village green. At one time the trees must have been cut down to make these habitations, but so long ago that no one remembered when.

The years had changed the forest but only a little. At the time of the Norman Conquest it must have covered almost the whole of Essex; but now there were the occasional big houses and the old villages, the churches, the dame schools, and several little hamlets.

It was not easy to communicate with Willie. If one spoke to him he looked like a startled deer; he would stand still, as though poised for flight. He did not trust anyone.

It is strange how some people enjoy baiting the weak. Is it because they wish to call attention to their own strength? Mrs. Dillon was one of these. She it was who had stressed the fact that I was not of the same standing as my companions. It seemed to me now that instead of trying to help Willie she called attention to his deficiencies.

Naturally he was expected to help about the house. He brought water in from the well; he cleaned the yard; and these things he did happily enough; they were a habit. One day Mrs. Dillon said: "Go to the storeroom, Willie, and bring me one of my jars of plums. And tell me how many jars are left."

She wanted Willie to come back plumless with a look of bewilderment on his face so that she could ask God or any of His angels who happened to be listening what she had done to be burdened with such an idiot.

Willie was nonplussed. He could not know how many were left; he could not be sure of picking out plums. This gave me a chance. I beckoned him and went with him to the storeroom. I picked out the plums and held up six fingers. He stared at me and again I held up my fingers; at last a smile broke out on his face.

He returned to the kitchen. I think Mrs. Dillon was disappointed that he had brought what she had asked for. "Well," she demanded, "how many's left?" I hovered in the doorway and behind Mrs. Dillon's back I held up six fingers. Willie did the same.

"Six," cried Mrs. Dillon. "As few as that. My goodness, what have I done to be given such an idiot."

"It's all right, Mrs. Dillon," I said. "I went and had a look. There are six left."

"Oh, it's you, Lenore. Poking your nose in as usual."

"Well, Mrs. Dillon. I thought you wanted to know."

I walked out of the kitchen, I hoped, with dignity. I passed Willie's little dog who was sitting patiently waiting for his master.

Whenever I could I would try to help Willie. I often found him giving me a sidelong glance, but he hastily averted his eyes if I caught him at this.

I wished I could help him more. It occurred to me that it might be possible to teach him a little, for he was not so stupid as people thought.

I used to talk about him to Cassie, who was very easily moved to pity, and she would try to do little things for him, such as showing him which were the best cabbages to pull from the kitchen garden when he was sent out for this purpose by Mrs. Dillon.

I was very interested in people's behaviour and I wondered why

Mrs. Dillon, who was comfortably placed herself, should be so eager to make the life of someone like Willie more of a burden than it already was. Willie was a frightened boy. As I said to Cassie: "If he could only get rid of that fear of people, he would take a step towards normality."

Cassie agreed with me. She invariably did. Perhaps that was why I liked being with her so much.

Mrs. Dillon was relentless. She said that Willie should be "put away" because it wasn't what was to be expected in a place like The Silk House to have idiots roaming about. When Sir Francis came she would speak to him on the subject. It was no use saying anything to her ladyship and Mr. Clarkson had no authority to get him sent away.

I believe she thought that a good way of attacking Willie was through his dog. There came a day when she said the dog had taken what was left of a leg of lamb from the table and run off with it. I was there when she was talking of it and demanding the death penalty for the dog.

Clarkson was very dignified. He sat at the table like a judge.

"Did you see the mongrel take the meat, Mrs. Dillon?"

"As good as," replied Mrs. Dillon.

"So you did not *see* the act?"

"Well, I'd seen that animal out there . . . his eyes on what he could steal and when my back was turned he was in like a streak of lightning, and he got the meat from the table and ran off with it."

"It might have been one of the other dogs," suggested Clarkson.

But Mrs. Dillon wouldn't have it. "Oh, I know who it was. No kidding me. I see him there with my own eyes."

I couldn't resist saying: "But Mrs. Dillon, you did not see the dog take the meat."

She turned on me angrily. "What are you doing here? You have to be into everything. Anyone would think you was one of the family instead of . . ."

I looked at her steadily. Clarkson was embarrassed. He said: "This is outside the matter. If you did not actually *see* the dog take the meat then you cannot be sure that he did."

"I shall call in one of them woodmen. I shall get him to take a gun to that creature. I'll not have him prowling round snatching the food I've cooked. It's more than a body can stand and I won't put up with it."

The matter did not rest there. People were taking sides. The dog should be destroyed. He was a miserable little mongrel in any case. No, let the poor little fellow keep his dog. He didn't have much of a life.

Poor Willie was distraught. He ran away taking his dog with him. It was winter and everyone was asking how he would look after himself. Mrs. Carter dreamed that he was lying in the forest somewhere . . . frozen to death.

May said she heard strange noises in the house; she thought she heard a dog howling. Jenny was walking through the woods and heard someone following her. She looked round and thought she saw Willie holding his dog. They were two ghostly figures and suddenly they disappeared.

Mrs. Dillon was disturbed. She was the one who had been persecuting him. She wasn't at all sure about that leg of lamb. It might have been one of the other dogs. She wished she hadn't asked one of the men to shoot the animal. She hadn't meant it really. It was no use blaming her; she was only doing her duty to the house.

There was great relief when Willie came back. He was unkempt and half starving. Mrs. Dillon made gruel for him and told him not to be such a silly happorth again . . . going off like that. Nobody was going to shoot his dog. It was just said in a manner of speaking.

They were a little kinder after that. So the incident had done some good and both Willie and the dog quickly recovered.

Life went on much as before. Julia was sometimes friendly but she could be suddenly imperious as though remembering that I was not quite one of the family. She would be impatient with Cassie who tired easily, but she was not averse to copying my work in the school room and asking me to supply certain answers to the work which Miss Everton set us. I suppose we got along tolerably well and I think that on the whole she was glad to have me there. I was more of a companion to her than Cassie could be. We practised jumping in the paddock and there was a certain friendly rivalry between us.

With Cassie it was different. She had to lie down in the afternoons. I used to take off her boots for her and sit with her and we talked. We played guessing games and sometimes I told her about Mrs. Halliburton's troubles or the trials of Lady Isabel in East Lynne. She enjoyed these conversations and wept quietly for the tribulations of those unfortunate ladies.

The boys were at school most of the time. We all looked forward to their coming home for the holidays, but when they did come, it was never quite as we had imagined it would be and often I was glad when they went back—when Charles did anyway. It was different with Philip.

Philip was rather like Cassie, with a kind and gentle nature. I expected they took after Lady Sallonger, who might have been like that before going through what she did with Cassie had made her rather peevish.

Charles was the elder brother—that meant about six years older than I. He was very lordly, and strutted about the house as though he owned it—which I supposed he would one day. He looked down on his brother and sisters, so it was not surprising that he had a contempt for me.

During the holidays the boys spent most of their time riding or fishing in the River Roding. They seemed to have so many exciting things to do from which we were excluded. I envied them their freedom. Philip, however, used to ride with us sometimes. He asked me questions about Grand'mère's work. He was very interested in it. He used to go and see her sometimes. She liked him, and told me that he had real feeling for materials and knew a good silk when he saw one.

"His father will be pleased with him when he goes into the business," she said.

"Charles does not seem interested at all," I observed.

"It could come. At the moment he feels himself to be the big man . . . very important. That is here . . . where his brother and sisters are younger than he is. Perhaps he is different with others, eh? We shall see. But it is good that there is Philip who will be a blessing to his father."

I noticed that Charles was quite interested in Grace the parlourmaid who was rather pretty. I saw them talking together on one occasion. Grace was giggling and was quite flushed; and he was being pleasant and friendly in a condescending way. So clearly he did not despise all females.

Once Charles did not come home. He was staying with a friend. Philip came alone and that was quite a pleasant holiday, for when Charles was not there Philip did not feel that he ought to hold us in contempt. He spent quite a lot of time with us.

I remember sitting by the lake with him and Julia and Cassie when he talked about the family and how wonderful it was that their ancestors had settled here all those years ago, driven from their homes because of religion.

"All we could do was weave our silk and so we arrived here without anything, for all we had we had left behind. We started up a silk industry in this country. Don't you think that was a wonderful thing to have done?"

I said fervently that I did.

He smiled at me and went on: "In a few years we were producing materials that were as good as anything that came out of France. It was hard work, but we wanted to work. We were all very poor for a long time and then we began to prosper."

"I'm glad we did," said Julia. "I should have hated to be poor."

"It's really an exciting story, don't you think so, Lenore?"

"Oh, I do. I do," I assured him.

"To come to a new country with nothing but your faith and hope and determination to succeed." His face shone with zeal. I thought: There is something very nice about Philip. I shall be sorry when he goes back to school.

"But there were endless troubles," he went on. "When the country started importing French silks the Spitalfields workers were near to starvation. People wanted *French* silks although those we were making were just as good. They just thought French silk sounded better than Spitalfields silk. My father told me all about the trouble they had. The people were very fierce. There were riots. The workers roamed the streets. There was no work for their looms. If they saw a woman in a calico gown they tore it off her. 'Silk! Silk!' they shouted. 'Everyone must wear Spitalfields silk!' "

"They must have been very fierce," I said. "I should not have wanted my dress to be torn off me however good the cause."

"They were fighting for their livelihoods. They had come over here leaving behind everything they possessed; they had set up their looms; they had produced beautiful materials; and just when they were beginning to prosper, the government allowed French silk to be brought into the country and people foolishly thought it was better and sentenced our workers to starvation."

"If their work was so good why did people want to buy the French?"

"English people always think foreigners do better work than their own people. Besides the French had a reputation. They thought French clothes and materials must be better than the English. In any case, they almost put us out of business."

"Why do you feel so strongly now?" I asked. "It is all over."

"I feel for those poor people because I know how they suffered. And it could happen again."

"Poor things," said Cassie. "It must be dreadful to be hungry. And the little children too . . ."

"They are the first to suffer," said Philip. "Oh, it has been a long and violent history. There was a time just over a hundred years ago when there was great trouble. The government had just signed the Treaty of Fontainebleau which allowed French silks to be brought into the country free of tax; and the workers were desperate. When the King was on his way to Parliament they decided to present a petition to the House of Commons. They were of the opinion that the Duke of Bedford had been bribed by the French to agree to the Fontainebleau Treaty. After they had marched to the House and forced an adjournment they went to Bedford House and attacked it. The guards were called out and the Riot Act read. The workers fled, but not before many of them had been trampled down by the horses. Many died. They had thought they had come to a safe haven when they left their homes, but they have had to fight all the way through to keep going."

"And they did," I said, "and all is well with them now."

He shrugged his shoulders. "One never really knows what difficulties are going to arise. That's how it is in life, Lenore."

"But people find a way out of their difficulties."

"Some do," he replied.

Julia yawned. "It is time we went back," she said.

I grew fond of Philip during those holidays. It was so different when Charles was not there. He used to come up to see Grand'mère. He would handle the bales of material knowledgeably and talk about the weave. He was very interested in the loom she had there.

"Do you use it much?" he asked.

"When Sir Francis has something he specially wishes me to do."

She talked of Villers-Mûre and the factory with the bougainvilleas on the walls and the big workroom with all the big windows letting in the light.

Philip was clearly absorbed by the subject. He talked about the new process of spinning which was turning what had hitherto been waste into good material.

"A certain Mr. Lister of Bradford has invented a special loom to do this," he told us. "It will revolutionize the trade because there must be quantities of chassum silk waste in many warehouses in London."

I did not understand a great deal of what they said but I liked to listen to them as they talked. Grand'mère's cheeks were flushed and Philip was talking enthusiastically. They liked each other and it is very pleasant when people whom one likes are interested in each other. Grand'mère made tea and we left the workroom and went into her little sitting room to drink it and continue talking. Philip told us how he would eventually be coming into the business. He found the waiting irksome. As soon as he had left the university he was to start. His father had promised him. He would have liked to dispense with the last stages of his education, but his father was adamant on that point.

"And your brother?" asked Grand'mère.

"Oh, he is bent on having a good time. I daresay he'll grow out of it."

"He has not your enthusiasm," Grand'mère commented.

"It will come, Madame Cleremont," Philip assured her. "After all, once he begins to understand something about this fascinating business, it couldn't fail to, could it?"

She smiled at him. "I am happy that Sir Francis has you to follow him. It must be a great joy to him."

"My brother will probably be good at another side of the business. It's the actual production of silk that intrigues me . . . the whole process. Those worms feeding on the mulberry leaves . . . spinning their cocoons to produce the most exquisite material in the world . . ."

He talked a great deal about processes which I did not understand. I sat there in a haze of contentment watching Grand'mère and Philip liking each other more every minute.

When he had gone she showed her pleasure. As I helped her clear away the cups she was singing softly to herself:

> *"En passant par la Lorraine*
> *Avec mes sabots*
> *J'ai rencontré dans la plaine*
> *Avec mes sabots dondaines*

Oh, Oh, Oh,
Avec mes sabots."

She always sang that when she was happy. I had asked her why once and she said she had always sung it as a child and it had always made her happy because the soldiers had thought the singer ugly. They did not know that a King's son loved her.

I said: "And did she marry the King's son?"

"We do not know. That is why I loved the song. He had given her a *bouquet de marjolaine.* If it flowered she would be queen. We do not know because the song ends before it tells."

She kept smiling at me. She said: "There is one who loves this work. He is like his father. Sir Francis is lucky to have such a son."

"You like him very much, don't you, Grand'mère?"

She nodded looking at me and smiling rather wistfully: and there were dreams in her eyes.

*   *   *

We were growing up. Julia was nearly seventeen. I was fifteen. Julia had changed; she was very anxious for us to know she was not a little girl any more.

She was to have a season in London.

Lady Sallonger talked of it often. It was one of our customs to take tea with her in the drawing room. I would often be there already, reading to her, and pausing now and then to thread the skeins of silk she needed. She was taking more and more of my time.

Julia and Cassie came down promptly at four o'clock and spent an hour with her. Clarkson would wheel in the tea trolly and Grace would stand by to pour out the tea and wait on us; but Lady Sallonger often dismissed her and dispensing the tea fell to my lot.

"Lenore can manage," she would say. Then it would be: "Lenore, a little more cream please. Oh, and do bring me one of those scones."

She would sit there, not eating, but crumbling the scone on her plate. The conversation at this time was all about Julia's coming out which would soon take place.

"Dear me, I should be there . . . but it is impossible. Lenore, my feet are quite numb. Just take off my slippers and rub them will you? Ah . . . that's better. Such a relief. In my state of health it is alas impossible. The dresses you will have to have, Julia . . . Madame

Cleremont will of course make them. She will have to get some patterns. Perhaps your father can send for them from Paris . . ."

Julia clasped her hands and listened ecstatically. She was longing to
be "out." She talked about it to Cassie and me. Balls, banquets . . .
gaiety . . . and armies of young men all seeking her hand in marriage.

I had heard Miss Logan, who knew of such things, talking to Miss
Everton. She said: "Well, of course, it's trade when all's said and done
. . . and that puts a damper on it. Mind you there's money . . . and
money talks."

So Julia was to be taken forth to the marriage market to display her
assets. She was young, quite pretty sometimes when she was in a good
temper, and very eager to find a husband but handicapped by that
label "Trade"—enhanced though by the other one: "Money."

Lady Sallonger said: "I have heard that the Countess of Ballader is
very good. Poor soul, she needs the money now that the Earl is dead.
He left her practically penniless . . . Gambling they say, and drink
. . . it swallowed up the estate and on his death it all came out. Poor
Countess. Of course she was not quite . . . to start with. Actress or
something. The Earl's third wife and he was in his dotage when he
married her. Well, now she has to eke out a living this way. She's
expensive but she was very good with Maria Cranley. Quite a plain
little creature but she married well . . . money mind you, not much
of the blue blood."

I could not resist saying that perhaps the money would be more
useful than blue blood.

"That's true, Lenore. Would you put another cushion behind my
back. That's better. I get so tired. And I have dropped my fan. Oh
there it is. And another cup of tea, Lenore. Take this scone away. Oh
dear, it seems to have gone all over the floor. Is that Madeira cake? I'll
have a piece . . . No. I think I'll try the fruit. And more cream
please. Yes, the Countess is considered to be ideal. She knows her way
about society and her origins make her pushing . . . and practical.
But everyone seems to have forgotten all that and the name Ballader
counts for a good deal. It is a great tragedy that I, as your Mama,
Julia, cannot do what should be done for you."

She then began to discuss what dresses would be needed.

"I shall have to ask Madame Cleremont to come and see me. There
will be so *much* to do. I don't know how I shall manage."

I could not help smiling knowing that Lady Sallonger would have very little trouble in managing, for others would do that for her.

There was talk of little else but Julia's coming out. Grand'mère was very excited about the dresses she would make for her. She did a good many sketches. I did one. Grand'mère said it should go down with the rest for approval, but she would not say it was mine until the choice was made.

Almost every afternoon we rode out together—Julia, Cassie and I. If there were three of us we were allowed to go without a groom providing we did not go beyond the little hamlet of Branches Burrow on one side and the King's Arms on the other.

The forest within five miles radius of the house was very well known to us, but to stray beyond the boundary would be most unsafe, for it was an easy place in which to lose oneself.

I shall never forget the horror of that day. We were riding through the forest and it was all so peaceful. The sun, shining through the leaves, made a dappled pattern on the ground and there was the lovely smell of damp earth in the air. Julia was talking—as she seemed constantly to be doing—of her coming out. Cassie looked thoughtful, possibly wondering with some apprehension whether she would have a season. I had no such fears to worry me. I was not sure whether I was pleased or sorry about that. I think Grand'mère was hoping I should be asked to share . . . not in Julia's perhaps, but in Cassie's, which I imagined would not be such a grand undertaking.

We were coming to the lake and as we approached it I heard sounds of shouting voices and shrieks of laughter.

"Some of the boys from the villages play round here," said Julia. "It's a favourite spot."

As we came in sight they saw us. There were scarcely boys being in their teens—sixteen or seventeen I imagined. There was a hush as we rode forward. I could not believe what I saw. Willie was tied to one of the trees.

I shouted: "Willie, what are you doing?"

The youths—there were about six of them—stared at us for a few seconds. There was something evil about them. I sensed that before I realized what they were doing.

One of them shouted: "They're from the house." And they all sprang into action and ran.

I leaped from my horse and went to Willie. He was incoherent, trying to speak to us, but he could not find the words. There was an expression of fixed horror on his face. Julia and Cassie had come up.

"Oh look," said Julia pointing.

Then I saw. It was the mongrel dog. He was tied to another tree. There was blood on his coat and he was lying very still.

I untied Willie. "What happened?" I cried. He did not answer. He ran to the dog and took it in his arms. It made no sound and was unaware of him so I knew it was dead. Those boys had killed it. How could they do such a cruel senseless thing?

"Tell us what happened," said Julia.

But still he did not answer. He stood holding the dog against him. I noticed that one of its legs was broken.

"Willie," said Cassie gently, "could you tell us what happened?"

Willie shook his head in abject misery.

"It was those boys," said Julia. "Oh they are wicked. Willie, what made them do it?"

But it was no use trying to speak to him. He could only think of one thing: his dog was dead.

There was no one Willie had ever loved as he had loved that dog; and no one had ever loved Willie as that little creature had. They had found each other, comforted each other and lived for each other. And now he had been wantonly killed by mindless boys whose aim had been to inflict pain on a helpless animal and a poor lad whom they considered to be inferior to themselves.

I did not know how we were going to comfort him.

Cassie was crying silently. I think that helped him to realize we cared.

"Willie," I pleaded, "if you try to tell us what happened . . ."

He spoke suddenly. "We was by the lake . . . sitting . . . looking. They came and laughed at us. I didn't look at them. Then one of them said: 'You do like the lake, don't you?' And they took me and tried to throw me in."

He looked at the dog in his arms and went on; "He bit him . . . when he laid hands on me . . . he bit him."

"I hope badly," I said.

"Then they put the ropes on me and they took him up and tied him to the tree and they threw stones at him."

"I shall tell Carter about this," I said. "They ought to be punished."

"It can't bring back the poor little thing," Julia pointed out.

"It will show them what happens to hooligans."

But I knew that Carter had no jurisdiction over boys who did not belong to our stables.

"We shall have to bury him, Willie," I said.

Willie began to walk away with the dog in his arms.

We mounted our horses and made our way to the stables where we found the head groom Carter and told him what had happened.

"Did you see what boys they were?" asked Carter.

"We didn't know them. They ran off when we appeared."

"He thought the world of that dog."

"That is why they did what they did," I said. "I wish we could find them. I think they should be severely punished."

"If it was any of my stable lads I'd see that they heard from me. None of them, I hope, would do such a thing."

"Willie will have to be gently treated."

"The Missus will see to that. We'll have to get rid of the dog. I fancy he might want to keep it. He's very simple in lots of ways."

We left him and went sadly home. We were all deeply shocked and Julia did not mention her coming out for a whole day.

* * *

I knew enough of Willie to realize that he would not want to give up the dog. He would rather have it dead than not at all.

It would soon be forcibly taken from him, and I decided to see what I could do. I found a little box of stiff cardboard and some twine and went in search of him. I did not think he would be by the lake but he was. He was seated beside that tree to which they had tied the dog and he was holding the animal in his arms.

I said: "Willie, we shall have to give him a burial. He can't be happy like that."

"They'll take him away from me."

"Yes," I said. "So let us give him a proper burial and then they won't." I held out the box to him. "He wants to rest," I went on. "He's tired. He must be left in peace to sleep."

To my surprise he put the dog in the box.

I said: "We'll bury him and I'll make a little cross. Here are these sticks, see? If I cross them like that and bind them up with twine they make a cross and that gives him a Christian burial."

He watched me and at any moment I thought he was going to snatch the box away.

I said gently: "Everyone has to die at some time. And when they die they must be treated with respect. They must be given an honourable grave. They want to rest in peace."

He was silent listening to me with a kind of wonder.

I said: "I know what we'll do. There's the mausoleum."

He looked at me not understanding.

"It's the house of the dead. You know it. It's not far from here. It is where the Sallongers go when they die. It's a beautiful place. You have seen the angels there. They are guarding it. We'll take him there and bury him, shall we?"

He continued to look at me in wonder and I put my arm round him and held him closely. He was trembling.

I said: "It is best. He will be at peace and you can come to visit him. You'll know he is there under the ground. You can sit by his grave and talk to him. It will seem as though he is there with you. The only difference will be that you cannot see him."

He went on studying me. It seemed a good plan. The dog had to be buried and I did not want it to be forcibly taken from him. We could dig a hole by the side of the mausoleum; that would give a certain dignity to the burial.

He was clutching the box tightly.

I stood up and said: "Come on, Willie. We'll do it now. Then you can stay and talk to him and you will know that he is at rest. He will be happier in his box. It is there he wants to be now."

I started to walk away, half expecting him not to follow, but he did. So I led the way to the family vault of the Sallongers.

It had always fascinated me since the first time I had seen it and Grand'mère had explained to me what it was.

"When a member of the family dies he or she is put in the mausoleum. In those coffins lie the bones of long dead Sallongers," said Grand'mère. "They were together in life and they remain so in death. Great families have these vaults."

I used to go and look at it—always trying to persuade Julia or Cassie to come with me. I was fascinated by the two angels with flaming swords—like those in the garden of Eden in my bible—guarding the place from intruders.

The iron gates were beautifully wrought and in the stone work of the walls figures had been carved. When I was small I fancied the faces changed as I looked at them. I sometimes dreamed of the place . . . that I was locked in there and could not get out and that the coffins opened and the long-dead Sallongers came out to look at me.

I said: "We will dig a grave here, Willie . . . by the walls of the vault and your little dog will lie close to the Sallongers. He will be happy there because his will be a real grave. We will put a cross on it and you will find it easily. Perhaps we will put some flowers on it and everyone will know that he is there and how much we cared about him."

Willie was nodding his head slowly.

I had brought a little shovel with me. I gave it to him and said: "You dig, Willie. He would want you to bury him. You were the one he loved best."

So that was how we buried Willie's dog.

I knew that he went to the grave often. He would sit beside it and appear to be talking.

The dogs in the stables often had puppies and I made Julia ask for one and I told her we were going to give it to Willie. This she was happy to do.

I knew we should find him sitting by the grass.

I said: "Hello, Willie. Here's a little dog. He has come to be with you . . . if you would like him to."

Willie stared at the dog without much emotion.

Cassie stroked him and said: "You'd like to be with Willie, would you?" She put her face close to the puppy and unexpectedly sneezed. Then she did it again.

"Once a wish, Twice a kiss," sang Julia.

"Then it's a kiss for me," said Cassie and sneezed again. "You're like pepper, puppy," she said. "You're making me sneeze. I'm going to call you Pepper."

"It seems a good name for a dog," added Julia.

I took the puppy and held it out to Willie. I said: "Look, Pepper, I think you and Willie are going to like each other."

Willie put out a hand and took the puppy. It gave a little bark and licked his hand. I saw a sudden joy come into Willie's face and I knew we had done the right thing.

"He's yours, Willie," I said. "He wants a home. Will you take Pepper and look after him?"

I am sure he stopped grieving after that.

* * *

Sir Francis came to The Silk House. There was always a good deal of ceremony when he arrived. The big carriage was housed with the gig and the dog cart which seemed to shrink into insignificance beside it. Cobb took up his quarters over the stables. I think he had the same effect on the grooms as Sir Francis did on the household. Cobb came from London and therefore considered himself greatly superior to poor country folk. Meals were more ceremonious. Lady Sallonger paid more attention to her toilette than ever, but she seemed to become more of an invalid and languished elegantly in her ribbons and laces on the sofa. Sir Francis sat beside her and called her "m'dear"; he patted her hand and listened patiently while she told him how she suffered. Clarkson became more dignified than ever and Mrs. Dillon was quite flustered in the kitchen, giving orders and cancelling them until Grace said she didn't know whether she was standing on her head or her heels.

He was closeted with Grand'mère for some time.

He did not stay very long . . . only for a few days, which I daresay was considered long enough by all concerned. There was a feeling of relief when Cobb, resplendent in the driver's seat, carried Sir Francis back to town.

Grand'mère talked about him to me after he had gone.

"He's got something on his mind," she said. "I have a fancy that all is not well."

"Was he angry about something?"

"Oh no . . . but I think he looked worried. He said trade was in the doldrums and we needed something to pull it out. Those were his words. We wanted something *new.* You couldn't stand still. We had to find something and it had to be good. The old lines were very fine but people craved for something new. 'What we have to find, Madame Cleremont,' he said to me, 'is some new method of weaving silk . . . something which will set the world alight . . . something no one else has.' I have rarely seen him in such a mood."

"Do you think he is worried about Julia's season? That must be very expensive."

Grand'mère laughed. "I think not, *ma chérie*. I think that is one small matter and Sir Francis has much business on his mind. No. It is merely that perhaps he has not made so much money this year as last. He thinks in big figures. Oh, he will be all right. It is just that he craves something new. It is what they all want . . . some invention which will set them way ahead of those who compete against them."

"And there is a great deal of this competition then?"

She raised her eyes to the ceiling. *"Ma chérie,* it is there all the time . . . and there is big competition between the house of St. Allengère and that of Sallonger. They have been rivals for years. One must do better than the other. The Catholic St. Allengères and the Protestant Sallongers. Can you not imagine the trials in the family when one branch takes up with a new religion. Religion is responsible for a great deal of trouble, *ma petite."*

"But there is friendship between them. They visit."

She pursed her lips. "It is . . . how you say it . . . an armed neutrality. Between these two there is great desire to outdo each other. One must be better than the other. It has been the story over the years."

"You were there. Did Sir Francis go to Villers-Mûre very often?"

"Very rare did he come."

"And you came back with him. I never really understood that."

"Oh . . . it was an opportunity . . . and since I come this is my home. I work with Sallonger . . . St. Allengère no more."

"There is so much I do not understand."

She took my face in her hands and looked at me tenderly.

"There is so much most of us do not understand, *chérie."*

In due course the house settled to normality, and all through that summer the subject of Julia's coming out dominated the household. The season usually lasted from Easter until August, and so Julia must be ready by the spring. The Countess of Ballader came to stay for a week or so to assure herself, I supposed, that Julia would be worthy of her tuition.

She was a tall woman of imposing presence and one was immediately impressed by her vitality. I gathered that the Earl had been some thirty years older than she was and that he had died five years after their marriage—leaving her little but her title. Her auburn hair seemed a little brighter than nature had intended it to be; her sparkling eyes were a deep shade of green; and although she was employed by the Sallongers to launch Julia into society, she implied that it was a great favour she was bestowing upon them.

Miss Logan said that the Countess was dubious about concerning herself with a family engaged in Trade; but no doubt she needed the money; and as Sir Francis was a rich man there had been no doubt in Miss Logan's mind that the Countess would take on Julia. Miss Logan assumed a new importance. She had been lady's maid to a Duchess at one time and she talked about Her Grace as though she were some sort of goddess. I used to hear her discussions with Miss Everton and I listened whenever I could without being detected.

The Countess had several sessions with Lady Sallonger. Sometimes we were there—Julia, Cassie and I. I noticed the Countess's big green eyes surveying us speculatively. At first she was inclined to bully Lady Sallonger but she soon realized that she had a worthy adversary there. Lady Sallonger had enjoyed a long period delegating responsibility to others and now she gently slid that onto the Countess's shoulders. They talked of balls . . . the lists of guests . . . the clothes. Julia would have to learn to walk more gracefully: her curtsy needed attention. The Countess would have to be sure that she was going to make a success of Julia's entry into society before she would undertake her debut.

"I have had success with all my girls," she announced.

Lady Sallonger smiled and said how fortunate she was to have her *health*. If only she herself were stronger. She even had the Countess bringing a cushion for her back, and picking up her fan which she had a habit of dropping at certain moments.

I was quite amazed and excited by it all.

I said to Cassie: "In two or three years it will be your turn."

Cassie shuddered.

"I suppose it won't happen to me," I went on. "I shall have to find a husband for myself if I want one."

"You're lucky," said Cassie.

"It's a long time yet for you, and you will have learned all about it from Julia when your turn comes," I told her soothingly.

There was a great deal of activity in the workroom. Julia was often there for fittings.

"Mightn't the things you make be out of fashion by next year?" I asked Grand'mère.

"I do not give such great thought to fashion," replied Grand'mère.

"I take what suits. Julia needs frills and ribbons . . . and that is best for her. I shall make for Julia . . . not for fashion. If only it were you . . . what a dress I would make!"

"It won't ever be me. I'm only Lenore remember, not Miss."

Then I wished I hadn't said that because she looked sad and vaguely frightened, so that I felt I wanted to comfort her. I put my arm about her and held her close to me.

"It would be wonderful if . . ." she began.

"If what?" I asked.

But she would not go on. I knew her well and I guessed that she was worrying because I was not to have a season, and she was wondering how I was going to find a rich and handsome husband.

* * *

It was that summer when Drake Aldringham came to The Silk House. From the moment he came he seemed to change everything. We had heard that Charles was bringing a friend home for part of the vacation. Philip arrived first. He knew of Drake.

"It's a great feather in Charles's hat that he got Drake to come," he said.

"Why?" we all wanted to know.

"Why?" cried Philip almost indignantly. "This is Drake Aldringham."

"What is so special about him?" asked Julia excitedly, for since this talk of her coming out she was becoming very interested in young men which I supposed was natural as soon she would be on show to try to lure one of them into marrying her.

"In the first place he's an Aldringham," said Philip.

"What's that?" asked Julia.

"Do you mean to say you have never heard of Admiral Aldringham? That's Drake's father."

"Is he very grand?" I asked.

"Well . . . not more than he can help."

That seemed non-committal. It was difficult to get more out of Philip.

The visit was discussed at tea that afternoon. I poured out tea and Philip carried his mother's cup to her. "Thank you, dear," she said. "A little more milk . . . and I will have a piece of bread and butter. And have they sent honey? Is it clear or thick?" It was thick. "Oh dear, send for the clear . . . and put the rug round me, will you Lenore. I know the sun is shining outside but it is chilly in here."

When the clear honey had been brought and toyed with and I had replenished her cup Lady Sallonger mentioned the coming visit.

"When did you think Charles and he will be here, Philip?" she asked.

"I don't know, Mama. They were going walking in the Lake District. There are several of them but I think very soon Charles will be home with his guest."

"I look forward to meeting him. I am sure he is most excellent. The Admiral's son . . . Isn't there an Aldringham in the government?"

"Oh yes, Mama, that's Sir James, Drake's uncle. They are a very notable family."

"Drake! What an extraordinary name!"

"It sounds like a duck," I said irreverently.

"It might be other things besides. What about the great Sir Francis Drake? As a matter of fact that is who he is named after."

"Fancy being named after a great hero of the past. It would make you feel you had to live up to all that glory."

"One thing," said Philip, "you would not be expected to defeat the Spanish Armada. There's another meaning. Drakon. It is an old English word. Draca; and the Latin, of course, is Draco. Dragon."

"How learned you are."

"I looked it up."

"Because of your Drake?"

"I thought it was interesting."

"I wonder what he will be like," said Julia.

"A great sea captain . . . or a dragon?" I suggested.

Cassie said: "He's probably very mild and meek . . . not a bit like Sir Francis Drake or a dragon. It often happens that people are not like what their names suggest."

"You'll be surprised," said Philip.

"Lenore, do bring me one of those jam tarts," said Lady Sallonger. I obeyed.

"Oh . . . it's raspberry. I *do* like black currant. I wonder if they have any black currant."

This was the usual practice so I rang and Grace appeared. Soon she returned with black currant tarts.

I smiled as Lady Sallonger took one which I was sure she would only nibble. If it had been black currant in the first place she would have wanted raspberry. But I expected they were accustomed to her vagaries in the kitchen.

I was almost certain that we should be disappointed when Drake Aldringham appeared. Then I began to wonder whether he would come at all. Charles had not said when he was arriving and as the days passed we gave up expecting him.

Charles came back alone. There was real dismay. We had heard so much about Drake Aldringham that we were patiently awaiting him. Charles said Drake had had to go to spend a few days with an elderly aunt and was coming to The Silk House as soon as he could get away.

Charles had changed. I was always amazed to see him and Philip when they came home; they seemed to grow so fast and to change with it—particularly Charles. He was quite grown-up now; he walked with a swagger and drawled faintly. He was playing the part of a worldly young gentleman. I was faintly amused. I saw his eyes following Grace with some appreciation. I heard Miss Logan say to Miss Everton that she would like to know what he got up to . . . or perhaps it would be better not to know.

Miss Everton sighed and said: "They don't remain young long." She spoke with feeling. I imagined she was thinking they would not be needing her at The Silk House much longer.

Philip was very different from Charles—much more serious. I thought Charles was not very interested in the family business—or ever would be. But he was enormously interested in the female form.

Once, to my horror, I caught his eyes on me as though he were considering . . . what? I could not imagine. But I did not like that seering glance and I felt myself growing hot under it.

I was in the garden where I used to sit with Grand'mère and I was alone, hoping that she would join me as she often did at this hour. I heard footsteps and looked up expecting her. But it was a young man.

He was very tall and very fair . . . quite good looking in a Nordic way. When he saw me he smiled pleasantly. "Oh, I say," he said, "I hope I'm not intruding."

"No," I replied. "What . . . do you want? Are you looking for someone?"

"For Charles Sallonger actually. There wasn't time to let him know. I've left my luggage at the house and as none of the family was in I said I'd look round the garden for a while. It's a lovely spot. I knew it was in the heart of the forest but I didn't imagine it quite like this."

"Are you a visitor? You must be . . ."

"Drake Aldringham," he said.

"I might have guessed."

"Are you . . . Julia?"

"No. I'm Lenore Cleremont." Clearly he did not know who that was, so I explained: "I live here. I'm not one of the family. My grandmother works here and it has always been my home."

He nodded. "It's a most interesting place. Coming here from the station I thought it was magnificent."

"Yes, I feel that, too."

"Charles tells me it is the country house. There is a place in London."

"Yes, in Grantham Square. I have only been there once or twice. Sir Francis . . . that is Charles's father . . . is there most of the time."

I liked his friendly looks and the fact that his manner towards me had not changed when he had discovered that I was not a member of the family.

"I daresay Charles or Philip will be in soon," I said.

"I thought of paying my respects to Lady Sallonger but they said she was resting."

"Oh yes, she would be at this time. She is very delicate."

He nodded.

"We have been eagerly waiting for you to come," I told him.

"How nice of you."

"We've talked about you a lot . . . about Sir Francis Drake and all that."

He grimaced. "You can imagine what it has been like going round all my life with a name like that."

"Inspiring, I should think."

"A little daunting. They are expecting me to go to sea."

"And you don't want to?"

He shook his head. "I want to go into politics."

"I am sure that will be very exciting. There is always something going on . . . and you are shaping the country's destiny."

He laughed. "You make it sound like a great responsibility . . . but it is rather like that. I've always wanted to know what was going on and how we fit into European politics. My uncle has talked to me a great deal. He knows of my ambition."

"It must be very satisfying to know what you want in life. It enables you to go straight for it. So many people are undecided."

"Very often one has to deal with opposition."

"But that makes it more exciting in a way. How does one begin in politics?"

"Well, you really start at University. I'm in all sorts of things . . . debating society and political club. I see a great deal of my uncle. I go to the House and see him there. It gets into your blood. I read the newspapers and form my opinions about what is going on. I discuss it with my uncle, who encourages me in every way. I'm lucky to have him. It's so thrilling to learn of these things. People are apt to shut themselves up in little cocoons. They know what is happening in their immediate circle. They know the Tay Bridge was destroyed. They know Gladstone had defeated Beaconsfield and is in power. They know Parnell is being tried for conspiracy. But they don't really know what is going on in Africa. What I mean is they don't know *why*. I'm talking too much. You must forgive me. I get carried away."

I said: "I'm very interested. I am sure you would make an excellent politician."

Just at that moment Grand'mère came into the garden. She was looking for me.

"Grand'mère," I said. "This is Mr. Drake Aldringham. He has arrived and there is no one to receive him."

She came towards us. She had great dignity. One would have thought she was mistress of the house.

"We have heard so much about you," she said. "I am sure Charles will be quite put out that he was not here to greet you."

"It was my fault," he said. "I should have let him know, but I thought it was quicker just to come."

"So you have been received by my granddaughter."

"Yes, we have been having a very interesting conversation. But I'm afraid I was talking a great deal about myself."

"That is the sign of a good politician," I replied, and he laughed.

We sat down by the pool and I went on to say: "Mr. Aldringham has been telling me about his ambitions, Grand'mère."

We talked about the forest and he said he had been very eager to see

The Silk House. It was such an unusual name. One would expect it to be made of silk . . . if that were possible.

"You know of course that the Sallongers are the biggest manufacturers of silk of the country," said my grandmother. He did not know, but he was interested and I told the romantic story of the Huguenot St. Allengères coming to England and becoming Sallongers. "They had to leave everything they possessed," I said, "and all they could bring with them was their knowledge of silk."

He thought it was romantic and exciting and he said he would enjoy his stay at The Silk House all the more because of the fascinating history behind it.

I could see that Grand'mère liked him. She had a very special look in her eyes; she smiled and nodded and talked volubly with a sprinkling of French among her words.

We could have gone on quite happily for a long time but Charles came out. He had returned to the house and was immediately told that his guest had arrived and had gone into the gardens so he had come to look for him and I guessed the sound of our voices had directed him to us.

He stood at the entrance to the garden looking in surprise at Drake Aldringham sitting between myself and Grand'mère chattering to each other like old friends.

"Drake . . . old fellow," he said.

Drake stood up.

"So there you are," he said. "I should have let you know but it seemed more sensible to arrive."

"It's good to see you. Sorry I was out and there was no one to receive you."

"Oh, but there was Miss Lenore and her grandmother. We have had a very interesting chat."

Charles gave a sharp laugh. He hardly glanced at us. He took Drake's arm and said: "Let's go in."

Drake looked over his shoulder and smiled at us. "I'll see you later," he said.

And they had gone.

Grand'mère looked at me, her eyes smiling.

"But he is charming. He is very . . . *intéressant* . . . I like him. He is a very nice young man."

"I thought he was quite pleasant."

"It is good that such come to the house," said Grand'mère.

She looked at me with dreams in her eyes. I was beginning to realize how preoccupied she was with my future. As we went back to the house she was humming *En passant par la Lorraine* under her breath.

* * *

The entire household was enchanted by Drake Aldringham. He was natural in his behaviour, so enthusiastic about everything and charming to everyone. Even Cassie came out of her shell and talked to him with ease. Lady Sallonger was delighted with him. She would have him sit beside her and talk.

"My dear boy, you must tell me *all* about yourself. It is so exciting for me. Here I am a prisoner . . . on my couch doomed to spend my life here and you . . . you have these wonderful plans. Tell about that uncle of yours . . . and of course of your father. When are you going to get into Parliament? You must be our member, mustn't he Julia? We would all work for him, wouldn't we?"

"Oh yes, we would," said Julia fervently.

Julia was already half way to falling in love with him, but I think she would have been with any young man who had presented himself at that time.

He had great charm and could respond to Lady Sallonger's mildly flirtatious conversation and be quite serious with Philip; I used to hear him laughing heartily with Charles; he was at ease and at home with everybody. He always had a special smile for me; and I would often find him sitting next to me when we were in the drawing room. I thought meeting me first had made a special friendship between us.

Julia was a little resentful of that. I understood. She wanted Drake's undivided attention and it was indefensible that I, not even a member of the family, should take it from her. When I sat with him, Cassie would often join us and it was amazing how she lost her shyness in his company. I often found Charles's eyes on me and I felt rather uncomfortable under his scrutiny. I thought he was implying that I should remember my place.

It was agreed that something must be done to entertain the guest and Lady Sallonger decided on a dinner party. We should ask about twenty guests and with the family that should make a considerable party. They might dance afterwards, just informally as the company would be comparatively small. There was a ballroom which was not used half enough but would be, of course, after Julia had come out. Lady Sallonger thought that several people who did not live very far away should be invited. They need not stay the night. But there could be one or two from London who would have to, of course. But The Silk House was commodious enough. She grew quite excited planning it.

I was commanded to bring her writing pad and paper. "Not that one. Lenore . . . the larger one in my bureau." Finally we had the right pad and the right pen and the compilation of the list began.

There was excitement throughout the house. I was to go to the party. Certain duties had been assigned to me.

"You will look after the Barkers, Lenore," said Lady Sallonger. "I don't suppose anyone will want to talk to them . . . and I don't think people like to feel neglected. It makes the party seem unsuccessful. Perhaps I should not have asked them. They are very, very rich . . . but it was all made out of building. People might forget that but Jack Barker won't let them. He talks about property developments and decay in the industry all the time. I'm only asking them because we need the number and they are near enough to go home afterwards."

Grand'mère was in a state of uncertainty. Before she had known that I would be there she was thoughtful. "It will be a sign," she said. "I want you to be there . . . I do so want you to be there."

So when I was told about the Barkers she was overjoyed.

"I shall make you a dress, *mon enfant.* You shall have such a dress as will make you shine among them all."

"Julia wouldn't like that," I reminded her.

"Oh, she would not know. She is lacking in style, that one. She does not know a perfection when she sees it. She is too fond of show and glitter . . . but that is not style. Oh no. That is not *chic* . . ."

She did make me a dress. It was my first grown-up dress. It was in flame coloured silk, which suited my dark hair; it had a tight bodice and short puffed sleeves; the glory was in the skirt, which flared out from the waist in numerous flounces.

There were tears in Grand'mère's eyes when she fitted it on.

"You look so like your mother," she said. "I could almost believe . . ."

I embraced her and said it was very grand, and it would be my favourite dress for the rest of my life.

The evening came and the guests arrived. Lady Sallonger received them on her couch. She looked very regal when they came to bow to her. Charles and Philip were with her and Drake Aldringham, of course. It was all very splendid.

It was to be a buffet supper and the tables were set out in the dining room. The musicians were already playing in the ballroom and Lady Sallonger had arrived there leaning heavily on Charles's arm. She had seated herself to watch the dancing.

I, of course, was with the Barkers. Mr. Barker talked all the time about his business. Mrs. Barker said very little; she sat arms folded over her ample stomach looking like a Chinese Buddha and watching her husband as though the words which came from his ever-open mouth were some divine gospel.

Still, it was fun to be there. I learned of the difference between building with bricks and with stones, of the difficulty there was to find workmen who knew their jobs, and how people did not work as they used to with all this talk of reform. Things had started to decline since every Tom, Dick and Harry could get the vote.

I was not paying very much attention but I took my cue from Mrs. Barker and just assumed an air of respectful absorption while my mind wandered.

I saw Drake Aldringham with Julia. Cassie was seated beside her mother. She could not dance because of her leg. Poor Cassie, I thought, she did not enjoy such occasions very much.

Charles looked in my direction and I was amazed when he sauntered over.

"Good evening, Mr. Barker, Mrs. Barker," he said. "I hope you are enjoying the occasion."

"Splendid, splendid," replied Mr. Barker. "This is a finely proportioned room. They knew what they were doing when they built this place."

"I'll grant you that," said Charles, giving me a conspiratorial look. "Alas, Mr. Barker, that you were not around at the time. I am sure if you had been it would have been even more splendid."

Mr. Barker looked pleased. "Oh, I would have brought a bit of modernity into it. That fireplace. Look at it. It must use up tons of coal. Should have been more shallow."

"I am sure you are right. I am going to take Lenore round the floor. She looks as if she is longing to dance."

I turned to Mrs. Barker. I felt it was strange that Charles should be so concerned about me.

Mrs. Barker said: "That's nice. Young people ought to enjoy themselves. We'll see you later, Miss Cleremont."

Charles had gripped my arm.

"There," he said, as he led me into the dance. "Ah, the waltz. I love the waltz, don't you?" He put his arm round my waist and drew me close to him.

My heart was beating fast. I was suspicious of him. I could not understand why he was being so genial towards me after the indifference—tinged with contempt—which he had so often shown me.

"I hope," he went on, "that you are grateful to me for rescuing you from those two old bores."

"Oh," I replied. "They are not so bad. Mr. Barker must be an expert builder."

"Why Mama had to ask them, I cannot imagine, and then to condemn you to look after them! Cruelty to the young, I call that. I say, Lenore, you look remarkably pretty tonight."

"Thank you. It's the dress."

"If you were to ask me I should say it is what is inside the dress."

His fingers crept up to the bare flesh of my neck and I felt a shiver run through me. He was aware of it.

"You are very young, Lenore," he said. "Just a little girl, in fact."

"I shall soon be sixteen."

"Dear me! What a great age! Sweet sixteen and never been kissed. Or have you?"

He was whirling me round at a great speed. I loved to dance. I used to dance with Julia. Miss Logan was teaching her. I imagined that when the season grew nearer she would have a real dancing master or mistress. Dancing was one of the social graces at which one must be proficient when coming out. I joined in the lessons to give Julia a partner and I always enjoyed the session. But I was not really enjoying this. Charles seemed quite different from the young man whom I had known before. I had always thought I was far beneath his notice.

We were passing a door and as we came level with it his grip tightened about my waist and he swung me out of the ballroom . . . all along the corridor.

I gasped: "What are you doing? Where are you taking me?"

"Patience," he sang out.

He opened a door and we were in a small room where the maids did the flowers every day. There was a sink and a tap. It was very cold and dark. I suddenly felt his lips on mine and I had rarely been so horrified.

"Let me go," I shouted.

"Why should I?"

"I didn't know . . ."

"You know. I think you are rather pretty. You're a babe, but babes can be taught and there are a lot of things I can teach you."

"I . . . I don't think I want to hear them. I want to go back to the ballroom. I have to make sure the Barkers get supper."

"The Barkers can take care of themselves for a while. Come on, Lenore. What's the matter? You know I like you, don't you?"

"I am sure you don't," I said. "You've always despised me."

"I never despise pretty girls," he said, attempting to insert his fingers into the neck of my dress.

"How dare you!" I cried. "I am going . . . now."

He barred the way. "Now come on. You can't tease me like this. I don't like girls who tease."

"And I don't like people who force themselves on others."

"Oh, you are a haughty piece, are you not?"

"I am myself and I choose people I shall talk to."

"You little bastard," he said.

I caught my breath and he laughed sneeringly. "Why so shocked? It's what you are. Why we have you in the house I don't know. Giving yourself airs . . . can't accept a friendly kiss . . . after leading me on."

I was silent with rage and astonishment.

He could not see my face because it was dark. He said in a more gentle tone: "Don't be silly, Lenore. I like you. You ought to be pleased about that. But of course you are. I'm going to give you a good time. We're going to be friends. This is just a beginning. It's a pity you sleep near your grandmother. Do you think the old lady would hear if I came up quietly?"

I cried out: "I cannot understand why you are talking to me like this."

"Because you're growing into an attractive girl and it is time you realized what good fun attractive girls can have."

My anger was turning cold. I knew that he was implying that

because of my lowly and less than respectable birth I should welcome the attentions of the son of the house. I had never liked him. Now I hated him.

"Please understand that I want to go at once and that I will have no more of this kind of behaviour."

"Oh, she is haughty, is she? Whom do you imagine you are? French scum . . . that's what you are. And because I want to be kind to you . . . show you what a gentleman can do for you . . . you give yourself airs."

"The trouble is that you are not a gentleman."

He gripped my arm roughly. "Listen to me, my girl. All I want from you is a bit of fun. That's what girls like you are meant for. You've no right in this house. Your grandmother may work for us but that does not mean that you can play the haughty lady . . . not unless you earn the right. Come on, Lenore, I'm telling you I like you. Give me a kiss. There's a lot I can show you."

I was in a panic. I was alone with him in this dark cubby hole. I brought up my hand sharply and hit him in the face. I had taken him by surprise and I heard his gasp of astonishment as he released me. I lost no time in slipping past him. I dashed out into the corridor. I did not stop running for I felt he might come after me. I sped up to my bedroom. I caught a glimpse of myself in a mirror. My face was flushed and my hair in disorder. I washed in cold water and was relieved to see that the red marks on my arms were beginning to disappear. I combed my hair with shaking fingers; but already I was feeling calmer.

Perhaps he had drunk too much claret cup. I could not believe that he really liked me. He felt towards me as he did towards the maids who tittered when he glanced their way and looked secretive as though there was some special understanding between them. He wished to treat me as he treated them.

I was very frightened but I must return to the ballroom for I should be missed. The party was not so large that absentees could fail to be noticed for long. I went down and slipped into the ballroom. No one looked at me in surprise. The Barkers were still alone. I went over to them.

"Did you enjoy your dance?" asked Mrs. Barker.

I smiled vaguely and asked if they would like to go in to supper.

As I conducted them to the dining room, I saw Charles. He was talking to Amelia Barrington, one of the daughters of our nearest neighbours. He looked right through me as though he did not see me.

"A fine room," Mr. Barker was saying. "There's a sign of damp up there. That wants looking into."

Philip joined us with Cassie. Cassie looked a little tired. She would be glad when this was over. It must be rather sad to sit and watch the dancing without joining in. Philip talked to Mr. Barker—or rather allowed him to talk and seemed quite interested in the building trade, or perhaps he was just being polite.

He told me afterwards that he had a lot of sympathy for those people who were dedicated to their work. It was exactly how he felt about silk.

I lived through the rest of the evening in a daze. I could not get that unpleasant encounter with Charles out of my mind.

When I finally retired Grand'mère came in to talk to me. She sat on the edge of my bed in her silk wrap which, because she had made it herself, was the essence of elegance.

"And what happened?" she asked. "Did you dance?"

"A little. Mr. Barker doesn't dance and I had to look after them."

"Did you dance with Mr. Aldringham?"

"No . . . he was with Julia quite a lot."

She looked disappointed.

"I danced with Philip just after supper, which I had with him and Cassie and the Barkers."

Grand'mère did not look very pleased. She said: "You are tired. You must go to sleep."

It was not so much that I wanted to sleep as to be alone to think over the evening, which meant that unpleasant encounter with Charles.

Grand'mère was disappointed. The young girl after her first ball should have been filled with excitement, bursting with the need to talk of the thrilling evening. And all I could do was think about those terrifying moments in the cubby hole. It was not that I wanted to. I just could not help it.

*　*　*

When I saw Charles the next day he did not seem to be aware of me. I began to feel relieved. He had forgotten. It was the way in which he behaved to any female whom he considered beneath him. Perhaps I had been unduly perturbed. He had tried and failed and he must have been very angry because of that stinging blow I gave him. It would have been a physical hurt as well as an insult.

The following morning Julia was annoyed because Charles and Philip had taken Drake off somewhere and it seemed they would be away for the whole of the day.

In the afternoon I went for a ride with her and Cassie. She was talking all the time about the party.

"It was really quite enjoyable," she said. "I can't wait to be 'out.' Then it will be all parties like that. Drake will be in London. He's bound to be asked to all the parties . . . or most of them . . . because of his father and his uncle. People are more respectful towards cabinet ministers than admirals."

"One wouldn't have thought so," I said, "when you consider the way in which they are vilified by the press."

"People take an interest in them because of that. There has to be a war for sailors to be made much of. I do hope Drake goes into politics. It will be most exciting."

Cassie said thoughtfully: "Do you think you will be there to see the excitement?"

Julia blushed. "I . . . I always thought I'd like to lead that sort of life. You know, all the thrill of elections . . . and going to the House and meeting people like Lord Beaconsfield and Mr. Gladstone. Mary Anne Wyndham Lewis was afterwards Lord Beaconsfield's wife. Everybody called her Mary Anne even when she became Lady Beaconsfield. It's frightfully romantic. She had lots of money. That was really why he married her."

"Very romantic," I said sarcastically. "Would you agree, Cassie?"

"Well, often those suitable marriages turn out very well in the end," said Julia. "Theirs did and she used to say that he might have married her for money, but after the years together he would marry her for love. Drake was most interesting about it. You would have loved it, Cassie . . . so would you, Lenore. But you had to look after those boring Barkers."

"Philip and Cassie came along and helped out. It wasn't so bad then."

"Theirs is a happy marriage," said Cassie. "Mrs. Barker thinks Mr. Barker is quite wonderful. It is rather charming to watch the way she listens to him, nodding her head all the time. I think if anyone said a word against him, or attempted to contradict him, she would be ready to slay them."

"That sort of marriage where one partner is subservient to the other is bound to be a success," I said. "I expect that is what every man is looking for."

"I don't think Drake would want that. He loves you to disagree with him. I've noticed that."

"I hadn't," said Cassie.

"Dear Cass, you haven't been with him like I have." She preened herself. "He is so amusing. I loved the story of Lord Beaconsfield's wife. I think he was plain Mr. Benjamin Disraeli then. She hurt her hand when she got into the carriage to drive with him to the House, where he was going to make an important speech. She did not tell him that she had crushed her hand in the carriage door when getting into it. The pain must have been terrible but she sat there smiling and chatting as though nothing was wrong because she feared he might be upset and that would spoil his speech. The pain must have been terrible."

"What a lovely story," said Cassie. "I like it very much, don't you, Lenore?"

"Yes," I replied. "But I was thinking that I would not want to be a shadow of my husband . . . like Mrs. Barker for instance. I should want to be myself. I might want to do something in life . . . quite apart from marriage."

Julia said: "Oh, I wouldn't want to be somebody else's shadow. Politicians' wives, though, have their place in society. Disraeli's Mary Anne used to follow everything that went on in the House and she used to sit up and wait for him to come home and she always had a cold supper waiting for him no matter at what time he arrived; and then he would tell her all that had gone on in Parliament. And Mrs. Gladstone is very well known in society. *She* always makes sure that *her* husband's material comforts are looked after. Drake says that in the home she is the one who gives the orders. So you see . . . it is a most exciting life."

"Why are you suddenly so interested in the political scene?" asked Cassie.

Julia blushed a little. "I suppose it is because I've been talking to Drake."

Cassie and I exchanged glances. It was clear to us that this was

Julia in love. It was to be expected. She was past seventeen and Drake would be about four years older, so both of them could be considered marriageable.

As we neared the house we met Drake with Charles. They had obviously been for a ride.

"Hello," said Drake. "Are you just returning?"

"We've been taking an afternoon's ride," explained Julia.

"The forest is beautiful," said Drake. He smiled at us all in his friendly fashion. Julia was gazing at him. She was rather obvious, I thought, and wondered if I dared tell her that it would be better to hide her feelings a little.

"Going back to the house now?" asked Charles.

Julia said we were.

I did not speak. Charles had not addressed me. He behaved as though I were not there. I wondered if he were going to ignore me from then on. I did not mind if he did. In fact I should be rather pleased.

We rode towards the house. Drake was between Julia and me.

He said: "It was a most interesting evening."

"It was, wasn't it," replied Julia.

"I saw you were very busily engaged," he went on, turning to me.

"Lenore had orders from Mama," explained Julia. "Mama was afraid people would find the Barkers boring. So Lenore had to look after them."

"That was very noble of you," said Drake.

"Not in the least. I was told to do it."

"Never mind," put in Julia. "You were there and you danced with Charles and Philip. We had a marvellous time, didn't we, Drake?"

"It was very amusing," he answered.

"What about you, Charles?" asked Julia.

"Oh, I had a very good evening," said Charles.

"Enjoying yourself with the young ladies?"

"Immensely," replied Charles.

We had come to the mausoleum.

"What an extraordinary building," commented Drake.

"It's the mausoleum," Julia explained.

"It's most ornate."

"It was built about a hundred years ago," explained Charles. "It's rather eerie, is it not?"

"Well, I suppose it would be," said Drake. "Is it open?"

"Good Heavens, no. It's opened very rarely . . . only when some-one is put in there, I suppose. Just think, I shall be there one day . . . Philip too. What a thought. You girls . . . well, I suppose you'll marry and you won't be Sallongers then . . . so therefore unworthy of the place."

"I've always been interested in mausoleums," said Drake. He had dismounted. "I want to look at it. That stone work is unusual. All that work . . . for the resting place of the dead."

"I call it the House of the Dead," said Cassie.

"That makes it sound quite frightening," said Julia with a shiver.

"I wouldn't like to walk past it at night," went on Cassie. "Would you, Lenore?"

"I think I should feel a little uneasy," I admitted.

"I wonder why they call it a mausoleum," said Julia. "It suits it, doesn't it? You couldn't imagine having a party in a mausoleum."

"I think the eeriness has become attached to the word because of what it implies," suggested Drake.

"I wonder who first called it that," said Cassie.

"I can tell you that," added Drake. "I was thinking of taking up archaeology at one time. If I fail as a politician, I might take it up again. It is called a mausoleum because of the tomb erected at Halicar-nassus to Mausolus, the King of Caria, by his widow. That was about 353 B.C. I believe it was large and magnificent and was recognized to be one of the seven wonders of the world."

"I'd love to see it," I cried.

He turned to me with a smile. "That would be quite impossible," he said. "It fell into decay during the thirteenth and fourteenth centuries. People took parts of it away for building material."

"The Mr. Barkers of the thirteenth and fourteenth centuries," I murmured.

"No doubt they didn't regard themselves as vandals. But when you are in London, Lenore, I'll take you to the British Museum. The site was discovered not so long ago—about 1857—and all that could be saved was brought to England. It has now been set up in the Mu-seum."

"How I should love to see it."

"One day you shall."

"I should like to see it, too," said Julia.

"It will be a great pleasure for me to take you both."

"And me?" said Charles.

"But, of course. I see I have succeeded in arousing your interest." He turned to Charles. "Is it possible to see inside?"

"I imagine so," said Charles. "There is a key somewhere. I daresay Clarkson knows where."

"Why don't you go and get it, Charles," suggested Julia. "Then we could all look now."

"I should so enjoy that," said Drake.

Charles said: "Very well, I will." And he strode towards the house.

"I hope I don't bore you with my enthusiasm," said Drake.

"It is rather different from the Barker lore," I said.

He laughed and Julia put in: "I think the past is so fascinating. You must have had lots of fun, Drake, discovering these things."

"It *is* fascinating. I should love to be involved in some spectacular discovery . . . revealing a lost city . . . some temple or tomb. Of course that sort of thing happens once in a lifetime. Most of it is a hard slog with no rewards."

"I can see that politics is going to win," I said.

He smiled ruefully. "I expect it will."

We talked a little while about old tombs and the party last night until Charles came back triumphantly holding up the key.

"Now," he said, "your ghoulish curiosity will be satisfied."

We had all dismounted and followed Charles past the angels with flaming swords to the gate. As we passed along Drake noticed the cross protruding from the ground.

"That looks like a miniature grave," he said.

"It is a grave," Julia told him. "A dog is buried there."

"One of your pets?"

"No . . . not ours," said Julia.

I explained: "The dog belonged to one of the boys from the stables. He was very attached to it and some wicked boys stoned it to death . . . not far from here. He was terribly upset. He is rather simple and loved the dog so much. How people can do such things I cannot imagine." I spoke passionately remembering it all. I still felt strongly about that accident. I knew that Willie often visited the grave and sat there talking to the dog. I had heard him. He had little Pepper now who comforted him a great deal, but I guessed he never forgot the other.

I was rather ashamed to feel that there were tears in my eyes.

"It was a foul thing to do," said Drake vehemently. "Only mindless idiots act so."

He took my arm, pressed it in sympathy and walked close to me towards the angels.

"Ready?" said Charles. "The great moment has come." He put the key in the lock and turned it with some difficulty. "It's stiff," he explained, "because it is opened so rarely . . . only when they are taking some poor Sallonger to join his forefathers."

"I should have thought the air inside will not be very good," said Drake.

"There is a little space open to the air . . . somewhere . . . I believe," Charles told him.

The door had swung open. We were confronted by steep stairs which led down into darkness. We descended in single file, Charles leading the way.

"Careful," he shouted. "Don't slip, any of you. You never know what could happen to you down here."

We went down and down. There must have been at least thirty steps. Then we were in the high underground chamber. We were confronted by an enormous piece of statuary of the Virgin and the infant Christ and another of a woman and two angels. Beside this group was a figure which was clearly meant to represent Satan. He appeared to be attacking the angels with the sceptre he carried. Presumably they were fighting for the soul of the deceased woman. It was indeed eerie, for there was only a shaft of light which came from high up in the wall through a gap in the stone and which I calculated must be at about ground level. Along the sides of the chamber were rows of coffins.

It was very cold and I began to shiver. I felt as though I were being caught up in the past.

"Impressive," whispered Drake. "Do you know it is built on the same lines as Mausolus's tomb? I've seen pictures of what it must have looked like long ago, before it fell into decay."

"How would you like to spend a night down here?" enquired Charles. "You, Cass . . . eh, what about you?"

"I think my hair would turn white overnight," said Cassie. "People's hair does, you know, if they are very shocked."

"It would be rather fun to see what you look like with white hair," said Charles. "What about leaving her here?"

"No," shrieked Cassie.

"Of course we wouldn't," Drake assured her. "It's only the darkness and the thought of the dead, you know. That's what makes it so ghostly. It's really just an underground tomb."

"I wonder what happens at night," said Julia. "Do you think they come out of their coffins and dance round here?"

"Not very pleasant just in their shrouds. The temperature is a little bleak," said Charles.

Drake was walking round examining the walls, and declared that it was all fascinating.

"We should open it to tourists," said Charles.

"But it's so chilly," added Julia.

"I think you are all cowards," said Charles. "But what can you expect from a parcel of girls?"

I felt the dampness seeping into my bones. I looked at the coffins on the ledges and thought there was room for many more.

Then I felt myself suddenly gripped by the shoulders.

"Gotcher," whispered a voice in my ear. "I am the ghost of the mausoleum. I am going to keep you down here as my bride."

I turned sharply and looked into the gleaming eyes of Charles. His face was very near my own and I was seized with trembling.

"Why, you are scared," he said laughing.

"Who wouldn't be, jumped on like that in a place like this," said Drake. "Stop playing tricks, Charles."

Charles answered: "I didn't think she would be so easily scared. You're a frightened little thing, Lenore, for all your bravado."

"Let's go," said Julia. "I've had enough. We've seen it. That was all you wanted, Drake."

"Yes, it has been most interesting. I'd like to come again. Next time we should bring candles."

"And warm coats," added Cassie.

Julia was making for the steps.

"I'll go first," announced Charles, "and lead the way."

"I'll take up the rear," said Drake.

"I was wondering who was going to be the last," said Charles. "You girls would all have been scared wondering who was coming to claw you back. Well, you have been ill-mannered enough to call uninvited at their private house."

"I'll make sure they don't get me," added Drake. "Come on. It is really chilly."

We were all breathing heavily after the climb up the steps and, blinking, came out in the fresh air.

"Well, I hope you enjoyed it," said Charles. "All present and correct." He glanced at me. "You look as if you've seen a ghost. I really do believe you thought you had."

"No," I replied. "It was just the suddenness of the attack."

He grimaced. "I'll have to get this key back to Clarkson. He was most insistent. See you shortly."

He rode away.

"It was quite an experience," said Drake, looking at me.

*   *   *

It was the afternoon of the following day. Drake had gone off with Charles and Philip on some masculine excursion early in the morning. Julia was in a bad temper because of this. She wanted to be with Drake all the time.

I took a book and was on my way to the pond garden when I met one of the young boys from the stables. He came running to me rather breathlessly. He said: "Oh, Miss, I was coming to the house to see if I could find you. I wanted to see you."

"What's wrong?" I asked.

"It's Willie. He's lost his dog."

"Oh no . . ."

"Yes, Miss. He's in a state about it. He's been in the forest looking for him all day. I think I might know where he is."

"Well, where is he?"

"He's in that burial place, Miss. People was there yesterday. P'raps he got in while the door was open. I thought I heard him there . . . through that slit in the wall. I put me ear there . . ."

"Well, have you told Willie?"

"Couldn't find him. I thought as you . . . being friendly with him like . . . and me not liking to go down on me own."

"Well, we must go and see."

He held up a key.

"I got it from Mr. Clarkson . . . I don't like to go in on me own . . . I thought as how you . . ."

It seemed possible that Pepper had gone into the mausoleum. It must have been when the door was open and we were all down there. I could imagine his sniffing round the place. He came there often with Willie.

I did not relish going into that dark underground place.

I said to the boy: "Come on . . . we'll both look round."

He hesitated.

"Oh come on," I said impatiently. "I shall be there. You won't be alone."

The boy unlocked the door leaving the key in the lock and we started down the steps, I leading the way. I picked my way carefully and warned him to do the same. I said: "The stairs might be damp and slippery."

He did not answer. Then I realized that he was not following me. I heard voices through the open door. I was relieved. Someone else was there.

"Pepper," I called. "Pepper, where are you?"

There was a shadow behind me.

I said: "He's probably hiding. He must have been rather scared when he found he could not get out."

I had reached the bottom of the stairs and turned. I went cold with fear. Charles was behind me.

"Charles!" I cried.

"The very same."

"How . . . how did you get here?"

"By the usual means . . . on my two feet."

"Where is the boy?"

"I sent him back. Oh don't worry, I have the key."

He held it up smiling at me.

I was determined not to show how frightened I was to be in such a place . . . alone with Charles. This was more than fear. It was like something out of a nightmare.

"Pepper," I called, "where are you?"

"The little beast is probably hiding. We'll find him . . . if he's here. Pepper. Come here."

There was no answer. Our voices in that strange place sounded unfamiliar.

"Well, if he is not here we'd better go," I said. "The boy thought he heard a dog down here and it seemed very likely as we had the door open yesterday and he comes here with Willie a good deal."

"I don't think he's here." He turned and looked at me. "You're scared," he said.

"I don't like this place."

"Not very cosy, is it? And you like it less because you're alone here with me."

I wondered if I could pass him and make a dash for the stairs. Could I reach the top before him? I knew I could not, for it was so gloomy one would have to pick one's way with care.

"You should not be afraid of me," he said in a soft voice. "I have told you I want to be your friend. But you won't let me."

"I do not want the sort of friendship you are suggesting."

"Oh, I know you are a very pure young lady. It's a pity. What are you afraid of?"

"I think we should go now. The dog cannot be here. He would come when called if he were."

"You think I'm going to attack you, don't you? That I am going to force you to submit to my evil desires. Is that not so? Confess. You think me capable of that, don't you?"

"Yes, I do."

He laughed. "You're a bold wench. Let me tell you that I do not have to beg for favours."

"I am sure you don't. So why don't you take from those who are willing . . . perhaps eager to give them?"

"There are plenty who are, I assure you. Therefore I will not do that which I could so easily do, for, my proud little bastard, you are at my mercy down here. What a setting for the ravishment. Surrounded by the dead."

"I am going now."

"Not so fast. You should be in terror that I shall rob you of your innocence . . . for innocent you are, are you not? Such a stinging blow that was, you gave me. I feel it still. No. I would not give what I have to offer to a slut who would not appreciate it."

"I can understand that. I am sorry I hit you. But you did provoke me. But now that we understand each other perhaps we can forget the incident."

"I do not forget insults so easily."

"I thought I was the one who was insulted."

"Because you have ideas above your station, little Miss Cleremont?"

"Perhaps," I said, "but I hope never to trouble you with them again."

"Then we will go."

He was on the stairs a little ahead of me. Suddenly he turned and said: "Listen. Did you hear that?"

I stood very still listening and turned to stare back down into the dark chamber. "No, I can hear nothing," I said.

Then I heard him laugh. While my back was turned he had been mounting the stairs. He started to run up them and he was well ahead of me. I heard the door shut with a bang just as I reached it. Then I heard the key turn in the lock.

A terrible fear came over me.

I was alone . . . locked in the house of the dead.

* * *

I went to the door and beat on it with my two fists.

"Let me out. Let me out," I cried.

He must have been very close to the door but I heard his laugh.

"You were very rude to me, you little bastard," he shouted. "You have to be punished for that. Stay there with the departed and think about the way you behaved to the son of the house which has been your benefactor for so many years. You ungrateful little beast. You have to learn, you know."

"No . . . no!" I cried.

The laugh was fainter now. He had gone leaving me here.

I sat down on the stone steps and covered my face with my hands. It was very dark now that the door was closed. I thought: This is not happening. This is a dream. I shall wake up soon.

But I knew it was not a dream. I knew he had thought of doing this to me yesterday, that he had lured me here. The boy must have been obeying his orders. There was no question of the dog's being lost.

I called: "Help! Help!" My voice sounded feeble echoing through the underground chamber. Perhaps if someone was right outside they would hear it. But who would be there? And how long should I stay here?

I was afraid to move from the stairs. I did not want to go down to the chamber where the coffins were. It was better there on the stairs where I could not see them.

They would miss me soon. Grand'mère would be worried. She

would insist on their looking for me. It could not be very long. But even a little time in such a place would be terrifying.

Why had I been such a trusting fool? I should have made the boy go down first, but I had been so eager to find Willie's lost dog. I would have done anything to restore him to his young master.

I sat staring down into the gloom. Silence can be frightening. I realized I was straining my ears for some sound from the dead.

I thought of stories of ghosts which I had heard. If there were ghosts anywhere in the world they would be in a place like this.

I heard myself praying incoherently: "Please God, let someone come now . . . quickly . . . now . . . *now.*"

I stood up. My legs were already numb. Again I banged on the door until my fists hurt. I knew the futility of that but I continued to do it. Suppose no one came . . . not until another Sallonger died and they opened the door to bring in the coffin and found me . . . dead.

But they would look for me. They must find me. But who would think of looking here? The stable boy would tell them. But no. He had been primed to do his part by Charles. My hatred for Charles momentarily overcame my fear. Why were people so loathsome? Why did they do such wicked things to other people? Those cruel boys who had stoned Willie's dog . . . Charles, who could do this to me because I would not submit to his lust.

I wondered how long I had been here. Was it fifteen minutes? Thirty? I was so frantic I could not think of what I must do. I had had no warning. I had been prepared for him to assault me. I would have fought him with all my strength if he had . . . but it had not occurred to me that this would be his revenge.

Was it likely that anyone would pass this way? When the evening came no one would. The servants never liked passing the place after dusk. Was I to spend a night here? And even when that was over . . . what then?

But they must come to look for me. Grand'mère would see to that. She would not have missed me yet . . . not until it was time for us to go to bed. Then she would grow alarmed.

I went again to the door and hammered on it in frustration. I called for help. How stupid of me. As if anyone would hear. It was so gloomy here. Down in the underground chamber there would be a faint light from that open slit high in the wall of the chamber but just above ground level outside. It was enough to let in a little air and a little light.

I felt an impulse to descend the stairs.

I stood in the underground chamber . . . dark, gloomy, the coffins on the ledges, the statues seeming, in my present mood, as though they had come to life. Satan's sceptre seemed to move. I had a notion that he was giving his attention to me.

I turned my eyes away and stared at the opening in the wall. Perhaps if I went close and shouted, I should be heard by someone. But what was the use? There would be no one there to hear me.

I could not bear to remain in the chamber with the gloom and the darkness and the presence of Death. Yet if I was to be heard I must be there . . . because of that gap. I stared at it. It seemed to offer me my only hope of communication with the outside world.

How long should I stay here? Surely Charles must realize what I was feeling. He would come back soon feeling he had punished me enough. I remembered what Cassie had said. Her hair would turn white overnight. I touched my hair tentatively. I could not be here all through the night. No one could be so cruel . . . not even Charles.

But people were cruel. I should never forget the boys who had stoned Willie's dog. Such pointless violence was the product of minds that had grown vicious because they were empty of everything else. But Charles was not like that. Charles had had education. This was not mindless cruelty. It was revenge.

I had repulsed him; and because of my humble birth he had objected fiercely to that—and he was teaching me a lesson.

I prayed again to the statue of the Virgin and the Child. I sat down on the lowest step and resisted the urge to run up to the top and shut out the sight of that gloomy chamber with its statues and remains of the dead.

I noticed the moisture trickling down the walls and saw two drops running parallel as though in a race. How could one notice such things at such a time?

I thought: Shall I die down here? Suppose they never find me. I remembered the bride who on her wedding day had hidden in a chest; the lock clicked and she could not escape. The players hunted for her . . . but she was not found . . . not until years later when someone opened the chest and found the remains of her in her wedding gown.

The story had always intrigued me. Poor bride! How had she felt when she could not get out? At least my case was not quite so hope-less.

He will come back, I assured myself. This is just to tease me. He will leave me here for perhaps an hour and then he will come and unlock the door and laugh at me.

How long had passed? I had no way of knowing. When one was in this state one was unaware of time.

Silence . . . that terrible silence. I listened, my ears strained for some sound . . . some indication that someone was near. I longed to hear a sound . . . any sound.

There was nothing.

I walked back to the stairs. I felt I was being watched by a ghostly unseen presence. There was still light coming through the gap. It must be fairly sunny outside. So it was not night yet.

When it was quite dark something would happen.

I sat on the lower step in despair.

* * *

Was it an hallucination or did I hear the barking of a dog? I was alert listening. Yes . . . faintly . . . in the distance. It was coming from outside. I went across the chamber and stood immediately below the gap.

"Help! Help!" I cried. "I'm in the mausoleum . . . locked in."

There was silence.

Then I heard the dog again. This time more distinctly and I shouted with all my might. I fancied a shadow crossed the gap.

"Help! Help! Get me out of here."

The shadow was gone.

I stood for some time straining my ears. But now I could hear nothing.

I felt limp with despair. Had someone really been there or had I imagined it? Perhaps in my present state I had heard what I wanted to.

The silence was back and I was in despair. I was shivering, whether with cold or fear, I did not know.

No one will come this way, I told myself. If they did they would not hear me. I would stay here for the night unless Charles came back. He *must*.

Time was passing. I felt faint. My feet were numb; so were my hands. I could feel the cold from the stones penetrating through my clothes.

Grand'mère would be unaware as yet. She would be busy in the workroom. That always absorbed her. When she knew that I was missing she would be frantic. She would insist on their searching everywhere. But who would think of the mausoleum?

Then suddenly I heard a noise. The stairs seemed less dark. It was the scrape of the key turning in the lock. There was a shaft of light as the door was flung open.

Then a voice said: "Lenore, are you there?"

I heard the barking of a dog. I stumbled up the stairs. I was caught in someone's arms.

"Drake . . ." I murmured. "Drake . . ."

Drake said: "It's all right now. My God, you're frozen."

The dog was barking and I was pulled through into the open. The fresh air seemed intoxicating. I felt dizzy. I thought I was going to faint.

"It's all right now. It's all right now . . ." It was Drake's voice. I saw Willie then . . . and I heard the dog again.

"I'll get you back to the house," said Drake.

Then I found myself sliding to the ground.

When I regained consciousness I was sitting on the step outside the gate and Drake was forcing my head between my knees.

"That's better. You poor, poor child. How did it happen? Never mind. It's all over now."

"Drake," I said.

"Yes, it's Drake."

"You've saved me."

"Come on. I'm going to get you back quickly. You want a warm bed and something to soothe you. Can you stand up?"

I did so totteringly. I was aware of Willie who was looking on in amazement.

"Not very steady," said Drake. Then he lifted me up.

"You can't . . ."

"But I can. You're as light as a feather. Come on. No time to lose."

We went across to the house.

I said: "Charles . . . he told you . . ."

"Charles?"

"Charles locked me in."

Drake did not speak; he just walked on in silence. As we came into the hall he said: "That was fine, Willie. You did well. Thank you. Miss Cleremont will thank you when she gets better."

"So it was Willie," I said.

"He heard you calling and had the sense to come to the house. I saw him and he told me, so I got the key and came at once."

I felt such relief that I could not speak.

I saw Mrs. Dillon and Clarkson.

"My goodness gracious me," said Mrs. Dillon. "Whatever next?"

And there was Grand'mère.

She took charge at once. I was to be taken up to my bedroom.

In a short time I was lying on my bed, covered with blankets and a hot water bottle pressed against my feet.

Grand'mère was seated by my bed.

I slept fitfully. I kept waking and thinking I was in the mausoleum. I cried out in fear. Grand'mère was there beside me all through the night. She gave me a soothing drink with herbs. And finally I passed into a peaceful sleep, confident that she would not leave me, so that if I woke in terror, I should be comforted by her presence.

*　*　*

The next morning I felt better, but Grand'mère insisted that I stay in bed. I had been chilled to the bone, she said, and I had had a terrible fright.

I told her about it, beginning with the episode at the party.

"It was his revenge on me, you see, Grand'mère," I explained.

"Mon Dieu," she murmured, "to think that he could do such a thing! He is one to beware of. But at least, *ma petite,* we now know the man we have to deal with. I wish I could get you away from here. Philip is a gentle, kindly boy . . . so different. But this one. Malevolent . . . that is what he is. But, *ma chérie,* it could have been worse. When I think of you alone in that place and what he might have done . . . I have always wanted to tell you about the dangers. You are not such a little girl now. You will catch the eyes . . . as you have done with Charles. I thank the good God that this was not worse. Oh, I know of your ordeal . . . of your terror. How could you not be afraid . . . to be shut up in that place? But this . . . it is over. It is a bad, bad dream . . . But when I think of what a man of his nature might have done . . . Then there would have been the great damage. That

would have been something for which I could have killed him. But for this I would too . . . but for that other . . ."

I knew what she meant and I knew that I had something for which to be thankful.

"There must be no more of him," went on Grand'mère. "He will be away soon and we shall be free of him. I cannot be happy while he is in the house."

"He hates me, Grand'mère."

"For wounding his vanity, for refusing him. Yes . . . he is a *montagne* of deceit, that one. He thinks he is handsome and irresistible. One must beware of such men. But at least we know what we have to deal with. It is a warning. Once you have recovered from this, you will forget it. It will fade. It is like a nightmare that happened to be real. But it sometimes is good to know the nature of people who live close to us. So . . . something good comes out of evil. We now know what we have to consider in this Charles."

"And we shall be together, Grand'mère."

"While I am wanted, I am here. When you are older you will have a husband and children . . . and grand'mères . . . they are not then of such importance. Never mind. It is natural and right that this should be so. But for the time . . . we are together, eh? And while I am with you I will watch over you . . . and you will tell me when you are afraid. I know that in time you are going to be happy. I want you to have all your mother missed. She was thoughtlessly happy . . . too trusting. Well, that is in the past and this is the present, and we must live in that."

I woke up next morning with a terrible fear for a moment that I was in the mausoleum. Then the familiar objects in my room began to take shape. Grand'mère came to my bed.

"You have had a good night's sleep," she said.

"You've been here all the time."

"I was quite comfortable dozing in the chair. Now I am going to get you something nice and soothing. Some porridge, I think . . . a little bread and butter. Mrs. Dillon suggested the porridge. She said it was soothing. They are all very anxious to help. Clarkson is annoyed because Charles took the key without asking him for it."

I ate the breakfast and said I wanted to get up but Grand'mère thought I should rest for a while.

"You were frozen to the marrow. I don't want you catching a cold."

I felt limp and unreal and was not averse to agreeing to stay in bed. She brought me *Jane Eyre* to read. I had read it before but I had enjoyed it so much and always felt so sorry for Jane that it made me feel how fortunate I was.

I told Grand'mère that she must not sit with me all day. It made me feel like an invalid, and if she were in the workroom, I knew that she was close.

"You've had a big shock," she said. "I feel that is more to be considered than the cold you endured in that place. You were there for three hours. Enough to chill anyone's bones . . . but the fact of your being there was probably the worst. So now you will rest."

Cassie came to see me. She stood by my bed looking at me with a kind of wondering tenderness.

"It's all right, Cassie," I said. "I'm not there now."

"I can't tell you how I felt when I heard that you were there for three hours. I should have *died.*"

"I thought I was going to die there."

"Your hair hasn't changed a bit." She was peering at me. "There's no white . . . and it should show . . . your being so dark."

"I think I'm getting over it now . . . though I dreamed of it last night quite a lot and when I woke up I had a terrible feeling that I might still be there."

"I can imagine nothing more horrible."

"There are more horrible things."

"You are very brave, Lenore."

"You should have seen me shivering . . . thinking of all sorts of horrors . . . watching for the ghosts . . . I was far from brave."

"There has been a lot of trouble," she said. "It has been terrible. Mama is most distressed. She is in her room with the curtains drawn and no one but Miss Logan is to go near her."

"What happened then?"

"Drake . . . and Charles . . . they fought. It was all about you. Drake got Charles on the ground and made him tell about locking you in the mausoleum. Charles said it was his affair and he was only teaching you a lesson. You needed to be taken down a peg or two because you gave yourself too many airs for a servant.

"Drake shouted at him and said he was a cad . . . and worse than that. He said he had sent that stable boy to get you in the place so that he could lock you in. Charles said he didn't deny it and what business was it of Drake's? Drake said it was every decent-minded person's business and as he was so fond of giving lessons he was going to get one himself. We couldn't believe it. They were quite different from what they are normally. Drake being bigger than Charles was able to pick him up as though he were a dog, and he just shook him. At the end he threw him into the lake. Julia was crying. I was near to it. I have never seen anything like it."

"What about Charles in the lake?"

"He walked out. He wasn't very far in but by that time Drake had gone back to the house. He packed his bag and presented himself to Mama and said he had to leave. He was called away suddenly. Mama was in a terrible state. But, of course, she had to say goodbye to Drake, and he came out and asked one of the stablemen to drive him to the station . . . and then he was gone."

"How . . . awful! What about Charles?"

"He's going tonight. He won't say where . . . except that he is going to stay with a friend and he will go straight on from there to the University."

"So . . . they've both gone . . . and it was all because of me."

"Drake couldn't stay in a house where he had had such a fight with his host. As for Charles, perhaps he is ashamed of what happened. Philip is very worried about you."

"Philip has always been kind to me."

"I think he will be along soon. He wanted to see you last night but Madame Cleremont said it was best you were not disturbed."

"What a dreadful end to the holiday!"

"I don't suppose anything like this has ever happened before, do you?"

"I should think it would be very rare."

When she left me I lay back thinking about Drake coming into the mausoleum, picking me up and bringing me back to the house. I should probably never see him again. He certainly would not come to The Silk House as Charles's guest. They must hate each other. I felt a mingling of feelings. I was gratified that he had defended me; it was almost like fighting in the lists or in a duel. It made me feel important and after the humiliation Charles had inflicted on me, I needed that. But I was sorry that I should not see Drake again.

Philip came to see me.

"My dear Lenore," he said, "this is most upsetting. What a terrible time you had!"

"It is good of you to come to see me," I answered. "You might have felt you didn't want to after all the trouble this has caused."

"You've heard then about Drake?"

"Cassie told me . . ."

"I'm so ashamed of my brother, Lenore."

"I always knew he was not as kind as you are."

"I think he is rather arrogant . . . going through a phase just now. He wants to assert himself. I'm sure it will pass. He is not such a bad sort really."

I smiled at Philip. He was one of those people who mean well towards the whole world and think everyone else is like themselves.

"How are you feeling now?"

"I'm being cosseted by Grand'mère, and everyone seems to be very kind. Even Mrs. Dillon said I must eat porridge."

He laughed, then he was sober. "It must have been very frightening for you."

"It was. And I should be there now if it wasn't for Willie and Pepper."

"Good for Willie. I suppose Drake felt he couldn't stay after such a violent quarrel with Charles."

"And Charles is going, too."

"He's going this evening."

"I'm afraid I've broken up the party."

"Charles did that by behaving like a brute. I'm not surprised that Drake was angry with him and gave vent to his anger, too."

"You can imagine how I feel to be the centre of it all."

"The centre of it is Charles's beastly vanity. He's had a big lesson."

"But Drake has been driven away."

"He wouldn't stay after that. How could he . . . as Charles's guest. He's had a good thrashing and been thrown into the lake. Don't be afraid of what Charles will do now. We shan't see him here for a while, I reckon. All you have to do is get well."

"I'm not ill . . . just shaken."

"It was enough to shake anybody. You'll be all right in a day or so. I'm going to look after you. Cassie and I have decided we must do that. My father is coming home soon. He wants to talk to us very seriously about the business. He'll want to talk to Charles as well as to me, of course."

"But Charles is leaving."

"I don't think Charles cares very much about the business. He happens to be the elder, but I am the one my father really wants to discuss things with. I'm going to persuade him to let me finish with my education. I want to go into the business . . . now."

"Do you think he will agree?"

"I have an idea he might. He is so pleased that I am interested in it. Charles isn't in the least and that upsets him. But at least there is one of us."

It was pleasant talking to him. I liked his enthusiasm and his kindness. There was something very natural about him. When he left me I felt a good deal better. I was glad Charles would be leaving that night and I should not have to see him again perhaps for quite a long time.

I was unprepared for Julia.

After Philip left she came into my room. She looked as if she had been crying and she was very angry. She stood at the foot of my bed glaring at me.

"It's your fault," she said. "I thought Drake was going to kill Charles."

"I've heard about it. I'm sorry it happened."

"You started it."

"I? I did not ask to be locked in the mausoleum."

"You told tales. You told Drake. I've watched you. You were always trying to get his attention . . . and you thought this was a good way of doing it."

"Julia, what are you saying? Do you think I wanted to be locked in that awful place? I was scared almost out of my wits. It was awful . . . with all those coffins."

"But Drake came and rescued you, didn't he? That was what you wanted."

"He came because Willie heard me there and went to find someone. It just happened that he found Drake."

"He's gone and I don't suppose I shall ever see him again." Her lips trembled. "We were getting on so well . . . and you had to spoil it."

"Julia," I said firmly, "it wasn't my fault. It was Charles . . ."

She just looked at me stonily and ran out of the room. I could see that she was ready to burst into tears.

I knew, of course, that she had felt deeply about Drake, and now she was blaming me because she had lost him.

The Engagement

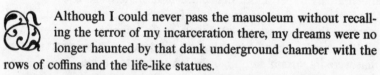Although I could never pass the mausoleum without recalling the terror of my incarceration there, my dreams were no longer haunted by that dank underground chamber with the rows of coffins and the life-like statues.

Charles stayed away for a long time. He even spent the next Christmas at the home of a friend, coming home on Boxing Day just to see the family and not even staying the night. Our first meeting was a little embarrassing, but he had obviously determined to behave as though that distressing incident had never taken place, and I was glad to do the same. He was distant, cool, but not unfriendly. It was the best way to behave.

Julia had recovered from her disappointment because at Easter she was to be presented at Court and such an undertaking demanded all her attention. I imagined she hadn't time to spare many thoughts for Drake. His name was never mentioned except by Lady Sallonger on one occasion who said: "What was the name of that rather charming young man who stayed here once? Was it Nelson or something?"

"Something like that, Lady Sallonger," I said.

"I'd like you to read to me now, Lenore. It will send me to sleep. I had a rather bad night. I think I want more cushions . . . not that green one . . . the blue is softer."

So Drake Aldringham seemed to have passed beyond our horizon.

It was decided that Julia should spend a week or so in London under the guidance of the Countess of Ballader. There were so many things she had to learn and she must be ready in every way for the great occasion.

Grand'mère was to go with her, so that she could study the current fashions, for although her work was excellent and she had that something which is called by the French *"je ne sais quoi"* and was entirely hers, there was a possibility that she might not be *au fait* with the very latest fashion. She might also acquire some new materials other than those which came to her from Spitalfields. Miss Logan, who knew of these matters having served in a very aristocratic family, assured Lady Sallonger that this was necessary.

I was with Lady Sallonger—as I often was now—when Grand'mère came to her. I was always struck by Grand'mère's dignity. It was so much a part of her and it demanded immediate respect.

"Forgive me for disturbing you, Lady Sallonger," she said, "but I must speak to you on a matter that is very important."

"Oh dear," sighed Lady Sallonger, who had an aversion to matters that were important and might be left to her to decide.

"It is this. I am to go to London. Yes, it is *necessaire* for Miss Julia to go. And we must see what is being worn and what we can do to give her the finest wardrobe of the season . . . yes, yes. I am happy for all this, but I could not go without my granddaughter. It is *necessaire* that I should have her with me."

Lady Sallonger opened her eyes very wide. "Lenore," she cried. "But *I* need Lenore here. Who will read to me? We are re-reading *East Lynne.* I need her to look after me."

"I know that Lenore is of great service to you, Lady Sallonger, but I could not work well if she were not with me . . . and this is for one week only . . . perhaps a day or so more. Miss Logan is very good. And there is Miss Everton. They can all serve you."

"It is quite impossible."

They looked steadily at each other—two indomitable women, each accustomed to having her own way. It was a tribute to Grand'mère's character and perhaps her unusual position in the household, that she won the day. Self-absorbed as she was, Lady Sallonger realized the importance of getting Julia launched into society. Grand'mère must go to London and it was clear that she would not go unless I went with her.

Lady Sallonger eventually pursed her lips into a pout and said: "I suppose I shall have to let her go, but it is not very convenient."

"I know how you appreciate my granddaughter," said Grand'mère with a touch of irony, "but I must have her with me. Otherwise I could not go."

"I do not see why not . . ."

"Ah, my lady, it is not always easy to see the 'why not' for what is necessary for others. *I* do not see why Miss Logan cannot look after you, and since Lenore is such a comfort to you, you will readily see why *I* cannot do without her on this very important occasion."

Grand'mère was triumphant.

"It is time you had a little rest from her," she said when we were alone. "She is demanding more and more of you. I can see that as the years pass . . . unless something happens to prevent it . . . you will be her slave. It is not what I wish for you."

I was very excited at the prospect of going to London. Cassie was downcast because she would not be accompanying us. There was a suggestion that she should come but Lady Sallonger had very firmly said that she would need her to share some of my duties with Miss Logan.

"It is only for a week or so," I told Cassie, "and I shall tell you all about it on my return."

So Julia and I set out with Grand'mère on a rather blustery March day, travelling by rail, which was far more convenient than going by carriage. Cobb met us at the station and took us to the house in Grantham Square.

I was very excited, riding through the streets of London. Everyone seemed to be in a great hurry and there was bustle everywhere. Hansom cabs and broughams sped through the streets at such a rate that I feared they would ride over people in their haste. But no one seemed to think this extraordinary so I supposed it was the usual state of affairs.

As we came into Regent Street Grand'mère was alert. She spoke the name of the shops aloud. Peter Robinson's . . . Dickens and Jones . . . Jay's. I caught glimpses of splendid looking goods in the windows. Grand'mère was purring like a contented cat.

Grantham Square was in one of the many fashionable residential parts of London. The house was tall, the architecture Georgian and elegant. There were steps to a portico with two urns on either side supported by flimsily clad nymphs and in the urns was a display of tulips. Cobb deposited us at the house and took the carriage round to the mews at the back.

There was a butler, a footman and several servants—slightly more than those we had at The Silk House. Sir Francis was not at home so we were taken to our rooms by the housekeeper who asked us to let her know if there was anything we needed. She was an authoritative looking lady and rather formidable in her black bombazine which rustled when she walked. Her name was Mrs. Camden.

Grand'mère and I were to share a room. It was at the top of the house and large and airy. There were two beds and a small alcove in which was a basin and ewer.

Grand'mère said: "I think we shall be comfortable here. At least we are together."

I smiled at her. I knew she was determined not to leave me alone in a house to which Charles might come back.

They were interesting days. Sir Francis arrived later that night. He was very courteous to Grand'mère. He said he had been delayed and hoped that we had been well looked after. The Countess of Ballader was arriving the next day and she would then get to work with Julia.

He wanted to take Grand'mère to the Spitalfields works to show her the new looms and the modern way of weaving, which was causing some distress to the workers, who always thought that when something new came in it threatened their jobs.

"There are always troubles," he said.

Grand'mère explained to him what a help I was to her and how I had a natural flair for matching styles with materials.

"She will be another such as yourself," said Sir Francis, eyeing me with approval.

"I think that may well be so," replied Grand'mère fondly.

I was so tired that night that I was asleep as soon as I got into bed and I awoke next morning to a feeling of excitement.

The Countess of Ballader arrived next day and took charge of Julia. She was to stay in the house while we were there. There was so much Julia had to learn. On those occasions when I saw her—and these were not often for she was almost always being put through her paces by the indefatigable Countess—I heard that on the great day she must have her hair dressed in such a manner as to support the three plumes, and a veil must be worn; her curtsy never seemed to please the Countess, though she could not see what was wrong with it. What was a curtsy anyway? One just bobbed down. Why should it be so difficult to learn? And her waist was not small enough; she had to be fitted for new corsets and she knew they were going to squeeze her so painfully that they made her red in the face; and that would be wrong too.

Poor Julia! Being launched into society seemed to be more a strenuous ordeal than a pleasant experience. But her excitement remained, though she did admit that she might be a failure at her first ball and she was terrified that no one would ask her to dance.

I had a happier time. Grand'mère and I explored London together. We looked in shop windows; we walked through the departments. Grand'mère noted the latest fashions . . . not only in the shops but on the ladies in the streets. There was a lack of *chic,* she said. She did not need to learn anything from them.

She bought a few materials and discussed with me how they should be made up.

Sir Francis took Grand'mère to Spitalfields. She came back preoccupied, I thought.

It was fun sharing a room with her, for we used to lie in bed and talk before we slept.

She said: "All this fuss . . . for one young girl. It seems an extraordinary custom, does it not? A girl cannot go into society and meet others of her class until she has been approved by the Court. And what is that encounter? A bob of the knees and . . . pass on. And yet there she is . . . in court gown, plumes and veil . . . after months of preparation. What do you think? Does it not make you laugh?"

"I think there is something rather obscene about it."

"Obscene? What is this?"

"Well, I mean parading her . . . showing off what she has in the hope that some man will think her worthy to be his wife."

"Ah. That is so. You think it is . . . how shall I say? . . . demeaning to our sex."

"Is it not?"

Grand'mère was thoughtful and at length she said: "It would seem to me, *ma petite,* that we have to fight hard for our place in the world. To be equal with a man one must be so much better, so much more clever. It is something I have always known. Here am I. I have a talent for materials . . . for style . . . and because of it I am a guest . . . or almost a guest . . . in the house of Sir Francis Sallonger. He treats me with respect always. He is, after all, a gentleman. But we have seen how precarious our position can be through the odious Monsieur Charles. We have to guard against that. Yes, this is in some way demeaning . . . this setting up Mademoiselle Julia on auction as it were, but, *ma chérie,* I find myself wishing that all this was being done for you because if you were launched into society you would have a chance of meeting people whom you could not otherwise. It is a great anxiety to me. I think of it often. Now . . . you are safe. I am here to guard you. But I am not young . . . and there will come a day . . ."

"No!" I cried involuntarily. The thought of life without Grand'mère was something I could not bear to consider.

"Oh, but I am well. I am strong . . . there are many years left to me yet. But before they are over my dearest dream is to see you settled. I want for you a husband not necessarily rich . . . but good. He must be good. I want to see you with little ones. For, believe me, they are the greatest comfort a woman can find. I had this comfort with my Marie Louise. Your grandfather was a good man. He died young and I was left with my daughter. When she died I thought I had died, too, for the world seemed to have nothing left for me until they put you into my arms . . . and since then, it has been us two against the world."

"Oh, Grand'mère," I said, "never talk about leaving me."

"There is only one thing in the world which could make me do that. Before anything in the world I want to see you happily settled . . . taken care of. I want to see that before I go."

"I can take care of myself."

"Yes . . . you will. That is what I tell myself. I took care of myself when I was left. I worked for the St. Allengères. I was important to them . . . my knowledge of silks, my talent for styles. I was of great use to them."

"And they let you go."

"Yes, because of you. I could not have stayed there in that close community where everyone knew the business of everyone else. They knew I had to get away . . . so they asked Sir Francis to take me."

"And he did."

"He was getting a bargain. He knew of my skills. And he did this because Monsieur St. Allengère asked him to. Although there is much rivalry between the branches of the family and religious differences . . . blood ties are strong and they go back through the centuries."

"How strange it is that there should be these two branches of that family . . . both engaged in business . . . meeting occasionally although they are rivals."

"It is . . . how you say? . . . symbolic. It is like the Church. There is a schism. One goes one way, one the other. With the Reformation came the split in the family. The Catholic side and the Huguenot side. They are opposed in religion and in business—although they are in different countries—they vie with each other. In England there is not the deep feeling for religion as there is in Villers-Mûre, I believe. Oh . . . there is contention between them . . . but they visit now and then, each wanting to know what the other is doing. They are the friendly enemies."

"And what of you, Grand'mère, for you are of Villers-Mûre?"

"My religion is to care for those I love. I am one of those who love someone more than a doctrine. Perhaps I am wrong but I could never care whether I worshipped in one way or another. I feel that God will understand."

"I know He will," I said. "And I will say that you are a better Christian than many who are outwardly devout."

"What a serious conversation! How did it start? Oh, I know. The parade of Julia. I hope she will do well and find the husband who satisfies all . . . most of all herself."

There was silence for a while, then she went on: "I had an interesting time with Sir Francis. They have some wonderful looms nowadays. He is very proud of them but . . ."

I waited and there was silence again.

"You were going to say something, Grand'mère," I prompted.

"Oh yes . . . that Sir Francis is a little . . . how shall I say? . . . anxious."

"What should he be anxious about?"

"There is one thing. I believe the business is not as prosperous as it was."

"But he is very rich. He has The Silk House . . . this house . . . and all those servants."

"So much to keep up. As you say . . . the house, the servants, the sons, the daughters and Lady Sallonger. He has many commitments, has he not?"

"He must be very rich, Grand'mère."

"Those who have much can lose so much more."

"Do you really think he is worried about money?"

"I daresay if he lost the business tomorrow he would still be comparatively rich. He has property and many assets, I am sure. But he is anxious about the business. He did hint that a great deal of silks are coming into the country. There are still echoes of the Fontainebleau agreement. You see, the French have always had a reputation and the very fact that a material is French gives it an advantage over that which is produced here."

"Did he tell you he was worried?"

"No, but he said that he needs desperately something which is new . . . something which is going to take the public by storm . . . something not too expensive so that it can appeal to a great number of people besides the *élite* . . . something that we can bring out in various forms . . . very special and very expensive for some . . . and in a cheaper version for everybody to wear."

"And will he do this?"

"My dear Lenore, the first thing to do is find this miracle material. He believes people are working on it in France. His people are too. Perhaps it is like a race. Who shall find it first and make it his own."

"Is this what he is uneasy about?"

"I am sure the business needs a boost. He must get back lost business. That is what I understand. I thought he looked a little tired. He was quite flushed and very breathless . . . and he talked to me with more vehemence than usual. *Mon Dieu!* Did you hear that? The clock is striking midnight. These night time chats are good, are they not, but we must not carry them on until the next day. Good night, my precious one."

I was soon fast asleep.

* * *

It was two days later when it happened.

It seemed almost as though Grand'mère had known it was coming. Sir Francis was taken ill. He had had a mild stroke from which it appeared he would recover; the unfortunate fact was that he was not in Grantham Square when it had happened.

He was in the house of a Mrs. Darcy in St. John's Wood. Mrs. Darcy had been terrified and had called a doctor at once. He had thought it advisable not to move Sir Francis immediately so he had remained in Mrs. Darcy's house for several days. His own doctor went there. Charles and Philip were sent for. If it had happened in Grantham Square it would have been so much easier, but the significant point was that he had been taken ill at two o'clock in the morning.

Charles took over quite efficiently. He thought it was imperative that his father be brought back to Grantham Square without delay.

This was eventually arranged and everyone breathed more freely, particularly when they knew that Sir Francis would recover.

The Countess was rather voluble to Grand'mère on the subject. A friendship had grown up between them and this seemed to include me. They were together a great deal discussing Julia's requirements and as the Countess agreed that Grand'mère could produce gowns which were more striking, and at the same time elegant, than any dressmaker she knew, there was an immediate rapport between them.

She said she would like to "bring me out." She thought I had more "originality" than Julia. Julia was too eager. "Trying too hard," she called it, "and showing it." "It's a social sin to show one's eagerness," she explained. "One must not miss an opportunity, of course, one must be alert, but assume indifference. It is not easy to achieve the right attitude but it is the way to success." And she thought I would do this better than Julia.

During our conversations she became very frank about herself and she had a racy turn of expression which was not exactly what one would have expected from a Countess.

"I was not born to the purple," she said, when she was in a confidential mood. "Plain Dulcie Dorman me. I had a way with me which the men seemed to like . . . particularly the old men. There are some who attract the young, some the middle-aged, but for me it was the old ones. I was on the stage. It was the only thing for a girl like me . . . good looking with her wits about her. The Earl saw me. He was quite a duck really . . . a bit doddering . . . all of thirty-five years older than I was. But he doted on me . . . and if there was one thing I liked it was being doted on. So I married him . . . and for five years I looked after him. Quite fond of him, I was . . . and there was I, the Countess, living with my old Earl in a house nearly as big as Paddington Station and as draughty. It wasn't exactly comfort, but I liked being a lady. Then he died and what was there for me? Debts . . . debts . . . debts and a distant cousin turning up to take the house. As for me, I was pretty nearly on my uppers . . . but not quite, so I looked about to see what I could do. I was at least the Countess of

Ballader and that was a good deal. So I took up this business of looking after girls. I soon learned about it and I'd had some good clients. And here I am. I've had my ups and downs . . . and I'm glad of it. I've been plain Dulcie Dorman who could high kick with the best . . . and I've been the Earl's lady. I've seen life from both sides, you might say. That's a help. It makes you understand people's troubles. One thing I've learned is don't judge or blame . . . because you can only get half the story, anyway. Take Sir Francis." She smiled at us benignly. "I liked him. I knew how things were. It's lucky it worked out fairly well. If he had *died* in the lady's bed, the fat would have been in the fire. Julia's presentation would have had to be postponed. Of course there haven't been the rigid conventions at Court since Albert died. He was responsible for that strict moral tone; he liked to visit the sins of the fathers on the children. Her Majesty is not really so strict. But if he had died in his mistress's bed, how should we have been able to keep the press away from such a spicy piece of news. Yes, that would have put a finish to Julia's debut."

"This relationship," said Grand'mère, "is it of long standing?"

"Oh years and years. It's been a steady affair. There's nothing promiscuous about Sir Francis. Poor Mrs. Darcy, she is very upset."

We were to extend our stay on account of Sir Francis's illness and we should be in London for at least another week. In one of our nightly chats, Grand'mère talked to me about Sir Francis.

"As the Countess says, one must not blame him," she said. "He is a good man. He loved Mrs. Darcy and she him. It was like a marriage."

"But what of Lady Sallonger?"

"Lady Sallonger is married to her ailments. You see how it is. After Cassie's birth she wanted no more children. There are needs in a man's life . . . and if he cannot have them where he expects to, he looks elsewhere."

"So Sir Francis looked to Mrs. Darcy?"

"That would seem so," she said. "He must not be blamed. He looks after Lady Sallonger. All her whims are granted. There was no unkindness . . . and unkindness is the real sin."

There flashed into my mind the memory of Charles running up the steps and looking back at me in the frightening darkness; I thought of the boys who had killed Willie's dog.

She was right. Unkindness was the real sin.

* * *

Charles was in the house but I had lost my fear of him. He treated me when we met in that cool manner which indicated that he had no interest in me and no longer felt rancour. It was different with Philip. He was pleased to see me.

The two brothers spent a great deal of time with their father, who, although confined to his bed, where he would be for at least a month, was well enough to receive visitors; and as he was anxious to talk to his sons, the doctor came to the conclusion that to try to prevent that would have distressed Sir Francis too much.

I gathered there was a great deal to talk about.

Grand'mère said that decisions were being made. Philip was very serious, but he was especially charming to me. When I came down to breakfast one morning he was there alone. His face lit up when he saw me.

He said: "I'm so glad you are here, Lenore. So much is happening really."

"You mean because of your father?"

He nodded. Then he gave me that very pleasant smile of his. "I always like talking to you. You always seem to understand. This is going to make a great difference. Both Charles and I have done with education from now on. Well, it's about time. It is really what I wanted and I have been urging my father to allow it for some time. Charles and I are going into the business at once."

"Yes, I rather thought that would be so."

"Our father is recovering but he will never be the same again. The doctor says he will have to take great care. This is a warning. So from now on we are in the business. Of course I didn't want it to happen this way. However, I want to talk to you some time." He looked round. "It's not easy here. Perhaps we could go somewhere."

"Where?" I asked.

"We could go down to Greenwich. I love the river. There is an inn there I know—the Crown and Sceptre. They say the whitebait there are the best in London." He grimaced. "I'd like us to go alone. But I suppose that is out of the question."

I did not answer.

"We'll have to have a chaperone," he went on, "or it would be considered improper."

"Well then, if you want to talk we might as well do it here."

"We'll take your grandmother along. She'll know what I'm talking about."

"That would be lovely."

Julia came down.

"Hello," said Philip. "Getting ready for the fray?"

Julia helped herself from the sideboard. "The Countess is quite a dragon," she said. "I get little peace."

"All in a good cause," said Philip lightly.

"You're lucky," said Julia, glancing at me. "You don't have to suffer like this. I shall never get my weight down and those corsets are killing me."

"I shouldn't eat all that bacon then if I were you," Philip advised.

"I have to keep my strength up. I think that lavender coloured brocade your grandmother has bought is lovely."

"It's beautiful," I agreed, "and have you seen the style it's going to be made in?"

"Oh no. They don't think it is necessary to consult me. Your grandmother and the Countess are like a couple of old witches doing this and that . . . and never letting me know a thing."

"I'm sure my grandmother would show you all the patterns if you wished to see them."

"Sometimes I'm sick of the whole thing, and I want to go home. Then there will be all the balls and things . . ."

"You'll love them," I said. "You know it is what you have always wanted."

"I *thought* I did . . . till now." She sighed and helped herself to more bacon.

"It won't be a young lady the Countess has to launch, it will be an elephant," said Philip with brotherly candour, for there was no doubt that she was putting on weight. I think her nervousness made her eat more than otherwise she would have done.

I left them at the table but Philip caught me up.

"Perhaps today," he said. "The late afternoon and we'll get there about half past six. You'll enjoy it. Ask your grandmother."

When I told Grand'mère she seemed very pleased.

"I like him," she said. "He's the best of the bunch."

Since she was so pleased I could look forward to the evening with even greater pleasure.

Philip was an expert with the oars. He said he liked rowing and had had plenty of practice at the University, so we could trust ourselves with him.

"I shall be in London a great deal now," he told us. "This morning I have been to Spitalfields. There is a lot to be learned."

Grand'mère said: "Your brother does not share your enthusiasm."

"True," agreed Philip. "In a way I'm rather pleased. I fancy it will give me a freer hand. I should hate interference."

"He will be a sort of sleeping partner," I said.

"Even the most prosperous business cannot afford sleeping partners," stated Grand'mère. "It is necessary for all to do their share."

"I don't think he has the feeling for silk . . . or for business. Charles ought to go into Parliament . . . or law or something."

"I am sure *you* will be successful," I told him.

His brow clouded a little. "Do you know," he said, "I think my father's stroke was brought about through anxiety."

"I think that could be very likely," agreed Grand'mère.

"Do you mean he was worried about business?" I asked.

Philip nodded. "Things are not quite what they should be. I wouldn't say this to anyone else, but you have always understood, Lenore, and as for you, Madame Cleremont, you are part of the business. No, certainly things are not what they should be."

"I gathered that from your father some time ago," said Grand'mère.

"It's these foreign imports," Philip explained. "Sales of our silks have declined and they go on declining."

"Do you think there should be a duty on foreign goods?" I asked.

He was thoughtful. "It would be useful, of course. We could then price our materials higher. We would not have to compete so rigorously. But whether one believes in free trade or not is a big question. One has to ask oneself whether one would wish for it on other commodities. It would hardly be fair to expect a tariff on what suits us. Do we want it on silk because we are limping along?"

"What we need," put in Grand'mère, "is to find some new style of weaving . . . something that produces a beautiful material . . . better in every way from what we have already."

"A secret method," I suggested.

"Exactly!" cried Philip, his eyes shining. "A secret method of producing something which has never been produced before with no one else knowing how it is done."

"Wouldn't they soon discover?" I asked.

"They might, but they would not be allowed to use it. There is such a thing as a patent. It prevents people by law from stealing someone else's invention."

"What a good thing!"

"First we have to find the invention," said Philip ruefully. "Oh, here we are."

We tied up the boat and climbed the stairs to the footpath.

"Greenwich has always appealed to me," said Philip, "because it was one of the headquarters used by the Huguenot refugees. I always wonder whether my ancestors came here before they went to Spitalfields. They even have their own chapel here. I don't think it is in existence now. And here is the Crown and Sceptre."

The inn had bow windows to enable those seated there to get a good view of the river.

"They are noted for their whitebait," said Philip, "so we must have that. Do you like whitebait, Madame Cleremont?"

"It depends," replied Grand'mère. "It has to be freshly caught, I believe."

"You can rely on that here."

The innkeeper's wife came up to talk to us. She knew Philip so obviously he was a frequent visitor. He would like to think of his ancestors coming here all those years ago.

"I was assuring my friends that the whitebait would be fresh," he said.

"Why, bless you," said the woman. "This morning it was swimming in the sea."

"And you have the secret of cooking them just as they should be."

"Oh, it is no secret. It is the only way to serve whitebait to my mind. I remember my mother throwing them into a layer of flour, all spread out on a cloth and shaking them to make sure they were all covered. Then they are thrown into a cauldron of boiling fat . . . just for a minute or so . . . then drain 'em off and they're ready to eat. Now you must be quick or they'll lose their crispness. Served up with a sprinkling of lemon and a dash of Cayenne pepper and they're a real treat. And they should be washed down with the right liquid . . . say, some punch or iced champagne."

"Which shall it be?" asked Philip.

We settled for the iced champagne.

Over this, Philip said: "My brother and I are going to France shortly. My father is hoping that our connections in Villers-Mûre will let us work there for a short while. He is sure that we have a great deal to learn . . . discover how other people do things . . . get new ideas for the business." He looked at Grand'mère. "It is your old home. What do you think? Is it a good idea?"

"It's always useful to find out how people do things in other countries," said Grand'mère.

"I wish we could produce right from the very start. I've often thought we should set up in India or China, which is the right sort of environment. In some parts of China I believe the silkworm is reared out of doors. That would surely get the best results. As it is we have to import our raw materials."

"Even in Villers-Mûre they have to have artificial heat for the mulberries," said Grand'mère. "It is really cheaper to have the materials brought into the country and concentrate on the weaving."

"Of course you are right," said Philip. He turned to me. "Are we boring you with all this talk, Lenore?"

"Not in the least."

"Lenore is interested in silk and I think she has a special feeling for the finished product," said Grand'mère.

"I expect you will be coming up to Town quite a lot now."

"Why?" asked Grand'mère.

"Well, Julia will be here."

"She will not need us," I said. "She will be involved in social activities."

"For which Lenore does not qualify," added Grand'mère.

"Oh, Lenore is too young as yet."

"I shall soon be sixteen," I said.

"You seem older, doesn't she, Madame Cleremont? So much more sensible than Julia."

"This is my upbringing," said Grand'mère. "Lenore is not in Julia's position. There will be no bringing out for her."

"I am glad of that," said Philip earnestly.

"Why?" asked Grand'mère sharply.

"I don't think it would suit Lenore . . . to be paraded. It's all right for Julia . . . not Lenore."

"You think Lenore is not one of the family and therefore . . ."

"I am thankful that she is not one of the family."

He took my hand and pressed it and I saw Grand'mère's eyes were shining. "I think," she said, "that you and I feel that there is something rather . . . how do you say? . . . special about my granddaughter."

"You and I seem to be in agreement about almost everything, Madame Cleremont."

Grand'mère sat back and lifted her glass. "To the future," she said. And I felt that the pair of them had sealed a pact.

We were all rather thoughtful on the way home and when we were in bed that night, Grand'mère said: "What a delightful young man Philip has grown into."

"He is always gentle and kind."

"So different from his brother. It is strange how people differ. Some say it is in their upbringing, but those two boys have been brought up together . . . and see what a difference."

"Yes," I said, thinking of Charles in the mausoleum.

"I believe he is fond of you. I mean . . . I *know* he is fond of you. What he said this evening . . ."

"What did he say . . . only that he was glad I was not one of the family."

"You know what he meant. He is in love with you. He is waiting to say so only because you are so young. Perhaps in a year . . . you'll be just on seventeen and . . ."

I laughed. "Oh, Grand'mère, you are romancing. Do you want so much to get me off your hands?"

"More than anything in the world I want your happiness. I want you to be cherished and loved. That is what I want . . . before I go."

"I wish you would not talk about going."

"I do not intend to go for a long time, but one must be practical. Look at Sir Francis . . . well one day and struck down the next. Oh, he has recovered they say, but he will never be the man he was. I should be so happy if I saw that everything was settled for you. Philip has always been fond of you. I have always known that he was the one. He has that wonderful enthusiasm for his business. He would be dedicated to his work, to his wife and his family."

"Grand'mère, I feel you are making a situation to fit what you want."

She shook her head. "Tonight he showed his feelings clearly. It was almost a proposal."

"I did not see it as such. I think he was just trying to be kind because he thought I felt left out of this presentation business."

"No. No. I am a happy woman tonight. I see the way ahead."

"Well, Grand'mère, I am glad you are happy."

"Good night, my child, and may the good God bless you."

I lay awake thinking about what she had said. I tried to recall every moment of that visit to the Crown and Sceptre. What had Philip said that was so revealing? I knew that he liked me. He had always been kind and friendly and I had looked upon him and Cassie as my best friends in the house.

Had there really been something significant about that conversation —or had Grand'mère tried to fit it into her dreams? I suspected her of that now and then.

And myself . . . married to Philip! Most girls think of marrying when they get into their teens. They dream of knights and heroes of romance. St. George . . . No, nobody wanted a saint. Sir Lancelot was more eligible. He had been a sinner but a great lover. Loving recklessly was more attractive than slaying dragons. People like Nelson . . . Drake . . .

Drake, of course. There had been something exciting about him. Julia had recognized it. What if it had been Drake who had said what Philip did at the table in the Crown and Sceptre? What should I be feeling now?

Quite excited. Well, I was excited now, for it was exciting to be loved . . . if that was what Philip had meant by those cryptic words.

* * *

The days passed quickly. Charles and Philip left for France, for Sir Francis had recovered sufficiently to resume his normal life; and Grand'mère with Julia and myself returned to The Silk House.

Lady Sallonger greeted me rather peevishly telling me that she had had a very bad time. Miss Logan's voice tired quickly, and Cassie did not put the same expression into the words as I did. We had remained away longer than we had said we would. She had all the anxiety of worrying about Sir Francis.

"If I could go to London and look after him I would be happy to do so," she said. "But here I am . . . a poor invalid unable to move from my couch . . . and everyone deserting me. No one seems to realize that I cannot move about. I am quite chilled. Ring the bell for them to put some more coal on the fire and is that window open? Well, please close it and bring me my red rug . . . I cannot endure this blue one . . . Oh, the fire, Henry . . . The red rug, Lenore . . . that blue one is so scratchy . . . and my skin is so delicate. See if you can find something to read to me."

So it went on. Grand'mère was right in saying that Lady Sallonger was getting more demanding than ever. She commanded that I be in attendance whenever I was not in the schoolroom.

I did manage to get to Grand'mère's room. I told Lady Sallonger that I was needed to help with Julia's clothes. The one thing which we had managed to impress on Lady Sallonger was the importance of Julia's coming out. She herself had "come out" so she knew all about it, although it was, of course, a much more demanding matter in those days when the Prince Consort was alive. Then things had been conducted with far more decorum. She had come out and been the success of the season. The offers she had had . . . !

I found her description of the London scene in her days more entertaining than sitting listening to her continual demands, so I encouraged her to speak of it and I learned what it meant to be a young girl in her days; and she grew quite animated remembering.

"There were afternoon parties where everyone was in full evening dress. Drawing Rooms, they called them. They had left those horrid little dark apartments in St. James's Palace and were held in the Throne Room at Buckingham Palace. We were selected with the greatest care in those days. Such a time it was . . . learning to curtsy and how to walk backwards. It was a nightmare . . . particularly with a train of about three or four yards in length. Those plumes and veils! And being stuffed into your corsets! It was agony for some of the girls. Of course I had a naturally slender waist. And all for a few minutes of being presented to Her Majesty. Oh dear, what days they were! And Sir Francis swept me off my feet before I had a chance with anyone else. I am sure I should have married a duke if I had not been caught up so quickly. How we danced in those days! My foot is going to sleep. Do massage it, Lenore."

So we were back to the familiar, and dreams of past glories faded.

But I did manage to spend some time with Grand'mère. Emmeline was constantly clothed in the most expensive garments. Cassie, who was often with us, was very fond of Emmeline. She made up stories and was sure that, when it was dark, the three dummies came to life and talked about the triumphs they had enjoyed before they were turned into dummies by some wicked witch. She was sure Emmeline smiled inwardly when she was swathed in blue silk.

Julia was happier now. She was back at home. She enjoyed the dancing lessons in which I always had to take part as the gentleman, which I enjoyed very much too. Cassie used to sit watching us, applauding. But I loved best being in the sewing room, taking a turn at Grand'mère's machine, feeling the softness of the silken materials and wishing they were being made for me.

Julia was getting fatter. I think anxiety made her eat even more than normal. I wondered what the Countess would say when she saw what weight Julia was putting on. Grand'mère was concerned that the dresses might not fit when the time came to wear them.

In due course Easter was with us and Julia was delivered by Miss Everton into the hands of the Countess and the real process had begun.

The workroom was very quiet. Cassie said Emmeline was sulking. Grand'mère made two dresses—one for Cassie and one for me—out of the material left over from Julia's needs. We called them our coming out dresses.

August came and the season was drawing to an end. No dukes, viscounts, baronets or even a simple knight had asked for Julia's hand. She was to come down to Epping for a few weeks' rest after her strenuous time, and then she would go up to London again, and under the excellent guidance of the Countess of Ballader make a fresh onslaught onto London society.

Philip and Charles had returned from France. Philip came to the house occasionally. He spent a lot of time in the big workroom. I would be there often with Cassie and he would talk enthusiastically about what he had seen in France.

He was worried about his father's health. Sir Francis would insist on going to Spitalfields and he did tire easily. Philip thought he should rest more—something which Sir Francis refused to do.

There was a great deal of excitement in London for Charles had produced some fantastic ideas which had been of inestimable value to those who were researching on new methods.

"Charles of all people," marvelled Philip. "Who would have

thought he was interested enough? He has contrived some formula. He said he has been working it out for some time. So odd. He gave no sign. I should never have thought he was such a secretive fellow . . . To keep something like that to himself! At first I was inclined to be skeptical . . . but it seems it is just the climax to something our people have been working on for years. I'm having a special loom made, Madame Cleremont, and I'm going to bring it up here to you, but this has to be secret until it is launched. I don't want any rivals to get a whisper of it. It is going to produce a certain weave which will bring a special sheen . . . not seen before. I think it is going to produce something quite different from anything we have done before. And to think that the clue to this perfection has come through Charles!"

The new loom arrived and Grand'mère used to talk to me about it every night when we were alone.

"Philip is so excited," she said. "I think we shall soon have perfected it. Who would have believed it of Charles! And the funny thing is now that he has given us the key which is bringing it to perfection he seems to have lost interest. Philip is most excited. I think we'll have made it in a few days now. We shall have to make sure it remains Sallongers'."

"There is that patent Philip mentioned at the Crown and Sceptre."

"That's right."

Philip had been at The Silk House for about two weeks. He was caught up in the excitement.

"This could be something quite unique," he kept declaring.

Then came the great day. Philip took the piece of silk material which Grand'mère handed to him and they looked at each other with shining eyes.

"Eureka!" shouted Philip.

He seized Grand'mère and hugged her. Then he turned to me, lifted me up and swung me round. He kissed me heartily on the lips.

"This is going to be the turn of the tide," he said. "We will celebrate."

"At the Crown and Sceptre," said Grand'mère, "with whitebait and champagne."

Cassie came in. She stared at us in amazement.

"It's a great occasion, Cassie," I cried. "That which has been sought has been found.

"Cassie must join us in the celebration," I added.

Philip took the material and kissed it reverently. "This is going to bring success to the Sallongers," he said.

"Don't forget the patent," I reminded him.

"Wise girl," he cried. "I shall see to it this very day. We need a name for it."

Grand'mère said: "Why not Lenore silk? Lenore has had a hand in it."

"No, no," I cried. "That would be ridiculous. It is Charles's really and yours, Philip . . . Grand'mère's too. I have just stood by and done the fetching and carrying. Let's call it Sallon Silk. That's part of the family name and we have alliteration's artful aid."

On consideration it was decided that that was a good name. And that evening we sailed to Greenwich and, as Grand'mère had suggested, celebrated on whitebait and champagne.

* * *

For some time we talked of little but Sallon Silk. It was an instant success and there were articles about it in the papers. Sallongers were commended for their enterprise and the prosperity they were bringing to the country. "There is no silk which can match its excellence," said the fashion editors. "Nothing from China or India, Italy or even France can compare with it. Sallon is unique and we should be proud that it has been discovered by a British company."

We used to talk about Sallon when we were in Grand'mère's workroom. Philip was often there discussing new ways of turning the invention to advantage. At the moment it was very expensive and a Sallon Silk dress was an essential of every fashionable wardrobe; but Philip wanted to use the method for producing cheaper material and so putting it within the reach of many more women to possess a Sallon Silk dress.

It was now being made in the factories. New looms had been installed for the purpose and Grand'mère, to her delight, was experimenting with an idea to bring out a cheap version.

She, Cassie and I were caught up in the project. Julia was in London where the Countess had moved into the house in Grantham Square and she was chaperoning Julia on her engagements.

We were into another year. I should soon be seventeen. Grand'mère had always implied that that was an age when wonderful things would happen.

Then the blow fell. Sir Francis had another stroke and this time it was fatal.

It was a bleak January day when they brought his body to Epping for burial. The coffin lay in the house for two days before it was taken to the mausoleum. There was to be a service in the nearby church and then Sir Francis would be brought to his last resting place.

The whole family was assembled at the house. Lady Sallonger assumed great grief which I felt could not be genuine for she had seen so little of him and never seemed to miss him. She insisted on going to the service to see the last she said of "dear Francis." She was carried down to the carriage, looking frail in her black garments and hat with the sweeping black ostrich feathers. She held a white handkerchief to her eyes and insisted that Charles should support her on one side and Philip on the other.

It was chilly in the church. The coffin stood on trestles throughout the service, then it was taken to the carriage and we made our slow ceremonial way to the mausoleum.

Standing there in the bitter wind memories came back to me. Several of the servants were there and I noticed Willie with the dog in his arms.

On the edge of the crowd was a stranger. She was dressed in black and there was a veil over her face. She looked tragic.

I knew at once who she was and I saw that Grand'mère did too.

"Poor woman," she whispered.

It was Mrs. Darcy.

* * *

The summer had come. Philip was often at The Silk House. Grand'mère used to grow pink with pleasure when she heard his voice. He talked to us about the business.

"There is no doubt," he said, "that the discovery of Sallon Silk has saved us from bankruptcy. Yes," he continued, "things were pretty bad. No wonder my father worried himself into an illness. The French were getting the better of us at every turn. They could produce so much cheaper and I suspect that they were cutting their prices just to wipe us out of the market. Well, we've retaliated. Sallon Silk has saved us."

"Charles must be very proud."

"He's not in the office much. He says he'll come when he's found some other invention which will revolutionise the silk industry."

"How very strange," I said, "that he, who is not really interested— or doesn't appear to be—should come up with this miraculous discovery."

"Odd indeed. I begin to think he must have a big feeling for silk after all. He is now having what he calls a good time. I have to say he deserves it and as long as he is ready to settle down in time, we'll let him continue."

Now that I was approaching my seventeenth birthday it seemed that I should be out of the schoolroom. I should have liked to work more with Grand'mère. I was getting more and more immersed into the excitement of the new discovery and I loved designing gowns which would suitably show it off. There were now several kinds of silk based on the new invention and Philip was introducing new colours which would suit it best. He was constantly involved with dyers and discovering where, because of the local water, the best results could be achieved.

I looked forward to the days when he came and we would sit in Grand'mère's room and talk. Cassie was often there. She would sit silently, listening, usually on a stool, her knees crossed and her hands clasped about them. She was very happy to be a part of the excitement.

My birthday was in November. Not a good time for a birthday, Julia had always said. It was too near Christmas. The best time for a birthday was in the middle of the year. She may have been right, but I was greatly looking forward to my seventeenth birthday, for it would be a sign that I had passed out of girlhood and was a young woman.

Had I been a daughter of the house there would have been a season for me; but of course there could not be one for a girl in my position.

Julia's season did not appear, so far, to have done a great deal for her. She was still, as Grand'mère cynically said, "on the market." She was quite discontented and, I think, a little deflated because she had had no proposal of marriage. As I said to Grand'mère, it must have had a demoralizing effect on a girl.

As for myself I was passing into a new phase. Lady Sallonger was very pleased about it. She was thinking up more tasks for me. "It is absurd . . . a girl of your age . . . going to the schoolroom every day. Why, I don't doubt you could teach Miss Everton a thing or two.

I want you to look at my tapestry. I think there is something wrong with the pattern." That meant her stitches were at fault, but she blamed the design, not herself. "You can come to me in the mornings when you leave the schoolroom. I feel so lonely when I am having my glass of sherry. I want you to talk to me."

I said to Grand'mère: "Lady Sallonger is going to find new ways of using my time when I leave the schoolroom."

"We must try to defeat her," replied Grand'mère.

My seventeenth birthday must be celebrated. She was going to arrange a very small party in her room—Cassie, herself and myself. She would mention it to Philip if he came home and perhaps he might like to join us.

The day came. It was a typical November day—the sort I always associated with birthdays. There was mist in the air and from my windows the forest seemed touched in mystery.

Lady Sallonger had given me a silk shawl which had once belonged to her.

She said: "We should have celebrated your birthday, Lenore, but for being in mourning for Sir Francis."

"I understand," I told her. "I really don't want a celebration. I'm just glad to be seventeen."

"Seventeen! I remember my seventeenth birthday. What a day! There was a party at the Hall. I wasn't 'out' then. You would have loved the Hall. It was very grand, very baronial. Of course there was a great fuss when I married Sir Francis. My people were against it. Trade, you know . . . and they guessed that I should have married right at the top. I could tell you some tales."

"I expect you will," I could not help replying.

She missed the irony. In fact I was sure she did not listen to anything anyone else said.

I told her the silk shawl was lovely. It was. It was handpainted with blue and pink butterflies on green leaves; but I was beginning to feel that it was not so wonderful to be seventeen if I were to be pressed into further duties.

In the afternoon Lady Sallonger developed a headache—a real one, which meant that she must stay in her room and lie in the dark. Miss Logan and I got her to bed and left her.

As I came out of her room I saw Philip coming up the stairs. He had just arrived.

"Oh, Philip," I cried, "how nice that you have come home on my birthday!"

"But of course I did. Where is my mother?"

"She has just gone to bed. She has one of her headaches."

"So you are free. I wanted to talk to you."

He opened the door of his mother's sitting room. "In here," he said, "where we can be quiet."

We went into the room. He shut the door and, putting his arms round me, kissed me.

"Happy birthday!" he said.

"Thank you, Philip."

"At last you have reached it."

"Yes, I'm seventeen. It does seem to have taken a long time to get there."

He took my face in his hands. "I promised myself that I would wait until then."

"For what?"

"I have something for you." He fumbled in his pocket and took out a velvet covered case.

"What is it?" I asked.

"For you. I hope you like it. If it doesn't fit they can do something about it."

I opened the case and there was a ring. It was splendid—an emerald surrounded by diamonds.

"I thought the green would suit you," he said. "Your eyes look a little greeny sometimes."

"This for me, Philip!"

"It's meant to mean something. An engagement ring."

He took my left hand and slipped it on the third finger. Then he kissed it. "It is what I've wanted for a long time, Lenore."

I was bewildered. Grand'mère had hinted at this, but I had never really believed her. I thought she was imagining what she wanted to happen.

"Lenore," he went on, "I've loved you for such a long time, and all this excitement we've had lately has brought us closer together. Do you feel that?"

"Why . . . yes."

"Then . . ."

"But Philip . . . I wasn't expecting this. I feel so . . . I don't know . . . so foolish really . . . so uncertain . . . not knowing."

"Didn't you know I was waiting for this day?"

"No."

"I thought it was so obvious. You look a bit shocked. It is just the surprise, isn't it? I mean you do care for me?"

"Of course I care for you. You've always been so good and kind to me. It's just, I suppose, that I am not ready."

I took the ring from my finger. "Philip . . . can't we wait?"

He shook his head. "I've waited long enough. I want you now. I want us to be married. I want to share everything with you. We care about the same things . . . you and your grandmother. I can't tell you what this has meant to me."

I put the ring back into the case and gave it to him.

"Just a little while please, Philip."

He smiled ruefully. "Not so long," he said. "Promise me . . . not for long."

"No," I said. "It won't be for long."

He went to his room, a little less exuberantly than he had come in; and I went upstairs.

Grand'mère came in.

"Was that Philip? Why, what's the matter? You look . . . how is it . . . not yourself."

"Philip has asked me to marry him."

Joy suffused her face; her eyes sparkled and the colour in her cheeks made her look like a young woman. "I am so happy," she said. "This is what I dream of. Now I am the happiest woman in the world."

"I haven't said I will, Grand'mère."

She drew back and stared at me in amazement. "What?"

"Well, it was so unexpected. I . . ."

"You mean you refused him!"

"Well, not exactly."

Her relief was immense.

"I was just so surprised."

"It doesn't surprise *me*. Why, you were meant for each other."

"But I am only seventeen, Grand'mère. I feel I haven't lived long enough."

"*I* know . . . and I'm old enough. He is a good young man. He will be a good husband. He has a purpose in life. I have prayed to God and the saints every night for this. What did you tell him?"

"He offered me a ring . . ."

She clasped her hands, smiling.

"He put it on my finger, but I couldn't . . . It was too soon."

"No, no. It is the right timing. Your birthday! What could be more romantic? Oh, Lenore, you are not going to be foolish, are you? If you turn away from him you will regret it all your life."

"I cannot be sure . . ."

"I can and I know what is best. Lenore, I beg of you, do not be foolish over this. You will never find one so good . . . so worthy. I know. I have seen much of the world."

"I want to forget it. He will be here soon and so will Cassie."

That evening stands out in my memory. There were just the four of us—myself, Grand'mère, Cassie and Philip—and that was enough.

How we talked! I thought of it afterwards, and how Philip's eyes were constantly meeting mine, and his were so loving and tender. I felt cherished and so happy to be with those who loved me dearly.

Philip talked a great deal about Villers-Mûre which enchanted Grand'mère. He had been deeply impressed with the place and not only with the production of silk. Grand'mère listened intently now and then joining in. I could see she was back in her childhood. Cassie sat silently clasping her hands about her knees gazing from one to the other of us and now and then sparing a glance for the dummies as though she really believed that they were part of the company. She was a fanciful girl, Cassie, and so glad to be included in our little circle.

Philip was saying that Villers-Mûre was almost more Italian than French.

"That is how it is with places on the border," said Grand'mère. "There were many Italians there and we were so near. There was bound to be some Italian blood among us, though we were under the French flag."

"There is a strong feeling for music there," went on Philip, "and I feel that came from Italy. Do you know, one could hear them singing in the fields and some of them had magnificent voices. It was often Italian opera. I remember once standing spellbound for a rendering of *La Donna e mobile;* and on another occasion I heard two singing a duet from *Trovatore."* He began to sing himself: *Ai nostri monti ritorneremo.* We applauded and he said: "You should have heard that as I did in the open air."

"Oh yes," said Grand'mère. "They loved the music. They loved to sing and dance."

"That's what I'm saying," said Philip. "They are light-hearted and merry, but very quick to anger I might say over something quite trivial. They can be really murderous. And then there is the French element . . . the realists versus the romantics. I can't tell you how fascinating I found it apart from their methods in the workroom."

"Was Monsieur St. Allengère frank with you?" asked Grand'mère.

Philip laughed. "Up to a point. They are naturally not prepared to give away secrets. I wonder what they think now that we have discovered Sallon Silk."

"Would they know about it?" I asked.

"Know of it? The whole world knows of it. It's a major breakthrough in manufacture. I expect they are grinding their teeth in fury because they didn't think of it first."

"What a good thing you patented it," I said.

"They'll get round that in some way, no doubt," said Grand'mère. "But we got there first and that is the big advantage."

Philip was thoughtful. "The most puzzling thing is that it should have been Charles."

"He has hidden talents no doubt," I said.

"He has never displayed them before. Even when we were there he seemed almost indifferent."

"Well, it shows how mistaken one can be."

"I should love to go back," said Philip. "I want to visit some of the Italian towns. I did see one or two of them briefly. Rome . . . Venice . . . and Florence. It was Florence which caught my fancy. It was so wonderful to go out to the heights of Fiesole and look over the city. I shall go back there one day." He was smiling at me. "You would enjoy it, Lenore," he added.

I was happy. He looked at me so lovingly and I had never seen Grand'mère so happy. I knew it was because of Philip's desire to marry me.

There was magic in that evening . . . sitting there with Grand'mère, dreams in her eyes, and Cassie looking so pleased with us all. Grand'mère and Philip exchanged glances as though there was some delightful conspiracy between them.

I wanted the night to go on and on. It was wonderful to be seventeen and no longer a child. Philip took my hand and pressed it. There was a question in his eyes.

Grand'mère was waiting, holding her breath, her lips moving as I had seen them do in silent prayer.

"Lenore," said Philip, "you will, won't you?"

And I said Yes.

What rejoicing there was!

Philip took the ring and put it on my finger. Grand'mère wept a little—but, she assured us, with pure happiness.

"It is my dearest dream come true."

Cassie hugged me. "You'll be a real sister now," she said.

Grand'mère poured champagne into glasses and Philip put his arms about me and held me tightly while Grand'mère and Cassie raised their glasses to us.

"May the good God bless you," said Grand'mère, "now . . . and always."

The Florentine Adventure

The news of our engagement was received in various ways by members of the household. Lady Sallonger was at first inclined to be shocked. I knew exactly how her mind worked and she always considered every situation as to what effect it would have on her. Her first reaction was that Philip should have looked higher. It was hardly seemly that his choice should have fallen on one who was, in her mind, rather like a higher servant. Madame Cleremont, it was true, was in a rather special position and she had made certain demands which had been accepted when she came, but she was only a servant after all. She was rather peevish. It was too much to present her with such a situation when poor Sir Francis had passed on and left heavy responsibilities on her shoulders. She was really too exhausted to deal with matters like this. People should have more consideration. Then she began to change her mind a little. I should be a daughter-in-law. I should be grateful to have risen to such a position in the household. She could make even more demands on my company; and I was useful to her. So perhaps it was not such a bad thing after all. At least it might have its compensations—and Philip was after all a younger son.

Julia was put out. It was galling to think of all she had gone through without having received one proposal yet, and without any help, on my seventeenth birthday I was engaged. Everyone would say that, in my position, it was as good a match as I could possibly make. So I had done well for myself and scored over Julia.

As for the servants they were dismayed. They did not care that someone who had occupied a minor position in the house should come to one of importance which would naturally fall to the wife of one of the sons. It was like the governess's marrying the master of the house, which had been known to happen now and then.

"It was all wrong," said Mrs. Dillon. "It was going against the laws of nature."

Cassie, of course, was delighted.

When Julia came home to stay for a weekend at The Silk House to see her mother, she was accompanied by the Countess of Ballader. That lady took me aside. She seemed genuinely pleased. "Well done," she said, with such approval that one would have thought that the whole purpose of a girl's existence was to get a husband. "I said from the start that I wished it had been you I had to handle."

Julia was cool to me during that weekend, and I was glad when she and the Countess left.

Then there was Charles. His attitude since Drake Aldringham had shown his contempt for him had been one of studied indifference. It was always as though he were unaware of my existence. He gave an amused smile when he was told of the engagement as though it were something of a joke.

Philip was as excited about the wedding as he had been about Sallon Silk. There was something single-minded about Philip; when a project lay ahead he was all enthusiasm to complete it. I liked that in him. In fact there was a great deal I liked about Philip. I believed I loved him, though I was not sure. I liked to be with him; I liked to talk to him; and best of all I liked the manner in which he treated me—as though I was very precious and he was going to spend his life looking after me.

Our wedding was to be in April. That gave us five months to prepare.

"There is absolutely no sense in waiting," said Philip.

Grand'mère had long conversations with him. She talked at great length about "settlements." I was appalled when I understood what she meant.

"Are you suggesting that Philip should make some payment?" I asked incredulously.

"It is done in France. There people face these facts. On the day you marry Philip he will settle a certain sum upon you and that money is yours . . . in case anything happens to him."

"*Happens* to him?"

"Ah, *mon enfant,* one never knows. One cannot be too careful. There is an accident . . . and what is a poor widow to do? Is she to be thrown on the mercy of her husband's family?"

"It is all so sordid."

"You must bring a practical mind to these matters. It will not concern you. It will be arranged with the lawyers and Philip and me . . . for am I not your guardian?"

"Oh, Grand'mère," I said, "I wish you wouldn't. I don't want Philip to have to pay money."

"It is just a settlement . . . nothing more. It means that once you are married to him you are safe . . . secure . . ."

"But I am not marrying him for that!"

"*You* are not . . . but there are those who must watch for your rights. We have to be practical and this is a matter for your guardian and not for you."

When I was alone with Philip I broached the matter with him.

He said: "Your grandmother is an astute business woman. She knows what she is about. She wants the best for you . . . and as I do, we are of one mind."

"But all this talk of settlements is so mercenary."

"It seems so, but it is the right thing to do. Don't think about it. Your grandmother shall have what she wants for you. I thought Italy for our honeymoon. When I was in Florence I thought of you often. I kept saying to myself: I must show Lenore that, so this is exactly what I am going to do. So agree that it shall be Florence."

"You are so good to me, Philip," I said emotionally.

"That is what I intend to be . . . always, and you will be good to me. Ours will be the perfect marriage."

"I hope that I shan't disappoint you."

"What nonsense! As if you could! So it is to be Florence then. It is so beautiful. It is the home of the greatest artists in the world. You sense it as you walk through those streets. We'll go to the opera. That should be a splendid occasion. You shall have a beautiful gown of Sallon Silk. Your grandmother must make it. A special one for the opera."

I laughed and said: "And you shall have a long black opera cloak and an opera hat . . . one of those which collapse and spring up and look so splendid."

"And we shall walk through the streets to our *albergo.* We shall have a room with a balcony . . . perhaps overlooking a square and we shall think of the great Florentines who have worked in this unique city and given the world its greatest art."

"It is going to be wonderful," I said.

* * *

The weeks sped by. I was so happy. I knew that Grand'mère was right. This was the best thing that could have happened to me. Philip was in London a great deal. He was going to take three weeks' holiday which should be our honeymoon. He could not make it longer.

Then we should come back to The Silk House for a while and later go to London. The house there was used jointly by Charles and Philip. Philip thought that later on we must have a place of our own. I thought so, too. The idea of Charles sharing our home was distasteful to me. I did not trust him. I never should again; and although he seemed to wish to forget that incident in the mausoleum, I could not entirely do so.

Grand'mère was blissfully busy making gowns for me. There was my wedding gown of white satin and Honiton lace. It was far too grand for the simple wedding we planned. But Grand'mère insisted on making it her way. Then there was my trousseau. She had listened to our talk of the honeymoon and how we planned to go to the Italian opera. She made me a dress of blue Sallon Silk and a black velvet cloak to go with it. When Philip came home from London, I wanted him to see it. He came up with something under his arm and when I stood before him in my Sallon Silk gown he unfurled a black cloak and put it on. Then he produced the opera hat.

We laughed. We paraded, arm-in-arm, round Grand'mère's work-room singing *La Traviata.* Cassie clasped her hands with glee and Grand'mère watched, happier than I had ever known her before. I guessed she was thinking how different my story was from my mother's.

It was to be a simple wedding. We both wanted that. There would be very few guests and soon after the ceremony we were to set out on our honeymoon.

Lady Sallonger was growing resigned though she was still a little resentful. "Three weeks," she said. "It seems such a long time. We shall have to finish *The Woman in White* before you go."

"Miss Logan would read it to you," I reminded her.

"She gets so hoarse . . . and she doesn't put the feeling into it."

"Cassie . . ."

"No, Cassie is even worse. She has no expression, and you don't know whether it is the heroine or the villain talking. Oh dear, I don't know why people want to have honeymoons. It can be so inconvenient."

"I am flattered that you miss me so much," I said.

"I am so helpless now . . . and with Sir Francis gone . . . there is no one to look after me."

"We all look after you as we always did," I protested. I was on a different status now . . . no longer merely the granddaughter of someone who worked for them but the prospective daughter-in-law. It gave me standing, and I intended to use it.

And so happily the weeks passed until my wedding day came.

It was a bright April day. The doctor who was a friend of the family "gave me away" and Charles was the best man.

As I stood there with Philip a shaft of sunshine came through the glass windows and shone on the plaque dedicated to that Sallonger who had bought the house and changed its name to Silk. Philip took my hand and put the ring on my finger and we vowed to cherish each other until death did us part.

We came down the aisle to the sound of Mendelssohn's Wedding March and I caught sight of Grand'mère's beaming face as I passed.

Then we went back to The Silk House and there was a small reception for the guests. We were congratulated and well-wished; and in due course it was time for us to prepare to leave.

Grand'mère was with me in my bedroom; she helped me out of my splendid wedding gown and into the dark blue alpaca coat and skirt which she had deemed ideal for travelling.

When I was ready she was beaming with pride and joy.

"You look beautiful," she said, "and this is the happiest moment of my life."

Then Philip and I set out for Florence.

* * *

They were days to treasure and remember for ever. I was happy. I now had no doubt whatsoever that Grand'mère had been right when she was eager for me to marry Philip. Now that we were in truth lovers, I had discovered a new happiness which was a revelation to me. This closeness to another person, this newly found intimacy was exciting, exhilarating and wonderful. I had never been lonely. Grand'mère had always been there, the centre of my life; but now there was Philip, and with him I had this special relationship. Philip was so good to me, anxious to make me happy. I was his first consideration. It made me feel humble in a way and very contented to be so loved. Grand'mère had known how it would be and that was why she had been so anxious for me to marry Philip.

Not only was he deeply enamoured of me, a gentle yet passionate lover, but he seemed to have an immense knowledge about so many subjects. I had always known that he was vitally interested in the production of silk—and I was learning that when Philip was interested, the smallest detail was of importance to him—but his love of music was great, and I had always been attracted by it, and when I was with him I came to a great understanding and therefore appreciation of it. He loved art. He was very knowledgeable about the painters of Florence, some of whom, like Cimabue and Masaccio, I had never heard of before. He was interested in the past and could talk so vividly of Florentine history that I almost saw it happening before my eyes.

As it was April there were not many visitors in Florence. I imagined that later on the place would be crowded for it was indeed one of the show places of Europe. There were very few people staying in the hotel which meant that we had the full attention of a staff which I was sure would be added to when the hotel was full.

The rooms were large and lofty; our bedroom had tiled walls of mauve and blue mosaic. The french windows opened onto a balcony so that we could look down on the street below. It was very large. I think it had once been a palace for there was a certain rather shabby grandeur about it. It was called simply Reggia. There was something about it which struck me as being rather eerie. I think I should have felt that more strongly if I had been alone. But as Philip and I were together I quite enjoyed the loneliness and that strange rather uncanny feeling that in this place strong emotions had occurred—some of them sinister, which added to the fascination.

They were golden days. Everything seemed exciting and amusing.

Philip had a way of looking at things to make them so. I had thought he was obsessed by his business—and to a certain extent he was. We used to wander round the streets looking in the shop windows which displayed silks. He could never resist stopping and sometimes going into the shops to enquire about prices, to feel the weight of the material and caressing it fondly with his fingers. I used to laugh at him about it and tell him that the shopkeepers would be annoyed with him because he never bought anything. "Well," he said, "that would be like taking coals to Newcastle."

I loved the little shops on the Ponte Vecchio. We would pore over the trinkets and sometimes buy a stone or a bracelet or a little enamelled box. There was so much to interest us.

We were looked after by a lively Italian. I did not know what he did in the hotel when it was full, but as there were so few guests he attached himself to us and became a kind of general factotum.

He brought our breakfast in the morning. He would draw back the curtains and stand surveying us with an indulgent smile. If we left clothes lying about he would hang them up, for he took a great interest in our clothes, particularly Philip's. He spoke a little English interspersed with much Italian and obviously he liked to practise it on us. We were very amused by him and as the days passed we began to encourage him to talk.

He was tall . . . about Philip's height; and he had dark brown hair and large dark soulful eyes.

He quickly discovered that we were on our honeymoon.

"How did you guess?" I asked.

He lifted his shoulders and raised his eyes to the painted ceiling.

"It is possibla to tella." He put an "a" on the ends of most of his words and uttered them in a singsong voice which was totally un-English.

"Verra nisa," he said. "Verra nisa." And seemed to think the matter was a great joke.

He looked upon us as his protégés. When we ate in the restaurant he would come down and stand with the waiter watching us eat. If we did not do justice to one dish he would shake his head and ask anxiously: "Notta nisa?" in that voice which made us want to laugh.

He was very dashing and dandy in appearance. One constantly saw him gazing at his reflection in mirrors with a look of complete satisfaction. His name was Lorenzo. Philip christened him Lorenzo the Magnificent.

As the days passed he came more and more loquacious. Philip had a certain understanding of Italian and between that and Lorenzo's English we learned a great deal. We encouraged him to talk. Everything seemed incredibly amusing and we laughed a great deal. It was the best sort of laughter that had its roots in happiness rather than amusement. I think we were both so glad to be alive.

Lorenzo sensed this and it was as though he wanted to be part of it. He wanted us to know what a fine fellow he was, beloved of the ladies. In fact, he conveyed to us, it grieved him that there were occasions when he had to shake them off. His hands were expressive and he made motions as though brushing away tiresome flies. He always placed himself conveniently near a mirror during these discourses so that he could throw glances at himself; he would pat his curls approvingly. But in spite of his blatant vanity there was something lovable about him and neither of us could resist talking to him.

As I said he was very interested in Philip's clothes. Once we had come into the room and found him trying on Philip's opera hat.

"Verra nisa," he said, not in the least abashed to be caught.

We tried not to show surprise, but we were never really surprised at anything Lorenzo did.

"It suits you," I said.

"In this . . . Lorenzo . . . he maka the big capture, aha?"

"I am sure you would. You wouldn't be able to brush them off. You would have to take flight."

Reverently he took the hat, collapsed it with almost childish pleasure and reluctantly put it into the box.

He used to tell us where to go and question us on our return. He was a source of great amusement to us. We laughed about his preening himself in Philip's hat.

"Have you ever seen anyone so vain?" I asked.

Philip replied that he was probably no vainer than other people, but he just did not hide it.

"He sees himself as the great lover," he went on. "Well, why not? It makes him happy. There is no doubt about that."

There certainly was not.

Sometimes we would sit in one of the open-fronted restaurants drinking coffee or sipping an aperitif. We would talk about where we had been that day and what we proposed to do the next and we never failed to talk about the latest exploits of Lorenzo.

Magic days in a magic city. When I think of Florence I think of the heights of Fiesole; I think of houses encircled by sloping hills covered with vineyards, gardens and beautiful villas; I think of the rather austere Florentine buildings which gave a certain sinister grandeur to the streets; I remember particularly the Duomo—the Cathedral—and the church of San Lorenzo with its magnificent marbles and decorations of lapis lazuli, chalcedony and agate; I discovered a statue of Lorenzo de' Medici—Lorenzo the Magnificent.

I swore it had a look of our Lorenzo. We tried to discover resemblances and asked ourselves whether our Lorenzo came here to study his famous namesake.

There was so much to see—a surfeit of riches. One should have lived there for a year and assimilated it gradually; the many palaces; il Bargello which had been a prison; the Palazzo Vecchio; the Uffizi and the Palazzo Pitti; we loved to linger in the Piazza della Signoria with its collection of statues and Loggia dei Lanzi under whose porticos were some of the most exciting sculptures I had ever seen.

The weather was gently warm but not hot. The skies were blue and gave an added beauty to those all imposing buildings.

While we were looking at the sculptures in the Piazza della Signoria, I noticed a man standing nearby. He caught my eye and smiled.

"What a wonderful collection," he said in English with a strong Italian accent.

"Beautiful," I answered.

"Where would you find anything like it outside Italy?" added Philip.

"I would venture to say nowhere," replied the man. "You are on holiday here?"

"Yes," answered Philip.

"Your first visit?"

"Not mine . . . but my wife's first."

"You speak in English," I commented. "How did you know we were?"

He smiled. "One has a way of knowing. Tell me, what part of England do you come from? I was there myself once."

"We are near Epping Forest," Philip told him. "Have you ever been there?"

"Oh yes. But it is beautiful . . . and so near the big city, is it not?"

"I see you are well informed."

"You are staying here long?"

"We have another week after the end of this."

He raised his hat and bowed. "You must enjoy what time is left."

When he had gone I said: "He was very affable."

"He liked us because we were admiring the sights of his country."

"You think that was what it was? He seemed quite interested in us . . . asking where we came from and when we were leaving."

"That," said Philip, "is just idle conversation."

He tucked his arm in mine and we went off in search of a restaurant where we could sit and watch the activity of the streets while we ate.

*　*　*

We went to the opera. I was wearing my blue Sallon Silk gown and Philip his black cloak and the hat for which Lorenzo had shown such fervent admiration.

Lorenzo came into our room on some pretext just as we were about to leave. He clasped his hands and stood regarding us with admiration; and I knew he was imagining himself in Philip's hat and cloak. He clapped his hands and murmured: *"Magnifico! Magnifico!"*

That was a wonderful night—the last of the wonderful nights. It seems incredible looking back that one can be so oblivious of disaster so close.

The opera was *Rigoletto;* the singing was superb; the audience appreciative. I was completely enchanted by the magnificent voices of the Duke and his tragic jester. I thrilled to Gilda's *Caro nome* and the quartette with the flirtatious philandering Duke intent on pursuing the girl from the tavern mingling with the tragedy of betrayed Gilda and the revengeful Rigoletto. I thought: I must tell Grand'mère all about this.

During the interval I looked up at one of the boxes and in it I saw the man who had spoken to us in the Piazza. He caught my eyes and recognized me, for he bowed his head in acknowledgement.

I said to Philip: "Look, there is that man." Philip looked vague. "Do you remember we saw him in the Piazza?"

Philip nodded vaguely.

As we came out into the street I saw him again. He was standing as though waiting for someone. Again we acknowledged each other.

"Perhaps he is waiting for his conveyance," I said.

We ourselves decided to walk to the Reggia.

That was an enchanted evening. I wanted it to go on and on. We stood, side by side, on our balcony for a while looking down.

"When there are no people in the streets they look sinister," I said. "One begins to ask oneself what violent deeds were done down there in days gone by."

"That would apply to anywhere," said practical Philip.

"But I think there is a special quality here . . ."

"You are too fanciful, my darling," said Philip drawing me inside.

* * *

We had spent the day walking and after dinner we were rather weary. Lorenzo had hovered about us while we ate in the almost deserted dining room.

"You do not go to the opera thisa night?" he asked.

"No. We were there last night," Philip told him.

"It was wonderful," I added.

"Verra nisa. *Rigoletto,* eh?"

"Yes. The singing was superb."

"And tonight you notta go again?"

"Oh no," said Philip. "Tonight we are going to retire early. We have some letters to write. We are rather tired so we shall have an early night."

"That is gooda . . ."

We returned to our room. We wrote our letters. Mine was a long one to Grand'mère telling her about the wonderful sights of Florence and our visit to the opera. Philip had had news from the factory and was absorbed in replying.

We sat on the balcony for a while afterwards and went early to bed.

Next morning breakfast was late in arriving and when it did come it was not brought by Lorenzo but by one of the others.

"What has happened to Lorenzo?" I asked.

His English was not good. "Lorenzo . . . has gone."

"Gone? Gone where?"

He set down the tray and looked blank, raising his hands in a gesture of helplessness.

When he had gone we talked about Lorenzo. What could have happened? It could not mean that he had gone altogether.

"I should have thought he would have told us if he were having a day off," said Philip.

"It's odd," I agreed. "But then Lorenzo is rather odd. I daresay we shall hear in due course."

But when we came downstairs no one knew of his whereabouts, and it was clear that they were as surprised as we were about his disappearance.

"He's on some romantic mission, I daresay," said Philip.

We went out and wandered about the city. We passed the Medici Palace and with our Lorenzo in mind we talked of that other Lorenzo, scion of that notorious family which had had sovereign power over Florence in the fifteenth century.

"Lorenzo il Magnifico," mused Philip. "He must have been a very great man to be universally known as such. Well, he was magnificent. He gave much of his great wealth to encouraging art and literature and made Florence the centre of learning. You know, he gave great treasures to the library which he founded; he surrounded himself with some of the most famous sculptors and painters the world has ever known. That *is* magnificent. I believe he became too powerful in the end and that is not good for anybody; and by the time he died in Florence he had lost some of his power. The sons of great men often do not match their fathers and there followed troublous times for Florence."

I could not stop thinking of our Lorenzo.

"I hope there is no trouble when he returns," I said. "I should imagine they will not be very pleased with him . . . walking out like that without saying where he was going."

We shopped on the Ponte Vecchio and walked along by the Arno where, Philip said, Dante had first encountered Beatrice.

I was rather glad to return to the Reggia because I could not get Lorenzo out of my mind.

There a shock awaited us.

As soon as we entered the hotel we knew that something was wrong. One of the waiters with two of the chambermaids came hurrying up to us. We had difficulty in understanding what they were saying for they all spoke at once and in Italian with only a smattering of English.

We could not believe that we had heard correctly. Lorenzo was dead.

It seemed he had been attacked soon after he left the hotel on the previous night. His body had been left in one of the little alleyways at the back of the hotel and discovered only this morning by a man on his way to work.

The manager came up.

"It is good that you are back," he said. "The *polizia* they wish to speak . . . I must let them know that you are here. They wish to speak . . ."

We were astounded, wondering why they wished to see us, but we were so stunned remembering the exuberant laughing Lorenzo now dead that we could think of little else.

Two members of the police arrived to talk to us. One spoke fair English. He said they had not identified Lorenzo for some time because he was wearing a cloak with a label inside and that label was the name of a London tailor. They had thought that the victim of the attack was a visitor to Florence. But he was not unknown in the city and was soon identified. They surmised that the object of the attack was robbery, but it was difficult to say whether anything had been stolen.

We were puzzled. Then I remembered Lorenzo's admiring himself in Philip's opera hat. I said I wanted to go to our room. I did so. The hat box was empty; nor was the cloak in the wardrobe.

I hurried down to tell them.

As a result we were taken to see the bloodstained cloak. There was no doubt whatsoever. It was Philip's. By that time the hat had been found. As soon as I saw it I guessed what had happened.

We were very upset for this touched us deeply. We had been amused by Lorenzo and enjoyed our encounters with him. I remembered that he had particularly asked us if we should be out that night, and knowing that we should not be, he had taken Philip's cloak and hat and so had been mistaken for a wealthy tourist and met his death.

It was so tragic and we felt deeply involved because he had been killed in Philip's clothes. I kept thinking of him, sauntering along, feeling himself to be a very fine figure of a man, irresistible to women. His vanity had killed him; but it was such a harmless, lovable vanity.

Poor Lorenzo—so full of life and so equipped to enjoy it and then, because of one foolish act . . . it was over.

That was the end of the honeymoon for us. We could no longer be happy in Florence. The place had taken on a new aspect. These streets with their fine buildings, full of shadows of a glorious past, were indeed sinister.

Wherever I went I saw Lorenzo . . . strolling out, pleased with life and himself, and then suddenly the assassin's knife had descended on him.

"I think," said Philip, "that it would be better if we went home."

Tragedy in the Forest

How different was our homeward journey compared with that on which we had set out. I was sure Philip, like myself, could not stop thinking of Lorenzo. He had come only briefly into our lives but I was sure that we should never forget him and that it was in Philip's cloak and hat that he had met his death.

I thought of him—setting out so jauntily, seeing himself as a sophisticated man about town . . . and then suddenly death striking him. I wondered if he had had time to realize what was happening to him and why. Perhaps . . . for one terrifying moment . . .

What a vicious attack it had been. He had been struck several times and nothing taken. That was strange. Perhaps it had not been robbery, but a long-standing quarrel. Perhaps the stories of his conquests had been true and there was some jealous rival. No. The cloak and the hat were significant. He had been mistaken for a tourist.

It occurred to me that it might so easily have been Philip and that really frightened me. I told him of my fears, clinging to him as though I was afraid to let him go.

He said: "This has changed Florence for us."

And I agreed.

So we came home.

Grand'mère was waiting for us, her hands clasped, her eyes anxious as she surveyed me. She was soon smiling: nothing could hide the contentment in my face.

"I am so happy . . . so happy," she said. "It is a dream come true. Oh, how rarely does that happen in this life! One plans . . . one hopes . . . and then it does not come. But this time . . . yes. You are happy, *mon amour*. He is good, is he not, this man? And good men are rare . . . and those who find them are fortunate."

"It was wonderful. I must tell you about Florence. The beautiful buildings . . . the pictures . . . the sculptures . . . everything . . . the lovely bridges over the river . . . the little shops there . . . the streets . . ." I trailed off. The dark, narrow streets where a man could go out jauntily . . . happily . . . in love with life and himself . . . and meet death.

"What is it?" asked Grand'mère, all concern.

I told her about Lorenzo and she listened intently. "And he was wearing Philip's cloak and hat?"

"Yes. He must have been mistaken for a rich tourist and that was why . . ."

"Mon Dieu . . . it could have been . . ."

I nodded. "That's what I thought. That is why we have come home earlier than we intended."

"Thank God you are safe. Thank God you are happy. This is how it must stay. I missed you. I thought of you all the time. I wondered. Marriage means much in a woman's life. There are some who did not find happiness in it, but I see you have and that makes me happy."

But what had happened to Lorenzo had thrown a shadow even over Grand'mère's contentment. I could see that she could not forget what might have happened to Philip.

Lady Sallonger was pleased to see me back.

"You have been away so long," she said. "Now I hope you are not going away again. That would be really thoughtless of you."

I was no longer subservient. I was a daughter of the house, married to one of the sons. Mrs. Philip Sallonger—no longer plain Lenore Cleremont.

I said: "Philip wants us to find a house in London. He will be there most of the time and of course I shall be with him."

"He can come here whenever he likes," she protested. "It is his home as well as the rest of us."

"I know. But we are going to have our own house."

"Tiresome," said Lady Sallonger. "Well, it will be some time before these things can be arranged. I have *The Moonstone* now. I heard it is most exciting. I thought we might start it this afternoon."

I could see that she wanted to bring me back into bondage, though I must say that one of my most agreeable tasks was reading to her.

But Lady Sallonger would have to realize that life had changed.

Cassie embraced me warmly. She said: "It has been so dull here, Lenore. I've been longing for you to come back. Your grandmother and I were counting the days. I had a calendar and used to mark them off. We were so pleased when you came home early."

She listened wide-eyed while I told her about Florence and the terrible thing that had happened to Lorenzo.

"If he hadn't taken the cloak it wouldn't have happened," she said awestruck.

"We don't know. But he did seem to have been mistaken for a tourist. On the other hand it might have been the outcome of some quarrel. He was always talking about his conquests and the Italians are a fiery people. They are always having feuds and vendettas."

"Romeo and Juliet and all that. But how upsetting for you."

"It was. If you had seen him, Cassie . . ."

"How I wish I had!"

"It was just horrible to think of that happening to him."

"Because he was wearing Philip's cloak. It might have happened to Philip."

"Don't speak of it."

"You do love him, don't you? I'm so glad. I love him too. This makes you really a part of the family."

"Yes, I am very glad about it and so is Grand'mère."

"So we are all happy."

Julia came to the house accompanied by the Countess. The latter greeted me warmly, Julia less so. She looked at me with grudging admiration. Really, I thought, this capturing of a husband became an obsession with these girls because so much was made of their coming out. I was lucky. It hadn't happened to me. My entrance into the world might have offended convention but it had given me Grand'mère and brought me to Philip. I must throw off the shadow Lorenzo's death had cast over me; I must accept my happiness and rejoice in it.

Charles arrived at The Silk House. He and Philip were closetted together for a long while while Philip, as he said, caught up with what had been going on during his absence. One of the managers came down with a case full of papers and Philip decided that he would stay at The Silk House with the manager and Charles while he sorted them out.

We had been home only three days when Madalenna de' Pucci arrived at the house. She came in a most unexpected manner.

We were dining. As Julia and the Countess were with us as well as Charles we were a larger party than usual. On what she called "her good days" Lady Sallonger dined with us, and she was wheeled into the dining room. This was one of those occasions.

We were half way through the meal when one of the servants came in and announced that there had been an accident. A carriage had overturned right outside the house. The occupants were foreigners and it was not easy to understand what they were saying, but it seemed they were asking for help.

Lady Sallonger looked alarmed. "Oh dear . . . how tiresome," she murmured. Charles said we had better go out and discover what it was all about.

In the hall stood a man. He was very dark and obviously harassed. He was talking at a great rate and in Italian.

We gathered that the carriage which he had been driving had overturned. His mistress, who was with her maid, had been hurt. He had been taking her to London.

Out in the road the carriage was lying on its side. The horses however were unharmed and standing patiently by. Seated on the roadside was a young woman; she was dark-haired and outstandingly beautiful. She was holding her ankle and appeared to be in some pain. Beside her sat a middle-aged woman who was wringing her hands and attempting to soothe her though the younger woman seemed calmer than she was.

Charles went to the young woman. "Are you in pain?" he asked.

"Si . . . si . . ." She lifted her beautiful eyes to his face appealingly.

"You must come into the house," said Charles. I could see he was impressed by her beauty.

"Shall we see if you can stand on it?" said Charles. "If you can . . . I think that means no bones are broken."

Philip said: "I'll get some of the men from the stables to see what can be done about the carriage."

The maid was talking volubly in Italian and the young woman got to her feet. She fell towards Charles who caught her.

"I think a doctor ought to see it," I said.

"That's the idea," added Charles. "Send one of the servants for him. Let him explain what has happened." He turned to the young woman. "Meanwhile you must come into the house."

She leaned heavily on Charles who took her in, the maid running behind them talking all the time.

Some of the men had come out and were looking at the carriage. Philip remained with them while I went with Charles and the women into the house.

"Has the doctor been sent for?" asked Charles.

"Jim has gone off to fetch him," Cassie told him.

"You are so kind . . ." said the Italian girl.

"Everything will be all right." Charles spoke soothingly, caressingly.

Lady Sallonger, left in the dining room, was querulously asking what was going on. She called to me and I went in and told her.

"What is going to happen then?" she asked.

"I don't know. They have sent for the doctor. She's hurt her ankle and Charles thought it ought to be seen to."

The doctor was soon with us. He examined the ankle and said he was certain no bones were broken. He thought it might be a strain. He must bind it up and he thought that a few days' rest might put it to rights.

Charles said she must stay at The Silk House until she was fit to walk. Meanwhile Philip was discovering where the little party had come from and what their destination was. They were Italians—that we already knew—and they were visiting relations in England. The young lady, Madalenna de' Pucci, had come from friends and was returning to her brother who was staying in London. They were going to return to Italy shortly.

A plan of action was decided on.

Charles insisted that she stay with us until her ankle was well. She protested weakly but Charles was adamant. She and Maria, the maid, should stay at the house. The carriage needed very little repairs and the men could do them immediately. The driver would take the carriage to London and explain to the brother what had happened, and in a few days Signorina Madalenna and her maid could return to London.

This plan was finally agreed on and a room was prepared for

Madalenna and an adjoining one for her maid. She was effusively grateful to us and kept talking of our kindness.

The excitement pleased the servants, who did all they could to make the newcomers welcome—so did the rest of us, especially Charles who was clearly taken with the Signorina's charms.

Only Lady Sallonger felt aggrieved to have a rival invalid in the house, but it was only for a few days and even she was reconciled and during the next few days she became quite pleased to have them there. She liked to talk to Madalenna about her ailments which, she assured the young lady, were far worse than anything she could imagine; and Madalenna, who did not understand half of what she said, was too polite to show anything but absorbed interest and deep sympathy.

I think we all enjoyed her stay. It was soon clear that her ankle was not seriously damaged; she was able to hobble to the table and to and from her room; and when we were in the drawing room she would have her ankle supported on a stool or sometimes she would lie on a settee. She was very graceful, elegant and obviously well educated.

Maria, the maid, was not so fortunate. She was quietly aloof. I supposed that was inevitable. The servants were suspicious of her. She was a foreigner who did not understand English—and that was enough to arouse their dislike. Moreover, she appeared morose; and even when kindly gestures were made they were met with something almost like hostility. She seemed to like the forest and used to go for long walks alone in it. She moved about the house silently; one would suddenly look up and see her though one had not heard her approach. Madalenna told us that it was the first time she had left Italy and she was bewildered; and that this accident should have happened had completely upset her.

Mrs. Dillon said she gave her "the creeps."

Our recent visit to Italy made us especially interested in Madalenna. She was eager to hear what we thought of Florence and her eyes shone with pleasure when we extolled its beauty and told her how fascinating we found it all. Once I was on the point of telling her about Lorenzo but I did not do so. The memory always made me feel sad. Moreover, I thought she might fancy it was a criticism of her country as a place where law-abiding citizens could go out into the streets and be stabbed to death.

She seemed drawn to me more than to either Cassie or Julia. I thought it was because I had recently been in her country. She wanted to meet Grand'mère and I took her up to the workroom. She was most interested in the machine and the loom and the dummies and bales of materials. Grand'mère talked to her about the work she did. She fingered the material tentatively.

"What beautiful silk," she said.

"That's Sallon Silk," I told her.

"Sallon Silk? What is this Sallon Silk?" she asked.

"It's the newest kind of weaving. Can you see the beautiful sheen? We're very proud of it. We were the first to put it on the market. It's a great invention really. My husband says it has revolutionized the silk industry. He is very proud of it."

"He must be," said Madalenna. "It is *interessante* . . . to find all this . . . in a house."

"Yes, it is, is it not?" I agreed. "My grandmother has been with the family for years. I have been here all my life."

"And now you are Mrs. Sallonger."

"Yes, Philip and I were married about six weeks ago."

"It is very . . . *romantico.*"

"Yes, I suppose it is."

"I hope," she said to Grand'mère, "that you will let me come again."

Grand'mère said she would be delighted.

Charles hovered round her. He liked to sit beside her when we were all in the drawing room; he would talk to her in his execrable Italian interspersed with English, which made her laugh; but clearly she liked his attentions.

When we were alone at night I asked Philip if he thought Charles was falling in love with Madalenna.

"Charles's emotions are ephemeral," he said, "but there is no doubt that he finds Madalenna very attractive."

"It is so romantic," I said. "She had her accident right outside the door. She might have had it five miles away and then he would never have seen her. It seems as though it was meant."

Philip laughed at that.

"Accidents can happen anywhere. There was a weakness in the harness."

"I like to think it was fate."

I should like to think of Charles's marrying for he still made me feel uneasy, and I often wondered if he still remembered that occasion when Drake Aldringham had thrown him into the lake.

Madalenna had been in the house four days when one evening the manager of the Spitalfields works came to The Silk House in some agitation. It appeared that there was a crisis at the works and the presence of both Charles and Philip was urgently needed.

Charles was annoyed. Usually he was ready to leave The Silk House after a short stay, but now that Madalenna was there he felt differently. He wanted to stay but it seemed his presence was necessary and he was finally persuaded that he had no alternative but to go.

I heard him explaining to Madalenna. "I am sure they could manage very well without me. But it will only be a day. I shall be back either late tonight or tomorrow morning."

"I shall look forward to that with pleasure," Madalenna told him; and Charles seemed reconciled, and with Philip and the manager, he left early the next morning.

Soon afterwards I happened to be sitting in my window when I saw Maria. She was walking towards the forest with quick, short, determined steps as though she were in a great hurry.

I watched her until she disappeared among the trees. I was rather sorry for Maria. She must find communication with the servants difficult and they were decidedly not friendly towards her. Her stay in the house was very different from that of Madalenna who had been made so much of—particularly by Charles.

It was mid morning when the carriage arrived. Cassie and I had been riding in the forest and had just come in when we saw it. I recognized it at once, as I did the coachman.

He descended from the driver's seat and bowed to me. He then implied that he must see the Signorina at once.

"Come along in," I said. "She is much better."

He murmured something about God and the saints and I imagined he was offering a prayer of thanksgiving to them.

Madalenna was in the drawing room resting her leg on a stool. Lady Sallonger was there drinking her glass of sherry she took at this time. Lady Sallonger was in the middle of one of her monologues which compared her present suffering with past glories.

As I entered with the coachman, Madalenna gave a cry and got to her feet quickly. Then suddenly she winced and sat down again. She spoke in rapid Italian, to which the man replied. Then she turned to us.

"I have to leave at once. It is a message from my brother. I must meet him in London. We leave for Italy tomorrow. It is necessary. My uncle is dying and calling for me. I hope to be there in time. We are so sorry to go like this . . . but . . ."

"My dear," said Lady Sallonger, "we understand. We shall be very sorry. You must come again . . . when your ankle is quite well. Then we can show you everything, can't we, Lenore?"

"Indeed, yes," I agreed. "Can I help you . . . packing or anything like that? Do you want to go immediately?"

"It is nearly time for luncheon," said Lady Sallonger. "Yes . . . you must stay for luncheon."

"I do not think . . ." said Madalenna. "My brother says we have to leave early tomorrow. We have to be soon in Italy. It may be that we shall go this night. No, there must be no delay. Lady Sallonger, how can I thank you? You . . . your family . . . for your goodness to me. There is no way of saying how grateful . . ."

Lady Sallonger said: "Oh, but we have enjoyed having you, my dear. It has been no trouble at all."

"I'll go and tell Maria," I said. "I saw her return from her walk a little while ago."

She was about to protest but I went on ahead of her. I ran up to the room, knocked on the door and walked in. Maria was startled when I entered. She had the travelling bag on the bed and she was putting things into it.

"Ah . . . I had come to tell you that the carriage is here . . . your driver is downstairs. Signorina de' Pucci wishes to leave at once."

She stared at me and of course she did not understand what I was saying. I could see she was taken aback. She had expected her mistress to come in—not me.

The odd thing about it was that she was packing—as though she knew they were about to depart. I thought there was something uncanny about her. Why was she packing? How did she know about the message?

But there *was* something strange about Maria.

Madalenna came in.

"Maria!" she cried and spoke in rapid Italian. Maria threw up her hands to the ceiling. I left them together, still puzzled.

Within an hour they were ready to go. Cassie, Julia and I with the Countess went down to wave them farewell. Madalenna again expressed her gratitude. She said: "I will write."

Then they were gone.

When Charles and Philip returned that night and Charles heard what had happened he went white with anger.

He glared at Philip. "There was no need for me to have gone to London," he said. "You could have done everything without me."

"My dear fellow, your presence was necessary. Don't forget we are partners. We had to have your signature on the documents."

"Where have they gone?" demanded Charles.

Julia said: "Her uncle is ill. They've gone back to Italy."

"I could have driven them to London."

"They went in their own carriage. The driver came down with it. Her brother had sent him."

"Where did they go?"

"To London, of course . . . for a night . . . perhaps not that," I told him. "She did say that they might leave for Italy tonight. They were in a great hurry."

Charles turned on his heels and left us.

I said to Philip that night: "I think he really did care for her."

Philip was inclined to be sceptical. He said: "He is just annoyed that the chase is over before the capture."

"Are you a little cynical about your brother?" I asked.

"Shall I say I know him well. In a few weeks he will find it difficult to remember what she looked like. He is not a faithful-to-one-woman-type like his brother."

"I am glad you are that type, Philip," I said fervently. "You were not in the least overwhelmed by the charms of the siren."

"There is only one for me today . . . tomorrow and for ever."

In my happiness, I could feel sorry for Charles.

Three days after their departure two letters came—one was for Charles, the other for Lady Sallonger.

Lady Sallonger could not find her spectacles so I was called upon to read hers to her. It was a conventional little note saying how Madalenna would never forget the kindness of being taken in and looked after so wonderfully. She could never express her gratitude.

The address was a hotel in London.

Charles's must have been the same. He went up to Town the next day and called at the hotel, but of course by that time she had left.

"That little episode is over," said Philip.

* * *

When Philip went to London, I was with him. I think Grand'mère was a little sad to see me go, but her joy in my marriage overshadowed everything else and it was a constant delight for her to see how it was between us.

The London house seemed different now. Before it had been rather alien—very grand, the Sallonger Town House. Well, now I was a Sallonger. The house belonged—at least partly—to my husband; and therefore it was in a way my home too.

The elegant Georgian architecture appeared less forbidding; the all but nude nymphs, who supported the urns on either side of the door, seemed to smile a welcome at me. Greetings, Mrs. Sallonger. I thought I should never get used to being Mrs. Sallonger.

The butler looked almost benign. Did I really detect a certain respect in the crackle of Mrs. Camden's bombazine?

"Good evening, Madam." How different from my last visit when I was plain Miss—not exactly a servant—but not of the quality either—a kind of misfit.

That had changed. The proud gold ring on my finger proclaimed me a Sallonger.

"Good evening, Evans. Good evening, Mrs. Camden," said Philip. "We'll get up to our room first I think. Please have hot water sent up. We must wash away the stains of the journey." He took my arm. "Come along, darling. If you're anything like me you're famished."

I was conscious on every side of my newly acquired status. I would tell Grand'mère about it when I saw her. We would laugh together and I would give an imitation of Mrs. Camden's very gracious but slightly hesitant condescension.

I loved being in London with Philip. He was so enthusiastic about everything. He talked unceasingly and it was usually about the business. I did not have to feign interest. He said he would take me to the works at Spitalfields. "It's wonderful," he said, "to have a wife who cares about the things I care about."

I vowed that I would learn more and more. I would please him in every way. I was so glad that Grand'mère had taught me so much.

My complete pleasure was spoilt by the presence of Charles. He was still sulking about Madalenna and seemed to think that we had deliberately refused to find out where she was going. Apparently his letter had been on the same lines as that she had written to Lady Sallonger—just a conventional thank-you letter; and he had no more idea where she had gone than we had. All he knew was that she had written from that particular hotel. Philip told me that Charles had been there several times but could get no information as to her address in Italy.

I would sometimes find his eyes watching me . . . almost speculatively and there was an expression in them which I could not fathom; but I did not think it was one of brotherly love.

I was glad when Julia and the Countess came to the house. Julia had had her little respite and was now once more in search of a husband.

I was becoming friendly with the Countess. She told me how much she admired Grand'mère who had made a niche for herself and kept her dignity; and now her granddaughter had married into the family. The Countess thought that was a very happy conclusion.

She and Julia went out a great deal. There was constant discussion about Julia's clothes. Often the Countess would call me in to ask my advice.

"You have a flair," she said.

She admitted that she had one, too.

I liked her very much; and one morning when Julia was in bed—she invariably slept late after her social engagements—the Countess and I talked together. She was very frank. She said she thought her work was rather futile. She would like to do something worthwhile. She spoke of Grand'mère. "What a dressmaker! None of the court people can compare with her. How I wish I could do something more to my taste."

"Have you any idea what?"

"Something in the dress line. I'd like to have a shop . . . all the very best clothes. I'd make it famous throughout Town."

I often remembered that morning's talk.

But at that period my time was mostly taken up by Philip. He gave me a book to read which he said would enhance my interest in silk and tell me something of its romantic beginnings. I found it fascinating to read how nearly three thousand years before the birth of Christ the

Queen of Hwang-te was the first to rear silkworms and how she prevailed upon the Emperor to have the cocoons woven into garments. So the art of silk-weaving became known in the time of Fouh-hi who lived a hundred years before the Flood. But this all took place far away and it was not until the sixth century A.D. that two Persian monks brought knowledge of the process to the Western World.

Philip would talk enthusiastically about the beginnings of the industry and how important it was that the worms should be fed on the right kind of mulberry. He greatly regretted that it was not possible to rear them effectively in this country and the importing of so much raw materials was necessary.

He took me to the works and I learned something of the processes through which the materials were put. I saw the large reels called swifts, and watched the people at work. I saw the manipulating of the hanks; and Philip was delighted to see my growing interest.

He took me to the shop. It was scarcely a shop by normal standards. It was more of an establishment, discreetly curtained and presided over by a certain Miss Dalloway who was the essence of elegance and known throughout the building as Madam. There I saw displayed some of the gowns which Grand'mère had made. They seemed like old friends and much grander here than they had appeared in the workroom on Emmeline, Lady Ingleby and the Duchess of Malfi.

I was even more fascinated by the place than I had been by the workrooms and I asked Miss Dalloway a great many questions. Since the introduction of Sallon Silk there had been a great rush of business. The place had a reputation and reputations were all important when it came to clothes. The label inside could be worth a fortune. People liked a dress because it came out of the Sallonger stable. Produce the same dress without the magic label and it would only be worth half the price.

I contested the point with her saying that if the two were the same, they must be of equal value. She smiled at me in her worldly-wise way.

"The majority of people need others to think for them," she explained. "Tell them something is wonderful and they believe it. If you were in the business you would see at once what I mean."

I talked to Philip about it afterwards and he agreed with Miss Dalloway.

"If one intends to be successful in life," he said, "there is one truth to be learned. One must understand people and the way their minds work, the way they think."

Oh yes, they were happy days; but I still felt a little uneasy about Charles. He was always polite, but I would be uncomfortable if I found his eyes on me.

He will always be there, I thought. It is his home as well as ours. Certainly his presence spoilt my pleasure in London.

Philip was very discerning. He knew of the Aldringham episode and that Drake had fought Charles and thrown him in the lake because of what he had done to me.

He said: "What we must set about doing without delay is finding a house of our own for we shall be living in London a great deal."

"Oh, that would be wonderful!"

"We should start looking right away. Houses are not all that easy to find and the search might take some time. I have one or two in mind which we could look at."

How I enjoyed those days! We looked at several houses—none quite to our taste.

"We must find exactly what we want," said Philip. "It must be somewhere near here."

There was a tinge of sadness for me as I looked at houses. Our home. But I would think about Grand'mère . . . still living at The Silk House. I knew she would miss me terribly, for all my life we had been together. She had never mentioned this; nor had she shown any sadness at the prospect of our separation; her devotion was entirely selfless. She believed that my marriage to Philip was the best thing that could happen to me and she was content for that reason.

Philip was very susceptible to my moods. He had known that I disliked living under the same roof as Charles and understood why although I had never told him of that encounter before the episode with Drake which had made him so angry with me.

Houses were fascinating. I would wander round the empty rooms, imagining the people who had lived there and wondering what had happened to them and where they were now. We found one house— not very far from the river; it had eight rooms—two on each floor, so it was rather small for its height and a room had been added to the top floor, with a glass roof and very large windows. We were told that the house had belonged to an artist and this had been his studio.

"What a lovely room!" I cried. "It reminds me of Grand'mère's at The Silk House."

"It would be an ideal workroom," said Philip. "It would suit her very well. And you see, there is a room adjoining which could be her bedroom."

I turned and looked at him. "You mean that Grand'mère would come and live with us?"

"Well, that is what you want, isn't it?"

"Oh Philip," I cried, "you have made me so happy."

"That is what *I* want."

Then I told him of how I had been worrying about her. She would have been miserable in The Silk House without me.

"I know you well," he replied, "so I knew what was on your mind."

"You are so good to me."

"It's practical," he said. "She can work there. It will be much more convenient than The Silk House."

"I'll tell her that. Oh Philip, I want to go back . . . now I can't wait to tell her."

* * *

What a happy homecoming that was! I think it made what happened afterwards the harder to bear.

The first thing I did was rush up to Grand'mère. She was in the workroom and had not heard our arrival.

"Grand'mère," I cried, "where are you?" And then I was in her arms.

She studied my face and was aware of my happiness.

"Oh Grand'mère," I said. "We've been house-hunting and we have found the very thing."

Why does one want to withhold good news? Why did I not burst out with it? Perhaps one feels that by hesitation one gives it greater impact; perhaps one wants to prepare the other for complete enjoyment. She had given no hint of sadness although the fact that we had a home in London would, she must think, mean more separations for we should come only infrequently to The Silk House.

I could withhold it no longer. "What decided us was the room at the top. It is rather like this one. The roof is glass. The light is wonderful. It is the north light. It was designed by an artist so that he could work there. The first thing Philip said was: 'This will be just right for Grand'mère.' "

She looked at me in puzzlement.

"Are you pleased?" I asked.

She stammered: "But . . . you and Philip . . . will not want . . ."

"But we do want. I could never be completely happy away from you."

"My child . . . *mon amour* . . ."

"It's true, Grand'mère. We have been together all my life. I could not have any change now . . . just because I am married."

"But you must not make these sacrifices."

"Sacrifices! What do you mean? Philip is the most practical man where business is concerned. He talks business almost all the time. He thinks of little but business. And I am becoming the same. He said it will be easier if you are in London. It was always rather a nuisance sending those bales right down here. You are still in the hands of your slavedrivers . . . and you will have to work . . . and work . . . in that room with the north light."

"Oh, Lenore," she murmured and began to weep.

I looked at her in dismay. "This is a nice homecoming! Here you are in tears."

"Tears of joy, my love," she said. "Tears of joy."

* * *

We had been home three days. What happened stands out in my memory as I hope nothing ever does again.

Philip and I had ridden out in the morning. The forest was beautiful in May. It was bluebell time and we constantly came across misty blue clumps of them under the trees.

As we rode along we talked excitedly about the house and how we would furnish it and how he hoped to find another material as successful as Sallon Silk.

He said: "It's wonderful to be able to talk to you about all this, Lenore. Most women wouldn't understand a thing."

"Oh, I am André Cleremont's granddaughter."

"When I think how lucky I am . . ."

"I'm lucky, too."

"We must be the luckiest people on Earth."

What a joyous morning that was! It made what happened afterwards all the more incomprehensible.

Lady Sallonger joined us at luncheon. We had arranged that she should not be told about the house just yet. She would not want me to go. She seemed to think that now I was her daughter-in-law she had an additional right to my services.

She was a little peevish because she had a headache. I suggested she go to her room instead of lying on the sofa in the drawing room. I would put some cotton wool soaked in Eau de Cologne on her forehead. She brightened up considerably; and when she went to her room I accompanied her.

I was with her quite a long time, for when I had ministered to her headache she wanted me to stay and talk until she slept; and it must have been almost an hour later when I was able to tiptoe out.

The house was very quiet. I went to our room expecting to find Philip impatiently waiting for me. He was not there. I was surprised for he had said something about our taking a walk together in the forest as soon as I was free of his mother.

There was a knock on my door. It was Cassie.

"So you're alone," she said. "Good. I wanted to talk to you. I hardly ever see you now. Soon you'll be going to London and staying there. It'll be your home . . . not this."

"Cassie, you can come and stay with us whenever you want to."

"Mama would protest. She is especially demanding when you are not here."

"She is demanding when I am."

"I am so glad you married Philip because it makes you my sister. But it does take you away."

"A woman has to be with her husband, you know."

"I know. I can't imagine what it will be like when you stay all the time in London. What am I going to do? They won't try to find a husband for me. They can't even find one for Julia. So what chance would I have?"

"One never knows what is waiting for one."

"I know what is waiting for me. Dancing attendance on Mama until I am old and just like her."

"It wouldn't be like that for you would never be like her."

"Do you remember that time when we were all up in your grandmother's room and we talked about having a shop together . . .

making wonderful clothes and selling them? Wouldn't that be lovely if we could take Emmeline, Lady Ingleby and the Duchess and all go off together? I used to dream we did and now you have married Philip and that has put an end to that."

"Cassie, when I go to London, Grand'mère is coming with us."

She looked at me in dismay.

I went on: "I have said that whenever you want to you can come and stay."

"I will come," she cried. "No matter what Mama says."

I told her about the house and the big top room which had been designed by an artist. She listened avidly and because I did impress on her that she would be welcome to visit us whenever she could she grew a little less melancholy at the thought of our departure.

I was expecting Philip at any moment, but he did not come. I could not imagine where he was. If he had been going out somewhere, surely he would have told me.

He had still not come back at dinner time, and the meal was delayed for half an hour; and still he had not returned.

We ate uneasily, for now we were beginning to be alarmed.

The evening wore on. We sat in the drawing room, our ears strained for sounds of his arrival. Grand'mère joined us. We were very worried.

We asked the servants if any of them had seen him go out. No one had. Where was he? What could have happened?

As the evening wore on so did our anxiety increase.

I was shivering with apprehension. Grand'mère put her arm about me.

I said: "We must *do* something."

She nodded.

Clarkson thought he might have had an accident in the forest . . . broken a leg or something. He could be lying somewhere . . . helpless. He said he would get some of the men together and organize a search.

I felt limp. In my heart I knew something terrible had happened.

It was nearly midnight when they found him. He was in the forest not so very far from the house.

He was dead . . . shot through the head. The gun was one of those from the gunroom of The Silk House.

* * *

I cannot bear, not after all these years, to dwell on that time. I was stunned by my grief. The most incredible tragedy had burst upon me. Why? I kept asking myself.

I, who had so recently become a wife, was now a widow.

The days and nights seemed to merge into one. Grand'mère kept me with her. I was in bed most of the time. She was knowledgeable about herbs and such things and she gave me something which made me sleep, so I slept and when I awoke it was as though to some nightmare from which I longed to escape in more sleep.

There was an inquest, and I was required to be present. I went with Grand'mère and Charles. He had come up hastily from London when he heard the news. I could not grasp what they were saying. My thoughts were far away . . . in the forest with the bluebells . . . he had been so happy; he had said we were the luckiest people on Earth, and now . . . what had happened? There were so many questions and no answers to them, but the conclusion was that Philip had apparently taken a gun from the gunroom, gone into the forest and shot himself for the evidence pointed to the fact that the wound had been self-inflicted.

It is impossible . . . impossible . . . I kept saying to myself. We were so happy. Everything was set fair. We were going to buy the house. How could he possibly do such a thing? If he were in some sort of trouble he would have told me. But he was not. He was happy . . . he was the happiest man on Earth.

The verdict was "Suicide while the balance of his mind was disturbed."

I would not accept it. It could not be true. I wanted to stand up in court and shout at them all. Grand'mère restrained me.

I allowed myself to be taken back to the house. She said she would look after me. She took me to bed, undressed me, and lay down beside me.

"It's not true," I said again and again.

She did not speak; she just held me close.

Days passed . . . grey days. Lady Sallonger wept genuine tears and wondered what she had done that God should punish her so. Charles was helpful. He managed all the formalities which such an event necessitated. We had to be grateful that he was there. Cassie tried to console me. Poor child, she was heartbroken. Philip had been her favourite brother.

"Why did he do it?" she asked.

None of us could answer that.

"He was so happy," I said.

"Charles says it was a brainstorm. People have them and then they do wild things."

"Philip was the calmest man I ever knew."

"Calm people sometimes have them."

"There must have been a reason," I said. "But what . . . what? Could he really have been so unhappy that he took his own life?"

I would not believe it. It was ridiculous. How unhappy did people have to be? How tired of this life to take that step to get out of it?

People talked about it . . . whispered about it. There must have been something. So recently married.

They looked at me wonderingly. There must have been *something*.

People revel in mysteries and when they cannot find solutions they fabricate them. I had been closest to him. I was his newly wedded wife. Surely I knew. Was it something concerning me? He had been passionately in love with me. Why should he have wanted to leave me . . . unless . . .

I began to think that in their secret hearts they were blaming me. Lady Sallonger . . . Clarkson, Mrs. Dillon . . . I could imagine the conversation in the servants' hall.

"Perhaps he found out something about *her* . . . Who is she anyway? Her sort has no right to marry into the family her grandmother is working for."

There were times when I did not care what they said. They were bound to gossip. All that mattered was that Philip was dead and that I had lost him for ever.

I was drifting along in a state of lethargy. I could not go on like that. Something had to change.

One night I awoke, startled. My body was damp with perspiration and yet I was shivering. It was a dream. I was in Florence. I was walking down a street. Ahead of me I could see a man in an opera hat and cloak. I saw the assassin creep up to him. He turned to face his assailant. It was Philip's face. I saw the knife raised. Then it was Lorenzo . . . and as he fell he changed into Philip.

It took me a few seconds to realize I had had a nightmare. It had all seemed so real.

I lay there for some time. Then I put on my dressing gown and slippers and went into Grand'mère's room.

She started up in bed. "Lenore, what is it?"

"I've had a dream," I said.

She leaped out of bed and took my hands. "You are shivering," she said.

"I shouldn't have disturbed you, but I had to talk. I had to tell you about it."

"Of course you did. Here. Get into bed."

I did so and she lay beside me holding me close.

"I told you about the man in Italy . . . Lorenzo who was wearing Philip's cloak and hat when he was killed. It . . . it seems clear to me suddenly. He was about the same height as Philip . . . from behind he would look exactly like Philip. It was not robbery . . . because nothing was taken. Someone must have come behind and stabbed him in the back . . . perhaps without realizing until later that they had killed the wrong man . . ."

"The wrong man. What do you mean?"

"Philip would never kill himself. I am sure that someone killed him."

"But the gun . . ."

"Would it be so difficult to stage a suicide . . . I believe now that Lorenzo was killed in mistake for Philip. I know he was murdered. I am sure of it now. I knew him so well."

"None of us know the secret places of other people's mind."

"You still believe that there was something about Philip which I did not know."

"Perhaps. But it is over. No good can come of going over all this. You should be getting your sleep."

"This dream . . . this nightmare . . . Grand'mère, it was a revelation. I am sure of it. Someone meant to kill Philip in Florence. They killed Lorenzo instead. And now . . . they have succeeded in killing him in the forest."

"Who would want to kill such a man?"

"I don't know. But someone did."

She stroked my hair. "I am going to make you a herb drink. It will soothe you. You need sleep."

I did not answer. It was impossible to convince me of something of which I was now so sure.

Obediently I drank from the cup she gave me.

"Now I am going to take you back to your own room. You will rest more comfortably there. And don't get up in the morning until I call you."

I went back to my bed.

The draught was effective and I soon slept, but when I awoke in the morning, it was still with the conviction that Lorenzo's death was in some mysterious way linked with that of Philip.

Oddly enough the thought helped me.

I no longer believed that Philip had killed himself because he found life with me intolerable.

Desperately I wanted to find out. How? I went over everything in my mind. That night in Florence. How we had stayed in. It was heartbreaking to recall how happy we had been. Lorenzo had taken advantage of the situation and slipped out in Philip's cloak and hat. Someone was lurking near the hotel waiting . . . following him through the streets and then . . . pouncing with the knife. He must have realized too late that he had the wrong victim. Was that why he had pursued the man he wanted? Was that why Philip had died in the woods . . . and by his own gun? How could that have been?

It was a theory which appeared to have few roots in reason. Whichever way I turned I was baulked. There was no one with whom I could discuss my suspicions. Grand'mère? Cassie? It all turned to the same thing. Philip had taken one of the guns from The Silk House gunroom and how could an unknown assassin do that? He had deliberately walked into the forest and shot himself.

There was only one explanation, but I stubbornly refused to accept it.

I brooded on it. I would wake in the night thinking I had the solution; then by the light of day it proved to be just nonsense.

I felt I was drifting. I could not go on like this. Grand'mère was very anxious about me.

"There has to be a change," she said.

And there was.

A suspicion had come into my mind. I hardly dared believe it. Then later it became a certainty.

I was going to have a child.

* * *

At first it was like a glimmer of light in my dark world. It seemed that I might not have lost Philip entirely. He might live on in our child.

When I told Grand'mère she was overwhelmed first with joy, then with anxiety.

"We shall have to take special care of you," she said.

Cassie was delighted. "A baby," she cried. "A dear little baby. Oh, isn't that the most wonderful thing?"

And it was. It changed me. It helped me to forget. Long periods of the day were spent in planning for the baby, talking of babies. Grand'mère remembered the birth of my mother. The servants' attitude changed. They looked forward to having a little baby in the house.

The serenity of pregnancy settled on me. My mind was now given over to such matters as layettes and the kind of cradle I should need. I was absorbed by it all. I was now to be a mother.

Lady Sallonger was a little peevish. She did not like the disruption of the household but it did give her an opportunity of recalling the terrible time she had had at Cassie's birth, which was perhaps not the most tactful conversation to indulge in with an expectant mother present.

The summer slipped away and autumn was with us.

Julia had found a husband. He was thirty years older than she was and he drank heavily; but he had one redeeming feature: he was rich. The Countess was overjoyed. At last her task was completed; and she passed on to her next client.

I was now finding exercise difficult. I used to sit in the garden when the weather permitted either with Grand'mère or Cassie, and our talk would be all of the baby.

I was in good health, the doctor said; and I was strong. All would be well.

A midwife was engaged; she would stay at the house until the appointed time. I was counting the days now. I felt everything would be different when my baby was born.

It was on a bleak February day when Katharine appeared. She was scarcely a beauty; she had a wrinkled cross-looking face, some spiky fair hair and a snub nose; but I thought her perfect; and each day she changed until in a week she was beautiful.

I had rarely seen Grand'mère so happy. Cassie thought it a great honour to be allowed to hold her. Lady Sallonger said I must have a nanny to give me more time to myself—which meant for her, of course; but I wanted to look after my baby myself.

"Nonsense," said Lady Sallonger, "only servants and those sort of people do that."

But I was adamant. This was my child. My consolation and entirely mine.

There was so much to learn that my time was fully occupied. I was glad that this was so. We called her Katie—Katharine being too dignified for such a tiny creature. And when I held Katie in my arms and watched her change every day, saw her first smile and that recognition which told me that she knew who I was and that she felt safe and happy when I was close . . . they were my compensation.

With Katie I could grow away from my grief. She was more than my beloved child; she was my reason for living.

The Salon

Katie was a year old when I decided I could no longer go on living at The Silk House. I had always felt that I was there on sufferance. Lady Sallonger could not forget that I was the granddaughter of a woman who worked for the family—as Grand'mère still did. Her machine worked doubly as hard now for she was constantly making little garments for Katie. I was expected to perform certain duties for her ladyship. I was still reading to her, fetching and carrying and making sure that she had her comforts. It was true Cassie was treated in the same manner, but although I was now her daughter-in-law, I was still made to feel like the poor relation.

She resented the time I spent with my daughter. If Katie needed me during one of the reading sessions, Cassie would come and take over from me—which did not please Lady Sallonger at all. I was really feeling very restive even before the fracas with Charles.

I had always known that he had some special feeling for me. There had been that occasion long ago when he had tried to make love to me and, of course, the affair of the mausoleum which had ended in his humiliation. I had an idea that Charles was the type of man who bore grudges. In which case he would remember the immersion into the lake and blame me for it. I had often found him watching me and that made me very uneasy.

In spite of being preoccupied with Katie's needs, I still thought a great deal about Philip's death, and the more I thought of it the more I remembered of Lorenzo; and I was becoming absolutely convinced that the assassin's knife had been meant for Philip.

I had made a habit of walking in the forest to that spot where his body had been found. The trees grew thickly there. I wondered whether that was the actual spot where he had died or whether his assailant had dragged his body there.

Everything had pointed to suicide. The position of the gun . . . the fact that it was one of the guns from the house . . . But even in the face of all that evidence, I still refused to believe that he had killed himself.

I knew that my theories would not stand up to the light of reason. Even Grand'mère believed there had been some dark secret in his life which he could not bear to have exposed; and she dismissed the death of Lorenzo as coincidental.

"You have to look straight at life," she said, "to see it as it is, not as you would have it. That is the only way to pick oneself up and go on."

So I kept my thoughts to myself. One day I would find some means of discovering. How? When? asked my commonsense. But I refused to listen to reason. One day I would know the answer.

I did not know why I thought I might find it in that spot where his body had been discovered. He was now lying in the mausoleum with his ancestors. If he could come back and tell me, it would be more likely that I could get into communication with him in this spot.

It was like visiting a grave. I thought: If these trees could speak they could tell me the truth. I used to look up into their leafy heights. "How did it happen?" I whispered. "You must have seen."

It was there that Charles came upon me.

"Hello, Lenore," he said. "You come here often, don't you?"

"Yes," I answered.

"Why? Is it a sort of pilgrimage?"

I shook my head and turned away, uneasy as I always was in his presence.

He caught my arm. "Don't go," he said. "I want to talk to you."

"Yes?"

"You must be feeling very lonely."

"I have my daughter . . . my grandmother."

"But missing Philip?"

"Of course."

"I always envied him."

"Envied him? Why?"

"I envied him you."

"I think I should go in."

"Not yet. Lenore, why are you so stubborn?" He pulled me towards him and held me firmly.

"I want to go back to the house," I said.

"Not yet." He smiled and kissed me. "Still a bit of a spitfire, eh?"

I struggled free. "Charles, I will not tolerate . . ."

"You must be lonely. I could change that."

"I told you long ago. You know what happened then."

His brow darkened. He was remembering Drake Aldringham, the magnificent friend whom he had been so proud to bring home and the manner in which Drake had left the house.

"You give yourself airs," he said. "Who are you, anyway?"

"I am Lenore Sallonger, your brother's widow."

"You managed to catch him. He was easy prey, wasn't he?"

"How dare you say such things!"

"Oh?" he said looking about him. "Do you think I'm afraid of ghosts? This is where they found him. Why did he do it, Lenore? What did he find out about you? Why? You must know if anyone does."

I turned to go but he caught me again. "I have always had a fancy for you," he said. "There's something deep in you. I want to find it. I want to know what caught Philip and what made him take his life. I know it was because of you."

"It was not. It was not," I cried.

There was a struggle. He was pulling at my blouse. Suddenly my rage gave way to terror. He had a distorted mind. I knew what was in it. He wanted to make love to me here . . . where Philip's body had been found. There was something macabre about it; something which appealed to his warped notions. I fought wildly. He was stronger than I. I prayed to myself: Oh God, save me. Help me escape from this evil man.

"You're not getting away now," he said. "Why should you? You come to our house . . . you live in luxury . . . You have to earn it, Madam Lenore. Don't be a little fool. You and I were made for each other. We are two of a kind."

My strength was failing. He had thrown me to the ground and was ready to leap upon me.

"Lenore!" The voice broke in on my terror like a sign from heaven.

It was Cassie. She had come to look for me. Oh God bless Cassie, I thought.

Charles stood back abashed, furious. I scrambled to my feet trying to adjust my torn clothes.

Cassie came into view.

"I guessed you'd be here. Why, Lenore . . . Charles . . ."

"Cassie," I said, "thank God you came. I'm going back to the house now. Come with me."

Together we walked back through the forest, Charles standing there, staring after us.

* * *

Cassie was horrified.

"He . . . he was attacking you?"

"Cassie, I shall never cease to be grateful to you for coming when you did."

"I'm . . . so glad. It was horrible. Charles . . ."

"I think Charles has always hated me in a strange way. I can't talk about it."

We reached the house.

"I have to see Grand'mère right away," I said. "You come with me."

Grand'mère was in the workroom. When she saw me she gave a little cry of horror. I fell into her arms. I was near hysteria. I stammered: "It was Charles. Cassie came in time or I think he would have . . . He was vicious. It was at that spot . . . where Philip was found. I think he found some satanic satisfaction because it was there."

"He did this to you? He tore your clothes?"

I nodded.

"You must tell me all about it."

"Cassie saved me," I said.

"I went to look for Lenore," said Cassie. "I know she goes there often. So I went and I saw . . ."

Grand'mère poured one of her concoctions into three glasses.

She said: "We have all had a great shock and what we have to do is think of what our next action will be."

Cassie looked from one to the other of us.

"I cannot stay in this house," I said. "It is his house. I would never feel safe again."

Grand'mère was nodding. "I have been thinking of this for some time," she said. "I have always known that we could not stay. Katie is now a year old and we are ready. We must be ready now."

I looked at her expectantly and I wanted to weep. She had always been there to solve my problems for me. Silently I thanked God for her as I had a short time before thanked Him for Cassie.

"You have your settlement," went on Grand'mère, "the money Philip settled on you. It is a tidy sum and I have saved a little. Perhaps it is enough."

"What is your plan, Grand'mère?"

"That we start our own establishment. We will have our dress salon. We will go to London and find the premises. We can work together. It is what I have always wanted . . . Independence. None could say I have not the experience."

"Oh, Grand'mère," I cried. "Could we?"

"We will, *mon amour*. We will."

Cassie was watching us intently. She said suddenly: "I want to come with you."

"My dear child," said Grand'mère, "it will be a venture. There are hazards."

"I believe in it," cried Cassie. "I have my little income. I can sew very well. *You* said so, Madame Cleremont. You won't have to pay me. I just want to be part of it."

"We shall have to see," said Grand'mère.

Cassie stood up and ran to the dummies. She embraced Emmeline. "I am sure they know," she said. "And they are very happy about it."

We found that we could laugh. And I thought: It is what I want. I cannot stay here any longer than need be. I must get right away . . . soon.

*   *   *

Life which had gone on in the same pattern since the birth of Katie was filled with events.

In the first place we had to see the lawyers about the settlement and to our satisfaction learned that it would be quite in order for me to invest it in a business. That was the first step. Charles conveniently and characteristically left the very day of our encounter in the forest. I think he might have been ashamed. I was glad of it. I did not know how I could have confronted him; and the thought that I was living in his house was irksome.

First we had to find premises. We had decided that we would say nothing to Lady Sallonger until this was done, for we should certainly have opposition from that quarter.

Grand'mère and I went up to London leaving Cassie in charge of Katie. She was quite capable and was given instructions to get into touch with me at Cherry's Hotel, where we were staying for two nights, if I should be needed.

We found the shop, just off Bond Street. It was smaller than we had visualized, but there was a sizeable room which would be suitable as a workroom, and a showroom. Moreover there was small but adequate living accommodation. The rent to us seemed exhorbitant, but after looking around we realized that we should have to pay highly for accommodation if we wanted it in fashionable London, which according to Grand'mère—and I agreed with her—was of vital importance.

So we had our premises. We bought some materials but Grand'mère had numerous remnants, left over from the bales which had always been regarded as her perquisites. She had been hoarding them for years with such a venture in mind. So we had some stock to start with.

We returned to The Silk House where Cassie was eagerly waiting to hear the result of our visit. Katie had behaved impeccably and there were no problems there. So we seemed set fair.

The next afternoon I decided to tell Lady Sallonger. Cassie was with me.

I said: "Lady Sallonger, I have some news. Grand'mère and I are going to set up in a shop."

"What?" she screamed.

I explained.

"How ridiculous!" she snapped. "Ladies don't set up in shops."

"But I always fancied you doubted my claim to that title," I said.

"You had better put such a notion out of your mind at once."

"We already have our premises."

She was really disturbed. It was somewhat gratifying to realize how very much she hated losing me. But, of course, there was nothing personal about that. It was only because of my usefulness.

Her first thought when she realized that we were in earnest was: "But what am *I* going to do?"

Grand'mère had had to give notice to the Sallongers since she would no longer be working for them. This caused a great deal of consternation. She received a letter from one of the directors asking her if she had really considered what this meant. They had taken her for granted for so long. The very fact that her home was at The Silk House had made them absolutely sure of her services. She had clearly been of great use to them; and they tried to persuade her to think again.

But we were determined. Charles had made it impossible for us to stay; and we both knew that this was what we wanted. There was so much to remind me of Philip in The Silk House and the best thing possible was for me to make a clean break.

Exciting times followed. There was settling into the new quarters with the rather small living rooms and the big workroom and salon. Cassie had wept and pleaded with her mother, but Lady Sallonger was adamant. Cassie must stay. If Grand'mère and I were going to be so ungrateful as to walk out after all she had done for us, at least her own daughter should not be permitted to do so.

So we had to say goodbye to a woebegone Cassie and to promise her that whenever she wanted to come to us she would be welcome.

Grand'mère was like a young woman. "This was always a dream of mine," she said. "I never thought I should be able to realize it."

Looking back I see how naïve we were. Grand'mère had made dresses in the past which had sold in Court circles; but they had had the Sallonger label attached to them. It was different without that name. She had wanted to call the shop Lenore's. "It is yours," she said. "It is for your future." But Lenore's was not Sallonger's.

We had the dresses but business was slow in coming.

We had one servant—a thin little Cockney girl called Maisie. She was eager and helpful and very fond of Katie; she was willing to work hard, but we needed more help.

I think that within six months we had begun to realize that we had taken on something which we were too inexperienced to handle. Grand'mère tried to be bright and optimistic but I could see she was worried.

One day she said to me: "Lenore, I think we ought to look into our finances."

I knew what she meant and I agreed.

We faced each other seriously. We had spent a great deal of the capital; and we were paying out more than we were taking in. "Perhaps," I said, "we are pricing our dresses too low."

"If we priced higher, should we sell?" asked Grand'mère. "We have to face it. Here we are in a fashionable part of London but we are not getting the high class clientèle who used to buy the dresses I made. Perhaps we should try something simpler . . ."

I could see that we had rushed into this without enough thought. Grand'mère could make the dresses but we needed an assistant. I had to look after Katie with Maisie's help. We had taken on more than we were able to manage. There were so many aspects which we had not considered and most devastating of all was the contemplation of our fast-dwindling capital.

"We can't go on until everything has been frittered away," said Grand'mère.

"What do you think we should do?"

"We will not go back to The Silk House."

"Never," I said vehemently.

"Perhaps I could ask Sallongers if I could work here for them as I used to at The Silk House."

"In these expensive premises."

"Perhaps we could find a little house somewhere . . . perhaps with a small workroom."

It was depressing and grew more so until one day we had a visitor . . . I went forward hoping for a customer and to my amazement saw the Countess of Ballader.

She embraced me warmly.

"It is good to see you," I said.

She waved her hands. "All this . . ." she said. "I saw the name Lenore's . . . and I'd heard through Julia that you'd gone off to work on your own. So this is it, eh?"

"Do come in. Grand'mère will be pleased to see you."

They greeted each other effusively and I asked what the Countess was doing now.

"I have a beauty this time," she explained. "Daughter of a multimillionaire. She has everything . . . face, figure . . . money . . . but alas no blue blood. It's my job to see that she gets it. I have an earl in mind but actually I'm looking for a duke."

She talked for a while and told us how weary she was of the social round and this profession of hers.

Then she looked at us sharply. "Not going well, is it?" she said.

Grand'mère and I exchanged glances. "No," I told her. "It is not."

"I'm not surprised," she said.

"But the clothes . . . they are just the same . . . just as good . . ."

"It's not the quality, my dear, that sells them. It's the aura. That's what you lack. You'll never make good this way, you know."

I think we must have looked as frightened as we felt for she went on: "Oh, cheer up. It's not the end of the world. All you have to do is go about it in the right way."

"We feel just hopeless at selling."

She looked round the place with something akin to distaste.

Then she said: "Listen. If you're going to get on in the business world, you have to know people. They can't make up their minds themselves. They have to be told. This is good. This is special. Tell them enough and in the right way and they'll believe it. Your dresses were a success at Sallonger's, weren't they? Every girl going to Court had to have her Sallon Silk dress."

"We have Sallon Silk here but nobody wants it. Grand'mère has made some beautiful dresses. They are still hanging here."

The Countess looked at us benignly. "I think," she said slowly, "that I can help you out of your troubles. Let me see what you have here."

We took her round and she examined our stock with care. "I see," she said. "Tomorrow I am bringing Debbie to see you."

"Debbie?"

"My protégée. She is a charming creature. You will love her. She is one of my best ever. A little aristocratic blood and she would have been perfect. But you can't have everything."

"Do you think she would buy one of our dresses?"

She smiled at us. "I think that is very likely. Leave this to me. I think things are going to change. You have one or two here which would fit her. We will see what can be done."

The next day, true to her promise, the Countess arrived with her protégée.

She was right. Debbie was beautiful. She had large greenish eyes with heavy dark lashes and dark brown curly hair; but it was her expression which was most appealing; there was a delightful innocence about her.

They arrived in a carriage with a resplendent coachman and a little page at the back to leap down and open doors.

The Countess could be very regal on occasions and this was one of them.

"This is Miss Deborah Mellor," she said; "Deborah, Madame Lenore and Madame Cleremont."

Deborah bowed her head charmingly.

"I have persuaded Madame Lenore to make your ball gown if she can fit it in."

"That is very kind of you," said Deborah.

"But first we are going to look round and see if there is some little thing we fancy."

"I should love that."

"As you know, Madame Lenore, Madame Cleremont and I are old friends. That is why they have agreed to give you special attention."

I wanted to laugh but the Countess was very serious.

"I wonder if you would be kind enough to show us one or two of your models," went on the Countess.

"With pleasure," I said. "Do come along, Miss Mellor."

"Oh, look at this!" cried the Countess. "I have not seen ruching done in this way before, have you, Deborah?"

"No, Countess, never."

"It would be most effective. We must try that one on. And the rose pink one, too."

What a morning that was! I shall never forget it. It was the beginning of a change in our fortunes; and we owed it all to the Countess. Deborah Mellor bought the two dresses and we had a commission to make her dress for a very special Court ball.

Of course, this was child's play for Grand'mère who had done similar things before and she was in her element.

Later that day the Countess called on us. She had brought with her a bottle of champagne.

"Fetch glasses," she commanded. "We're celebrating. This is the start. Oh, you innocents! I am going to turn you into wily business women. Debbie is delighted. She is so grateful to me for bringing her to you. She says your clothes are ravishing. I explained the smallness of your premises as being due to your insistence on exclusiveness. You only make for the very best . . . the top people. You would not look at anyone else. She will see that the word is spread. Now, my dears, you will have to be ready. You need assistance. You must find an expert seamstress—two I think— There are thousands of them in London looking for work. Debbie will talk about you. So shall I. And I shall bring people to you as a special favour to them."

"I can't believe it is as easy as that," said Grand'mère.

"Everything is easy when you know the way. Look round you. Things are good mainly because people believe them to be good. Mind you, you have to have something to build on. You can't do it on rubbish. But if you have two articles of equal value side by side, and ask for an opinion you will find the one which has the right aura— though in all other ways it is exactly the same as the other—will be acclaimed, and that without, ignored. It is the world all over. People have to be told that something is good . . . and if it *is* good, they will agree. But don't tell them and they will think nothing of it. Lenore's models are good . . . so we are off to an excellent start. We are going to make Lenore's the most sought-after dressmaker in London."

We could not help laughing and our spirits rose when we considered the sales she had brought us, though we did not, at this stage, entirely believe her.

But how right she was proved to be.

The ball gown was a startling success; the duke proposed. "It was a lucky dress," said Deborah.

"She looked ravishing," said the Countess afterwards. "Everyone wanted to know who her dressmaker was. I said, 'I am not telling . . . we don't want to share her.' But, of course, I let it slip. People are asking me for introductions."

"It seems incongruous," I said. "There we were begging for business and now they are begging us."

"It's the way of the world," said the Countess.

And from that time we began to prosper. We were able to engage new seamstresses. We took the premises next door which gave us better living accommodation. The label Lenore on a garment meant high fashion.

We made Deborah's wedding dress. She looked very beautiful and fervently we wished her happiness with her duke. She had been our saviour. No. That was the Countess; and during that year she continued to bring clients to us.

One day she called and said: "I had a nice present from Mellor *père* for getting his daughter satisfactorily settled and I have never been very attracted by my way of earning a living. I rather fancy myself selling . . . in a place like this."

"Do you want to come in with us?" I cried.

"Well, what do you think?"

"We can never be grateful enough to you, can we, Grand'mère?" I said; and Grand'mère agreed with me.

"I'd put the Mellor present into the business. Then I can be a partner. It will give you more time with Katie."

So the Countess joined us.

Soon after that Lady Sallonger died. She passed quietly away in her sleep. I felt saddened, for in spite of her demands I had been quite fond of her. Grand'mère and I went to The Silk House for the funeral.

There was nothing now to keep Cassie from us, and she made haste to join us. She settled in with ease and both Grand'mère and I were happy to have her support as well as that of the Countess.

Within five years of our coming to London we were firmly established. Often I thought of Philip and those happy days we had had together. Katie was very like him—a constant reminder. But I was growing away from unhappiness. I had my daughter, Grand'mère and good friends; moreover I was discovering that I was quite a good business woman. I had a flair for design; I could choose material; I could see ahead and plan what should be done.

The Countess had shown us the way and Lenore's was becoming one of the leading court dressmakers.

* * *

As we became more and more successful Julia was a frequent visitor to our showrooms. She had changed a great deal. Her tendency to put on weight had stayed with her and she was what is called "buxom." Her colour had heightened and Grand'mère thought she had fallen into her husband's habit of drinking heavily. She was very amused by our progress.

"I could not believe it," she said. "Everyone was talking about Lenore's . . . wonderful models . . . wonderful hats . . ." (We had started hats at the Countess's suggestion—not many, just a few to match the costumes.) "And all the time it was you!"

She spent a good deal of money with us, for her husband was wealthy. I often thought of the old days when she had been so dismayed at her inability to make a capture during her season.

The Countess thought she had done very well. As she said: "After all, John Grantley has the money and he does not stint her."

I could believe that Julia was very pleased with life . . .

Then her husband died and she became a wealthy widow. She evidently savoured her freedom with relish.

"Certainly she came very well out of the marriage market," commented the Countess.

She gave what she called "soirées" at her elegant house near Piccadilly. Her guests were mostly politicians with a sprinkling of what she called "the bohemians," artists, musicians, writers and such like. Occasionally I was invited. She would engage a violinist or a pianist—always a fashionable one—to perform for us; those were her musical evenings; then there were card evenings and some dinner parties. Julia was fast becoming a leading hostess and entertaining far more frequently than she had done during her husband's lifetime.

Cassie was enjoying being in London. She worked very hard and Grand'mère said she was a great asset. For a brief period Julia tried to find a husband for her—a project which horrified Cassie, and as Julia quickly tired of her projects when they did not find immediate success, she soon stopped trying very hard.

I did not play cards and I did not care for a great many of Julia's friends; many of them were gamblers and heavy drinkers; but I did enjoy the musical evenings. Julia realized this and those were the ones to which I was invited.

Katie was now seven years old. She was a beautiful child with a sunny nature—not exactly pretty but her charm was great. She loved the whole world and thought the whole world loved her. I was very proud of her. Every night I would read to her before she slept; and then I would sing a hymn to her, for she loved hymns; and I would lie beside her, her hand clasped in mine. And I think that then I was really happy again.

I thought: If we can go on like this I shall be content.

Julia had sent an invitation to one of her musical evenings. I was wondering whether to go or not but Grand'mère said: "You know you do enjoy them. I should go if I were you. Cassie would like to go with you."

So Cassie and I went.

I shall always remember it—that elegant room with the palms in the corner, and the grand piano on the dais and Julia, the gracious hostess in a violet coloured velvet gown trimmed with écru lace which Grand'mère had made for her.

Julia had commanded a middle-aged gentleman to look after Cassie, who would have preferred to be without his care. The pianist played Chopin and this was followed by polite applause. I sat through the playing and thoroughly enjoyed it and as the applause died down, I saw a man coming towards me. He was tall, extremely good-looking and vaguely familiar. He was smiling at me quizzically.

"We have met before," he said.

Then I knew.

"Yes," he went on. "Drake Aldringham and you are Lenore. I would have known you anywhere. Mind you, you have changed. I'm delighted to meet you again."

He took my hand and held it firmly.

"I left in rather a hurry. Do you remember?" he went on. "There was no time to say goodbye."

"I remember it well."

He laughed. "It's a long time ago." Then he was serious. "I know about you . . . and Philip. Julia told me. I'm sorry."

"And what of you?" I asked.

"I've been abroad. That is . . . until just about a year ago. My father has interests on the Gold Coast. Well, now I'm back . . . to settle. At a by-election I recently became Member of Parliament for Swaddingham."

"How interesting."

"I think so. I'm enjoying it. It is what I always wanted, but my people thought I ought to travel a bit first . . . see the world. Perhaps they were right. Well, here I am."

"Do you live in Swaddingham?"

"I have a house near . . . fortunately it is conveniently in reach of my constituency. I also have a place in Town . . . not far from here. It behoves a member of Parliament to be stationed in two places—near those who have elected him and the House. I hear you have become a successful dress designer."

"With my grandmother and Cassie . . . you remember Cassie? . . . and the Countess of Ballader."

"So you are really an important business woman now."

"Well . . . a business woman."

"A rare species."

"Oh, it is always difficult for women. They have to work twice as hard as men to be equal with them."

"Very unfair, but I believe true. I have often thought of you."

"Have you?"

"Yes. You were at the source of the trouble really. I behaved abominably marching off like that. I ought to have been bold and stayed."

"How could you? You were Charles's guest."

"It was a foul thing he did. It makes my blood boil even now."

"It was good of you to take up the cudgels on my behalf."

"Not much good . . . after the deed was done."

"Thank you, anyway."

"I should like to come along and see your place. Is that permissible?"

"Certainly. Gentlemen do call—though usually in the company of ladies."

"Perhaps I should get Julia to bring me along."

"That would be an excellent idea."

"Julia says you have a little girl."

"She is seven years old now. She is enchanting." I felt myself glowing as I always did when I talked of Katie.

"I should expect that of her," he said, smiling at me.

Julia had come up.

"Oh Drake . . . so you found Lenore."

"Yes, we have been reminiscing."

"That's ancient history."

"Not all that ancient."

"Why, Drake, we were all children then. Do come and talk to Roskoff. He plays divinely but he is hard going conversationally. I'll see you later, Lenore."

He smiled at me and went off with Julia.

I felt rather excited.

I did not have a chance to talk to him again. Cassie wanted to leave and as we never stayed long after the music was over, I went with her.

I said: "Did you see Drake Aldringham?"

"Drake Aldringham?" she repeated. "Wasn't he . . . ?"

"Yes, the one who came home with Charles that time. There was trouble and he threw him in the lake."

"I remember. It was because Charles shut you in the mausoleum. So he was here tonight?"

"Yes. He's apparently a friend of Julia's."

"How strange! But I suppose it is not really. Julia knows so many people. She's bound to meet everyone sooner or later."

When we reached home I told Grand'mère of the encounter. She always liked to hear how the evening had gone.

"I was so surprised to see him," I said.

"You recognized him then?"

"Oh yes. He is the sort of person one would. There was something about him. Do you remember how proud Charles was because he had deigned to spend the holiday at The Silk House? That was what made what happened so awful."

"I wonder if you will see him again," said Grand'mère, looking at me intently.

"He said he would call," I told her. "With Julia."

* * *

He did call—and with Julia. Grand'mère and Cassie came out to meet him and I introduced him to the Countess.

"Isn't it odd to see Lenore here like this?" said Julia. "Who would have believed it all those years ago?"

"We have all changed since those days," I reminded her. "Would you like some coffee? We very often have it at this time of the morning."

"Yes please—and I should like to see everything."

"Oh Drake," cried Julia. "You're not interested in fashion."

"I'm interested in Lenore," he said.

"It is rather marvellous," commented Julia, "to think they have done all this."

"Very clever," said Drake, smiling at me.

Grand'mère was welcoming.

"The Countess of Ballader brought me out," said Julia.

"I've given up those activities now," the Countess told him. "This is more to my taste."

Cassie said she would go and make the coffee.

We sat in the reception room with the red carpets and white furniture—chosen by the Countess who said we must have an aura of luxury about the place.

I found Drake's eyes on me. I guessed he was comparing me with the frightened little girl who had been locked in the mausoleum.

"And how is business?" asked Julia.

"Flourishing," said the Countess.

"Well, your gowns are absolutely the latest thing," replied Julia. "I was talking to Lady Bronson only yesterday and she said she had misguidedly bought a new dress . . . *not* a Lenore . . . and, my goodness, she realized her mistake."

"Let us hope," put in the Countess, "that she has the good sense not to repeat her folly."

"I want a new morning gown," said Julia. "I'll look round while I'm here."

We talked lightly. Drake told us about his place in the country. "It's quite a small manor house. It's been in the family for years. My aunt lived in it, but she died a little while back and it seems ideal for me because of its geographical situation."

"Very fortunate that it should be so near your constituency," I said.

"Couldn't be better. My place in Town is very small. I get down to the country when I can."

"It must be fascinating to be at the heart of affairs," I said. "We just read about them in the papers whereas you are on the spot."

"It is what has always fascinated me. I was amazed when I got in first time. That was a bit of luck. I happened to be in the right place at the right time."

"That's the secret of success in life," added Grand'mère, "to be in the right place at the right time."

"It happens so rarely," I added.

"And when it does we should be grateful. I seized the opportunity with both hands."

"When would you like to select your gown?" the Countess asked Julia.

"Why not now?" asked Julia.

"Come. I will take you round."

Julia left with the Countess, and I felt more at ease when she had gone. There was something about her attitude to Drake Aldringham which disturbed me. I fancied she was watchful of him and of me when we talked together.

"You are a Liberal," I said when she had gone, "so at the moment out of power."

"We shall remedy that at the next election."

"And then Mr. Gladstone will return to office. Will it be for the third time?"

"For the fourth."

"He is getting rather old, is he not?"

"He is the greatest politician of the century."

"The view of the faithful follower! I believe there is one in a very high place who would not agree with you."

"You refer to Her Majesty, the Queen."

"I am right to do so, am I not?"

"She is a lady with firm fancies and prejudices. Unfortunately she had one of the latter against Mr. Gladstone."

"Wouldn't that affect his position as Prime Minister?"

"Of course. I cannot understand why she is so much against him."

"I suppose we are all drawn to some people and feel an antipathy towards others."

"Do you?"

"I like most people, but there are some whom I could never like."

I was thinking of Charles. Even before the mausoleum incident I had felt uneasy about him.

"Mr. Gladstone is not exactly a courtier in the sense that Lord Melbourne was. The Queen, as a girl, was absolutely devoted to him."

"And later to Disraeli," I added.

"I could never understand that. But he had a way with words."

"Hasn't Mr. Gladstone?"

"As an orator . . . not as a flatterer. Gladstone is a great man . . . and one who will put his political future in jeopardy for the sake of what he believes to be right. Such men are rare."

His eyes shone with enthusiasm. I liked his zest. I was finding it a very interesting morning.

Grand'mère said we must excuse her as she had something important to do. She said to Cassie: "I shall need you." And that left me alone with Drake.

We talked naturally and easily. I told him about the shop and how I had no wish to remain at The Silk House—a widow with a child to care for. I had longed for independence and the time had come when it seemed advisable to move. "So I sank my capital in the enterprise."

He listened intently. He asked no questions about Philip's death, for which I was grateful. I told him how difficult our start had been and how alarmed we had become at one stage until the Countess came to our rescue.

He said: "This business means a great deal to you, doesn't it?"

"It's our livelihood."

"But it is more than that, I fancy. It represents freedom and something you have always wanted to prove."

"What is that?"

"That a woman can do as well as a man."

"I hadn't thought of it, but I suppose you are right."

"I know. You hate injustice. You seek the truth. You want hard logic to prevail."

"I suppose that is so."

"I share your view. That is why I am in Parliament. I want justice . . . for everyone. I won't subscribe to a point of view because it is the accepted one. I will stand out for what I believe to be right. That is what Mr. Gladstone is doing. He has become very unpopular over his Home Rule for Ireland bill. That was what let Salisbury in with the Conservatives at the last election."

"I find it all fascinating," I said.

"We must meet sometimes, so that we can talk. I'm in London frequently. What do you say?"

"I should like that."

"Then we will."

Julia came back and joined us.

"It really is divine," she said. "Pale lilac with ribbons of a deeper shade . . . not quite heliotrope . . . lavender, would you say?"

"It suits you to perfection," said the Countess. "I'll have it sent."

"You look very earnest," said Julia, glancing from Drake to me. She seemed surprised to find us alone and I felt I had to explain.

"My grandmother had some urgent work and Cassie had to help her."

"We have been having an interesting discussion," Drake told her. "About politics," he added.

Julia grimaced. "You've no need to tell me that. I would have guessed. It's your pet topic, Drake. You hardly ever talk of anything else."

"I suppose you're right." He looked at me. "I hope I didn't bore you."

"Far from it."

"Lenore is always polite," said Julia.

"I'm not being polite, only truthful," I protested.

"Drake is devoted to his leader, aren't you, Drake?" said Julia.

"For very good reasons," added Drake.

"It's a pity some people don't share your devotion," said Julia laughingly.

"Many do," Drake retorted.

"I think a lot of people wonder about those nightly adventures of his," said Julia slyly.

Drake turned to me. "Julia is referring to Mr. Gladstone's crusade for the rescue of fallen women."

"Yes," said Julia. "He used to prowl about at night looking for ladies of easy virtue."

"In order to save them," said Drake quickly. "He is a very good man. Of course he is getting old now, but for forty years he used to go once a week through Piccadilly to Soho and the Thames Embankment which was where such women could be found. He would offer to take them home with him and give them supper and a bed and in the morning he and Mrs. Gladstone would talk to them about their way of life and try to persuade them—and help them—to renounce it."

"It was a very dangerous sort of philanthropy," said Julia. "There were bound to be those who suspected his motives."

"Which makes it all the more noble of him." Drake turned to me. "Don't you agree?"

"Yes, I do. People are too ready to suspect others and put the worst construction on events."

I was thinking of those looks which had come my way after Philip's mysterious death. Why had he killed himself? people wondered. When a man who was recently married did such a thing surely his wife must somehow be concerned.

"Lenore is determined to support you," said Julia.

"I say what I feel."

"Well, Drake, *I* feel we must be going. These are business hours, are they not?"

He stood up and held out his hand to me.

"It has been an interesting morning." He held my hand firmly. *"Au revoir."*

"Where are the others?" demanded Julia. "We must say goodbye to them."

I called them and they came. We went out to the door with them where Julia's carriage was waiting.

As we watched them drive away it occurred to me that Julia had displayed an almost proprietorial manner towards him. And they seemed to know each other very well.

I remembered how she had felt about him all those years ago, and how angry she had been with me for being the cause of his departure.

I thought: I believe she is in love with him. She seems softer, different. She was a little in love with him long ago.

"What a charming man!" said the Countess.

"He was very attractive as a boy," added Cassie.

"I like him," said Grand'mère. "There is something good about him." She smiled at me fondly. "I hope he comes again."

* * *

We had a meeting every Friday evening to discuss the week's business and talk over any new idea one of us might have. The Countess used to pay periodic visits to Paris. "Paris is the centre of fashion," she used to say. "We must go there and see what they are up to."

On one or two occasions Grand'mère had gone with her. The Countess was adept at choosing styles which she wished to incorporate with changes—improvements, she called them; Grand'mère was concerned with the practical side; and she would say if what was suggested was possible.

I was unable to go because I did not want to leave Katie. After these trips Grand'mère always seemed to have been rejuvenated. I suppose a visit to her native land did that for her; moreover, she was passionately interested in fashion.

On this occasion the Countess astounded us with an announcement. "We should open a place in Paris," she said.

We stared at her. Open in Paris! We were doing very well in London, expanding every year, growing generally, becoming well known in Court circles.

"Well," went on the Countess, "most of the best houses have something over there. I'd be there most of the time till we'd built it up. I know how to manage that. We'd have the French touch for our clothes over here. 'This, Madam, has just been brought over from our Paris establishment' . . . and so on."

"And the cost of setting up a place over there?"

"It's not going to be cheap."

"And where would we get the money?" asked Grand'mère.

"We'd borrow."

I flinched and Grand'mère turned pale. "Never!" we said simultaneously.

"Why not?"

"Who'd lend the money?"

"Any bank. We have the security of this place . . . a prosperous concern."

"And the interest on the loan?"

"We'd have to work hard to pay it."

"I was always against borrowing," said Grand'mère; and I nodded in agreement.

"Do you want to stay as we are forever?"

"It is a very pleasant niche we have found for ourselves," I reminded her.

"But expansion is the very breath of successful business."

"I believe there have been occasions when it has been their ruin."

"Life is a matter of taking risks."

"I want none of that," said Grand'mère.

I backed her up in this. The thought of borrowing terrified me.

"How long would it take before a Paris place was profitable?" I asked.

"Three years . . . four . . ."

"And all that time we should have the interest on the loan to pay off."

"We'd manage," said the Countess.

"What if we didn't?"

"You are prophesying defeat before we begin."

"We have to look facts in the face. I could see us ruined and I have a child to think of."

"When the time comes I want to launch her into society."

"In the meantime I have to feed and clothe her, educate her too—and that is of the utmost importance to me."

"You are really rather unadventurous," said the Countess.

"I call it cautious," I replied.

"So you are both against me?"

We nodded.

"Well, we shall have to shelve the matter."

"We'll do that," I said.

"Meanwhile," went on the Countess, "when I am in Paris I will scout round and see what's to be had."

"Whatever it is we can't afford it."

"You never know," insisted the Countess.

We went on to discuss other matters.

Grand'mère and I talked about her scheme together when we were alone.

"She's right, of course," said Grand'mère. "The important houses do have branches in Paris. It is the centre of fashion and therefore carries a certain prestige. It *would* be wonderful if we could sell our clothes over there. That would be triumph indeed . . . and so good for business here. We could do so much better . . ."

I said: "Grand'mère, are you getting caught up in this idea?"

"I realize its merits, but I am against borrowing as I always have been. I'd rather remain as we are than have to worry about loans. Remember how it was when we started and how we thought we were not coming through?"

"I shall never forget."

"We are cosy. We are comfortable. Let's leave it at that."

But we both continued to think of the matter and every now and then it would crop up. It was clearly on our minds. The Countess was silent, brooding. I began to think that in time we might come round to her way of thinking.

A week or so later the Countess and Grand'mère went on one of their periodic trips to Paris.

Meetings in the Park

One of the greatest blessings of our prosperity was that I could devote more time to Katie. I had engaged a governess for her—a Miss Price—a very worthy lady, who took her duties seriously; but I often took Katie off her hands, for the child loved to be with me as much as I did with her.

We used to walk together each afternoon after her lessons. Sometimes we went to St. James's Park where we fed the ducks; sometimes we visited the Serpentine. Katie was a very gregarious person and made friends with the other children very quickly. I liked to see her enjoying the companionship of people of her own age.

It was two days after the departure of Grand'mère and the Countess and we were sitting on a bench engaged in the sort of conversation Katie and I often had together which consisted of a number of "whys" and "whats" when a man stopped, lifted his hat and said: "So I have found you."

It was Drake Aldringham.

"I called at your place," he said, "and Miss Cassandra told me that you would either be in St. James's Park or here. Unfortunately I went to the wrong one first, but at least I am now rewarded."

I felt a great pleasure to see him.

I said: "This is Katie. Katie, this is Mr. Drake Aldringham."

She gave him a direct look. "You're not a duck," she said. "You're only a man."

"I can see I have disappointed you," he replied.

"Well . . . I've heard them talking about a drake."

I was embarrassed but he looked pleased to learn that he had been the subject of our conversation.

Katie gave him one of her dazzling smiles. "Never mind," she said. "I'll try not to take it to heart."

I could see that he thought her charming and I was happy about that.

"We like it here, don't we, Katie," I said. "We come often."

"Yes," said Katie. "It's like the country . . . but you can hear the horses' hoofs and that makes it nicer.

"Grand'mère is in France," she told Drake.

"Yes," I added. "She and the Countess have gone to Paris."

"Some day," Katie said, "I shall go. With Mama, of course."

"Of course," he said. "Are you looking forward to that?"

She nodded. "Have you been?"

He told her he had. He talked to her about Paris and she listened avidly. A small boy came up. He was often in the Park with his nanny and he and Katie played together. I could see that she wanted to go now and play with him for she looked at me expectantly.

"Yes," I said, "but not too far. Keep where I can see you, or I shall be after you."

She turned, smiled at Drake and was off.

"What a delightful child!" he said.

"I am so lucky to have her."

"I can understand how you feel."

My eyes had filled with tears and I was ashamed of myself for showing my emotions.

"She must have been a great consolation."

I nodded. "She always has been that. I can't imagine what I should have done without her."

"I am so sorry it happened. It must have been devastating."

"To have lost him in any way would have been that, but . . ."

"Don't speak of it if you would rather not."

I was silent for a few minutes. Oddly enough I did want to talk about it. I felt I could with him.

I said: "People thought he killed himself. Everyone thought that. It was the verdict of the coroner. I shall never believe it."

"You knew him better than anyone."

"How could he? We were so happy. We had just decided to buy a house. Why should he be so happy and then a few hours afterwards . . . do that? It doesn't make sense."

"There was nothing you knew of . . ."

"Absolutely nothing. It was all so mysterious. I have a theory that someone intended to kill him . . . and had tried before."

He listened intently while I told him the story of Lorenzo who had gone out in Philip's clothes.

"How very odd!" he said.

"They seemed to think I knew something which I did not divulge. It made me so unhappy. There was nothing . . . nothing . . . Everything was perfect . . ."

He put his hand over mine and pressed it.

"I'm sorry," I said. "I got carried away."

"I shouldn't have brought it up."

"You didn't."

"I'm afraid I did. Perhaps one day . . . you will grow away from it."

"I have done that to a certain extent. Katie has helped me. And yet . . . she is so like him sometimes . . . that it reminds me. I think I shall never forget."

"You would not, of course. But you are happy . . . in a way."

"Yes, I suppose so. I have Katie, Grand'mère . . . good friends . . ."

"And the business," he said. "You are a dedicated business woman and that means a lot to you."

"It has. It was not until a year after Philip's death that we started. I could not go on living in that house. It was Charles's house and I could not forget that."

"Of course."

"The Countess has been invaluable to us. She is really a very lovable person. I am certainly very lucky."

"And the prosperous business has been a great help."

"It was not always prosperous. We were innocents, Grand'mère and I. The Countess is very worldly and I think we are becoming so under her tuition."

"Don't grow too worldly," he said.

"One must be to succeed in our kind of business . . . or in any for that matter."

"Success means a great deal to you."

"It has to. It means giving Katie the sort of education I want for her . . . launching her into society . . . giving her every chance."

"You are an ambitious Mama."

"I am ambitious for her happiness. And we are talking too much about me. Tell me about yourself and your constituency and everything a good member of Parliament has to do."

So he talked very amusingly and interestingly. He told me of the letters he received from some of his constituents. "A member of Parliament is expected to be a genie of the lamp," he said. He talked too about his travels abroad, of life in the sweltering heat of the Gold Coast; how he had dreamed of coming home; and how delighted he was at last to see the white cliffs that he started to sing out loud to the amazement of his fellow travellers.

So we passed a pleasant hour watching Katie running and jumping and looking over her shoulder every now and then to smile at us.

It was a long time since I had felt so happy.

When we left he walked back to the house with us—Katie between us, each of us holding a hand.

He said how much he had enjoyed the meeting.

"Do you go to the park every day?" he asked.

"Quite often."

"I shall look out for you."

He bowed and smiled down at Katie. "I hope I'm forgiven for being only a man."

"It was silly of me," she said. "I ought to have known. Ducks don't visit, do they?"

"No. They just quack." He illustrated his remark with a little noise which did resemble that made by ducks. It greatly amused Katie. She quacked herself and went into the house quacking.

Cassie came out.

"Oh," she said. "That Drake Aldringham called."

"I know," I told her, "we saw him in the park."

"I told him you were there and would be somewhere near the water whichever park it was."

"Well, he found us."

"He's a very nice man," said Katie. "He quacks just like a real one . . . only he isn't one, of course . . . only a man."

Cassie was beaming.

"I'm glad he found you," she said. "He was so disappointed when I told him you were out."

And the next day we saw him again.

In fact he made a habit of meeting us in the park.

* * *

Two weeks later Grand'mère and the Countess returned home. They had been away longer than usual. I thought Grand'mère looked preoccupied. I knew her so well and she was never able to hide her feelings, so I realized that something had happened—good or bad, I was not quite sure; but it certainly had made her thoughtful.

The Countess was exuberant as she always was after her visits to Paris.

"I saw just the place that would suit us," she said, "in the Rue Saint-Honoré . . . quite the right spot. Small but really elegant."

"We have made up our minds that we can't take the risk," I said.

"I know," she replied sighing. "Such a pity. Chance of a lifetime really. You should see it . . . a lovely light workroom; and I could imagine the showroom decorated in white and gold. It would have been perfect."

"Apart from one thing," I said, "we haven't the money and Grand'mère and I are determined not to be in debt."

The Countess shook her head mournfully but said no more.

When I was alone with Grand'mère, I said to her: "Come on. You must tell me what happened."

She looked at me in surprise.

"I know it is something," I said. "I can see it in your face. So you had better tell me."

She was silent for a few minutes, then she said: "The urge came over me. I had to go. I wanted to see it all again. I left the Countess in Paris and went to Villers-Mûre."

"So that was it. And it has made you thoughtful?"

"There is something about one's birthplace . . ."

"Of course. It was a long journey for you."

"I made it."

"And how did you find it there?"

"Very much as it always was. It took me back . . . years. I visited your mother's grave."

"That was sad for you."

"In a way. But not entirely. There was a rosebush . . . someone had planted it. I had expected to find the grave neglected. That cheered me a great deal."

"Who had done it?"

She lifted her shoulders and raised her eyes. There was a sad brooding look in them.

"Perhaps it was unwise to go," I said.

"Oh no . . . no . . ." She dismissed the subject. "Cassie tells me that Mr. Aldringham called."

"Yes, I have met him now and then in the park. Katie's taken quite a fancy to him . . . and he has to her."

"I liked him when we met."

"Yes, I know."

She smiled at me. "I'm glad you've been seeing him." Then she added cryptically: "You can't go on mourning for ever."

It was my turn to change the subject. "The Countess I am sure thinks that in time we shall come round to her way of thinking."

"I will never agree to borrow."

"Nor I. So it seems a waste of time to look at shops in Paris."

"She was right about us in the beginning and we did have to spend a little to get things going."

"That was different. We were desperate then. Now we have a steady business. I would not want to go through that anxiety again."

"There is only one way I would agree to go into it," said Grand'mère.

"And that?"

"If we had the money. If some benefactor invested in us."

"That is quite impossible."

"Unlikely but not impossible."

She was thoughtful again and I said: "Grand'mère, what's on your mind?"

"Only that that shop in the Rue Saint-Honoré was very enticing."

"Put it out of your mind. There is plenty of work here for us."

"I can't wait to get on with it." She kissed me. "It's good to be home," she said.

* * *

We had settled down to the old routine. Katie and I met Drake frequently, and I looked forward to those meetings. They formed a certain pattern. We would often find him waiting for us. Katie would run up and give a quack to which he responded. It was the recognized greeting between them. The same joke would amuse Katie again and again.

She would play with her friends while we talked. There was much to tell each other. I found I could talk to him freely and I was sure he felt the same about me. He spent a certain amount of time at Swaddingham.

"I wish you could see the house," he said. "It's an Elizabethan manor. It was an inn at the beginning of the fifteenth century, then it became a private residence and enlarged, so that while part of it is Saxon, the lower floors are entirely Tudor. There is quite a bit of land. So I am a sort of squire. If ever I lost my seat in Parliament I should devote myself entirely to my squiral duties."

"Would you like that?" I asked.

"It would only be second best." He looked at me seriously. "Sometimes one has to settle for that."

"That's true. At least you have a second string. In that you are fortunate."

"I wonder if you and Katie would visit me at Swaddingham?"

"It sounds exciting."

"Perhaps you and your grandmother could bring Katie."

"I am sure we should enjoy that very much."

"Well, when the House is in recess we'll go. One can never be sure when one is going to be called in for some important vote . . . so that would be the best time."

"Do invite us."

I told him about our dilemma.

"The Countess is rather different from Grand'mère and me. She is full of energy . . . something of a gambler. She wants to expand and open a place in Paris."

"And you do not? You surprise me."

"I do want to . . . very much, but I dare not take risks."

"Is it such a risk?"

"It's an enormous one. We should have to find the shop and it would be a very high rent in the right quarter. Then we have to stock it . . . and get staff. We should have to do it in style now. When we opened here we were just beginners and we could start in a humble way. We could not do that now. The Countess wouldn't hear of it. She would say it would do us more harm than good. We have to do every-thing in grand style. Grand'mère and I see exactly what she means. If it worked it would be wonderful; but if it failed we could be ruined. Grand'mère and I do not take such risks."

"I think you are probably wise."

"Who shall say? The Countess thinks we are unenterprising."

"Better be that than bankrupt."

"I agree."

"So you are in a dilemma."

"Not really. Grand'mère and I are adamant."

"But regretful," he said.

"Yes, regretful."

We were talking animatedly when Julia came along. She was styl-ishly dressed in a costume of midnight blue edged with sable. She looked very elegant in a type of riding hat with an ostrich feather trailing over the brim. I had seen the costume and the hat before for they had both come out of our showrooms and when I saw them, my first thought was: Grand'mère has genius.

Julia opened her eyes with surprise; but I immediately thought that this did not express her true feeling, and I had a notion that she had come out here to find us. It must have been that we had been seen together by some of her friends and that our meetings were a matter of some interest. As a widow with a child I was not expected to lead such a restricted existence as a young unmarried woman and the fact that I had been seen at the same spot on several occasions with an eligible bachelor would cause some speculation.

"Well, fancy finding you here! Of course . . . you come with Ka-tie. Children do love the parks." She sat down beside us. I felt insignif-icant in my simple walking costume beside her in all her glory.

"I like to take a walk now and then," she said. "Exercise is sup-posed to be good for you. I have the carriage waiting for me not far off. I thought, Drake, that you were in Swaddingham."

"I shall have to go down in a day or so."

"Of course. You have to get them all in a good humour before the election. When do you expect it?"

"In the not too distant future."

"I'll come and help," said Julia.

"That's kind of you."

"I find politics fascinating," she went on. "All that going among the people and kissing the babies . . . and you're half way there."

"It's not quite as easy as that," said Drake with a laugh. "Our opponents might be good baby-admirers, too."

"Poor Drake! He works so hard," said Julia, laying a hand on his arm. "He really is wonderful."

"You have too high an opinion of me."

"I am sure that would be impossible. You must come and dine tomorrow."

"Thank you," he said.

She smiled at me. "Sorry I can't invite you, Lenore. You see, it is so difficult. There is a shortage of men . . . and a woman on her own . . ."

"Oh, I quite understand."

"You ought to get married. Don't you agree, Drake?"

"I think that is a matter for Lenore to decide for herself."

"Of course these things can be helped along."

I looked at my watch and said it was time I was going. I called Katie who came running up.

"Hello, Aunt Julia."

"Hello, my darling." Julia kissed Katie effusively.

"You smell nice," said Katie.

"Do I, dear? You must come and see me some time soon."

"When?" asked Katie.

"We must wait to be asked definitely, Katie," I said.

"We're asked now."

"Aunt Julia will tell us when she wants us."

"But she said . . ."

"We really must go," I insisted.

"Of course," said Julia. "We'll excuse you, won't we, Drake?"

"I'll escort Lenore and Katie home," said Drake.

Julia pouted. Then she said brightly: "I'll tell you what. We'll ride in my carriage."

I was about to protest when Katie cried: "Oh yes . . . please."

And so we rode home.

Julia had somehow conveyed to me that she was displeased by my meetings with Drake. I remembered in the past how very taken she had been by him. She still was, I could see.

I was not sure of Drake. I think he was not pleased by the intrusion.

Katie was, however. She kept talking about the horses and sang clopetty-clop all the way home.

* * *

After that we often met Julia. She knew, of course, the time we should be there, and she would find us somewhere near the Serpentine; or if we were in St. James's Park she knew we should be feeding the ducks.

"I do enjoy my little walks," she said. "So good for one. And it is such fun to come upon familiar faces and sit down and talk."

She dominated the conversation and managed to discuss people whom I did not know, so that I was often excluded.

I wondered what Drake was feeling. He was too polite to betray this, and sometimes I wondered whether he was pleased to see Julia. He did smile quite often at her inconsequential chatter. It was very feminine, I supposed, and perhaps he found that attractive.

She had a way of disparaging me through supposed compliments. "Of course, Lenore is such a wonderful business woman. I could never be that. It must be wonderful to be so self reliant . . . such a wonderful manager . . . like a man really . . . Lenore doesn't need any looking after."

I don't know why I should let it annoy me, but it did. She was, of course, calling attention to her own helpless femininity which was supposed to be so attractive to the opposite sex.

In any case those mornings were spoilt, and because I felt so bitterly disappointed I tried to analyse my feelings for Drake.

I so much enjoyed being with him; I was intensely interested in all he was doing and I felt I should like to share in it.

In his turn, he was interested in the shop. The Countess had said I must not call it "the shop." It was "the Salon." "What's in a name?" I had asked. "A tremendous amount," she had retorted. "I have often told you that it is not so much what things are as what people believe them to be. A shop is somewhere where things are sold over the counter. A salon is where artists deign to sell their work."

"I'm learning," I replied. "The Salon it shall be."

When I had told Drake this he had been very amused. He had listened intently to the story of our beginnings. He was so interested in everything I was doing. He enjoyed being with Katie and it was clear that she was fond of him. I had a cosy feeling that when we had walked back with Katie in between us, holding our hands, the Countess, who had seen us, had felt some approval. "You looked . . . right . . . like that," she said.

As for Grand'mère, she had never been one to hide her feelings and her opinion was obvious.

I was very touched to consider how her one thought, throughout her life, had been to care for me. She had been heartbroken when Philip died; she had seen through my marriage all her dreams coming true. But I had been without Philip for a long time and she was visualizing another dream with Drake at the centre of it.

It would have been impossible for me not to consider which way I was going. Drake's persistent visits to the park, our growing friendship, the manner in which a special light came into his eyes when he saw us—they were all significant. There was a possibility that he was falling in love with me.

He was eager for me to go down and see the manor at Swaddingham and we were to pay the visit the first weekend after the Parliamentary recess.

And myself? I could never forget Philip and that honeymoon in Florence which had ended so tragically, and since my feelings for Drake were beginning to grow into something very serious, I thought of those days more and more.

I had grown up considerably since my marriage. I had been young, simple and innocent. I had known little of the world then. Perhaps Philip had been a little like that, too. We were like two children. Could we have gone on like that? I had suddenly been brought face to face with tragic reality. I had become a mother and there was now one person in my life who was more important to me than myself. I had learned something about the seriousness of making a living for myself and my child; and our close approach to failure and possible penury had matured me considerably. The worldly Countess had taught me a great deal about people. I no longer lived in that ideal world which I had believed lay ahead of Philip and me; there were things in life which were ugly and these had to be recognized and fully faced.

Now I was asking myself how deeply had my love for Philip gone; and had I built it up to such proportions since his death? Had I told myself I could never love a man again?

Had I really known Philip? Could it be possible that there had been some dark secret in his life and that he took his life rather than allow it to come to light? Was that just possible? No, I could not believe it. Philip had been good and true and innocent . . . as I was. Then why had it happened as it did? And if he had not shot himself who had and why? There was only one conclusion: Either Philip shot himself or someone else did. And in any case there must have been some dark secret in Philip's life of which I had known nothing.

I had loved Philip, but then, had I really known him? With him I had first learned the meaning of love between men and women. Our relationship had been tenderly romantic. But he was dead. Perhaps it was time that I ceased to mourn him. My meetings with Drake were beginning to tell me that I was not meant to lead the life of a nun.

When I watched him, coming towards me, my spirits lifted. I tried to see him dispassionately: a tall man dressed with quiet, good taste; he had always been distinguished looking as a boy; now that was accentuated. I admired him very much; I was happy to sit close to him and I was pleased when he touched my hand. Yes, I was attracted by him for the days when I did not see him were dull days and I found myself looking forward to that Swaddingham weekend with a joy that resembled Katie's.

Julia came to the Salon. She always arrived in style with her carriage, her obsequious coachman and the little boy who was equally eager to please.

I dreaded her visits which was foolish. She was a very good customer. As she said, she simply adored clothes.

She was a great spender—so different from the Julia of our childhood. She had had her tantrums then and had always been self-indulgent, but she had lacked this overwhelming confidence which being a rich widow had brought her.

The Countess always greeted her effusively.

"I am so glad you came in. I was just saying to Madame Cleremont that the burgundy velvet is just *you*. I said to her that before we show it to anyone else Julia must see it."

Then she would hustle her off to the showroom where there would be tut-tutting from the Countess because of Julia's growing waistline. The burgundy dress had fitted but only just. "My dear child . . . (The Countess often fell back into that relationship they had shared during Julia's launching.) "You must cut out this penchant for food."

And Julia would giggle and become almost a girl in the Countess's company.

Of course she bought the dress as the Countess intended she should. Then she sought me out.

"Charles is getting married," she told me.

"Oh . . . really?"

"It's about time. *Un mariage de convenance.* You know what I mean. I hear that Sallonger's are not doing so well now. Charles is not like Philip, you know. He needs money and he'll get it. She's a little older than he is and not the most beautiful woman in the world, but my dear, she is gold-plated."

"I hope it is successful."

"She'll get what she wants . . . a husband . . . and he'll go his own sweet way . . . as he always has done. I told him once he was a ruthless philanderer. He just laughed at me and said, 'Fancy your noticing that, little sister.' "

"Perhaps he'll settle down."

"What! Charles? Do you believe that? I wish I could find someone for Cassie."

"Cassie is happy enough."

"You'll probably get an invitation to the wedding."

I did not answer and she went on: "You're seeing quite a lot of Drake Aldringham, aren't you?"

"We meet in the park, as you know, as you are often with us."

"He's very much a man of the world, you know."

"Yes, I suppose so."

"A little like Charles in a way."

"Like Charles?"

"Well, men are mostly alike . . . in one respect."

I stared at her in amazement.

"With women, I mean. I know him very well and in spite of all this . . . clever business and so on . . . you're a little innocent in some ways."

"I don't know what you are suggesting."

She laughed. "Don't you? Just think about it then. Drake is a very great friend of mine . . . a very *close* friend . . . As a matter of fact . . . Never mind. Do you really think that burgundy velvet suits me? I wish the Countess wouldn't go on so about my weight." She looked at me archly. "Some people tell me they like it. It's warm . . . and friendly . . . and womanly. I don't think men really like those beanpole types."

She was looking at me a little scornfully. It was true that I was very slender. Grand'mère worried that I did not eat enough.

I was glad when Julia went; and then I kept turning over in my mind what she had said.

I hated to think of Julia as a rival. Yet she did not like our meetings in the parks; she was eager to tell me he was *her* friend . . . *close* friend, she had pointed out. What did she mean by that? Was she warning me in comparing Drake with Charles?

I thought Julia was jealous, and I remembered her fury of long ago when she knew that Drake had left after a quarrel with Charles; and that had been on my account.

*   *   *

It was a few days later when I first noticed the man in the park. He was sitting on a bench near the one which we occupied and whenever I glanced casually his way he seemed to be looking in my direction. I fancied I had seen him there before.

He was of medium height, dark-haired, greying at the temples; he might have been about forty years of age, distinguished looking in a foreign way. It was something about the cut of his clothes as well as his looks which made me feel that he was not English.

Julia had joined us as usual. Katie played happily; Drake, who had been talking animatedly before Julia's arrival, was now restrained.

I was beginning to think that as Julia resented my friendship with Drake so much, and made a point of joining us, I should find some excuse not to come. Cassie would be only too happy to take Katie to the park.

The next day I saw the man again. He really did seem to watch me intently. I might have thought I had imagined this but Julia had noticed.

"I do declare Lenore has an admirer," she cried.

"What?" said Drake.

"The not-so-young gentleman over there. He can hardly take his eyes from her. I saw him here yesterday. Lenore, have you a secret lover?"

"I have no idea who he is," I said.

"Well, he is gazing at you with a kind of rapture."

"What nonsense! I am sure he is unaware of us."

"Of *us,* my dear, but not of you."

I felt I wanted to get away.

I said: "I have to go back early today, Katie," I called.

Katie was disappointed to be called from play, but she was of such a happy sunny nature that she never sulked.

"Come along," I said.

Drake rose and stood up, prepared to leave.

"Don't come if you'd rather stay," I said.

Julia laid her hand on Drake's arm. "We'll sit here for a little while," she said, "and then I want you to come back to luncheon, Drake. There will be just a small party. I'm counting on you."

I did not wait for more. I took Katie's hand and hurried her away.

She cried: "Look at that little duck, Mama. He's ruffling his feathers. I think he's rather angry. Perhaps he's hungry. Oh, I wish I had some bread to give him."

"Next time we'll bring some," I promised.

"Your face is red," she said. "Are you angry?"

"Of course not."

"Not with Aunt Julia?"

"No."

"Then with Quack-Quack."

"No, darling, I'm not angry at all."

"You look angry."

"No. Just in a hurry."

I was aware of footsteps behind, and I thought for a moment that Drake was coming after us. I glanced over my shoulder. It was the man whom Julia had said was watching me.

I felt a touch of uneasiness. I was in a very sensitive mood today. Of course he wasn't following me. Why should he?

We left the park and crossed the road. We turned the corner. I glanced back. The man was still behind. As we went in he passed slowly on the other side of the street.

* * *

It seemed that there would be an election in the following year. Everyone was saying that surely Gladstone must retire now that he was eighty-two—certainly not of an age to lead the country.

Drake was very excited at the prospect of an election and thought the Liberals had a fair chance. In spite of his great age Gladstone was popular with the people. They called him the Grand Old Man and the People's William. It was true that the Grand Old Man refused to give up.

Drake was very busy and I saw less of him. It was growing too cold to sit in the park. Katie and I walked there and Julia did not appear because she knew Drake was working in Swaddingham.

The proposed weekend had had to be postponed—but only briefly, Drake had insisted.

Charles was married that autumn. I had an invitation to his wedding which I wanted to refuse; but Cassie naturally had had to go to her brother's wedding and she begged me to go with her. We had made the bride's gown and the Countess was also invited.

It was a grand affair in St. George's Hanover Square and later there was a reception at Claridges. Charles looked very pleased with himself and the bride seemed happy. Her gown was exquisite and I saw the Countess watching, her eyes glittering, probably speculating as to how much business this would bring us.

Julia was there looking splendid. She spoke to us briefly.

"It will be your turn next," she said to Cassie.

"I've no wish to have a turn," retorted Cassie promptly.

"If you are so persistent in clinging to your spinsterhood, no one will bother to take it from you," warned Julia.

"I like things as they are."

"There is nothing like a wedding to bring satisfaction to both parties . . . like today," commented Julia.

"I hope they'll be happy," I said.

"They will if they are sensible. She has been longing to find a husband and Charles is desperately in need of a wife. Miss Money Bags is just the right answer to his prayers." She laughed at me. "You're shocked. You know you are easily shocked." She looked round. "Drake's not here. He wasn't invited. Charles wouldn't, would he? Charles never forgets old scores. I told him he was vengeful. After all, how many years is it since Drake threw him in the lake?"

"I expect Drake was too busy to come," said Cassie. "He has the election to think of."

"Voters like their members to have wives," said Julia. "It's a recognized thing. A member has a great deal to do. He needs a wife." She looked at me archly. "I must tell him so. I know just the sort he should have. Someone who knows the world and has the money to entertain lavishly . . . someone who can mix and go about with him . . . looking pleasant."

I did not answer.

"He'll come round to it," she went on. "As a matter of fact, I believe he is considering it now and . . . with a little help from me . . . I believe he will choose the right one."

"Let us hope for his own sake that he does," I said.

"I mean the woman who can help him along. Drake is very sensible, you know. Not the sort of man who would fall in love with the beggar maid. Drake will fall in love judiciously."

"What a clever thing to do," I said.

"Oh, Drake *is* very clever. The great thing in his life is his career. I wouldn't be surprised if he were not dreaming of stepping into dear old Gladstone's shoes. Oh, not yet, of course. The Grand Old Man it seems is not finished and there are many stepping stones to be crossed. But Drake would always have his eyes open to the main chance. You'll see. He'll marry a woman who knows how to be a social hostess—and a little money will not come amiss."

"I should hate to think a friend was so mercenary."

"You misinterpret my words. Now when did I say he was mercenary? I call it wisdom. Look at Disraeli. Now he was a clever man. He married his Mary Anne for her money. He needed that money. If you're going to climb the greasy pole—Disraeli again—you need to be well protected with money if, when you get to the top of it, you're going to stay there. This happy pair will soon be going off to their honeymoon in Florence. Why does everyone go to Italy for their honeymoon?"

My thoughts were back there, I was walking along the banks of the Arno. I was reliving that night when Lorenzo had disappeared.

"It is one of the most beautiful places in the world," Cassie was saying. "That is why it is so suitable for honeymooners. That wonderful art . . . It must be magnificent."

"Charles won't be interested in art. He will just be counting his blessings; and his bride will be telling herself how lucky she is that Papa's money was able to buy her such a handsome husband."

I looked at Cassie. "I think I should like to go now," I said.

"You must see the bride and groom off on their honeymoon," Julia reminded us. "It's not etiquette to go before that. They won't be long now."

Cassie said: "I want to see her in the mulberry coloured suit. It really is beautiful."

"Strange how you have become one of London's leading dressmakers."

"It's my grandmother's genius and the Countess's knowledge of salesmanship which has made us that."

"Still, it bears your name, and I think you have a great pride in the place."

"Of course I have."

"It will be wonderful if we go to Paris," said Cassie.

"We shan't," I said sharply. "We haven't the money."

"Your grandmother thinks we shall and so does the Countess. And you want to, don't you, Lenore? I have seen your eyes sparkling at the thought of that shop in the Rue Saint-Honoré."

"Go to Paris!" cried Julia. "That would be marvellous. We should all be popping over to buy."

"We should still have the Salon in London."

"Oh, but there is something about a garment bought in Paris. Even if it were exactly the same as one you bought here you would feel it was different. It would have the Paris touch."

Cassie and I exchanged glances. Those were almost exactly the Countess's words.

Julia laughed. "Do you know, I am sure you will get that Paris salon because you are determined to. Something will turn up, you see."

"Wouldn't it be wonderful if it did?" said Cassie.

"Look," cried Julia. "I didn't realize the bride had disappeared and here she is all ready. That mulberry is . . . wonderful. It makes even her look pretty. Those silver grey ruffles at the neck and sleeves are a touch of genius."

There was great excitement over the departure of the newly married pair; and finally the carriage left.

I turned to Cassie and said: "We can go now."

* * *

I received a letter from Drake. He was working very hard in the constituency and there was a great deal to do. He missed our meetings in the park and he wanted to know if I with Katie, Cassie and my grandmother—and the Countess if she wished to come—would care to spend Christmas at Swaddingham.

We were all delighted at the prospect, but the Countess had already had an invitation to the Mellors' country house and she thought she ought to take it. So it would be just Grand'mère, Cassie, Katie and I who should go.

I was delighted at the prospect of seeing the Manor House at Swaddingham. Those meetings in the park seemed a long way in the past and I had been realizing more and more every day how I missed them.

"We're rather a large party even without the Countess," I said. "I wonder if there will be any other guests."

"Well, you could hardly be asked without a chaperone," said the Countess, "and that must be Madame Cleremont. And you couldn't go without Katie—and Cassie would then be on her own which would be quite out of the question. A thoughtful gentleman would think of that—so it was one and all. You must have a special gown for the occasion, Lenore."

"I'd thought of that," said Grand'mère. "Scarlet velvet would be nice." She looked at the Countess who was nodding in agreement.

Secret glances passed between them. I knew them well enough to understand what they were expecting. And of course it concerned Drake and myself.

* * *

Katie and I walked in the park, she hugging a coloured ball in which she took great delight. She had to wait until we were in the park before she could bounce it and as soon as we arrived she began to throw it and run forward to catch it.

She chanted a little ditty to herself—laughing, smiling and giving out a little cry of mock-despair when she failed to catch it.

I thought back nostalgically to those days when it had been warm enough to sit about. There were fewer children here now. The nannies no longer sat on the benches knitting or chatting with one another about their charges.

I was thinking of Christmas. Grand'mère was engrossed in the red velvet gown. It would be a gown to make me look my best.

I was very much looking forward to the visit. I had missed Drake more than I had realized I should. I could imagine myself sharing his enthusiasms. And the salon? Well, I should keep my interest in that, of course.

I had a strong feeling that during this Christmas Drake was going to ask me to marry him. And if my premonition was right, was I going to say yes? I knew that therein lay happiness. I had, though, not quite recovered from Philip's death; but I knew too that I could do no good by brooding on it. I needed a fresh start and Drake, with whom I was already falling in love, was the man to lead me to it.

Kate gave a shout of dismay. She had bounced her ball too high and it had gone over a low iron fence enclosing rose bushes which even at this time of the year sported a few blooms.

I ran up to Katie but someone was there before me. He was leaning over the fence and rescuing the ball with his walking stick. Katie stood beside him, jumping up and down in her glee because she saw that he was going to retrieve her ball.

He had taken it in the crook of his stick and drew it towards him; then he lifted it up and with a bow handed it to Katie.

"Oh, thank you," she cried. "You are so clever. What a wonderful stick. Is it magic?"

"Ah," he said in a foreign accent. "Magic? Who shall say?"

Katie studied him with grateful eyes. She turned to me. "I have the ball back, Mama."

He turned to me. My heart gave a jolt. It was the man I had noticed previously and who appeared to have been watching me.

I stammered: "It was so kind of you. Thank you."

Katie went on jumping while he looked at me searchingly. I had a notion that the meeting was not accidental.

I said: "I . . . I think I have seen you before in the park."

"Yes," he replied. "I come here. It is great *bonne chance* that I am here when the ball goes over the fence."

"I am sure my daughter thinks so."

"She is most charming."

"Well, my grateful thanks. She would have been so unhappy to have lost her ball. Come along, Katie. I think you should not bounce it so high near the fence."

Katie held the precious ball tightly in one hand and took mine with the other.

"Thanks again," I said to the man. "Good day."

He took off his hat and stood bareheaded bowing, the wind ruffling his greying hair.

As I walked off I could sense his eyes following me. He was French, I thought, judging by his accent; and he had charming manners.

Katie kept talking about him. "He was rather a funny man."

"Funny?"

"He talked funny."

"That was because he was a foreigner. But he was good with the ball."

"Yes," agreed Katie. "He pulled it up with his stick. He is a nice man."

When we reached home Katie told Grand'mère about the man who had recovered her ball.

"That was nice of him," commented Grand'mère.

"He was a foreigner. He talked like you . . . Grand'mère . . . a bit like you. He said *bonne chance* when he meant lucky."

"Oh . . . French," said Grand'mère.

"He was very charming and polite," I told her.

"Of course," she said.

* * *

We arrived at Swaddingham two days before Christmas Eve. Drake was at the station to meet us. He was delighted to see us. Katie could not keep still, so excited was she. Grand'mère was quieter than usual but there was a look of intense happiness on her face.

"I hope you are going to like my manor," said Drake. "I'm growing more and more devoted to it. My sister Isabel and her husband Harry Denton are staying over Christmas. Isabel said I needed a hostess and has offered herself for the part. I think you'll like her. She is longing to meet the famous Lenore . . . and you all of course . . . not forgetting Katie."

Katie gave him her dazzling smile and bounced up and down on her seat.

She said: "Riding in a carriage is very nice. I like horses."

"We ought to teach you to ride," said Drake.

"Oh yes . . . yes . . ."

"Riding is not very easy in London," I pointed out.

"It's easy here."

He smiled at me and I felt happy.

I was fascinated by the house when I saw it. It was predominantly Tudor—black beams with white-washed panels in between, the upper part projecting beyond the ground floor.

Drake had pulled up. He sat for a few seconds watching the effect the house had on me.

I turned to him smiling. "It's wonderful," I said. "I could really feel I was back three hundred years."

"That's the effect it has. Isabel complains of the inconvenience of the kitchens and so on. But I wouldn't change one little bit of it. I'm so glad you like it."

He leaped down and helped us all out.

The big oak door opened and a woman came out. She was fresh complexioned and sufficiently like Drake to tell me that this was his sister Isabel. She smiled warmly.

"Welcome," she said. "I'm so glad to meet you at last. Do come in."

We went into the hall, which had a high vaulted roof. There was a fire blazing in the enormous fireplace.

"Are you cold and hungry?" she asked. "Oh, here's my husband. Harry, come and meet our guests."

Harry Denton appeared to be in his mid-thirties. He had a charming, easy manner and I liked him on the spot—just as I had Drake's sister.

I felt this was going to be a very happy Christmas.

Isabel insisted on our drinking a glass of hot punch to warm us up. "Then you shall go to your rooms."

"Punch?" cried Katie. "How can you *drink* punch?"

"You'll see," Isabel told her.

I said that Katie might have a little . . . watered down.

Katie was very intrigued. She thought she was in a very exciting household where people were named Drake—although she had accepted that one by now—but not to drink *punch!*

"What a funny house," she said.

"Darling, it's a wonderful house," I admonished.

"Yes . . . but funny."

Isabel showed us our rooms. We went up a staircase of solid oak. Drake could not resist telling us that the staircase had been put in for a king's visit, for King Henry VIII had actually stayed at the house for two nights. That was when the house had been transformed and changed from a dilapidated Saxon dwelling into a Tudor house. On one side of the newel was engraved the Tudor rose and on the other the fleur-de-lys.

We came to a landing. Here were our bedrooms—a small one each for Grand'mère and Cassie, and for Katie and me a much larger room with a high ceiling and a floor which sloped, and windows with leaded panes looking out onto a garden.

"Are we going to sleep here?" whispered Katie.

I told her we were and she was awestruck.

Hot water was brought into the bedrooms as soon as we arrived.

"Could you be down in half an hour?" asked Isabel. "That will give you time to wash and unpack perhaps." She smiled at me. "I'm so glad to meet you at last. Drake has talked so much about you."

"Are you here often?" I asked.

"Yes. Since Drake was elected. He needs a hostess here. Harry and I like it. This house is part of my childhood. It has been in the Aldringham family since soon after it was Tudorized . . . so you see how we feel about it."

"I can well understand."

"I'll be pleased to show you over it, but I daresay Drake will want to do that. He's so proud of the old place. It has quite a history. Charles the First stayed in one of the bedrooms when he was being chased by Cromwell's men. Of course he stayed in lots of houses . . . but we preserve his room. We never use it. It's just as it was when he slept in it."

"It must be wonderful to belong to such a family."

"Well, we all belong to our families, don't we? There is a family tree in the hall. I must show it to you. It goes right back to the sixteenth century. Collect the others when you're ready and come down to the hall."

Katie had been listening intently.

"What's Cromwell's men?" she asked.

I said: "I'll explain later. It's a long story and there isn't time now."

"Will they come chasing us . . . like they did that First man?"

I laughed. "Nobody's going to come chasing us. It all happened a long time ago."

When we went down to the hall Isabel was waiting for us. She said dinner would be served in about ten minutes.

I learned that Harry had a fairly large estate some thirty miles from

Swaddingham. He had a good manager so it was easy for him to get away.

"It means," said Isabel, "that we can almost always come here when Drake needs us. There is a certain amount of entertaining to do now that he is an M.P. He has to keep the constituents happy. There are all sorts of meetings here. Of course, he is in London a good deal, but I always tell him that I'm available when he needs me. I've always been something of a mother to Drake. He was only eight when our mother died. I was thirteen. I felt years older than he was. And that's how it has always been."

"I'm sure he's very grateful to you."

"Oh . . . he's my favourite man . . . after Harry, of course. I hope he will marry as happily as I have. Drake is a very special person."

I had a feeling that she was assessing me and that she was coming to the conclusion that I was to be that one; and as she looked pleased I guessed that she approved of me. She was certainly very charming to me.

Katie was allowed to join us for dinner for I did not feel she should be left alone in a strange room. She was delighted to be sitting at the table with the grown-ups; and as she was placed between Drake and me she felt quite at home.

That was a merry meal, sitting in that ancient room with its exquisite linenfold panelling and the leaded windows. Candles guttered in the brackets and in the large candelabrum in the centre of the table.

We talked about the house, its gardens, its grounds and stables. Katie listened avidly. Drake said that the next day he would find a pony for Katie and would give her a lesson in the paddock. She was wildly excited at the prospect and asked a great many questions. We were all very amused by these; but eventually she grew sleepy and was desperately trying to keep awake so as not to miss a moment of this exciting adventure; but it was hard work.

I said I would take her up to bed and stay with her so that I should be there if she awoke.

She murmured something about her pony as I kissed her goodnight and she was soon fast asleep.

I sat for some time at the window looking out. There was faint moonlight which showed me the outline of the distant trees. I was looking down on a lawn surrounded by flower beds which no doubt would make a glorious show in summer.

I was falling in love with the house and I had a notion that this was what Drake intended me to do. I was visualizing myself as mistress of it, helping Drake with his political work, making his career my main interest, just as I had made the salon mine; but Drake's career would have to be my first concern if I married him. I was only really part of Lenore's. Grand'mère was the creator of those superb creations and it was the Countess's shrewdness and connections which were of such vital importance. I could easily step aside or take a minor role . . . Grand'mère would understand. It was what she wanted; and I believed the Countess wanted the same.

I was physically tired but mentally alert. I went to bed and lay there wakeful for some time. A great excitement gripped me. I was certain that Drake had brought me here to ask me to marry him. He was showing a certain caution; and I guessed this was because he would be asking me to give up my business—at least to a large extent—and he was not sure how I should feel about that. I felt there was a certain restraint in him and I could only think that was the reason.

After breakfast next morning, Isabel took us round the house. It was larger than I had thought. We began with the kitchen with its enormous brick oven and roasting spits.

"Made for the days when people had gargantuan appetites," said Isabel. "Mind you I have dared to introduce a little modernity so that we can cook without too much inconvenience."

We explored the outhouses which included a buttery and a laundry.

Then we came to the main hall with its stone walls and vaulted ceiling.

"We use this when there are many guests," Isabel explained. "Sometimes we have to give dinner parties for the dignitaries of the neighbourhood. For smaller occasions we use the dining room. On Christmas Day there will be several guests so we shall eat Christmas dinner here. These stairs lead up to the dining room and the drawing room; and then on the next floor are the bedrooms. There are twenty of them, of varying sizes; and above that is the long gallery which goes across the whole length of the house; above are the attics and servants' quarters."

Drake had joined us. "You're stealing a march on me, Isabel," he said. And to us: "You must see the gallery. It's the oldest part of the house . . . the remains of the Saxon section. It was not changed when the lower part was renovated."

I stood there in that gallery. There was an eeriness about it. Even though it was bright daylight there seemed to be shadows.

"The windows are so small," said Drake. "We could have them changed but that would be frowned upon. Of course we can't change the character of the place which we should do if we altered anything."

"Is it haunted?" asked Cassie.

Isabel and Drake exchanged glances.

"Did you ever hear of any old house which was *not* supposed to be haunted?"

"So it is," said Cassie.

"It's the old part of the house you see, and in a house where people have been living for centuries there are bound to be legends."

Cassie shivered. I looked at Katie. I did not want her to be frightened but she was looking out of the window where she could see the stables. She said there was a man on a horse. Drake went over to her.

"Yes, that's the stables," he said. "Your pony is there."

He stood beside her talking to her.

"Who sleeps up there?" asked Cassie.

"The servants," Isabel told her.

"Have they ever . . ."

"We don't talk about it. You know what people are? They build up things in their minds and start imagining things."

Grand'mère asked about the pictures.

"They are all members of the family," said Drake who had joined us with Katie.

"Are you here?" I asked.

He shook his head. "Our family home is really in Worcestershire. My father's sister came here a long time ago and it was reckoned to be her home. She was unmarried and devoted herself to the house and the affairs of the neighbourhood. And when I was as they say 'nursing' Swaddingham, it seemed a stroke of good luck that this place was in the family. I came here for a while and lived with her. She was a martinet . . . a woman of great character; but we liked each other; and when she died the house passed on to me."

"I think it is a wonderful house," I said.

Drake smiled at me happily. "I'm so glad."

True to his promise he took Katie riding. She was in a state of bliss;

and it was such a joy to see her seated on the pony and Drake himself holding the leading reins and taking her round the paddock. With Grand'mère and Cassie I watched.

"Look at me," cried Katie. "I'm riding."

That was such a happy morning.

After luncheon, Katie was tired out—I think with excitement more than anything else. I thought she should have a rest, so she went to bed. Drake asked if I would care to go for a ride with him. I said I should love to. I had ridden a great deal when I lived at The Silk House but there had been few opportunities to do so since.

Grand'mère said she would like to rest too and Cassie volunteered to go and sit in my room so that if Katie woke she would not find herself alone in a strange house.

Drake procured a suitable mount for me and we rode off.

"I want to show you the neighbourhood," he said. "It's rather beautiful. You wouldn't believe you were so near to London. It couldn't be more convenient for me."

"No, and your sister is so helpful."

"I was hoping you would like her. Isabel is a good sort."

"I think she is charming."

"She likes you very much."

"She hardly knows me yet."

"She has heard of you . . . from me. She is full of admiration for your enterprise. I told her about all that. She thinks it is wonderful to have achieved so much."

"I must say I have enjoyed my work."

"Do you think people ever succeed in anything they don't enjoy?"

"Perhaps not."

"Still worried about that expansion?"

"Well, we do have it on our minds. The Countess talks of little else, and I know Grand'mère thinks we ought to do it. So do I for that matter . . ."

"Yes, you are deeply immersed."

"We have been lucky. Knowing the Countess was the best thing that could have happened."

"It was a way of escape . . . from your unhappiness."

"Yes, exactly that."

"But you are growing away from that now."

"One does . . . in time, I suppose."

"But you still think a great deal of the past?"

"It is there. One can't escape from it."

"I understand. Do you think . . ." He paused and I waited for him to go on. But he seemed to change his mind. "This is where our land ends," he said.

"It's quite an extensive estate."

"It needs a lot of managing. Fortunately I have a good man. It's a part time job with me."

"The main one being politics."

"Yes, but I don't have to worry. If I'm detained in London everything goes on smoothly here."

"You seem to have it all worked out beautifully."

"I have been so anxious for you to see it . . . and to realize what it is like here . . . and in London. I have to do a lot of entertaining in both places. My sister of course is a great help here . . . but she does have her own home."

"She is so fond of you."

"Yes. She has always been the little mother."

I felt I wanted to sing. He was going to ask me to marry him; and I was going to say Yes. Life was going to change. He would be a good father to Katie. Children needed a father—and some women—like myself—needed a husband.

We had come to a field. I said: "Let's gallop." And we did across the field, pulling up sharply before a hedge. It was most exhilarating.

I thought I understood. He was going to ask me to marry him but he was hesitating. He would ask me before I left. He wanted me to understand all that marriage with him would entail. He wanted to be absolutely sure that I could forget the past. That was why he had been so eager for me to come here for the Christmas holiday. He could not forget that I was Lenore and that my name was that of one of the most exclusive dress establishments in London. He wanted so much to be sure . . . for both of us to be sure. I had to convince him that although I was dedicated to a successful business, I should consider love and marriage more important.

It had been a most happy afternoon but there was an unpleasant surprise awaiting me.

We returned to the stables, a groom took our horses, and we went into the house. Isabel was there with a woman splendidly attired in sables. It was Julia.

She rushed forward to greet Drake.

"Here I am," she said. "It is so good to see you."

Drake looked bewildered.

"I shall stay only until after Christmas. Of course we had to spend that together. I understood perfectly what you meant when you said you had to be here."

"Hello, Julia," I said. "I had no idea that you were coming here."

"Well, Drake and I understand each other. He was very insistent on my knowing that he was spending his Christmas here so I knew what he meant and that he was expecting me. Drake dear, I'm sorry I couldn't come before. There was the Harringtons' dinner party last night. I had to go. They insisted. Otherwise I could have come yesterday."

Isabel said: "We shall have to get a room ready."

"How sweet of you."

"And you have your maid with you?"

"Annette . . . yes."

"She will have to sleep in one of the attics. There is one she could have."

"How kind! Drake, you are very remiss, you know. Why didn't you tell Mrs. Denton that I was coming?"

"It is a surprise to me."

"Oh Drake . . . when you told me . . . I thought it was understood . . ."

"Well, now you are here . . . Isabel will see to everything."

"Isn't that nice? I love this old place. It's so quaint. And Cassie is here?"

I nodded.

"I'm so pleased. Families ought to be together . . . especially at Christmas."

The visit had changed now. Julia had spoilt it.

*　*　*

Christmas! It should have been such a happy time. The carol singers came as soon as it was dark. They stood outside with their lanterns and rendered all the well-loved carols: "Once in Royal David's City"; "Come All Ye Faithful"; "Good King Wenceslas" . . . and many more.

Katie was delighted and sang with them and afterwards helped to hand round the mulled wine and mince pies. That night she went to bed at her usual time and was soon fast asleep. The house had become like home to her.

After we had dined that evening we went up to the long gallery where a fire had been lighted.

"We always come up here on Christmas Eve," Isabel explained. "We roast chestnuts and drink port wine. One always feels one has to cling to old traditions which have been passed down through the centuries."

"It's rather eerie," said Julia. "That old gentleman looks as though he is going to step out of his frame and give us a good talking to."

"He certainly looks rather severe," agreed Drake. "That's great great grandfather William. He was an admiral. There is a strong naval tradition in the family."

"And some of these old gentlemen must be rather cross with you, Drake, for not carrying out the family tradition."

Cassie said: "Are you afraid they might show their displeasure in some way?"

"They have been in their graves . . . for a long time."

"Some say they live on afterwards," said Cassie, "and some come back."

"Even if they did I intend to do what I want to with my life as they did with theirs," Drake told her.

"Why do they always connect revenants with old houses?" I asked. "You rarely hear of haunted cottages. It is always big houses."

Grand'mère said: "The dead are dead . . . and however much one wants to have them back one cannot." I knew she was thinking of my mother and Philip.

"This is actually the haunted gallery, isn't it?" asked Cassie who appeared to be fascinated by the subject.

"Supposed to be," said Drake.

"Is there some story . . . ?"

Drake looked at Isabel who said: "Well, there is."

"Do tell us," begged Cassie.

"Cassie," I warned, "you won't be able to sleep tonight."

"I don't care. I long to hear."

"You tell them," said Drake to his sister.

"Well, the gallery is supposed to be haunted by a young girl . . . one of our family, of course. She was sixteen years old and it happened about two hundred years ago. She was in love with a young man and her father would not allow her to marry him. Instead he had found another husband for her—a rich ageing man. In those days girls had to obey their parents."

"As they do not always do now," added Grand'mère.

"I daresay there were some who did not then," I suggested.

"Well, Anne Aldringham did. She said goodbye to her lover and married the man of her father's choice. After the wedding all the guests came back here for the celebrations." She closed her eyes. "Sometimes when I come up here I fancy I can hear the minstrels' music. They were dancing downstairs in the great hall and suddenly they found that the bride was missing."

"It's like the mistletoe bough," murmured Cassie.

"Not quite. They were not playing hide and seek and she was not locked in a chest where she stayed for a hundred years. She came up here and jumped out of a window. It is said to be that one." Isabel pointed. "She jumped to her death."

"Oh, poor poor Anne," murmured Cassie.

"She should have run away with her lover," said Julia. "I should." She looked tenderly at Drake who did not meet her eyes.

"Well, she did not," went on Isabel. "Instead she jumped out of that window."

"And now," suggested Cassie, "she haunts the place."

"On certain occasions, it is said. When any of the family is about to marry someone who would bring him or her unhappiness, she is supposed to come through that window and walk along the gallery wringing her hands and crying 'Beware! Beware!' "

"Have you ever seen her?" I asked Isabel.

She shook her head.

"So presumably all the marriages have been happy," said Cassie.

"If you believe the story, yes. I don't think the ghost is going to appear for us."

Julia was looking steadily at me. "What a cheerful subject for a Christmas Eve. I hope my room is well away from the wailing lady."

"You wouldn't hear her down in your room," consoled Isabel.

"Thank Heaven for that."

"Let me give you some more port," said Drake.

"Oh, isn't this cosy!" Julia smiled round the company. "Christmas in this wonderful house . . . with wonderful people . . ." She lifted her glass. "Happy Christmas . . . to all."

Her eyes had come to rest on Drake and they stayed there.

* * *

On Christmas morning we went to church. Julia came with us rather to my surprise, but she did seem as though she were determined not to let Drake out of her sight more than was possible.

I felt vaguely uneasy. I would never forget her fury when we were children and she had realized that Drake had left The Silk House because of me. She had looked quite murderous then.

I was now convinced that she wanted to marry Drake. I was sure he had not invited her although she had suggested that he had, or that she had misunderstood something he had said and had interpreted it as an invitation. It was too far-fetched. If he had wanted her to come why should he not have asked her outright in the normal way. The truth would be that Julia had discovered that I was at Swaddingham and had determined to come too.

I knew that she was drinking a great deal. It was becoming obvious in her high colour and her occasional aggressiveness and in the rather unguarded remarks she would make when she was a little less than sober.

I wondered if Drake was aware of this. He was always extremely courteous and, after the initial shock of finding her here, had played the perfect host.

There was the traditional Christmas dinner eaten at midday; turkey followed by Christmas pudding brought ablaze to the table and served with brandy butter—and then of course mince pies. Several of the neighbours, friends who supported Drake as their member of Parliament, were present; and there was a great deal of conversation about political affairs, and an election which seemed imminent.

After lunch we rested awhile.

I was very grateful to Drake for taking a little time to lead Katie round the paddock in the afternoon—a source of great delight to her; and I liked to see how happy she and Drake were together.

There were more guests in the evening when we had a cold buffet supper and minstrels came in and played. There was dancing in the long gallery which lost its eeriness with so many people present.

Drake had to dance with all the female guests and I had only one with him. He asked me if I was enjoying my stay and I assured him that I was. He said he was glad. He had so much wanted me to come down and see everything. He wanted me to tell him frankly what I thought about the life a politician was expected to lead.

"You know what I think of that," I told him. "It must be one of the most interesting professions possible."

"Even better than running an exclusive dress salon?"

"That has its points," I replied.

"I'm sure it has."

"Isabel is wonderful in the way she copes with everything."

"She has done it all her life. First at home, then with Harry and now with me. Isabel is a wonderful person."

"I know. Nothing ruffles her. She was quite unprepared for Julia and did not show it."

"Yes. She certainly did not."

I was waiting for him to assure me that he had not invited her. It was important to me that he should not have done so.

But he said nothing and I could not ask.

Later I saw him with Julia. She was very flushed and laughing all the time; and he was smiling as though he were enjoying the dance. One would never really know what he was feeling.

When I went to my room that evening Katie was fast asleep. I bent over and kissed her lovely innocent face. I prepared slowly for bed. I knew I should find sleep difficult. A sense of disappointment was still with me. It had come with Julia's arrival.

I kept thinking about Drake and Julia. I kept seeing them dancing together. She had a proprietorial manner towards him, and he did not seem to resent this. Or did he? He did not show his feelings; his manners were impeccable; he had to play the perfect host. Had he invited her? I was unsure.

I could not sleep. I lay staring out of the window. I looked over at Katie sleeping peacefully. She was mine entirely and while I had her I must be happy . . . no matter what. But my disappointment and frustration stayed with me.

Suddenly I was wide awake. Something was happening upstairs. I got out of bed and put on my dressing gown and slippers.

I went out and up the stairs to the long gallery. A few candles had been lighted and they burned fitfully in their sconces. I saw Isabel. She was seated on a settle, a young girl beside her. The girl was crying.

"It's all right," said Isabel, when she saw me. "Patty was feeling a little hysterical."

The girl said: "But I heard it, M'am. I heard it distinct. It was awful ghostly like . . ."

Drake had come hurrying up.

"What on earth is happening?" he demanded.

Isabel said: "Patty's had a nightmare."

"Oh no it wasn't . . ." said Patty.

Three of the other maids emerged from the shadows.

"I heard it too," said one of them. "Oh, it was terrible. I never heard the like . . . Someone was crying something awful. She said, 'Beware! Beware! . . .' Three times she said it. Oh, it was terrible, M'am. I was shivering for it turned terrible cold sudden like."

"That was because you were only in your night things."

Julia had come to the top of the stairs. Her hair was hanging about her shoulders becomingly and she was clutching a pale lavender negligee about her.

"What's wrong? Oh, my goodness. What has happened? That poor girl. She looks scared out of her wits."

"Patty has had a nightmare," repeated Isabel.

Patty shook her head, her teeth chattering.

"I was wide awake, M'am . . ."

"I think a little brandy, Drake," said Isabel. "Oh, there's Harry. Harry, Patty's had some sort of dream. The girls are all upset. Do bring some brandy. It will quieten them down."

Mrs. Gratten, the cook, appeared. She sailed in majestically in spite of the fact that her hair was in curl papers.

"What is it?" she said to one of the girls. "What's wrong with Patty?"

"She's a little hysterical, Mrs. Gratten," said Isabel. "There's no need for everyone to get so excited. I think they were probably frightening themselves with ghost stories before going to bed."

"No we wasn't, M'am," said one of the girls. "Nobody said nothing about a ghost. It just came into Patty's head. And I heard it, too. It wasn't fancy. It was the real thing. You could tell."

Julia said: "It wasn't that ghost you were telling us about . . . the one who comes in through the window and weeps and cried 'Beware'?"

"Yes, M'am, that's it," said Patty. "I heard her footsteps all along the gallery. She was crying something awful and she said 'Beware.' That was it."

"Oh, here's Harry with the brandy," said Isabel. "Thank you, Harry. Now you girls, drink this and get to bed."

"I'll see to them, Mrs. Denton," said the cook. "I don't know what things are coming to . . . rousing the household like this."

"But it was the ghost, Mrs. Gratten," insisted Patty. "It was truly."

Drake said: "I think we all need a little fortification. Come down to the drawing room."

We followed him down. He poured out the brandy and very soon Isabel joined us.

"I hope all this didn't wake Katie," she said.

"No. I looked in. She was sleeping peacefully."

"Oh . . . good."

"What an extraordinary thing," said Julia. "After we'd been talking . . . What do you think that girl really heard?"

"Someone has been telling her the story, I should think," I said.

"That is very likely," agreed Isabel.

"It really was rather strange," went on Julia. "In any case you'd better take it as a warning, Drake."

Drake raised his eyebrows.

"Well, isn't it something to do with an impending marriage . . . warnings and all that? You're the only marriageable member of the family. Don't you agree with me?"

"I always thought Patty was the hysterical type."

"It was odd all the same," said Julia. "The brandy is deliciously warming."

"A little more?" suggested Harry.

"Oh yes please," said Julia.

I said: "I am going now. I don't want Katie to wake up and find me not there."

"Poor Lenore," consoled Julia. "You look really shocked. You don't believe in ghosts, do you?"

"Do you?" I asked.

Julia laughed and lifting her hand swayed from side to side. "Not really. But it is rather odd. I wonder if that girl overheard us talking . . ."

"I daresay she had heard the story somewhere. Good night."

I left them.

Katie was still sleeping. I knew I could not hope to. I lay in bed for some time listening to the noises of the house . . . the boards which creaked as they always did in old houses . . . and the wind seemed to moan in the trees and to whisper softly "Beware."

*   *   *

The rest of that visit was something of an anticlimax. Everyone seemed embarrassed except Katie. She wanted her riding lesson which Drake gave her, and she seemed completely happy.

Isabel made Patty stay in bed for the next day.

"The poor girl is really shaken," she said. "She's the hysterical type."

Everything had turned out so differently from what I had expected. I could see that Grand'mère was disappointed and Cassie seemed merely bewildered. It was rather a relief to leave—but Katie felt very sad.

"It has been lovely," she said, flinging her arms round Drake. "Take care of Bluebell till I come back."

Drake assured her that he would make sure that the pony was well cared for.

We left Julia there. She was one at least who had enjoyed Christmas.

*   *   *

It was about two days later when Grand'mère said that she wished to talk to me alone for she had something very important to say to me.

"Lenore," she began, "you know that I went to Villers-Mûre not long ago."

"Yes, Grand'mère."

"When I was there . . . I met someone."

"Who?"

"I met . . . your father."

"Grand'mère!"

"It's true."

"I thought you did not know who my father was."

She was silent. "I have told you something of our family history. It is not always easy to explain to a child. To talk of it was most upsetting and I am afraid I was something of a coward."

"Tell me now."

"You know that your mother, my daughter Marie Louise, was a girl of exceptional beauty. It was natural that she should attract men. We were humble. I was left a young widow and had to work for my living and like most people in Villers-Mûre I worked at the St. Allengère establishment, and when Marie Louise was old enough she was given a place there. You know what happened. She fell in love. You were born. She died . . . perhaps of fear and grief. Women do die in childbirth even when the future is bright for them. I do not know . . . All I know is that she died and I was heartbroken . . . for she was my life . . . Then I realized that she had left me you . . . and that changed everything."

"Yes, Grand'mère, you have told me this."

"You knew that the great Alphonse St. Allengère arranged for me to come to England to work for the Sallongers. The reason he did that was because he did not want me to remain where I was."

"Why?" I asked. Grand'mère was finding it difficult to tell me this; she was not her usual loquacious self.

She frowned and said: "Because your father was his youngest son."

"So . . . you did know who my father was!"

"Marie Louise told me . . . just before you were born."

"And he would not marry her?"

"He was only a boy. Seventeen years old and I can tell you Alphonse St. Allengère is a very formidable man. The whole of Villers-Mûre went in fear and trembling of him. He held our lives in the palm of his hand. Everyone dreaded his frowns, his sons no less than any others. There was no question of a St. Allengère marrying one of the girls who worked in the factory. Your father did his best. He truly loved Marie Louise, but his father was adamant. He was sent away to an uncle who owned a vineyard in Burgundy. When I went to Villers-Mûre I made enquiries. By great good fortune he was on a visit to his family so I was able to talk to him. I told him about you . . . how you were now a widow with a young child. He was very touched."

"I knew there was something. I could see it in your face when you returned."

"He is in London now."

I stared at her.

She nodded happily. "Yes, he has said he must see you. Naturally he wanted to know his own daughter. He is coming here."

She looked at me intently as though to assess the effect of this bombshell. I have to admit that I was astounded. To be brought face to face with a father one has never known could be a shattering experience. I was not sure whether I looked forward to it or dreaded it.

Grand'mère went on: "It is not natural for those who are so close to be strangers to each other."

"But after all these years, Grand'mère . . ."

"*Ma chérie,* he longs to meet you. You could make him very happy. He has come all this way to see you."

"When is he coming?"

"This evening. I have asked him to dine with us."

"But . . . this is so unexpected . . ."

"I thought it wise not to tell you until it was all arranged."

"Why?"

"I did not know how you would feel. Perhaps there would be some resentment. All those years he has not seen you . . . The years of struggle for us. He is a very rich man. He owns vineyards in various parts of France. The St. Allengères are always successful whatever they take up. His father is proud of him now. It is a different matter from when he was young."

"I do not greatly care for this father of his . . . my grandfather, I suppose."

"He had great power. And sometimes that is not good for people. He is old now but he is still the same Alphonse St. Allengère. He still rules Villers-Mûre and is undoubtedly the greatest producer of silk in the world."

"And tonight . . ."

She nodded.

I was so overcome that I found it difficult to analyse my feelings. Should I tell Katie? What should I say to her? "This is your grandfather." She would ask interminable questions. Where had he been all this time?

Fortunately she would be in bed before he came and I should have a chance of meeting him and perhaps breaking the news gradually of how a grandfather had appeared out of the blue.

I dressed carefully in a scarlet gown and waited in trepidation for his coming. Grand'mère was rather agitated, too. I was glad that the Countess and Cassie were present. They helped to subdue the emotion which Grand'mère and I were feeling.

At the appointed hour the doorbell rang. Rosie, our maid, announced him.

"Mr. Sallonger," she said, finding it impossible to pronounce his name and giving the anglicized version.

And there he was.

I looked at him in amazement. He was the man I had seen in the park, the one who had retrieved Katie's ball and had appeared to be watching me.

* * *

What an exciting evening that was! So much was said that it is difficult for me to remember now and in what order. I remember his taking both my hands and looking into my eyes. He said: "We have met before . . . in the park."

I nodded in agreement.

"I was on the point of making myself known many times," he went on, "but I hesitated. Now . . . we are together at last."

How amazing it was, I thought, that when I had seen him in the park I had believed him to be a stranger; and he was in fact my father!

During the dinner, at which Cassie and the Countess were present, he talked about his vineyards. He spoke in English and now and then had to grope for the words he needed. He wanted to hear of our salon and the Countess was most voluble on the subject.

She talked amusingly of our clients and the manner in which they followed each other like sheep. One had a Lenore gown and they all must. It was inevitable that she should come to the matter which was uppermost in her mind.

"By hook or by crook I shall get us to Paris," she said. "That is the centre of fashion and worthwhile houses must in time have connections there. It is an essential in the long run."

"I can see that," he said. "And at the moment you have not this . . . connection?"

"No, but we will."

"When do you propose to set up there?"

"When we have the good fortune . . . and I mean fortune . . . so to do," said the Countess. "I'm all for it but my partners are cautious. They want to wait until we can pay for it. The good Lord knows when that will be."

He nodded gravely and Grand'mère abruptly changed the subject.

After dinner, the Countess and Cassie left him alone with me; and then we spoke in French of which language I had been made fairly fluent by Grand'mère; and of course she was in her natural element.

"I have thought of you often," he said. "I have wanted so much to find you and when your grandmother came to Villers-Mûre and I happened to be visiting my family home it seemed like Providence. She told me a great deal about you. How you had this wonderful business. The St. Allengères always prospered in business."

"Our prosperity is largely due to the Countess, is it not, Grand'mère? She is a superb saleswoman, and she showed us what innocents we were. We should have foundered without her."

"I want to know a great deal about your business. But first let us talk about ourselves. You must understand that I truly loved your mother. It was the shame of my life that I let myself be sent away. I should have stood by her. I should have defied my father. But I was young . . . I was weak and foolish. I was not strong enough. I should have married her. Instead I let them send me away."

Grand'mère nodded.

He looked at her and said: "How you must have reviled me when I did."

"Yes," said Grand'mère frankly, "I did. Marie Louise did not blame you. She defended you to me. She said you did what you had to do. Your father was determined and he is a very powerful and ruthless man."

"And still is," he added grimly. "It was good for me to escape from his domination. I found my life among the vines rather than the mulberries. But it is all so long ago."

"And nothing can bring Marie Louise back."

"Perhaps she would have died in any case," I said.

They were silent.

Then he told us how he had gone away to stay with his uncle who owned a vineyard and how he became interested in wine. "I threw myself into the work," he said. "It was a solace. My uncle said that I should be a good vintner. So I stayed with him. Then I had my own vineyards. I worked hard. I married my wife who brought me property, and now we have our family."

"And you are happy?" I said.

"I do not complain. I have a son and a daughter."

"I saw Marie Louise's grave had not been neglected," said Grand'mère.

"I always go there when I visit the family. And I have paid one of the peasants to look after it. If it is possible that she could be aware she will know that I have not forgotten."

He and Grand'mère talked of my mother for a while—how pleased and proud she would have been of me and Katie—whom he had found enchanting. It had delighted him to realize that she was his grand-daughter.

"And you have suffered," he said to me. "Madame Cleremont has told me of your husband's death and how you have devoted yourself to that dear child."

"She is a great joy to me," I told him.

We fell into silence again and after a while he said: "I was interested in what the Countess was saying about your salon, and how she thought you should open in Paris. She is right, you know."

"Oh yes, we know she has a point, but my grandmother and I are against it . . . for the time being at any rate. We have not been so very long in business here and once . . . in the beginning . . . we came near to disaster. That has made us cautious."

"But," he said, "it is a move you must take."

Grand'mère was watching him intently and I had a notion that she knew what he was going to say.

It came. "Perhaps I could be of assistance."

I looked at him in astonishment.

He went on: "It is something I should dearly love to do. I am not a poor man. I have my vineyards. We have good years when all goes well; the weather is kind to us, and the leaf hoppers and the rot worms decide to leave us alone . . . Then we make good profits. I have not done too badly. I would take it as a privilege if you would allow me to help with this Paris addition."

"Oh," I said quickly, "that is good of you but, of course, we don't want to borrow money . . ."

"How right you are. What does your Shakespeare say: 'Neither a borrower nor a lender be . . .' But I was not thinking of a loan. You are my daughter. Should there not be these things between a father and his daughter? Let me finance this Paris branch . . . as a kind of dowry to my daughter."

I drew back in horror. I looked suspiciously at Grand'mère. She was sitting with her eyes downcast and her hands in her lap. She dared not let me see her face because she knew it would be shining with triumph.

"I could not accept that," I said sharply.

"It would give me great pleasure."

"Please think no more of it."

He looked at me sadly. "I see you do not accept me as a father."

I stammered: "I have met you for the first time tonight. We cannot count those meetings in the park. And you offer this! Do you realize what such an undertaking would cost?"

"I am of the opinion that it would not be beyond my means."

"No, no," I said. "It is out of the question. We have a very profitable business here. It is adequate. It gives me a very good return on the capital which my husband left me. I can bring my daughter up if not in luxury—which might not be good for her in any case—in comfort."

"We will think about this."

"No. Please forget it. It is most generous of you and I thank you sincerely. But I cannot accept it."

He bowed his head.

Because I wanted to change the subject I asked him a great many questions about his vineyards. He was full of enthusiasm for them. He talked vividly about the vagaries of the climate and the effect it had. The weather was the great enemy but like many enemies, it could be a good friend. They would despair when the summers were too wet and they prayed in the churches for a warm and sunny autumn which had more than once saved the harvest. He made me feel the excitement of the *vendange.*

"You will come and see it," he said. "You and the little one. Now that we have found each other we shall not lose each other again. The little one would love the vineyards."

"I am sure she would."

"And what happiness that would bring us."

"But your wife and family?"

"My wife died two years ago. She was older than I. Our marriage worked well enough. My son Georges and my daughter Brigitte are both married. I believe they would be happy to meet you."

I said: "We must come then." I turned to Grand'mère. "Don't you agree?"

She nodded emphatically.

It was late when he rose to go. "I will see you tomorrow," he said. "I may call, may I not?"

"You must call whenever you wish," said Grand'mère firmly.

* * *

She came to my room when I was in bed. I knew she would so I was prepared for her. She looked young for her age, with her hair in two plaits like a schoolgirl's, and her plain but elegant dressing gown.

"What a night!" she said. "One to remember."

"It is not every day a girl is presented with a father she has not known before. You arranged all this, didn't you, Grand'mère?"

"Well . . ." she began.

"I know you too well," I said. "Besides, your face always betrays you. It is the most expressive face I know. You went to France intending to find him. You told him he should see me, now didn't you?"

"He didn't need any persuading."

"Then what about all those years . . ."

"How could he know where his daughter was?"

"So you told him where I was and that he must come and see me."

"As soon as he knew, he wanted to see you."

"And did you by any chance mention the salon . . . and the fact that there was a question of opening in Paris?"

"The Countess did that over dinner."

"But was it entirely a surprise to him?"

"Well, I might have mentioned . . ."

"And now he has made this offer. I fancy it was not something he did on the spur of the moment."

"Why this catechism? Is it not good that he should wish to do this thing?"

"So you suggested it to him?"

She lifted her shoulders. "He wanted to know how you did . . . what was happening . . . It was natural that he should wish to hear of his daughter. Oh, enough of this. You must take the money."

"Grand'mère, I couldn't! It is like begging. It is shameful. It is like asking a price from him because he deserted my mother."

"You think of yourself, *ma chérie*. You must think of others. This will give him great pleasure. Why should he be denied that because of your pride?"

"Grand'mère, you surely do not want to take his money!"

"Most gladly, would I. It will give us what we need . . . that salon
in Paris. I have always known it was necessary for us. I have always
said to myself 'Some day' . . . and now it has come and you are
turning away from it."

"I can't take it, Grand'mère."

"So we are all to suffer for your folly. You, I, the Countess, Cassie
. . . and your father."

"But surely . . ."

She shook her head. "Think of that man. He is beside himself with
contrition. He wants a chance to right the wrong he did your mother.
It has been on his conscience for years. If he could do this thing he
would be so happy. He would feel that he had made some recompense.
But Madame Lenore . . . she says No. My pride, my precious pride
. . . must come first."

"Grand'mère, how can you put it that way?"

"I put it the way it is. Now I go, my obstinate little mule. Good
night. Pleasant dreams. Dream of all the good you could do and which
you are refusing because of that foolish pride which is no good to God
or woman."

"Good night, Grand'mère."

She turned at the door and threw me a kiss.

"May the good God keep you, my precious one," she said.

* * *

When the Countess heard of my father's offer she clapped her
hands in glee and threw her arms round Grand'mère's neck.

"Do not be too happy," said Grand'mère. "Lenore has decided not
to accept."

"What?" cried the Countess.

"Something called pride."

"Oh no!"

"Yes . . . alas," said Grand'mère.

Grand'mère sat rocking from side to side, a smile playing about her
mouth.

"That poor man," she said, "that loving father. He is covered in
shame because of all that happened years ago. Now he has found her
and wants to show her how happy he is. He wants to bestow this
outward sign of his joy . . . and his daughter says 'No. You must go
on reproaching yourself. I am not going to release you one little bit.'

Poor man. Pride is a cruel thing. It is one of the seven deadly sins, you know."

"It isn't like that, Grand'mère. I know now that you sought him out just for this. You were determined to find him because we needed this money to open the Paris branch. Confess."

"I meet him. He wants to know what his daughter is doing. I tell him . . . and how could I not tell him of this? He listens . . . most intently . . . and he says to himself, 'Ah, here is a chance for me to right the wrong I did to my poor Marie Louise. This is her daughter . . . hers and mine . . . I will make her happy. I will give her this money for her business. I have plenty. I can do this with ease. But alas she will not take it. Her pride stops her.' Never mind his remorse, his sadness. That must not be helped because of this pride . . . this strong stubborn pride . . ."

I could not help laughing and very soon the others joined in.

The Countess wanted one of her celebrations. "Cassie," she called, "bring a bottle of champagne."

"But I have not agreed . . ."

"This is too great an opportunity to miss. You could not be so cruel to us all."

"But don't you see?"

"I see the future. I see that Paris salon. What we have always lacked can be ours."

Cassie came in with the champagne.

"What's happened?"

"Lenore's father has offered to put up the money for the Paris salon."

Cassie's face was alight with joy. She put down the tray and turned to me.

"Lenore," she said, "it's wonderful."

I thought: You, too, Cassie.

And in the end I gave way.

* * *

Now there was bustle and excitement. I was gradually being convinced that I had done the right thing. My father was constantly at the salon. He listened to our plans with enthusiasm.

Julia called.

"The most wonderful thing has happened," the Countess told her. "We are going to open in Paris."

Julia listened wide-eyed.

"We have a benefactor," said the Countess gaily. "Lenore's father is putting up the money."

"Lenore's father!"

"Yes, he has appeared . . . out of the blue. He is charming and generous."

My father came in while Julia was there and was introduced to her.

"I've seen you before," she said.

"You were with us in the park," I reminded her.

"Oh yes, I remember. The admirer. We joked about it. We said Lenore had an admirer."

"So she has," said my father.

"How wonderful! You must tell me all about it."

The Countess could not stop talking. Even I was quite caught up in the project now, and when I saw the joy my acceptance had brought my father, I began to think they were all right.

"You are wise," said Julia. "Most of the houses have Paris branches. You will go zooming ahead now."

She talked of Christmas. "It *was* a pleasant time, wasn't it . . . until that girl had hysterics in the gallery. Everyone seemed to take that to heart. I suppose they think a lot about that sort of thing in the country. I expect Drake is working hard down there. He said he had to do a bit of 'nursing.' This is the time to do it. He has to be ready for this election . . . letting them all know how much he cares about them."

She kissed me effusively and went off.

That very day it was arranged that I should go with the Countess and my father to Paris. We were going to stay there until we had found the premises and set things in motion.

I was now as eager as any of them; my father was so happy. He would be of great help, said the Countess; not only was he a business man, but he was also French, and we should have to remember that we were in France.

"We are not likely to forget it," I told her.

She clapped her hands and murmured: "Paris"—as though Paris was heaven.

* * *

So I left Katie in the charge of Grand'mère and Cassie and with my father and the Countess I set out. From the moment we left the Gare du Nord, I was caught up in the excitement of that most enchanting of cities and I was convinced—as was the Countess—that our venture was going to be a success. It was comforting to be in the care of my father, for the city was a little bewildering. He had taken on all the arrangements; he knew exactly what we should do first. He was in high spirits and I realized how happy I had made him—as well as the others—by accepting this offer.

He hustled us into a cab and gave the *cocher* instructions to take us to our hotel in the Rue de la Fayette. I shall never forget that ride through the streets of Paris where everyone seemed so full of vitality. We passed markets where I glimpsed barrows on the pavements; the cafés and restaurants where, in the summer, my father told me, I should see people eating and drinking at the tables in the open air as they liked to live out of doors. The traffic seemed to move in all directions and the drivers shouted to each other above the hubbub of the streets.

My father pointed out landmarks as we went along.

"Oh, you will love exploring Paris. I shall show you Montmartre . . . Notre Dame . . . Oh, there is so much I shall show you."

"First," the Countess reminded him, "we have to find our premises."

"Ah yes, I do not forget, dear Countess, that is the object of our visit."

Soon we were installed in our hotel. I had a large high-ceilinged room with a balcony from which I could look down on the street. We should retire early, my father suggested, and tomorrow we would begin the search.

I was excited to be here but at the same time I was thinking of Katie and wondering whether she was missing me. I was thinking of Drake and that Christmas visit which had turned out so differently from what I had expected. I was, of course, thrilled by the prospect of the opening in Paris but my home and my heart were in London. Was that because Drake was there? Oddly my feelings for him seemed to have intensified since Christmas. Before that I had been uncertain, but the overwhelming disappointment I had known when he did not ask me to marry him, had shown me my true feelings. Julia's arrival had spoilt everything—as had that strange matter of the girl who had thought she saw a ghost.

Now I must give my mind to this Paris project. I thought: I will see them set up and then . . . I will marry Drake. I would always have an interest in the business, but my first and foremost care would be for my family. Katie . . . and Drake. I looked forward to more children . . . a son . . . another daughter. My life would be with my family. I would be a politician's wife; and I had heard someone say once that if a marriage was to be a success there was not room in it for two careers.

We were up early next morning. Coffee and brioches had been sent to our rooms, so we were soon ready to venture out on our search. My father had secured the addresses of one or two properties and we sallied forth. One was not very far from our hotel and we walked to it.

There is something invigorating about the streets of Paris. It was a bright morning, quite warm for the time of the year. There was a smell of coffee in the air; people were already in the streets and the traffic was building up.

My father said: "Are you beginning to get the feel of Paris? As soon as the opportunity arises I shall take you to one of the highest points in the Ile de la Cité—that is the top of Notre Dame, and from there you will be able to look down on the centre of Paris."

"Thank you," I said, "that would be wonderful."

The Countess was impatient. We had come here for business and she was anxious for us to get on with that.

During the days that followed we looked at several premises—all of which were not quite suitable. My father did take me to a number of interesting places and sometimes the Countess accompanied us, but more often she was looking at shops and studying fashions. She was always bursting with ideas of what she should do.

"She is a very invigorating lady," said my father, "but sometimes it is well to escape from her. Yes?"

I agreed with him. I found his company very pleasant. We were discovering each other. He was very tender to me, always anxious to make up for the years of neglect; and I was beginning to admire him, for he was undoubtedly a man of great ability. The Countess thought so. She demanded a certain amount of his time when they talked business with intensity . . . costings . . . possibilities of starting and increasing business. It was quite fascinating to hear them and I realized more and more that I should never be as dedicated as she was. She had one interest: the success of business; I had others.

I was able to give myself up to the pleasures of Paris. We walked a great deal together—my father and I. We would stroll arm in arm along the banks of the Seine and he would talk to me of the history of the country he loved so much. He showed me the Palace of the Tuileries and that exciting monument which Gustave Eiffel had set up only a few years before. It seemed enormous towering over Paris—its chief landmark now.

"Only a part of the high cost was borne by the state," he said in his practical businesslike manner, "the remainder by Monsieur Eiffel. He hopes, I hear, to get the money back—and of course more in admission fees—over the next twenty years."

"Do you think he will?"

"I am not sure. He is now in trouble over some breach of trust over the Panama Canal. Monsieur Eiffel is a speculator . . . and that can be a dangerous thing to be."

"I do agree. That is why . . ."

"I understand. It is wise to be cautious . . . and rather than speculate and lose it is better not to speculate at all. Then some say . . . nothing venture nothing have."

"There is a homily for every kind of action," I agreed. "That is why it is difficult to choose the right thing to do."

He told me a little about his family—which was, after all, my own.

"My father is a very hard man," he said. "He has ruled the family for many years . . . and he still does. He believes himself to be just and acts according to his beliefs. But he has little pity for anyone . . . and little understanding of human frailties. He is a tragic man, really. He is the most powerful man in Villers-Mûre and surely the most unloved. Everyone goes in fear of him . . . even now, I could tremble before him. I become a different person in his presence. That is why I rarely go to Villers-Mûre now. I have a vineyard bordering on it. It is one of my best vineyards. I think he has a little respect for me now as I have broken away from the family and done well in my own way without his help. He wouldn't admit it . . . but it is there. It is for that reason that I am received at his house."

"After all these years he still remembers!"

"He will remember for ever. He never forgives or forgets. One has to displease him once and that is enough. My sisters and my brothers were all in awe of him . . . still are. The villagers tremble at his approach and get out of the way as quickly as possible."

"He sounds like a monster. Surely nowadays . . ."

"He lives in the past. His great preoccupation is silk. He is the greatest silk producer in the world. That is what he has always aimed to be and that is what he intends to remain."

"He must be getting old now."

"He is seventy."

"And he still behaves like a tyrant."

He nodded. "It is a sort of tradition throughout the village and the factories. After all Villers-Mûre *is* the silk works. People depend on him. If they lose their livelihood they will starve. So he has become the master of them all."

"He sounds like a monster," I said. "I had hoped to meet him one day."

"That is hardly likely. He would never receive you."

"Would he not want to see his granddaughter?"

"He would not recognize you as such. He is strictly religious . . . if you can call what he has religion. He will not tolerate what he calls immorality. He says he is determined to keep Villers-Mûre pure. When the girls marry he calculates the time elapsing between the ceremony and the birth of the first child. If it is not nine months there is an enquiry."

"I do not feel exactly endeared to him."

"That matters not as you will never meet him."

"It's a pity. I should have liked to see Villers-Mûre."

"You will come very close to it when you visit me in my vineyard. My sister who is married and lives close by will welcome you."

"So it is just this old man whom I shall not see?"

He nodded. "Cheer up. You are happier without seeing him. He spends a great deal of time in church . . . goes to Mass every day and twice on Sundays. It is a strange view he has of what is right. It hardly conforms to the Christian Faith. I believe he would like to set up the Inquisition in France. He thinks that all those who are not members of the Catholic Church are sinners. He has never forgiven that branch of the family which broke away all those years ago . . . they were the Huguenots . . . though he is following what they are doing in England. Oh, he is still aware of the family . . . even though they have gone away and adopted another country and even call themselves Sallongers. He will see them when they come to France. He always hopes to bring them back to the Catholic Church."

"It is always very interesting to hear about one's family, and before this I had had only Grand'mère."

"She is a good woman," he said. "She stood up to my father. The only person who ever has. I think he has a grudging admiration for her. He it was who sent you with her into England to be with that branch of the family there who call themselves Sallongers. And now . . . you have married one of them."

Each day I learned more and we grew closer.

Meanwhile the Countess had found exactly what she wanted. It was a shop, small but elegant and close to the Champs-Elysées.

"A good spot," declared the Countess. "It is just the thing."

She was eager for my father to see it, which he did and approved wholeheartedly.

I loved the Champs-Elysées, the Cours la Reine and the magnificent Arc de Triomphe. I loved to see the children at play in the gardens. I thought: I will take Katie there. She shall have a hoop to bowl. It must be beautiful in the summer when the little tables with their brightly coloured umbrellas are brought out.

I was drawn into the excitement of planning for the salon. There were fewer jaunts. My father was almost as excited as the Countess. She herself was working tirelessly. She could not wait to get everything in motion; she chafed against the delays; she wanted to see those splendid creations of Grand'mère's in that window and several seamstresses working away in the room behind the showroom.

Completing negotiations took longer than we had thought it would. We had been away for six weeks. I felt it was an age since I had seen Katie and I was longing to get back. I had bought her several presents including a big doll which was unlike any doll I had seen before. It was an elegant Parisian lady with clothes which came off and on; and when she closed her eyes, which she did when she was held backwards, her beautiful lashes lay luxuriantly against her pink-tinted china cheeks.

It was wonderful to be going home. I was on deck for the first glimpse of the white cliffs.

Then there was the journey to London.

They were waiting for us when we arrived. Katie flung herself into my arms.

"Oh Mama . . . it has been such a long time!"

"We shall never be parted again for so long," I promised her.

And there was Grand'mère ready to welcome me . . . but all was not well. Grand'mère's looks betrayed that.

"How is everything?" I demanded.

"Very well. Very well," she replied too vehemently, so that I knew that she was not telling the truth. Grand'mère's face always betrayed her.

There was a great deal of talk. The Countess was bursting with news of our wonderful find in Paris. Soon we should be opening. The formalities drove her mad. Why could not the buying of premises be a straightforward affair? There had to be this . . . and that . . . and it was all quite maddening.

Cassie was delighted to see us.

"We've been waiting and waiting to hear that you were coming home, haven't we, Katie?"

Katie nodded. She kept close to me holding my hand as though to prevent my going away again. I was very touched.

I had the news from Grand'mère that night after everyone had retired. I went to her room and demanded to know what was wrong.

She looked at me steadily for a few moments and then she said: "Drake is getting married."

"What?" I cried.

"To Julia," she added.

I could only stare at her, all my dreams of the future suddenly dissolving round me.

"She is sending invitations to the wedding. It is to be in two weeks' time."

I could think of nothing to say except "So . . . soon."

"Yes. It seems it was a hasty decision."

She did not meet my gaze.

I said: "Oh . . . well . . . good night."

I had to be alone. I was completely shattered. I felt suddenly numb with misery. I had not realized until then how very much I had cared for him.

* * *

I don't know how I got through the next day. It was hard to keep smiling for Katie. She wanted to know all about Paris. I told her much of what my father had told me. I knew that both the Countess and Cassie were shocked, by the manner in which they meticulously avoided any mention of Drake.

I was bitterly wounded. I thought I should never believe my own instincts again. I had been sure that he loved me.

It was quite impossible to keep up the pretence with Grand'mère.

The next night she came to my room after the household had retired, in the way she always did when there was something to say between us two alone.

She said: "My darling, you need not pretend with me. I know how you feel. This is one big shock to you. I wondered how best to break it. I am afraid I did it clumsily."

"No . . . no, you did not. I had to know quickly."

"And you cared for him?"

I nodded.

"I did not understand. I thought perhaps it was something you knew . . . I thought perhaps you had told him you would not marry him . . . and he had turned to her. I thought you cared for him . . . and I was happy about that for I thought he was a good man. Oh, *mon amour,* do not bottle up these feelings. Let go . . . It's only the old Grand'mère . . . You and I are too close for pretence."

"Oh Grand'mère . . . dear Grand'mère. I feel so . . . so lost and bewildered. I do not know what I feel."

She came to me and held me in her arms rocking me as though I were a baby.

She said: "It will pass. All things pass. It is better that you do not marry such a man. He is clearly fickle . . . not what we thought him."

"Just because he prefers Julia."

"But he showed so clearly that he loved *you.* Then to do this . . . it is not understandable. He came back the day after you left. He called that very day. Cassie saw him. I made her tell me everything that took place. Poor Cassie! She thought she had done some wrong. He was only in the place five minutes. He asked for you. Cassie said: 'She has left for Paris. She has gone with Monsieur St. Allengère and the Countess. They are going to look for premises for a salon there. They are very excited about it.' She said those were her very words.

She said his face went very white. He said: 'I understand. I can't stay. I must leave at once.' She said he would not see me. She said he was not exactly curt but determined to go immediately."

"How very strange. He had always been so friendly with us all."

"He did not call again. And a little while ago there was this announcement of his engagement to Julia. She came here for her wedding costume."

"Oh . . . no!"

"I could not turn down the order. It would have looked so odd. It would have betrayed us. The thing is made now. She's taken it. I hated doing it. But . . . what does it matter anyway?"

"Did she say anything about me?"

"Oh yes. She chattered all the time. Wasn't it wonderful that you were going to Paris at last? She knew it was what you had longed for. Wasn't life wonderful . . . full of surprises? And now she was going to be married to that wonderful Drake Aldringham. She said it would be such fun. She had always wanted to be in politics . . . which she would be with Drake. It would involve a great deal of entertaining. Every man wanted a woman behind him . . . the right sort of woman. She was going to devote herself to his career."

"She is certainly a practised hostess."

"I think that is why he is marrying her."

"Do you think he would be so calculating?"

She nodded slowly.

"We have been quite mistaken in him and this is a blessing in disguise. Julia went on about you. She said you should not remain a widow. 'Do you know what I plan to do?' she asked. 'I am going to find a husband for her.' "

I covered my face with my hands.

"I know, my dearest. There was something about her . . . something malicious. Oh, I do not trust her. She is what you say . . . a snake in the grass, that one. Never mind, ma chérie. They deserve each other. There will be little happiness there."

"They will understand each other," I said. "I obviously did not understand him."

"He is marrying Julia for her money."

"Somehow I can't believe that, Grand'mère."

"It is the general belief. Lady Travers was in here a few days ago. You know how she talks. She knows everything that is going on.

Naturally she talked about Julia's coming marriage. 'Poor Julia,' she said, 'past the first flush of youth but still of an amorous nature. She was always angling for Drake Aldringham, and at last she has made him see what she can do for him.' I said, innocently, 'What can she do?' 'Drake has the seeds of something in him,' she said. 'He is ministerial material . . . might even aspire to the premiership . . . most of them do. Julia knows this. Wouldn't she like to be the P.M.'s wife! She sees herself as a Mary Anne Disraeli or a Catherine Gladstone. I am sure she would not be in the least like either of them. But at least she has money. And that is what Drake lacks. His family are rich enough but Drake has a special pride and wants to get on without parental assistance.' I said, 'But he doesn't mind marrying someone for it.' 'That, my dear Madame Cleremont, is quite another matter.' I said I could not see that but she waved that aside. 'She will be able to entertain all the right people. Although she hasn't an inkling of what politics are about she will be an adept at pressing him onwards. We shall see. So this is the perfect timing—with an election in sight. The people love a wedding. Julia wants Drake and Drake wants Julia's money—the right combination for a successful marriage. She will have to stop her drinking. She is going too far with that. But perhaps Drake will be able to stop her.' "

"Grand'mère," I said. "I can't believe Drake is marrying her for her money."

"I can think of no other reason for his doing so."

"Oh, Grand'mère," I said, "what am I to do?"

She stroked my hair. "There is only one thing you can do, *ma chérie,* and that is go on. Remember how it was when Philip died? You thought you had reached the lowest then. But time helped, did it not? And here there seemed a chance of happiness . . . but it was not to be. Now we have the Paris project. That is going to make us all very busy; and there is darling Katie who is so happy because you are back. The poor child has been moping and asking every day when you were coming home. He has failed you, Lenore, my love, but there are those who love you here."

I wept a little. I felt I could not hide my feeling from Grand'mère. She brought me one of her soothing concoctions and insisted on sitting with me until I slept.

* * *

The Countess could talk of nothing but Paris. She was so busy making plans that she did not notice the change in me—or perhaps I was good at hiding my feelings.

Katie was, as ever, a solace to me. She wanted me to tell her more of Paris. "I shall be there, shall I not?"

I said she certainly would. I told her about the children playing with their hoops in the gardens.

My father had returned to Paris to continue with the negotiations. I should join him there with the Countess and Grand'mère. Cassie would stay behind and we had a good manageress who could look after everything for a few weeks.

Our invitations arrived for Julia's wedding.

"I can't go," I said.

Grand'mère was silent; and I knew that meant that she thought I should. I tackled her with this.

She replied: "You cannot . . . how you say . . . wear the heart on the jacket for everyone to see. Cassie must go. She is the sister . . . and what of you? You were brought up with them. People will say, 'And where is Lenore?' And . . . 'Was she not angling for the young man herself? Is it jealousy then . . . envy? It is certainly odd that she is not at the wedding.' "

"It is monstrous that people should know so much of our private lives."

"Not odd at all . . . they being so observant and we living as we do."

"If I go . . ."

"I will make you a beautiful costume for the occasion. Velvet I think . . . trimmed with sable. I have a beautiful length of blue velvet . . . such a lovely shade . . . not too bright . . . subtle. It will suit you to perfection. A small hat with an ostrich feather . . . I know the thing."

"I shall hate going."

"I know. Just put in an appearance at the reception. You can come away quickly. The press will be there. After all he is a rising politician and she is well known for her parties in social circles. 'The bride looked exquisite in her Lenore costume . . . One notable absence was Lenore herself who is a close connection of the bride.' That must not be. Lenore must be there for it will be noticed."

"You are right, Grand'mère."

She nodded, pleased.

I had felt since I had heard the news that I was living in a dream from which I was going to wake up. Drake was not going to marry Julia . . . He couldn't . . . not after all the signs he had given me. I thought often of our meetings in the park and how they had enlivened the days. And now . . . that was over. Those encounters which had meant so much to me had meant nothing to him.

On the wedding day I dressed in my blue velvet and set the little hat with the ostrich feather on my head.

Grand'mère and the Countess clapped their hands when they saw me.

"Perfect . . . perfect . . ." murmured the Countess.

She herself was elegantly arrayed, of course, for she would be at the reception. Julia was her protégée; she had seen her into her first marriage and was, I knew, dismayed, now that she was embarking on the second. Like Grand'mère she had designated Drake for me.

I did not go to the church. That was something I could not have endured. The reception was held in Julia's drawing room which was large enough for the occasion.

I glimpsed Drake standing beside her helping her to cut the cake and while the speeches were made and the toasts drunk. It struck me that he did not look very happy although he was smiling.

I felt my heart leap in dismay when he caught my eyes from across the room. I lowered mine. I could not trust myself to look at him.

I thought: I must get away. I looked for Cassie. She was talking with a group of friends. I would make my way to her and ask her if she were ready to leave.

Then he was at my side.

"Lenore," he said.

"Oh . . ." I steeled myself to look at him. "Drake. Congratulations."

"Mine . . . to you."

"To me?"

"On the Paris opening."

"Oh, you have heard of that?"

"Oh yes. Everyone is talking about it. What a stroke of luck for you."

"Yes . . . isn't it?"

"So good to have rich friends."

"My father will have a stake in the business."

"Your *father?*"

"Surely you knew. Didn't Cassie tell you when you called?"

"Cassie said you were in Paris . . . getting things going over there. I didn't know about your father."

"You saw him in the park."

He looked bewildered.

"Don't you remember? He watched me several times. We noticed him. Julia called him my admirer."

He repeated: "Your father."

"It is a most romantic story. I had never seen him before. My mother died when I was born. They weren't married and his family sent Grand'mère to England with me."

Again he said: "Your father . . ."

"What's the matter, Drake, you look stunned."

"Julia said . . ." He stared at me. "We must talk. We must get out of here."

"You can't leave your wedding reception. In a little while you will be leaving for your honeymoon."

He said quietly: "I had no idea that the man was your father. I thought he was . . . your admirer . . . that you were taking money from him for this Paris project which was of so much importance to you."

"You thought . . ."

"Yes," he said, "that he was your lover."

"What an idea! How did you get it? Surely you did not think . . . How could you? I hesitated to take the money from my father but Grand'mère and the Countess persuaded me . . . and he was so eager because he was ashamed of what he had done all those years ago and the fact that he had only just come back into my life."

"This is . . . impossible." He looked round helplessly. "What have I done?"

I was beginning to understand. He had believed that I had a lover, that I had become the mistress of my admirer in the park in order to advance my business. And how had he come to accept that calumny? Because Julia had told him.

I hated her then with her highly coloured face beaming triumphantly at the guests. She had won.

I felt stifled. "I want to get away," I said.

"No," he insisted. "I have to talk to you. I have to explain."

"There is nothing more to explain, Drake."

"There is everything to explain. You must have known."

"Known what?"

"That it was you I cared for. I have been such an idiot. I wanted to tell you. I thought you were still hankering for Philip . . . that it was so much on your mind that you could not decide to marry again. It was you I wanted. What am I going to do?"

"You will be a good husband to Julia," I said, and added a trifle bitterly, "She will give the right parties and you will meet influential people. That is what an ambitious politician should do. Perhaps in time she will be able to say as Lord Beaconsfield did: 'He married me for my money but if he could do it again it would be for love.' "

"Money!" he cried. "There is an obsession with money!"

"It is a very useful commodity."

"You think I married her for her money!"

"As you thought I had given myself for it."

"There has been a terrible misunderstanding. Oh, Lenore, we must meet."

"I don't think we should meet alone."

"There is so much I have to tell you."

"I know that you thought I had taken a rich lover in order to set up business in Paris. That you could think I could do such a thing appals me. You could not have known me at all. I understand your shock. And then you just say, 'She has bartered herself for money, and so will I.' You thought your method was respectable . . . more so than the one you attributed to me—but even if it were so you would have been equally immoral in my eyes."

"Lenore . . ."

I said: "We are becoming too vehement. This is supposed to be a lighthearted party. You should be telling me about your honeymoon. Where is it going to be? How you hope the weather will be clement . . . and so on, and so on . . ."

"When I heard," he went on, "I was shattered. I called at the house. It seemed to confirm what Julia had told me."

"But Julia *knew* he was my father. She knew he was putting up the money."

"How could she . . . ?" he murmured. "I shall hate her now."

"You are speaking of your wife."

"Yes, God help me."

"How could you!" I cried. "Oh . . . how could you?"

"It happened," he said. "I was . . . shattered . . . bewildered . . . maddened . . . when I called at your place and was told you had gone to Paris . . . with that man. I knew the Countess was with you. I imagined that she would be arranging the premises while you were making love with your lover to pay for the venture . . ."

"Drake!"

"I know . . . now. I should have thought more clearly. I walked about the streets for a long time . . . trying to tell myself that I had had a lucky escape."

"As I have been telling myself . . ." I said.

"How could we, Lenore . . . either of us!"

I said nothing and he continued: "I went to Julia. I dined with her. I drank too much. So did Julia. She often does. It seemed to me the best way of forgetting. Next morning I found myself in her bed. I was so ashamed. I wanted to get right away. I went back to Swaddingham. I stayed there trying to get the episode out of my mind . . . She wrote to me. There was going to be a child . . . the result of that night. There was only one thing I could do . . . so I did it."

"Oh Drake . . . what a mess we have made of everything."

"What shall we do?"

"There is only one thing we can do. We must go on from here. I am a little happier now knowing that you did love me . . . that comforts me a little. I was not mistaken in that."

"I love you. I have always loved you. It started at that moment when I brought you out of the mausoleum."

"This is so strange," I said. "Here we are declaring our love at your wedding reception when you have just been married to someone else. Was there ever such a situation before?"

He took my hand and pressed it.

"Lenore, I shall never forget you."

"That is something we must do as quickly as possible . . . forget each other."

"It is impossible."

"Hello, Lenore." It was Julia. "Is all well? Drake is looking after you?"

"I must go," I said coolly.

"So busy with the Paris project! We understand, don't we, Drake? We shall have to go and change soon."

He was silent. There was a look of abject misery on his face, and when she took his arm I saw him shrink.

I said: "I will go and find Cassie. Goodbye." And I left them.

Carsonne

The Paris salon was my salvation. For a whole year I worked steadily. I did not want to think about Drake. Grand'mère was as ever a constant solace, always thinking of what was best for me. The Countess briskly refused to allow me to be sorry for myself. The Paris salon was, in her eyes, a more worthwhile acquisition than a husband. My father was comforting, too. He was so eager to make up for all the years when we had not known each other. And there was Katie. She was so excited by what was going on, and to see her little face alight with interest and listen to the endless questions, made me feel that whatever my loss, I had a great deal to live for.

They nursed me through that time, and the days became tolerable although at night I would feel sad and find myself brooding on what might have been. I had loved Philip, youthfully, romantically. There had not been time for us to discover the flaws in our natures which living together might have disclosed. We had existed in a state of euphoric idealism. Could it have gone on like that? Perhaps not. But our love would always remain in our minds as it had been . . . not as it might have turned out to be. And he had died tragically, unexpectedly . . . and no one knew exactly why; and now when there had seemed the chance of a more mature relationship with a man whom I admired, respected and loved, events had been so contrived that I had lost him, too. Sometimes I felt that I was doomed to lose my lovers and to bring disaster on them. Philip had died by a gunshot wound and Drake had fallen into what could be a worse fate; he was married to a woman whom he hated.

I must try to forget that my dream was shattered and start again.

In a way I was lucky, for this project which demanded my deeply involved attention would help me.

Grand'mère had decided that it would be a good idea if I went to Paris. We had a good manageress in London and with Cassie to help we could leave her in charge. That meant that Grand'mère, the Countess and I, with Katie, went to Paris.

From time to time the Countess would return to London to make sure that everything was working smoothly there and then she would come back to us.

Katie was delighted with Paris. I had engaged two governesses for her—one French, one English, for as she might be living in France for some time she must become proficient in the language, but at the same time she must not neglect her English studies. Miss Price was earnest and conscientious and just a little prim, a contrast to Mademoiselle Leclerc who was voluble and high-spirited. She came from Lyons where, she assured me, the best French was spoken.

Katie was rather a serious child. She greatly enjoyed the company of Mademoiselle but I think she had a greater respect for Miss Price who imposed strict rules. Katie's loving nature enabled her to adjust herself to the two and I was amused to see how she changed in their company; she could be quite sedate with Miss Price and frivolous with Mademoiselle Leclerc. I was pleased with the arrangement.

With Mademoiselle she would take her hoop into the gardens; they would ride in steamers along the Seine; she would make the acquaintance of other children there and was soon able to chat with them. With Miss Price she took quiet walks along the river, looking at the books on the stalls and visiting places of historic interest. Miss Price made a point of studying the history connected with the places they visited and afterwards Katie would pass on what she had learned to me and I was pleased and gratified by the knowledge she was acquiring.

There were a few initial difficulties to be smoothed out, but the Countess was adept at dealing with such matters and sooner than I had expected we were establishing ourselves.

I thought of home. In the election which had taken place soon after Drake's wedding Gladstone had triumphed though without the large majority for which he had hoped and—much to the Queen's disgust—went to Osborne to kiss her hand. "A deluded old man of eighty-two,"

she called him, "trying to govern England with his miserable demo-
crats. He was quite ridiculous."

"This will be a step up for a certain party," commented the Countess.

I wondered what he was doing. Whether he was finding Julia's
social expertise a compensation for a lack of love.

"But they'll be out soon," said the Countess. "It's Gladstone's obsession with Ireland that will be their downfall."

I used to wonder a great deal about the child who had been so
casually conceived. I wondered whether it would prove a consolation
to Drake. It was some time before I heard that there had never been a
child—so the very reason why Drake had married Julia had not existed.

I longed for news. I was thinking of Drake a good deal. I heard that
Gladstone's Home Rule Bill though it had passed through the Commons had been rejected by the Lords.

Another year passed and I was still thinking of Drake. We were so
busy that there was time for little else beside the salon.

My father paid periodic visits to Paris. He was a great help to us—
not only financially—for he was as eager as any of us to see the business a success.

Katie was a delight to him—especially when she could chatter in
his own language. He was constantly urging me to visit his vineyards.
Katie would love it, he said. And how right he was.

He had several but his favourite was the one in Villers-Carsonne,
which was very close to Villers-Mûre. I had an idea that this was the
one he loved best because it was close to his old home and the country
was the scene of his childhood. His voice softened when he spoke of it;
but it was not to it that he took us first, but to one not so far from
Paris.

He thought Katie would be interested in the *vendange.* In fact, she
was quite enchanted, and she thoroughly enjoyed those weeks we
spent there. She was learning to ride. My father set one of the grooms
to teach her and when she was not joining in the harvesting of the
grapes, she was riding with the groom. My memory went back to
those days when she had ridden round the paddock at Swaddingham
with Drake and I was sad watching and thinking of what might have
been.

Her happy face was some consolation to me. It was a great occasion when she was let off the leading rein. My father said she was a born horsewoman and as much at home on a horse's back as on her own two feet. He would ride with her round the vineyard—he on his big black horse, she on her pony while he told her about the grapes, answering her interminable questions with pleasure; and afterwards she would come and tell me everything.

This was one of the more old-fashioned of his vineyards and here they trod the grapes in the ancient manner. I think he had wanted Katie to see this and it was his reason for bringing us here.

He would talk to her as though she were an adult—which won her heart—explaining to her that at most of his vineyards he used a machine to crush the grapes. It had two wooden cylinders turning in opposite directions and in this machine not a single grape escaped. But some liked the old ways best and preferred to do what had been done through the centuries.

What a night that was! The grapes, which had been laid out for ten days on a level floor to take the sun, were put into troughs, and the villagers sang as they danced on them, crushing them while the juice trickled through into the vats which had been placed below to catch it.

It was magic to Katie, and perhaps to all of us. My father's eyes were sentimental as he watched her—her hair flying loose, her eyes alight with excitement.

"You must always come to the *vendange,*" he said.

Katie was reluctant to return to Paris, but soon she forgot the regrets and was content again.

I remember the day when one of our English clients came to Paris. She was Lady Bonner, a noted hostess, who was said to know more of other people's private lives than any other woman in London. She was voluble and always eager to impart the latest scandal.

She knew of my connection with Julia and asked if I had heard from her lately.

I said that we had not.

"Oh dear me! Quite a scandal. Poor Drake, what a mistake he has made! Of course, it was her money. He needed that. He is an ambitious man. Mind you, he comes from a wealthy family, but he has that sort of pride that says No, I will make my way on my own. Making his way meant marrying money . . . and so he did that. But what a burden the poor man found he had taken on. She drinks . . . you know."

All I said was: "Oh?"

"Oh yes, my dear. Surely you knew. It was always a problem with her and now it has become really serious."

"There was to be a child . . ." I began. "Perhaps having lost it . . ."

"A child! Good Heavens, no! That's not Julia's line at all. It was this function. She was so intoxicated . . . She staggered when she was talking to Lord Rosebery . . . and if Drake hadn't been there to catch her, she would have fallen flat on her face. You can imagine the talk. Poor Drake was overcome with embarrassment. This could cost him a post in the government . . . if there ever is a stable one. He thought her money would help . . . and so it would if she had been the right sort of wife. They all think they are going to get a Mary Anne Disraeli. He made a big mistake, poor man, and it may well cost him his career."

"But he is an able politician," I protested.

"Only half of the battle, my dear."

She went on talking of the London scene but I was only half listening. I was thinking of Drake who had blundered into such a disaster.

Poor Drake, he was no happier than I was—in fact he had not the consolations which I was so grateful for.

Cassie came to Paris now and then and often the Countess went to London. We were now making a profit in Paris and business was flourishing in London where our name had been greatly enhanced. We were a big name in the world of fashion.

Three years had passed since Drake's marriage to Julia and Katie was now eleven years old.

One day my father said: "I am going to take you to Villers-Carsonne."

He had often seemed a little secretive when he mentioned it and I had the feeling that there was some reason why he was not eager to talk of the place, let alone take us there.

Now he seemed to have come to the conclusion that the time was ripe. He sought an opportunity, when we were alone, to talk to me.

"You may have wondered," he said, "why I have not suggested you come to Villers-Carsonne before."

I admitted that I had.

"It is near the place where I was brought up. It is my favourite vineyard. There we produce our best wines. I am there frequently, but I have never taken you there. Why? you asked."

"I did not," I said, "but I will."

He hesitated for a while and then he said: "This is because I have much to tell you. Your grandfather, Alphonse St. Allengère, is well known throughout that part of the country. They say that he *is* Villers-Mûre. It may be difficult for you to understand but Villers-Mûre resembles a feudal community. In Villers-Mûre my father is the lord of all, the *grand seigneur.* Monsieur le Patron. He is as powerful as a medieval king. It is a restricted community. Almost everyone depends on the silk manufactory; he owns that manufactory; and therefore they owe their livelihoods to him."

"He sounds formidable."

He nodded gravely. "He would not receive you, Lenore."

"I realize that he does not accept me as his granddaughter. But should that prevent my going to your vineyard? That does not belong to him, does it?"

"It is mine. He does see me when I am there. Because I have done well and not through his help he has a certain respect for me. I am an undutiful son, he implies, but grudgingly, he allows me to call on him."

"I think I should be inclined to refrain from calling."

"One does not. He has a certain quality . . . and as much as one resents his attitude one finds oneself obeying."

"I am quite prepared not to be received."

"My sister Ursule will be delighted to meet you."

"Will she be allowed to?"

"Ursule does not live at the house in Villers-Mûre. She lives in Villers-Carsonne. She was disowned long ago. She defied him, you see."

"Forgive me, *mon père,* but your father seems to be a man it is better not to have to meet."

He nodded. "Ursule was disowned shortly after I was. Louis Sagon, her husband now, came to the house to restore my father's pictures. He painted a portrait of Ursule and fell in love with her—and she with him. My father had other plans for her. He forbade the match. They eloped and as a result she was cut off from the house. She married Louis Sagon and they settled in Villers-Carsonne. My father has never seen her since. She was more courageous than I was."

"And she is happily married?"

"Yes. She has a son and a daughter. She will want to meet you. We see a great deal of each other when I go to the vineyard."

"So that was two of you who were disowned."

"Yes. Two of us disappointed him. My elder brother, René, however was a comfort to him. He is taking over a great deal of the work at the manufactory, although of course my father is still head of affairs there. René is a good son. And he has produced two sons . . . and there were two daughters . . . twins . . . One of them, Heloïse, died."

"Long ago?"

"Twelve years or so."

"She must have been young to die."

"Just seventeen. She . . . drowned herself. It was a great blow to us all . . . and especially to Adèle, her twin sister. They had always been close."

"Why did she do this?"

"Some love affair. It was all rather mysterious."

"It seems to me to be a very sad household, but then I suppose it would be with a man like your father ruling over it."

He agreed sombrely. "I want you to be prepared before you come."

"I shall not think of my grandfather. If he does not wish to see me, then I have no desire to see him."

"Ursule has expressed her eagerness to meet you. She is always urging me to bring you."

"Then I shall look forward to meeting her. She is, of course, my aunt."

"You will like her, and Louis Sagon. He is immersed in his work and appears to have little interest in anything else, but you will like him. He is a quiet, gentle, kindly man."

"I shall be content with meeting them—and forget all about my ogre of a grandfather."

In spite of the fact that he had prepared me in a way for what I must expect, my father seemed to view the proposed visit with some trepidation.

I said goodbye to Grand'mère and the Countess, and Katie and I set off with my father.

* * *

We travelled by train and it was a long journey from Paris. Katie was in a state of high excitement. She kept to the window, my father beside her, pointing out landmarks as we went along. We passed through towns and farmlands, past rivers and hills. There was great interest when we saw vineyards and my father would cast a knowledgeable eye over them; we glimpsed several ancient castles—grey-stoned with the pepper-pot towers which were such a feature of the country. My father was growing a little subdued as we drew nearer and nearer to his birthplace. I fancied he was suffering a certain uneasiness and I wondered whether he was asking himself whether his father would hear of my presence and what his reaction would be.

They were to send a carriage to the station of Carsonne to take us to the house. He told me that they would know exactly when we should arrive as there was only one train a day.

It was a small station.

"We are lucky to have it," he said. "The Comte de Carsonne insisted on it. He is a very influential man. It was something of a fight, I believe, but the Comte usually gets his way in such matters."

As we came into the station my father waved his hand towards a man in dark blue livery who was standing there.

"Alfredo!" he called. He turned to me. "He is Italian. Some of the servants are. We are very close to the borders and that makes us somewhat Italianate in certain ways."

Alfredo was at the door taking the luggage.

"This is my daughter, Madame Sallonger," said my father, "and my granddaughter, Mademoiselle Katie Sallonger."

Alfredo bowed. We smiled at him and he took our bags.

My father was evidently a man of some importance in the neighbourhood if the respect which was shown him was any indication. Caps were touched and welcomes offered.

Then we were in the carriage driving along.

The vineyard was spread out before us. People were already gathering the grapes and we saw the labourers with their oziers, so carefully poised as not to damage the grapes with too much motion.

My father said: "We are in good time for the *vendange.*" At which Katie expressed her pleasure.

Ahead I saw the *château.* It stood on what looked like a square platform surrounded by deep dykes.

"How grand!" I exclaimed.

"Château Carsonne," said my father.

"And does this Comte . . . the one who insisted on bringing the railway to Carsonne . . . live here?"

"The very same."

"Does he actually reside there?"

"Oh yes. I believe he has a house in Paris . . . and probably in other places, but this is the ancestral home of the Carsonnes."

"Shall we meet them, these Carsonnes?"

"It is hardly likely. Our families are not on the best of terms."

"Is there some sort of feud?"

"Hardly that. My father's land borders on theirs. There is a sort of armed neutrality . . . not open warfare . . . but both sides ready to go into action at the least offence from the other."

"It sounds very warlike to me."

"It is hard for you with your English upbringing to understand the fierce nature of the people here. It is the Latin blood . . . and although you were born with it, your upbringing has evidently brought down its boiling point."

I laughed. "It all sounds very interesting."

"We shall soon see my place. Oh, look. Ahead of you."

Katie leaped up and down with excitement. My father put an arm about her and held her against him.

It was like a miniature *château* with the now familiar pepper-pot towers. It was of grey stone and there were green shutters at the windows, several of which had wrought-iron balconies. It was charming.

As we drew up I saw a man and a woman standing at the door as though to receive us.

"There is Ursule," said my father. "Ursule, my dear, how good of you to come over to greet us. And you, Louis." He turned to me. "This is your aunt Ursule. And this is her husband Louis." He smiled at them. "Lenore," he said, "and her daughter, Katie."

"Welcome to Carsonne," said Ursule. She was dark-haired and not unlike my father. There was an air of kindliness about her and I liked her immediately. Louis was, as my father had said, a very gentle man. He took my hands and said how pleased he was to see me.

"We have been urging your father for a long time to bring you here," said Ursule. "Come along in. We live half a mile away. I had to come over to welcome you."

We went into the house and were in a long panelled hall with a great fireplace round which gleamed brass ornaments.

"I have arranged which room Lenore shall have," said Ursule. "I thought it better not to leave it to the servants, and Katie shall have the one immediately next to hers."

"That is thoughtful of you," I said. "We like to be close."

Katie was taking everything in as Ursule took us up to our rooms. Mine was low-ceilinged with pale green drapes and bedspread and there were hints of green in the light grey carpet. It was a charming restful room and what delighted me was the communicating door between it and Katie's.

In mine there was a balcony. I opened the french windows and stepped out. In the distance I could see the towers of the Château Carsonne and the terracotta coloured roofs of the houses in the little town closeby. And there below me were the ever-present vines.

I felt touched in some odd way. Beyond the *château* lay Villers-Mûre—the mulberries and the manufactory . . . the place where I had first seen the light of day. I suppose one must be moved by the sight of one's birthplace, particularly when one has never seen it before.

Hot water was brought and we washed and changed our clothes. Katie kept exclaiming at something new she had discovered.

She said: "Isn't it exciting to find a grandfather in the park? You're always finding out something about him. Other people's grandfathers are rather *dull*. They've been there all the time."

"Some people might like it that way," I commented.

"I don't. I like it our way."

After we had eaten a meal in the courtyard we were taken back into the house to meet the servants. There were quite a number of them. Ursule explained everything to me as we went along.

"We eat in the courtyard until it gets too cold. We like the fresh air. And it can be very hot sometimes. Georges—your father's son . . . your half-brother really . . . comes here quite frequently. He has his own place now about fifteen kilometres away. His sister Brigitte has recently married and lives in Lyons. I daresay you'll meet them sometimes. I am so glad you and my brother are together. He has never forgotten your existence and when your grandmother came here and sought him out he was so excited . . . so happy. So it is wonderful to see you here."

"He has been so good to me."

"He feels he can never make up."

"He has to me . . . more than I can say."

She asked if I could ride and I told her that I could.

"That is good. It is not easy to get around any other way and you should see a little of the countryside."

"I should like to see Villers-Mûre."

She did not speak for a moment. Then she said: "I haven't been there for over twenty years."

"Yet it is so near."

"Did you know the story? I displeased my father when I married. It is not forgotten."

"It seems . . . terrible . . . all that time."

"That's the way it is."

"Have you never tried to become friendly again?"

"It is clear that you do not know my father. He is a man who prides himself on keeping his word. He has said he will never see me again— and that is what he will do."

"He must miss a great deal in life. He must be very unhappy."

She shook her head. "He has what he wants. He is the Seigneur of Villers-Mûre. He is the king in his domain and all must obey him or suffer the penalty he inflicts upon them for disobedience. I believe he is content. Well, I have never regretted choosing the way I did."

"So you never go there?"

She shook her head. "Never."

After Ursule had shown us the house, my father took us on a little tour round the vineyards. We ate once more in the courtyard and we sat long over the meal until it was dark. The night air was scented and as we sat watching the stars appear in the sky, a bat flew back and forth . . . low just over our heads; and we still sat on.

My father, I knew, was very content, that at last we had come. Ursule and Louis were staying for a few days. "To see you settled in," said Ursule. "Your father needs a hostess at times and this is one of them."

We talked desultorily about the little town of Carsonne which was almost on the borders of Italy, and where the air was just right for the cultivation of the grape.

We were growing drowsy on my father's best wine which he had had brought up from his cellar for the occasion and I noticed that

Katie was finding it difficult to keep her eyes open, so I suggested we go to bed.

I saw Katie into her bed. "I'll leave the communicating door open," I said. "Then we shall be close."

I think she was rather glad of that. Perhaps she felt that there was something rather eerie about the countryside after dark. By the time I had tucked her in and kissed her goodnight she was almost asleep.

Then I went to my room. I undressed, but before getting into bed I opened the windows and went out onto the balcony. It looked dark and mysterious—the stars brilliant in the clear air; and seeming closer than it did by day. There it was—the Château Carsonne, arrogant, mighty, menacing in a way. I found it difficult to withdraw my gaze from it.

Finally I went to bed but I found sleep elusive. I kept thinking of all the events of the day and when I did sleep it was to be haunted by dreams in which my wicked grandfather loomed large and the Château Carsonne was a prison in which he had decided to shut me up because I had dared come into his territory against his wishes.

When I awoke the dream lingered. It made me feel very uneasy and the first thing I did on rising was to go out to the balcony and look at the Château Carsonne.

* * *

A few days passed with rapid speed. Ursule and Louis departed, Ursule insisting that we visit them soon. I assured her that there was little I should like more. We were good friends already.

"We are always in a little turmoil here at the time of the *vendange*," said my father. "An excitement grips the household. It is the culmination of a year's hard work . . . all the trials we have undergone . . . all the anxieties as to whether or not there would be a good harvest or no harvest at all . . . that is over, and this is the achievement."

"It's understandable."

"If you knew what we have suffered. It has been a little damp this year and we have had to keep a watch for mildew. Apart from that it has been a fairly good season. And now it is over and everything is being gathered in. Hence the jubilation and the anticipation of the great climax."

There were horses for both Katie and me and we loved to ride round exploring. Katie was quite a good rider by now, but at this time her chief interest was in the wine harvest.

She liked to go off with my father and he liked to have her with him; this gave me an opportunity to ride out alone.

I knew that Katie was safe and happy with my father and so I could give myself up to the complete enjoyment of exploring the countryside.

It was some four days after our arrival when the whole countryside seemed to be taking its afternoon siesta. I donned my riding habit and went down to the stables.

My father had suggested I use a certain chestnut mare. She was smallish and not over-frisky, but at the same time she had spirit. We suited each other; and that afternoon I rode out on her.

I found myself going in that direction where lay Villers-Mûre. There was one point where I could ride up to the top of a ridge of hills and look down on the valley. It was becoming a favourite spot of mine and I knew that one day I should be tempted to ride down the slopes and into that village.

On this afternoon I went to this spot. From where I was I could see the mulberry bushes and the manufactory with its glass windows in the distance. It did not look like a factory. A small stream ran past it and there was a bridge over it on which creepers grew; it was very picturesque. I could see the towers of the big house and I wondered what my grandfather was doing at that moment and whether he was aware that his granddaughter was close by.

One day, I thought, I *will* ride down there. I will find the house where Grand'mère lived with her daughter; and I wondered if my mother had ever come up here and stood on this very spot, where she and my father had met, where I had been conceived. This was the place of my birth and I was forbidden to go to it.

I turned away. The sun was hot this afternoon. Away to my right the thicket looked cool and inviting and I could smell the redolence of the pines. I turned the chestnut towards the thicket. The trees grew more closely together as I progressed. It was beautiful . . . the smell of damp earth . . . the sudden coolness and the scent of the trees. I rode on deeper into the wood. I wondered how far it extended. It had seemed quite a small wood when I had first seen it and I was sure that if I went on I should emerge soon.

I heard the bark of a dog. Someone was in the woods. Or perhaps it was just a dog. The barking was coming nearer. It sounded fierce, angry. Then suddenly two Alsatian dogs were visible through the trees. When they saw me they gave what sounded like a yelp of triumph and they were bounding towards me. They stopped abruptly, looking straight at me, and their barking was truly menacing. I felt the chestnut quiver. She drew her head back. She was very uneasy.

"Go away," I cried to the dogs forcing a note of authority into my voice which seemed only to enfuriate them the more, for their barking intensified and they looked as though they were ready to spring at me.

To my relief a man had come riding through the trees. He pulled up sharply and stared at me.

Then he said: "Fidele. Napoleon. Come here."

The dogs stopped their barking immediately and went to stand beside his horse.

In those few seconds I noticed a good deal about him. He was riding a magnificent black horse and he sat it as though he were part of it. He reminded me of a centaur. His eyes were very dark and heavily lidded and his eyebrows were firmly marked. His hair under his riding hat was almost black. His skin was fair which was one of the reasons why he was so striking. It made such a contrast to dark hair and eyes. His nose was what I call aggressive—long, patrician, reminding me of the pictures I had seen of François Premier. His mouth was the most expressive part of his face. I imagined it could be cruel and at the same time humorous. He was one of the most striking looking men I had ever seen and that was the reason why I could take in so much in such a short time.

I knew at once that he was a man of power who set himself above others and he was as accustomed to obedience from those about him as he was from his dogs. He was now studying me with those strongly marked eyebrows slightly raised. His gaze was penetrating and I felt uncomfortable beneath it. I was vaguely irritated by the intensity of his inspection and I could not refrain from showing my displeasure.

I said: "I suppose these are your dogs."

"These are my dogs and these are my woods and you are trespassing."

"I am sorry."

"We prosecute trespassers."

"I had no idea that I was doing so."

"There are notices."

"I am afraid I did not see them. I am a stranger here."

"That does not excuse you, Mademoiselle."

"Madame," I said.

He bowed ironically. "A thousand apologies, *Madame*. May I know your name?"

"Madame Sallonger."

"St. Allengère. Then you are connected with the silk merchants."

"I did not say St. Allengère but Sallonger. That was my husband's name."

"And your husband . . . he is here with you now?"

"My husband is dead."

"I am sorry."

"Thank you. I will now leave your woods and apologise for the trouble I have caused if you and your dogs will allow me to pass."

"I will escort you."

"There is no need. I am sure I can find my way."

"It is easy to lose oneself in the woods."

"They did not seem to me to be so very extensive."

"Nevertheless . . . if you will allow me."

"Of course. You will want to make sure that I leave your property at once. I can only say I am sorry for the intrusion. It shall not happen again."

He approached me. I patted the chestnut and murmured words of reassurance. She was still disturbed by the dogs.

"She seems restive," he said.

"She does not like your Fidele and Napoleon."

"They are a very dutiful pair."

"They look vicious."

"They could be in the course of their duty."

"Which is to keep trespassers from your land."

"That among other things. Come this way."

He rode beside me and we went through the woods, the dogs docile now, accepting me and the chestnut as approved by their master.

He said: "Tell me, Madame Sallonger, are you visiting this place?"

"I am here with my father, Henri St. Allengère."

"Then you *are* one of them."

"I suppose so."

"I see. Then I believe I know exactly who you are. You are that one whose grandmother took her to England which accounts for your accent and that somewhat foreign aspect."

"I'm sorry for the accent."

"Don't be. It is charming. You speak our language fluently, but there is just that little betrayal which gives you away. I like it. As for your foreign ways . . . I like those too. *Vive la différence.*"

I smiled.

"Now," he went on, "you are asking yourself, who is this arrogant man who has dared accost me and driven me from his woods? Is that so?"

"Well, who is he?"

"Not a very pleasant character, as you will have gathered."

He was looking at me expectantly but I did not answer. That amused him. He laughed. I turned to look at him. He was like a different person now. His eyes were brilliant . . . full of laughter. His mouth had changed too: it had softened.

"And you would be perfectly right," he said. "My name is Gaston de la Tour."

"And you live hereabouts?"

"Yes, close by."

"And you own the woods of which you are very proud and eager to keep to yourself."

"Correct," he agreed. "And I resent others using them."

"They are so beautiful," I said. "It is a shame to keep them to yourself."

"It is because they are beautiful that I want to. You see, I am entirely mean-spirited."

"What harm do people do in your woods?"

"Little, I suppose. But let me think. They might damage the trees . . . start fires. But the real reason is that I like what is mine to be mine alone. Do you think that is reprehensible?"

"I think it is a common human failing."

"You are a student of nature?"

"Aren't you?"

"I am self-absorbed . . . a quite impossible creature really."

"You have one virtue."

"Pray tell me what good you have discovered in me?"

"You know that you are . . . your own words . . . quite impossible. To know oneself is a great virtue and so few of us have it."

"What a charming trespasser you are! I am so glad you took it into your head to come into my woods. Please tell me, Madame Sallonger, how long will you stay among us?"

"We have come for the *vendange.*"

"We?"

"My daughter and I."

"So you have a daughter."

"Yes. She is eleven years old."

"We have something in common. I have a son. He is twelve years old. So we are both . . . parents. There is something else. You are a widow. I am a widower. Is that not interesting?"

"I don't know. Is it? There must be a great many widows and widowers in the world. I suppose they meet fairly frequently."

"You are so prosaic . . . calm . . . logical. Is that the English in you?"

"Actually I am French by birth, English by education and upbringing."

"The latter probably forms one's nature more than anything. I'll tell you something. I know exactly who you are. I was eight years old at the time. So you now know my age. In a place like this people know the business of others. It is a place where it is impossible to have secrets. There was a big furore. Henri St. Allengère and the young girl . . . one of the beauties of the place . . . the wicked old man who blighted their lives. Blighting lives is a habit of old Alphonse St. Allengère. He is one of the ogres of the neighbourhood . . . quite the most monstrous."

"You are right in thinking he is my grandfather."

"Condolences on that point."

"I see you do not like him."

"Like him? Does one like a rattlesnake? He is well known throughout this neighbourhood. If you go to the church you will see the stained glass windows restored by the benevolence of Alphonse St. Allengère. The lectern is a gift from him. The roof is now in excellent condition. Through him war was declared on the death watch beetle; the church owes its survival to him. He is God's good friend and man's worst enemy."

"Is that possible?"

"That is something, my dear Madame Sallonger, which you with your knowledge of human nature, will be able to decide more easily than I."

I said: "It is a long way through the woods."

"I am glad of it. It gives me a chance to enjoy this interesting conversation."

I was suspicious suddenly. It had not taken me long to reach that spot where the dogs had found me. He saw my look, interpreted it and smiled at me ingratiatingly.

"Where shall we emerge?" I asked.

"You will see."

"I am not very familiar with this terrain. I want to be able to find my way back."

"You will be safe with me."

"I think I should be back now. They will wonder what has become of me."

"Leave this to me."

"I seemed not to have gone so far."

"The woods are beautiful . . . you said you thought so."

"I did. But I had no intention of lingering."

"I give you permission to come to my woods at any time you like."

"Thank you. That is generous of you."

"I have my good points."

"I feel sure you have."

"Then I have managed to vindicate myself during this brief encounter."

"But, of course. You have been most courteous after the first shock of finding me. Now if you will show me the way out of the woods . . . quickly . . . I shall be most grateful."

"Your gratitude is something I appreciate. Come along."

The trees were thinning. We were out in the open and ahead of us lay the *château.*

I caught my breath and said: "It's magnificent."

"The home of the Comtes de Carsonne for hundreds of years."

"I know. I was told of them. I saw it when we arrived and was most impressed."

"It is one of the finest and oldest *châteaux* in this part of the country."

"I understand the present Comte is in residence quite often."

"Yes. Though he is often in Paris."

"I suppose so. Are those his vineyards?"

"Yes. Quite small compared with those of Monsieur St. Allengère
. . . but, of course, there is something special about the *château*
wine."

"There would be, I suppose. I think I know where I am now.
Thank you for rescuing me from those monsters of yours."

"You mean my good and faithful hounds?"

I nodded. "And thank you for escorting me through the woods."

"You are so gracious. I will attempt to be the same. I repeat; please
come to my woods whenever you wish."

"That is indeed kind of you."

"It may be that I shall meet you there."

I did not answer. When I had thought that he was detaining me I
had been faintly alarmed, now I was sorry that the encounter was
over.

We paused side by side on the slight hillock while I looked round
me.

"There," he said, "are your father's vineyards. Go straight down
the hill, cut across the field there and you will be there."

"I see. And thank you. Goodbye, Monsieur de la Tour."

"Au revoir, Madame Sallonger."

I knew he was watching me as I rode off and thoughtfully I made
my way. I was tingling with pleasure. It had been very amusing. He
had made quite an impression on me. I could not say that I liked him.
I did not admire arrogant men. Neither Philip nor Drake had been
like that. Philip had been essentially gentle; Drake was, too. This man
was quite different, and all the time I felt he had been making fun of
me; and there was something sensuous about the manner in which he
had regarded me—something, too, in the tone of his voice. I thought
he was too much aware of me . . . physically, and that the banter
was leading to something. He made me uneasy and yet at the same
time he had stimulated and excited me.

When I approached the house I saw my father. He was coming
from the stables.

"Lenore," he called, "I'm glad you're back. I was getting anxious."

"Is something wrong with Katie?"

"No . . . no. She's all right. I heard that you had ridden off and I
thought it was time you were back."

"I had quite an adventure. You know the wood . . ."

He nodded.

"I explored, and two savage looking dogs appeared. I thought they were going to attack me. Marron was quite put out." I patted her as I mentioned her name and felt her response.

"Dogs!" said my father.

"Horrible brutes. Fortunately their owner was with them. He called them off and told me I was trespassing. The woods apparently belong to him. He talked for a while and said his name was Gaston de la Tour. Do you know him?"

He stared at me. "Gaston de la Tour," he said, "is the Comte de Carsonne. The woods do belong to him . . . so does most of the place."

"You mean to say that this man is the Comte himself? He didn't say . . . just that he was Gaston de la Tour."

"I am sorry you encountered him," said my father.

"It was quite amusing."

"He would be, of course, if the mood took him."

"After his first accusation of trespassing he was quite friendly . . ."

My father looked anxiously at my flushed face. "Well, you probably won't see him again. It's better not. He does not enjoy a very good reputation . . . with women."

"Oh, I see." I laughed. "I can quite believe that."

I left Marron to the groom and went into the house with my father, thinking of the wicked Comte.

*　　*　　*

The grapes were all gathered and the process had been completed without mishap. They were now lying on the level floor absorbing the sun. Every day the sky was examined with a tinge of anxiety, but each morning the sun rose and shone benignly on the gathered fruit. All was well.

Katie was growing more and more excited. My father had shown her the great cylinders which he had had installed to crush the grapes. She was a little disappointed because she had been fascinated by the treading. However, he explained, that this way was more effective.

Then came the first blow. The itinerant workers who arrived at this time of the year to add to the work force, did not come. My father was furious when he heard the reason.

"They are at the *château,*" he said. "The Comte's *vendange* is usually a week or so later than ours; we are a little more exposed to the sun here and that means we start earlier. This year he has decided to begin at the same time—hence, he has ordered the workers who usually come to us, to go to him."

"Do you mean to say that those who have been coming to you for years, just go when he beckons them?"

"It is the Comte, you see. He expects complete obedience."

"But what of their loyalty to you?"

"I don't blame *them.* They have been commanded and they have to go."

"How mean of him!"

"He wants us all to realize that he is the master here. Most of this land belongs to him. There is only mine and of course Villers-Mûre which is beyond his jurisdiction. But he likes to remind us of his power."

"Can't you explain to him that you must have those men?"

"I would not dream of asking favours of him. We will manage without."

"Can we?"

"I think we shall do what we have to."

My father set about reorganizing the workers; and then the second blow fell. He used wooden horse-drawn carts to transport the workers from place to place and one of these was involved in an accident. The horse bolted, jumped a hedge, broke a leg and overturned the cart, injuring four of the workers.

The horse had to be shot; the foreman had broken a leg, one of the workers an arm and others suffered from cuts and bruises.

My father was in despair. "It would seem," he said, "that there is a curse on the *vendange.*"

Then the unexpected happened. While my father—in the depth of despair—was trying to reorganize everything, a cart arrived with ten men—some of them the itinerant workers who had deserted us at the Comte's command.

I saw the cart arrive and hurried down to see what had happened now. My father came and joined me.

One of the men stepped down from the cart.

He said: "The compliments of Monsieur le Comte. He has heard of your ill luck and he has sent us to work for you while you need us."

My father stared incredulously. "But . . ." he stammered, "I don't understand. And why did you desert me in the first place?"

"The orders of Monsieur le Comte, Monsieur St. Allengère. We could not disobey them. But now he has sent us. He has heard of the accident and wishes to help you. When we have finished here we are to return to the *château* for his *vendange.*"

My father's emotions were mixed. I could see that he was fighting with himself. He wanted to refuse the Comte's offer, but the sight of those men and what they could do for him was too much, and his common sense prevailed over his pride. Here was a chance to save the wine harvest and it would be folly on his part to refuse it.

He murmured: "It is good of the Comte."

"We'll get to work immediately, Monsieur St. Allengère."

They scrambled down. They did not need instructions. They knew exactly what to do.

I followed my father into the house. I laid my hand on his arm. "So all will be well?"

"I cannot understand his motives."

"He is sorry. He has heard of the accident. He knows all the difficulties. I daresay he is sympathetic."

"You don't know the man. We are rivals. I am sure he would be delighted if my harvest was a failure."

"Perhaps you misjudge him."

My father shook his head. "He has his reasons, I daresay. He always has his reasons."

Katie had come up and was listening with that singlemindedness which was a habit of hers.

"Is he really an ogre?" she asked.

My father nodded grimly.

"I'd love to see him. He lives in that castle. Is he a giant?"

"There aren't any giants now, Katie," I reminded her.

Katie looked disappointed. "Does he eat people?" she asked.

"In a manner of speaking," replied my father.

"Oh, let's forget him," I said. "We have a complete work force now and can go ahead."

My father agreed with me, but he did not like the fact that salvation had come through the Comte.

* * *

That was a memorable night. All was safe and there was an air of jubilation everywhere. After what had been a calamitous beginning we had come through to a satisfactory end. The whole of the neighbourhood seemed to have gathered there. Lights from lanterns and torches flickered in the warm evening air. On the grass before the house the fiddlers were playing folksongs: people were singing as they danced. Katie was beside me, silent with wonder.

There was last year's wine for all, and cakes made of nuts and fruit. The singing grew louder as the evening progressed and the dancing more vigorous. I sat down on a bench and watched them and I was moved to hear some of the songs Grand'mère had sung to me when I was little.

> "En passant par la Lorraine
> Avec mes sabots . . ."

Someone was beside me. He sat down. I turned and my heart gave a leap of surprise, consternation and I admit, a certain excitement.

I heard myself stammer: "The Comte de Carsonne."

"In person," he replied, putting his face near mine. "Please say you are glad to see me." He took my hand and kissed it. He looked at Katie. "Don't tell me. I know. This is the delectable Mademoiselle Katie. I am enchanted to meet you, Mademoiselle." He then took her hand and kissed it.

I could see the excitement bubbling up in Katie's eyes. Her hand had never been kissed in that manner before—and by such an obviously important gentleman.

"I know who you are," she said. Katie was never at a loss for words.

"Then we are well acquainted already."

"Are you really an ogre?"

"I think the answer is probably yes."

"You're not a giant, though."

"I'm sorry about that."

"Do you eat people?"

"Do I look like a cannibal?"

"What is a cannibal, Mama?"

"Someone who eats people," I said.

"They do not form a regular part of my diet," he told her.

"Would you eat me?"

"This is a silly conversation," I said. "You know it is, Katie."

He laughed and taking her by the chin smiled at her. "Not for breakfast," he said.

"Dinner then?"

"I should have to fatten you up."

"Fee, Fi, Fo, Fum," chanted Katie, "I smell the blood of an English girl."

She giggled.

I said to him; "Did you want to see my father?"

"No. I wanted to make sure that all was well and that he had overcome his bad luck."

"He was grateful to you," I said.

"If all is well, I am satisfied." He added, "What do you think of this?" He waved his hand. "This . . . ceremony?"

"It is very interesting."

"Quite amusing . . . briefly, for the lady of business from London and Paris."

"Quite amusing."

"I see that Mademoiselle Katie is entranced. Mademoiselle, I should like to show you a true *vendange* . . . just how it has been done for the last hundreds of years . . . the way they do it at my *château*. Will you honour me by attending?"

"Do you mean to come to yours? Oh yes, please. We will, won't we, Mama?"

I said: "We shall have to see."

"But why can't we go?"

"We must see what plans your grandfather has for us."

"He hasn't any."

"Then," said the Comte, "it is arranged. Madame Sallonger, Mademoiselle Katie, you are to be my guests. It will be in three days from now."

Katie clapped her hands.

"I promise not to eat you," he added.

Katie lifted her shoulders and giggled.

My father had seen us and came speedily towards us.

"Monsieur le Comte."

He rose smiling urbanely as though it were the most natural thing to call casually on an enemy of years' standing.

"I'm glad all went well, St. Allengère."

"I have to thank you," began my father stiffly.

"Don't think of it. It was the only thing to do. I heard about the accident. What a time for it to happen! I guessed your predicament and so I sent the men."

"They came just in time."

"Then I am content."

"I am indebted to you," went on my father.

The Comte waved his hand. "Madame Sallonger and Mademoiselle Katie have just agreed to come to the *château vendange.* That is ample reward for the little service I have been able to render."

My father looked stunned. He said: "I am sure the Comte will want to look round. Would you care to come with me, Comte?"

"With pleasure."

He was smiling secretively as he bowed first to me, then to Katie; and we watched him walk off with my father.

"He's not a giant," said Katie. "But he's better than a giant. He makes me laugh. I like him, don't you, Mama?"

I was silent.

She looked disappointed. "He doesn't really eat people. That was only a joke."

"Oh?" I said.

"I like him," she added, almost defiantly.

I did not see him again that night.

I was glad to be alone in my room. There was no doubt that he was disturbing. I wondered why he had sent those men and why he had actually put in an appearance tonight. First he had shown his power by commanding the itinerant workers to come to him and then he had made the grand gesture. I thought it had all been rather contrived.

I lay awake for a long time thinking of him.

In the morning, when we were alone together, my father said: "The Comte is acting very strangely . . . to turn up like that, as though we had been fast friends for years. We have never had any communication whatsoever."

"Well, he did send the men over."

"Why? In the normal way he would have snapped his fingers at us. He would have been glad if our harvest had been spoilt. We are, in a measure, rivals. Moreover his family have had a long-standing feud with ours."

"Not you personally."

"My father and he are at daggers drawn. If they could do each other an ill turn there would be no hesitation. Why this sudden *volte face?*" He looked at me searchingly and I felt myself flushing. "You met him, of course."

"Yes, in the woods. I told you."

"I think this must be something to do with you. You will have to be careful, Lenore."

"Don't worry about me."

"I think he may well be planning to pursue you. He is said to be susceptible and you are attractive."

"He seemed to like Katie."

"I expect that is part of the act. He apparently has little interest in his own son."

"Katie was greatly taken with him. He played along with her little game of ogres and cannibalistic tendencies. He seemed amused."

"I don't like it. I have looked forward so much to your coming here, and now I think I shall be relieved when we return to Paris."

"Don't worry," I told him. "I am not a young and innocent girl. Remember I am a widow with a child."

"I know. But he is said to be a very attractive man."

"I am sure he sees himself in that light."

"I fear others do, too."

"I tell you not to worry."

"But you have promised to go to his *vendange.*"

"Katie more or less accepted before I could intervene."

My father shook his head. "I don't like it," he repeated.

"All will be well," I assured him.

And I was thinking: *I* did like it—although I was sure my father was right and the Comte probably thought that I should be an easy conquest.

I was greatly looking forward to proving him wrong.

* * *

That night will always stand out clearly in my memory. At the time there seemed something unreal about it. I can shut my eyes even now and recall it in every detail. The air was so clear that the stars seemed close above; it was warm and windless. The voices of the revellers came to us from a little distance away—singing to the accompaniment of violins, accordions, triangles and drums.

But most of all I remembered the Comte. He had somehow arranged that he and I should be apart from the others and we sat in a small courtyard about whose grey walls bougainvilleas bloomed and there was a smell of frangipani in the air. I sipped the special wine which he had had brought from his cellars and nibbled the cake which had been made for the occasion and which was a feature of the *vendange*.

From the moment he had sent his carriage to conduct Katie and me to the *château* it had been an enchanted evening. It was a somewhat cumbersome vehicle although very dignified with his family's arms engraved on it. My father had been concerned and I had reassured him. I should be all right and Katie was with me. I said we should return at midnight and he muttered something about its being late for Katie to which I had said she might stay up for once and no harm would be done.

He was certain that the Comte was set on a course of seduction. I was largely in agreement with him, but I had no intention of becoming the easy victim of a philanderer; and I felt I had been serious too long and should be none the worse for a little light entertainment which I intended this to be.

How magnificent was the castle! It overwhelmed one with its antiquity. As we approached the platform on which it stood a feeling of anticipation swept over me. This night was going to be like no other. The high round tower of the main wing encircled by a corbelled parapet, the cylindrical towers which flanked the building, the thick massive walls, the narrow slits of windows . . . it all seemed to me entirely medieval. I felt that I was passing into another world.

The Comte greeted us with his son Raoul beside him. Katie and the boy eyed each other speculatively. Katie took the initiative and said: "Hello, Raoul. Do you really *live* here?" Then she wanted to know whether they poured boiling oil down on their enemies.

"Oh, we have more subtle means of dealing with them nowadays," said the Comte.

As I stood in that ancient hall, I felt the past closing in on me and the Comte was an essential part of it—the overlord, the all powerful *seigneur* who believed that he could claim the *droit de seigneur* now, as his ancestors had undoubtedly done in the past.

I looked about at the weapons hanging on the walls, the great fireplace over which was displayed the arms of Carsonne, the embrasures in which there were stone benches, clearly centuries old. It was impressive indeed.

The Comte had arranged everything as he had intended it should go. He said he knew that Katie was eager to observe the manner in which they conducted the wine making at the *château*.

"Here we observe tradition," he said. "Everything must be done as it was hundreds of years ago. You will want to see the treading." He told Raoul that he must look after his guest. He summoned Raoul's tutor, Monsieur Grenier, to take charge of the two of them. The housekeeper, Madame Le Grand, appeared and was presented to me. She would make sure that the children's wine was well watered. She knew they were longing to taste the *vendange* cake.

So tactfully was it all arranged that Katie went off happily with them, which left me alone with the Comte.

It was an unforgettable scene.

We saw the men with their laden baskets marching to the troughs in which the grapes were to be trod to the sound of music. They must have been about three feet deep when the treaders appeared.

The Comte was watching me closely. "You are thinking this is unhygienic. Let me assure you that every precaution has been taken. All the utensils have been disinfected. The treaders' legs and feet have been scrubbed. You see, they are in a special sort of short trousers . . . all of them, men and women. This is how it has always been done at the *château*. They will sing our traditional folk songs as they dance. Ah, they are beginning."

I watched them, dancing methodically as their feet sank lower and lower into the purple juice.

"They will go on till midnight."

"Katie . . ."

"Is very happy with Raoul. Grenier and Madame Le Grand will see that she is all right."

"I think I . . ."

"Let us enjoy a little freedom for a while. It is good for us . . . even the children. Have no fear. Before midnight strikes you will be safely on your way. I give you my word. I swear it."

I laughed. "There is no need to be so vehement. I believe you."

"Come with me. We will escape the turmoil. I want to talk with you."

And so I found myself in the scented courtyard on that starlit night

. . . alone with him . . . and yet not alone . . . for we were within sound of the revelry and every now and then the night would be punctuated with a sudden shout; and there was the constant music in the background.

A servant appeared with wine and the *vendange* cake delicately served for us with little forks and napkins embroidered with the Carsonne crest.

"This," he said, "is vintage *château* wine which I have served only at special occasions."

"Such as the *vendange.*"

"That takes place every year. What is special about that? I meant the day when Madame Sallonger is my guest."

"You are a very gracious host."

"I can be charming when I am doing what I like to do."

"I suppose we all can."

"It is those other occasions which indicate the character and betray our faults. I want to hear about you. Are you happy?"

"As happy as most people, I daresay."

"That is evasive. People's contentment with life varies."

"Happiness is rarely a permanent state. One would be very fortunate to achieve that. It comes in moments. One finds oneself saying, with a certain surprise, I am happy *now.*"

"Are you saying that at this moment?"

I hesitated. "I am very interested in all this. The *vendange*, the *château* . . . It is all so new to me."

"Then can I conclude that if it is not quite happiness, it is a pleasant experience?"

"It is certainly that."

He leaned forward. "Let us make a vow tonight."

"A vow?"

"That we will be absolutely frank with each other. Tell me, do you feel drawn to this place?"

"I wanted to see it properly from the moment I had my first glimpse of it. You see, I was born close to here. There has always been a mystery about Villers-Mûre. I am excited to be near it."

"I was born here in this *château*. So our birthplaces are very near. Tell me, how do you feel about your grandfather?"

"Rather sad."

"Don't let yourself be sad on his account. I find a certain pleasure in contemplating him. I feel very strongly about him. He is the sort of person I dislike most. It is more amusing and interesting to have deep feelings about people and I am one to have such feelings. I hate or I love . . . and I do both most intensely."

"It must make life rather exhausting."

He looked at me steadily. "Your upbringing would have been very different from mine. The English are less formal than we are, I believe. Yet they cloak their feelings in assumed indifference. I call it a kind of hypocrisy."

"Perhaps it makes life easier not to have to cope with the intense hatred and love you mention."

He was thoughtful. "Perhaps," he said. "I was interested to see your Katie and my Raoul together. She is quite uninhibited."

"That is a natural characteristic."

"As Raoul's solemnity is with him."

"Katie has always had absolute security. She knows she can tell me anything. I am always there to help her. I think it makes her spontaneous. It gives her confidence."

"You mean Raoul has missed that?"

"You can tell that better than I."

"I have not been such an exemplary parent as you have."

"I have done what is natural."

"I believe that child means everything to you."

"That is true."

"She is a lucky girl."

"I should like to believe that."

"You were brought up by Madame Cleremont."

"Yes. I also was lucky."

"A good woman."

"You speak as though you know her."

"I know most that goes on here, and there was a scandal at the time she left. Your mother was once the beauty of the neighbourhood. I was a child but I had long ears and I used them to good avail. So I knew that Henri St. Allengère was in love with the village beauty and that wicked old Alphonse had refused to sanction the match, that there was a child on the way, and Henri could either desert the girl or get out. Henri decided to desert the girl. Poor Marie Louise. She lived with her mother who cared for her and they said broke her heart when Marie Louise died giving birth to a daughter."

"I was the cause of the trouble."

"The innocent cause." He smiled at me. "When your grandmother wanted you recognized and made demands on the old tyrant, he did not want you here so he passed you off to those English connections—the breakaway Huguenot branch of the family. Madame Cleremont was the bait. She was a genius at the machine and a highly respected member of the St. Allengère work force. He would give her to the Sallongers if they would take the child as well and allow her to be brought up in their household. So he rid himself of an encumbrance and a perpetual reminder of his son's misdemeanour. And then you married one of the Sallongers, and that should have been the happy ending. But something went wrong."

I felt the pain of memory—those days and nights in Florence . . . each day falling more and more in love with Philip . . . and even the horrible experience of Lorenzo's death.

"Now you are looking sad," he said. "You are remembering your marriage."

"It ended so disastrously. It was so brief." I found myself telling him about Philip's disappearance from the house and the discovery of his body in the forest.

"Why?" he asked.

"I do not know. I can never know. We were happy. We had just bought a house. It is a mystery."

I told him of that terrible time, of the verdict at the inquest.

"It is incredible," he said. "It must have been some secret which he could not bear you to know."

"I will never believe that he killed himself. Sometimes I wonder if someone killed him."

"Why?"

"Because if he did not kill himself that was the only solution."

I told him about Lorenzo's death.

"You see," I went on, "I sometimes think . . . although I didn't at the time, of course . . . only after that happened to Philip . . . that someone was going to kill Philip and mistook Lorenzo for him."

I could see that he was astonished.

"It certainly throws a different light on everything," he said. "Do you think you will ever forget?"

"I think I never shall."

"Have you ever tried to probe the mystery?"

"I have pondered on it endlessly, but there seems no reason. I had to come to the conclusion that there could only be one answer, but knowing him, that seemed impossible."

"No one will ever match up to him. He will be in your memory always . . . just as he was in those weeks of your marriage. You were not long enough together to discover the flaws. They say those whom the gods love die young."

"Do you believe that?"

"It means that they have eternal youth because that is how they live on the minds of those who knew them."

"You speak enviously. Surely you are not regretting living on?"

"Not I. I would take all the risks of my sins being revealed. You have told me about your husband. I will tell you about my wife. You know that in families like mine these things are arranged."

"I had imagined so."

"When I was eighteen a wife was found for me."

"I am surprised that you allowed yourself to accept such a situation."

"I rebelled. I was not enamoured of the young lady. But she was a daughter of one of the greatest houses in France. We still have our great houses, you know, in spite of *Liberté, Egalité and Fraternité.* We still keep up the old traditions. There are a few of us who escaped the holocaust of the last century. Carsonne was lucky. Perhaps we were too tucked away. Perhaps our local peasants were too lethargic. The *château* was untouched. After all, we are almost on the Italian border. We survived and so did some others. These families stick together, as they did through the days of the Napoleons . . . till the end of the monarchy and so on. So I must marry one who was chosen for me. My father explained that I should not be downhearted. I must do my duty and produce the heir to Carsonne and he must have the requisite amount of blue blood in his veins. Once that was done, I could, as my father said, take my pleasure where I would. All French noblemen must do their duty by their wives and are then free to enjoy their mistresses. It is a way of life."

"Very acceptable by your sex, I am sure."

"You are right. So I married. My poor Evette. She was only a child, barely seventeen, hardly suited to childbearing . . . no more fit to be a mother than I was a father. However, we did our duty and Raoul duly appeared. Alas in doing hers, Evette lost her life. And so I became a widower."

"Did they not think you should marry again and produce more blue-blooded heirs?"

"They did. But I did not. I had done my duty. I was now my own master for my father had died. The married state was not for me. I enjoyed my freedom."

"But surely you would not have allowed marriage to have impaired your freedom?"

"I suppose not. I am one who will go his own way. But still, I am content to remain as I am enjoying being pursued by those who fancy the title of La Comtesse and have a respect for an ancient *château*. But always I elude the capture."

"I daresay the pursuit is hot and strong."

"It varies. And you, dear Madame Sallonger, you, too, prefer the solitary state?"

"I think it preferable to an unhappy married life."

"Surely there must have been much pursuit in your case?"

I was silent thinking of Drake. On this night he seemed more remote than he had for a long time.

"I see I have aroused unpleasant thoughts. Forgive me." He attempted to fill my glass.

"No thanks," I said, "I have had enough."

"My special vintage?"

"It is quite potent."

"You find it so? Perhaps it is the night air, the scent of the flowers, the company?"

"Perhaps," I said.

"I should like your grandfather to see you sitting here with me now. It gives me great pleasure to contemplate how angry he would be."

"So that pleases you?"

"Enormously. I do not need anything to make me enjoy your company more, but if I did, that would."

"Do you dislike him so very much?"

"Infinitely more," he assured me. "There is a feud between our families. A vendetta. I dislike him more than anyone I know. There are some sinners whom I find tolerable . . . myself for instance. What I cannot endure is the virtuous villain. Your grandfather is one of those. He is cruel, ruthless, selfish. His work people live in fear of him—and so does his family. He believes that he and God are the greatest friends and allies. He thinks his place in Heaven is secure. He will oust Jesus Christ from his place on the right hand of Lord God Almighty when he gets—as he is sure he will—to Heaven. In fact, I expect he believes they will send a special company of angels down to fetch him. He takes Mass once a day; his household is subject to long prayers while he reminds them of their evil ways and how he—as God's emissary—is waiting to spring on every misdemeanour and to make sure that the sins they do by two and two are paid for one by one. In his own chapel he communes with a god who is made in his own image and is therefore as unpleasant as he is. I assure you the Devil's Own are preferable to such a man."

I found myself laughing.

"He has been our enemy for years," he went on, "and my father passed his loathing on to me. *Viva Vendetta.*"

"How you hate him. Surely he must have some redeeming features?"

"I can think of only one. He is your grandfather and therefore indirectly responsible for your existence."

I was silent and he went on: "You are fortunate that he does not wish to see you. Have you met your aunt Ursule?"

"Yes, and her husband."

"Ursule had the courage your father lacked at the time. He broke away afterwards but he should have done so in time to live happily ever afterwards with Marie Louise. Just imagine if he had! You and I might have known each other long ere this. Ursule certainly had courage. My father helped her and Louis Sagon. He gave Sagon work restoring his pictures and they had a house which my father said went with the job. He did it all to spite old Alphonse. They are a tragic family and it can all be traced back to that old man. Then there was the matter of Heloïse. That is not so long ago. She was René's daughter. He had two daughters—Heloïse and Adèle. He also has a son Patrice. Patrice is like his father, obeying the old man without question. Patrice is the heir to the St. Allengère properties . . . after René, of course. They have worked hard for it, which means never offending the tyrant and absolute obedience to his commands. Perhaps they think it worth it."

"Tell me of Heloïse."

"She was so pretty . . . a gentle girl. She drowned herself in the river. It is quite shallow so there was no question of an accident. She just gave up. It was said that she was betrayed by a lover. It was a great blow to René. He doted on her. She meant more to him than Adèle. There was nothing gentle about *her*. She was close to her sister . . . had always protected her. *Mon Dieu,* one would need protection in that household. She went away to Italy. She was very interested in the silk production. They said that although she was a girl she played a big part in the business so she went away to study Italian methods. It was while she was away that this happened to Heloïse."

"And Heloïse's lover?"

"There is a bit of a mystery about him. Heloïse would not name him. If she had, Adèle would have tried to kill him. She is a passionate woman and when her sister died she was almost mad with grief."

"And so the lover was never discovered? Surely in a place like this it would be difficult for him to hide his identity?"

He was silent and the thought occurred to me suddenly; You were the man!

I felt bemused. He was dangerous, but he was fascinating. I knew his reputation and still I was attracted to him. I thought I must go. I should be warned. He was looking at me penetratingly as though he were trying to discover what was in my mind.

I said: "It is getting late."

"The time has flown. Time is so perverse. It flies when one wishes it to stay and slows down when one is longing for it to go. This has been a wonderful evening for me."

"It has been interesting, but I must find Katie. It is long past her bedtime."

I stood up and he stood beside me. He took my hands and drew me towards him. He was standing very close. I was not short but he was some six inches taller and I had to look up to him. I was very eager to let him know that I was unmoved by his proximity.

"It has been such a pleasant evening," I said coolly. "Thank you so much."

"It is I who should thank you." I thought in that moment that he was going to kiss me and I felt alarmed, particularly as I realized that it was not so much of him that I was afraid, but of myself.

Impatiently I tried to shake off the effect he was having on me. I knew him for a practised philanderer. Why had I allowed myself to be attracted by him? Why was I hoping that he would kiss me and declare his passion? Perhaps I had been alone too long. Perhaps I wanted a normal married life. I had tasted that . . . and it had been taken from me. I had thought of Drake . . . but not quite like this.

He drew me to him suddenly and kissed me lightly on the forehead. I withdrew my hands and tried not to show surprise or emotion. I pretended to understand that this was a French custom for hosts to kiss their lady guests chastely on the brow.

I said rather briskly: "Now, I must find my daughter."

He took my arm, holding it lightly as he led me towards the revellers.

Katie was there with Raoul and Monsieur Grenier.

"Isn't it wonderful?" she cried when she saw us. "It's the best *vendange* I have ever seen."

It was clear that she had made friends with Raoul and that he was delighted by her companionship. Poor boy, I thought, no doubt he does not have a very good time with such a father. I expected that he had always to remember the duties which would be his one day. He would have to be skilled in all the manly pastimes; he would have his tutor to please. Katie's attitude to life must be a revelation to him.

Katie was over-excited. I thought: It is indeed time we left.

The Comte sent for the carriage. He himself would escort us back and Raoul should accompany us. I sat next to Katie and put my arm about her. She lay against me and I could see that her lids were forcing themselves down in spite of her efforts to remain awake. The jogging of the carriage would soon send her to sleep.

I was aware of the Comte's watchful eyes. Raoul sat rather stiffly beside his father. I imagined he was always thus in the Comte's company.

At length I said: "We're here."

Katie opened her eyes and was immediately wide awake remembering where she was.

"Raoul," she said, "may I come and see your falcon? You promised to show it to me. May I come to the *château?* I haven't seen it really."

The Comte spoke for his son. "Please come whenever you wish, Mademoiselle Katie. There will always be a welcome for you."

Katie smiled rapturously. "This is the happiest night of my life," she declared.

The Comte smiled at me triumphantly.

My father was clearly relieved by our arrival. He had rather obviously been waiting for us.

"Grandfather," cried Katie, "it was *wonderful*. You should have seen them dancing on the grapes. The purple juice splashed right up their legs . . . and they went down and down . . ."

"I am gratified indeed," said the Comte.

We said farewell and I listened to the carriage rumbling off into the night.

"I expect you are tired," said my father.

"Very."

"I'm not," said Katie.

"Then you should be," he told her. "You should have been in bed hours ago."

"It's midnight," said Katie. "It's the first time I've been up at midnight."

"Come on," I commanded. "You're half asleep."

And she was asleep almost before I could help her into bed, but as far as I was concerned sleep was elusive. It had been a memorable night and somehow significant. This worldly French nobleman was different from anyone I had ever known before.

Then I thought of Heloïse who must have been led through ecstatic weeks . . . perhaps months . . . before she knew that she had placed her trust in a faithless lover.

I tried to remember his face when he had talked of Heloïse. Could he have been the man? He would have been at hand.

I knew I must be very careful.

* * *

The carriage came for Katie the next day. Madame Le Grand arrived with it. She assured me that my daughter would be well looked after. Monsieur le Comte had instructed her that she was to take care of her so that I need have no qualms.

I said: "I am not sure whether I should allow her to go."

"Oh, Mama," protested Katie, "I *want* to go. I want to see Raoul. He's promised to show me the *château* and his falcon and dogs."

"I personally will see that no harm befalls your daughter, Madame," Madame Le Grand assured me.

I thanked her and I did not see how I could protest after that.

When she had gone my father came to me.

"This is so strange," he said. "Our families have never been on these terms."

"Isn't it rather foolish to keep up these old feuds?"

"My dear Lenore, the Comtes of Carsonne have kept up the feuds as firmly as any of us. It is this change of front that I do not like. It is since you came across him riding."

"There is this friendship between his son and Katie."

"Which he has contrived."

"But they are two children. It is good for them to be together. They liked each other at once. Poor boy, I don't suppose he has many companions of his own age."

"They are no doubt bringing him up to be like the rest of them—to think they are divine beings set there to rule over us all."

"That seems to be what he thinks of the St. Allengères. Oh really, father, these family feuds went out with Romeo and Juliet."

"I think we should return to Paris. I daresay they can do without us here. It is not fair to leave everything in the salon to the Countess. When the barrelling is done and everything is safely in the first cellar, I shall be ready to leave."

"When will that be?"

"At the end of the week, I should think. We'll go back then."

I agreed that we should.

In the late afternoon Katie was returned. She was full of the day's adventure.

"They have a keep, Mama. Do you know what a keep is?"

I said I did.

"We explored the *château* with Monsieur Grenier who told us a lot of history . . . but it was interesting because it was all about the *château*. Then he took us riding. They have an *oubliette*. Do you know what an *oubliette* is?" She did not wait for my reply, for she was eager to tell me. "It means forgotten. They used to push people down there . . . it's like a dark, dark cave . . . There is only a hole in the floor above . . . They are left down there . . . to die . . . forgotten, you see."

"What a gruesome place it must be."

"Oh it is," said Katie delightedly. "Raoul has a falcon. He is going to teach me what has to be done. We went to the parapets. You can see right across to the mulberries and those buildings by the little river. St. Allengères live there. It sounds a bit like us."

Halting the flow, I said: "Katie, we are leaving at the end of the week."

"Oh no, Mama . . . just when I am having such a good time."

"All good times come to an end, Katie."

"They don't have to . . . if you don't let them."

"We have to go, Katie."

"The end of the week," she said blankly; and was downcast for about five minutes.

The next day the carriage came to take her to the *château* again.

* * *

That day I went out riding myself. I thought: Two more days and I shall be away from here. I had expected it to be a memorable experience. I had thought so often of my birthplace where my mother had lived and died giving birth to me. But it had been complicated by the Comte. He had cut across my expectations and added something to the adventure.

I was not surprised that day to meet him. I had a fancy that he had lain in wait for me, certain that he would catch me some time.

He rode up to me on his big horse which he had been riding in the woods on the first day we met.

"Good day, Madame Sallonger," he said. "What a pleasure to find you."

"Thank you."

"I heard you are leaving soon."

"My daughter must have mentioned it."

"Raoul is desolate."

"Oh, he will find another playmate."

"How could he find another Katie? I, too, am desolate."

"You will soon forget we ever came here."

"That statement is completely false and you are aware of it."

"I think you flatter us both."

"I speak from the heart." I smiled lightly and he went on earnestly. "I feel we could be good friends . . . if you would allow that. I have thought a great deal about you since we have met."

"I am honoured but it seems strange that I should have given you such food for thought."

"It is quite natural when you consider that you are different from anyone I have ever met."

"Well, no one person is absolutely like another."

"Most of them arouse little interest in me."

"That is because you are self-absorbed."

"Do you really think that?"

"Perhaps I speak rashly. I know so little of you."

"I think you would find it interesting to discover more."

"What a pity I shall not be here to make those discoveries."

"You could stay, I suppose."

"I do have my business to attend to."

"Are there not others who can do that?"

"Naturally I could not stay away indefinitely."

"I believe you have been eluding me."

"Why should I do that?"

"Perhaps because you are a little afraid."

"Are you so formidable?"

"Very, I expect."

"Perhaps to those who depend on your bounty, but, Monsieur le Comte, I am not in that category."

"You are afraid of me in a different way. My reputation has been whispered to you. I am the notorious enemy of your family."

"I know you are my grandfather's enemy, but why should his enemies be mine?"

"So . . . I am your friend?"

"A pleasant acquaintance, shall we say?"

"Is that how you rate me?"

"This is, I believe, our fourth meeting. How could I rate you in any other way?"

"But each has been no ordinary encounter."

"No. The first time you set your dogs on me, the second you were the gracious host and now we have met by chance . . . Oh and there was another when you came uninvited to my father's house."

"I shall be sad when you depart."

"How kind of you to say so," I said lightly.

"I mean it. Please persuade your father that he must stay another week . . . and we will meet each day."

"I fear that would be a great encroachment on your time . . . and mine."

"Stop this banter. You know how affected I am by you. You intrigue me. You are so cool . . . so sure of yourself . . . yet I suspect hidden fires within you."

"You talk of me as though I am a smouldering bonfire."

"I think I am falling in love with you."

"Monsieur le Comte is pleased to jest."

"I never jest about matters which are serious to me. Do you intend to mourn your husband for ever?"

I was silent. I was so much enjoying this encounter with him. It stimulated me. It made me feel young as I had not felt since the days of my marriage with Philip. I wanted to go on with this battle of words. There was an element of danger in it which only added to the excitement. I knew he was an expert in such encounters. He attracted me. I supposed any woman would have been attracted by him. He was so essentially worldly, but perhaps chief of all he emanated power and that, I believe, is an irresistible element of sexual attraction. He was so obviously a man who had been accustomed to having his own way and was adept at getting it. I thought about the frail Evette and all the women to whom he must have made easy and competent love. That he intended to add me to their list had been obvious for some time. That should certainly not be. And yet . . . I could not resist this flippant interchange. I felt this was a kind of mental seduction—exciting to indulge in, and wise, because there would be no after effects.

Certainly I had very much enjoyed all our encounters.

Then suddenly I thought of Heloïse lying in the shallow river. Had it been like this with her in the beginning?

He was saying: "I could show you the way to a new life. Bring you out of the past. I could give you a chance to put all that behind you."

Was he right? I wondered. Had I lived too long in the past? I might have been Drake's wife now. I think I might have been happy with Drake. Drake was gallant and kindly, a man one could trust. He would have been a tender husband and a good father to Katie.

Of course the Comte had charmed Katie, but that was superficial charm. He was using Katie as a means of approaching me. How different Drake had been!

"What are you thinking now?" he asked.

"Of returning," I replied.

"Do you think you will escape me so easily?"

"Escape? Why do you use the term? I am not your prisoner."

"No," he said. "It is I who am yours."

I laughed.

"You are a cruel woman," he said.

"You did ask that I should be frank. I understand you. I know your motives. I am not one of your village maidens to be carried away by your family crest . . . nor am I one of those ladies of your acquaintance who make a bid for a title and an ancient *château*. Neither of these things would mean anything to me."

"And what about their owner?"

"As I said, I hardly know him. He is . . . an amusing acquaintance."

"So I do amuse you?"

"You know you do."

"And you enchant me. You know you do."

"You are of the world, Monsieur, and so am I. I am not in the first flush of youth. Nor are you. I just want you to know that you are wasting your time in looking for an easy conquest in this direction. There must be plenty of other easier prospects."

"You misunderstand me."

"I understand you very well. I will tell you the truth. I have enjoyed our meetings, but I do not attach any significance to them."

He sighed. "I see how difficult it is to convince you of my feelings."

"Not difficult at all. I understand perfectly. I shall really have to go back now. I have preparations to make."

"Suppose I were to ask you and your father to a musical entertainment at the *château*. I could get some well-known musicians to play for us. Do you like music?"

"I do. But we could not accept your invitation. We have to leave at the end of the week."

"I am interested to discover what happened to your husband. I think the matter should not be dismissed lightly. I think we should try to solve the mystery. Once you know the truth you will cease to think so constantly of him. You will grow away from the tragedy. You will see that life is for living not brooding over the dead and dreaming of what might have been."

"This has very little to do with my relationship with you."

"Oh, it has, I am sure."

"I am taking this turning back. It is a short cut to the house."

As it came into sight with its surrounding vineyards I pulled up.

"In case I don't see you before I go, I will say goodbye."

"This sounds like dismissal."

"That's absurd. It is just . . . goodbye."

He took my hand and kissed it.

"This is not the end, you know," he said.

And I felt a lightness of heart for I should have hated it to be the end.

I withdrew my hand.

"*Au revoir,*" he said.

I turned and rode away.

When I am busy in Paris I shall forget all about this, I told myself. What would involvement with him mean? A brief love affair. Not marriage. The idea of marriage with him was a disturbing thought. It would be stimulating and exciting. But he had never mentioned the possibility of marriage. That was another reason why I should get away.

Of course he had no intention of marrying. The only time he had talked of it was in connection with Evette whom he had married to please his family. He had produced the heir and he would never want to enter the bonds of matrimony again. Although why a man such as he was should have such an aversion to it I could not understand, for he would never keep his vows if he did not want to. He would be a typical French husband . . . courteous, paying attention to his wife and doing what he called his duty and then being off to take pleasure with his mistresses.

That was *mariage à la mode* according to the worldly ways of the French nobility.

It was not for me.

* * *

Before I left I wanted to see my mother's grave. I knew that she was buried in the graveyard of the little church of Villers-Mûre. My father had not wished me to go near his old home. I think he feared what my grandfather's reaction might be if he heard that I was there. I did not want to involve him but I was determined to go.

The day before we were due to leave, I set out.

I came to the hill from which I could look down on the St. Allengère property. I could see the village close to the manufactory, and the little river winding its way past the stone buildings and under the little bridge. It was a charming sight.

I could see the spire of the church and I made my way down the hill towards it.

There was no one about. I expected they were all at work. I came to the church and tethered my horse outside. I entered and my footsteps, echoing on the stone flags, broke the silence. It was awe-inspiring to think that this was the church where my mother and Grand'mère must have sat so often together. The windows were magnificent. There was the Jesse window presented by a Jean Pascal St. Allengère in the sixteenth century; and the parable of the loaves and fishes by Jean Christophe St. Allengère a hundred years later. There was St. John the Baptist. 'Presented by Alphonse St. Allengère.' I stood staring at his name. My grandfather! I remembered what the Comte had said about him and could not help smiling.

The name St. Allengère appeared in several places. They had been benefactors of the church throughout the ages. I was trespassing. I should not be here. My father did not wish it. I wondered what my grandfather would say if he knew I had ventured into his territory.

I felt suddenly warm so I took off the scarf I was wearing. I studied the ornate altar, the lectern . . . another gift to the church from my pious grandfather. There was evidence everywhere of his generosity.

This was his church. The castle would have its own chapel, I supposed, so the Comte would never come here. He would be quite different from my grandfather; if his flippant conversation was an indication of his beliefs he was certainly not devout.

I came out into the fresh air and made my way to the graveyard.

Ornate statuary had been placed over many of the graves. There were angels in plenty and figures of the saints. Some of them were so large and lifelike that one almost expected them to speak.

I did not think my mother would be among those with the elaborate sculptures, but there among the most magnificent were the burial grounds of my ancestors. The name St. Allengère was on many of the headstones. I went to the most ornate of them all. Marthe St. Allengère; wife of Alphonse 1822–1850. So that was my grandmother. She had been young to die. I daresay childbearing and life with Alphonse had taken their toll. I walked on and found the grave of Heloïse. There was no elaborate statue there. It was an inconspicuous little grave, but all the plants on it had been well tended. There was a white urn from which grew pale pink roses. Poor Heloïse! I wondered about her. How she must have suffered. I thought of the Comte. Of course he may not have been the man involved with the tragic girl. I was being unfair to him to be so sure that he was he. I had no reason for doing so except that he was the man he was. Heloïse was a beautiful girl, and I knew that he would take great delight in seducing the daughter of the enemy house.

I passed on. It was some time before I found my mother's grave. It was in a corner among those of the less flamboyantly decorated. It just said her name, Marie Louise Cleremont. Died aged 17. I felt an intense emotion sweep over me and I saw the rose bush which had been planted there through a haze of tears.

Her story was not unsimilar to that of Heloïse. But she had died naturally. I was glad she had not given up. I had robbed her of her life. Had she lived, we should all have been together, she, Grand'mère and I. Poor Heloïse had been unable to face life. Hers was a different story although it had begun as my mother's had with a lover who had failed her. A lesson to all frail women.

I turned away and started to make my way back to the church door where I had left Marron. In doing so I had to pass the St. Allengère section and I was startled to see a man standing by Heloïse's grave.

He said, "Good day," and as I returned his greetings I could not resist pausing.

"A fine day," he said. Then: "Have you lost your way?"

"No. I have just been having a look at the church. I left my horse tethered at the door."

"It's a fine old church, is it not?"

I agreed that it was.

"You are a stranger here." He looked at me piercingly. Then he said: "I believe I know who you are. Are you staying by any chance at the vineyards?"

"Yes," I told him.

"Then you are Henri's daughter."

I nodded, and he looked rather emotional.

"I heard you were there," he said.

"You must be . . . my uncle."

He nodded. "You are very like your mother . . . so like her, in fact, that for the moment I could believe that you were she."

"My father said there was a resemblance."

He looked down at the grave.

"Have you enjoyed your visit here?"

"Yes, very much."

"It is a pity that it has to be as it is. And Madame Cleremont, she is well?"

"Yes, she is in London."

"I have heard of the salon. I believe it prospers."

"Yes, now we have a branch in Paris. I am going back there tomorrow."

"I believe," he went on, "that you are Madame Sallonger."

"That is so."

"I know the story, of course. You were brought up by the family and in due course married one of the sons of the house. Philip, I believe."

"You are very knowledgeable about me. And you are right. I married Philip."

"And you are now a widow."

"Yes, I have been a widow for twelve years."

The scarf which I was carrying had caught in a bramble. It was dragged from my hands. He retrieved it. It was silk, pale lavender, and similar to those we sold in the salon.

He felt its texture and looked at it intently.

"It is beautiful silk," he said. He kept it in his hands. "Forgive me. I am very interested in silk naturally. It is our life here."

"Yes, of course."

He still kept the scarf. "This is the best of all silks. I believe it is called Sallon Silk."

"That is true."

"The texture is wonderful. There has never been a silk on the market to match it. I believe your husband discovered the process of producing it and making it the property of the English firm."

"It is true that it was discovered by a Sallonger, but it was not Philip, my husband. It was his brother, Charles."

My uncle stared at me incredulously.

"I was always of the opinion that it was your husband. Are you sure you were not mistaken?"

"Certainly I am not. I remember it well. We were amazed that Charles should have come up with the formula because he had always given the impression that he was by no means dedicated to the business. My husband was . . . absolutely. If anyone should have discovered Sallon Silk it should have been him. But it was most definitely

Charles. I remember it so well. It was a brilliant discovery and we owe it to Charles."

"Charles," he repeated. "He is the head of the business now?"

"Yes. It was left to the two of them, and when my husband . . . died . . . Charles became the sole owner."

He was silent. I noticed how pale he was and his hands shook as he handed me back the scarf.

He lifted his eyes to my face and said: "This is my daughter's grave."

I bowed my head in sympathy.

He went on: "It was a great grief to us all. She was a beautiful gentle girl . . . and she died."

I wanted to comfort him because he seemed so stricken.

He smiled suddenly: "It has been interesting talking to you. I wish . . . that I could invite you to my home."

I said: "I quite understand. And I have enjoyed meeting you."

"And tomorrow you are leaving?"

"Yes. I am returning to Paris tomorrow."

"Goodbye," he said. "It has been most . . . revealing."

He walked slowly away and I made my way back to Marron.

* * *

Our last evening was spent with Ursule and Louis in their little house on the Carsonne estate.

It was a pleasant evening. Ursule said how she always looked forward to Henri's visits and she hoped that now I had come once I would come again.

I told them how interesting it had all been. I mentioned to them that I had been to the graveyard to see my mother's grave and had there met René. At first my father was taken aback but then he was reconciled.

"Poor René," he said. "Sometimes I think he wishes he had had the courage to break away."

"He is our father's puppet," replied Ursule rather fiercely. "He has done all that was expected of him and his reward will be the St. Allengère property in due course."

"Unless," said Louis, "he does something to earn the old man's disapproval before he dies."

"I am glad I chose freedom," said Ursule.

Later they talked about the Comte.

"He's a good employer," said Louis. "He gives me a free hand and as long as I keep the Carsonne collection in order I can paint when I will. Occasionally he arranges for me to have an exhibition. I don't know how we should have come through without his father and now him."

"He does it all to spite our father," said mine.

"The Comte has a fine appreciation of art," said Louis. "He respects an artist and I think he is not unimpressed by my work. I owe him a great deal."

"We both do," said Ursule. "So Henri, do not speak harshly of him in our household."

"I admit," said my father, "that he has been of use to you. But his reputation in the neighbourhood . . ."

"That's a family tradition," insisted Ursule. "The Comtes of Carsonne have always been a lusty lot. At least he doesn't assume the mask of piety like our own Papa . . . and think of the misery *he* has caused."

"I daresay de la Tour has caused discomfort in some quarters."

"Now, Henri, you are referring to Heloïse and you don't really know that he had anything to do with that."

"It's clear enough," said my father. "He has been making himself agreeable to Lenore."

"Then," said Ursule to me, "perhaps you should beware."

"Katie has formed a friendship with his son Raoul," went on my father. "She has been over there today. He sent the carriage for her. I'd like to tell him to keep away."

"Oh, you must be more diplomatic than that," said Ursule. "In any case you with Lenore and Katie are leaving for Paris tomorrow, so you will all be out of harm's way."

I was interested to hear what they had to say about him. In fact, it is all I remember of that last evening with Ursule and Louis.

The next day we left for Paris.

* * *

The Countess was there. Grand'mère and Cassie were still in London.

"Why," cried the Countess embracing me. "You look rejuvenated. What has happened to you?"

I found myself flushing.

"I enjoyed seeing the place," I said.

"We went to the *château,*" Katie told her. "There was a falcon there and ever so many dogs . . . little puppies some of them. They have an *oubliette* which they push people into when they want to forget them for ever more."

"I wish we had one here," said the Countess. "Madame Delorme has brought the mauve velvet back. She says it is too tight. She could be the first one to go in, if I had my way."

"If you leave them there they will die," said Katie.

"Good idea!" replied the Countess. "But we want to hear all about this visit."

Katie burst into a vivid description of the *vendange.*

"The best one was at the *château.* They danced in the tubs, Countess. Great big tubs and the juice was all over their feet and legs. But they scrubbed them before they started. It was a purple mess."

"As Madame Delorme's velvet will be by the time we have altered it to fit her increasing bulk."

She talked a great deal about what had been happening in the salon during our absence, and I noticed that she kept watching me as though she thought I was harbouring some secret.

I had not been back three days when there was a caller at the salon. The Countess received him and came hurrying to me, beaming.

"A gentleman to see you. He wouldn't give his name. He said he wanted to surprise you. What manners! What an air! Who is this man?"

"I had better go and see," I said; but I knew before I saw him.

He was smiling at me almost sardonically.

"My dear Madame Sallonger, I was in Paris and I could not return to Carsonne without looking you up."

The Countess was beside me, bubbling over with excitement.

"The Countess of Ballader," I said. "The Comte de Carsonne."

"Well, I am delighted to meet you," said the Countess.

"And I you, Countess."

"You would like some refreshment?" she said. "A little wine?"

"The Comte is a connoisseur of wine," I said. "He produces his own. I don't think we have anything suitable for his palate."

"Whatever you offered me," he said, "would be nectar. I am so happy to be here in Paris."

"A favourite city of yours, Comte?" asked the Countess.

"At the moment . . . my favourite."

She left us together, smiling secretly.

I turned to him.

"Please look pleased to see me," he begged.

"I am so surprised."

"Are you? Surely you did not think I would allow you to escape so easily."

"It is not a matter of escape."

"Forgive me. An ill chosen expression. I am delighted to see you. You have a very elegant establishment here."

"One must be elegant in Paris."

"I accept the compliment on behalf of the city. While I am here I am going to show you a good deal of it."

"I have been here some time, you know."

"I know. But I am sure I can surprise you."

"I have no doubt you will attempt to do that."

The Countess returned with a bottle, some glasses and wine cakes. "Come into the sitting room," she said. "It is more comfortable."

She poured the wine into two glasses. "Now," she went on, "I am going to leave you two as I am sure you wish to talk together."

"How kind you are," said the Comte.

She gave him a dazzling smile. I could see that she was a little fascinated by him and that she had decided that he was for me. Her profession had fitted her for selecting husbands for the unmarried in her circle and she was already planning for me.

She quite clearly did not know the Comte.

"What a charming lady," he said.

"Yes. I have known her for some years. She used to bring people out, as they say. That is, she prepared them for presentation at Court, and helped them to find the right husbands."

"What a useful lady she must be!"

"She no longer does that, of course. She is now one of the directors of our salon. How long are you staying in Paris?"

He smiled at me, lifting his shoulders. "Who can say? So much depends on . . . circumstances."

"Where do you stay?"

"I have a place in the Rue du Faubourg Saint-Honoré just before it becomes the Rue Saint-Honoré at the Rue Royale."

"I know the place."

"It has been the family's Paris residence for about fifty years. Our old *hôtel* was burned down during the revolution."

"Are you in Paris often?"

"When business . . . or pleasure . . . brings me here."

I heard Katie's voice. She was arguing with the Countess.

"Your mother is busy."

Katie peeped round the door. "Oh," she cried in delight. "It's the Comte." She ran forward and held out her hand to be kissed.

The Comte responded gracefully.

"Where is Raoul?" she asked.

"Alas, he is in Carsonne."

"Why didn't you bring him with you?"

"I have important business here and he has his duties in Carsonne."

"That's a pity."

"I will let him know what you said. He will be gratified."

Mademoiselle Leclerc came in. She was obviously looking for Katie.

"This is Mademoiselle Leclerc, Katie's French governess," I said.

I was ashamed of the twinge of annoyance I felt as I saw his eyes upon her—assessing her, I thought. She was very pretty and younger than I. I noticed the effect he had on her; she flushed and her eyes seemed to brighten. One would never be sure of him, I thought.

Mademoiselle Leclerc said she had come to take Katie for a walk.

"Go along now, Katie," I said.

"Shall you be here when I come back?" she asked the Comte.

"I hope to be," he said.

She looked pleased and went off with her governess.

"What an enchanting child she is," he said. "She could only be yours. I should like her to see more of Raoul."

I was still thinking of the governess.

"So while I am here," he went on, "I shall show you Paris."

"As I told you, I am no stranger to it."

"I mean the real Paris . . . which only a native can show you. I can think of so much I want you to see."

I was wonderfully happy during the days that followed. I knew that I was falling under his spell and I told myself I need have no fear. I was not an innocent girl. I would always remember the sort of man I was dealing with . . . polished, worldly, looking for new sensations and fresh woods to conquer. I would always remember that and pride myself on my common sense.

But everything seemed different when he was around. He was indefatigable in his attempts to please me and the days were a kaleidoscope of shifting emotions . . . too delightful to set aside. I could be happy and carefree as I had not been for years, catching his moods, but always at the height of my pleasure I was aware of the warning voice. Every now and then the image of Heloïse lying in the shallow water came to me. There was my mother, too. She had loved recklessly and unwisely. I could understand their feelings. It would be easy to give way to moments of recklessness with a man like this.

But mostly I gave myself up to the sheer enjoyment of those golden days. I learned a great deal about him. There was a serious side to his nature and his life was by no means given over entirely to sensual pleasures. He was deeply knowledgeable. He was something of a connoisseur of art. He was well versed in his country's history and to be with him was to share that interest. His love of his country was fierce —and yet he was essentially critical which made discussion especially interesting. I felt I was learning a great deal about many things, including myself.

I looked forward to our meetings. I knew my father was anxious but I assured him he had no need to fear. He did though. The Countess was in a fever of excitement. She was completely fascinated by the Comte. He knew exactly how to treat all women and to adjust his attitude to what he believed would please them best.

He brought presents for Katie, flowers for the Countess. He deferred to my father. He was anxious to be on good terms with the entire household. It was part of his strategy.

He took us to the opera to see *Orpheus in the Underworld*. He told me it was a particular favourite of his because of the fun it poked at the gods. It was a delightful performance and we all enjoyed it. Even my father was laughing; and when we drove home the enchanting music was ringing in my ears. I told myself that it would be among my favourites ever after.

The Countess was eager that I should enjoy my expeditions. I said I should be working, but she would not hear of it.

"We can manage perfectly well," she insisted. "After all, we did while you were away. This is just an extension of your holiday. Plenty of time for work . . . later."

Those days sped by at an incredible rate. I knew I should never forget them. Paris is one of the most delightful cities in the world, and under the guidance of the Comte it was an enchanted place. Sometimes Katie accompanied us; but more often we were alone.

We climbed to Montmartre, he holding my arm as we mounted the steep streets. We visited the Cathedral, that rather bizarre oriental building which has always been so much a landmark of Paris. He talked of St. Denis, the patron saint of France, and the martyrs who had been put to death here. He showed me the great bell—Françoise-Marguerite or La Savoyarde de Montmartre which was nine feet tall. He made me listen to its unusual timbre. I had been here with my father when I first came to Paris but everything seemed to have acquired a new and exciting quality now. I was seeing much which I had seen before without noticing. He brought a new light to everything and that which had been insignificant had become of absorbing interest.

His sense of the past was ever-present. He talked sadly of the Revolution which had destroyed the old way of life, and bitterly of the masses and of his ancestors who had suffered at their hands. Only extraordinary good fortune had saved his branch of the family.

"The blood lust," he said, "the bile of envy . . . the desire to destroy because this one has something which that one lacks." He took me to the Conciergerie, into the vaulted Salle Saint Louis called the *Salle des Pas Perdus* on account of the fact that those condemned to die passed through it on their way to the guillotine. He was grim when we saw the cell in which Marie Antoinette had spent her last days. "Subject to humiliation inflicted by petty tyrants," he said with venom.

Then I saw a different side to him. He was surprising me all the time.

His knowledge of art was profound as I discovered when we visited the Louvre. He showed me new aspects of pictures I had seen before. He was fascinated by Leonardo da Vinci and we stood for a long time in the Grande Galerie while he discussed the *Virgin on the Rocks.* Of course he had much to say on the Mona Lisa which had been in the country since 1793; and he told me how François Premier, who had cared deeply for artists, had brought Leonardo from Italy that he might have first claim on his works. "He was an artist *manqué,"* he said, "as perhaps I am. But I am afraid there are a good many *man-ques* in my life."

"One which is not, is the wisdom to know it," I told him.

Such happy days! I shall never forget them. Each morning there was a fresh adventure. This, I told myself, is the way to live. But I reminded myself a hundred times a day, it was ephemeral. There had to be an ending . . . soon.

But I clung to each moment, savouring it to the full. I had an uneasy feeling that I was becoming his victim as he had all the time intended that I should. I had lost sight of that fact in discovering new sides to his nature.

We went to Père-Lachaise—so much a part of Paris. I had often wondered who Père-La Chaise was and he told me that he was the fashionable confessor of Louis XIV and that the cemetery was so named from his house which had stood where the present chapel now did. We looked at the monuments and the graves of the famous.

"A lesson to us all," he said. "Life is short. The wise make the most of every moment."

He pressed my arm and smiled at me.

I very much enjoyed the open spaces. I loved the elegance of the Parc Monceau which seemed to be full of children with their nurses and unusual statues of people like Chopin with his piano and figures representing Night and Harmony, of Gounod with Marguerite. The children loved them and when I took Katie there she was loathe to be drawn away from them.

It was one day when we were together in the Jardin des Plantes that I realized these halcyon days were almost over. We sat on a seat watching the peacocks and I remembered once saying to him that in certain moments one realizes that one is completely happy. This was such a moment.

I said to him: "I shall have to go home soon."

"Home?" he said. "Where is home?"

"London."

"Why must you go?"

"Because I have been away so long."

"But is not Paris your home, too?"

"One can only have one real home."

"Are you telling me you are homesick?"

"I just have the feeling that I must go. It is a long time since I saw my grandmother."

"I hope you will not go just yet. These have been pleasant days, have they not?"

"Very pleasant. I am afraid I have taken up a lot of your time."

"That time has been spent in the way I wished it to be. You know that, don't you? These meetings have been as agreeable to me as I hope they have been to you."

"I will be frank," I said. "You have a motive, and it may be that you are wasting your time."

"My motive is pleasure. I find it and that is never a waste of time."

I was silent. I could hardly refuse him that which he had not asked for . . . except in a subtle way.

"Why are you pensive?" he asked.

"I am thinking of home."

"I cannot allow that. Where would you like to go tomorrow?"

"Tomorrow I shall prepare to go home."

"Please stay. Think how desolate I shall be if you leave."

"I fancy you would quickly find some other diversion."

"Is that how you think of yourself . . . a diversion?"

"No. It is what I intend not to be."

"You know my feelings for you."

"You have made them plain."

"You have enjoyed our excursions?"

"They have been most illuminating."

"You will miss them when you go away."

"I daresay I shall. But I am very busy in London. There will be so much to catch up with."

"And then you will forget me?"

"I shall think of you, I am sure."

He took my hand. "Why are you afraid?" he asked.

"Afraid? I?"

"Yes. Afraid, you . . . afraid to let me come too close."

"I think I may be different from most of the women you know."

"You are indeed. That is one of the things about you which I find so attractive."

"So therefore I do not react as you are accustomed to expect."

"How do you know what I expect?"

"Because I realize the sort of life you have led."

"Do you know me so well?"

"I think I know you well enough to deduce certain things."

He gripped my arm. "Don't go," he said. "Let us get to know each other . . . really well."

I knew what he was suggesting and I was ashamed that it presented some temptation. I shook him off angrily. A love affair? It would be torrid, wildly exciting . . . until it burned itself out. Such an adventure was not for me. I wanted a steady relationship. A few weeks . . . perhaps a few months . . . of passion were no substitute for that.

Suppose he had suggested marriage? Even then I should have hesitated. My common sense told me that I should have to think very dispassionately before I entered into any form of relationship with him. But of course he was not suggesting marriage. He had married once for the sake of the family, and he wanted his freedom now . . . no encumbrances. He had a strong and healthy heir. He had done his duty to Carsonne. No more marriage for him. He would be free.

I thought: Why have I let this go so far? Why have I allowed my emotions to become involved? I had and I greatly feared that I could be overwhelmed by him.

I looked at the proud peacock, his beautiful feathered tail arrogantly displayed, and the pale little peahen trotting along behind him.

Somehow that gave me strength.

Never. Never, I told myself.

I stood up. I said coolly: "I think it is time that we were going."

Blackmail

Katie and I returned to London, my father accompanying us because he did not want us to travel alone. I knew that he was relieved because we were going for he had been deeply affected by the Comte's pursuit—particularly after he had appeared in Paris.

"You enjoyed your visit?" he asked me tentatively.

I replied that it had been one of the most interesting periods of my life, at which he was silent.

It was wonderful to see Grand'mère again. I noticed her studying me intently, and at the earliest moment she found an opportunity of speaking to me alone.

She said: "You look different . . . younger. I saw the change in you the moment you arrived."

I told her that I had seen René in the graveyard. "I went there to look for my mother's grave," I explained.

"So you saw your father's brother. Did he speak to you?"

"Yes. He was quite friendly. He was at Heloïse's grave. He knew who I was. He had heard that I was at my father's vineyards and he recognized me. He said I was very like my mother."

She nodded emotionally. "I wonder what he thought to see you there. I don't suppose he told the old man. There would have been trouble if he had."

"He really seemed more interested in my scarf than in me."

"Your scarf?"

"Yes. I dropped it and he picked it up and saw that it was made of

Sallon Silk. Then he talked about Philip. He thought he had discovered it. He was really taken aback when I told him it was Charles."

"That family thought of little else but silk. They must have been really put out when someone other than themselves discovered the Sallon method. But something else happened?"

"Do you remember the *château* there?"

"Carsonne. Of course. Everyone knows the *château* and the de la Tours."

"I met Gaston de la Tour."

"The present Comte!"

I nodded. "Oh," she said blankly.

I told her about the encounter with the dogs and our being invited to the *vendange* and how Katie and his son had got on so well together.

"Well, that was interesting," she said, watching me intently.

"I met him in Paris."

"You mean he followed you to Paris."

"No. He was there when we were."

"And you saw something of him."

I nodded.

"I see. So that is it."

"What do you mean, Grand'mère . . . that is it?"

"I mean he is responsible . . . for the change in you."

"I do not know that there is any change."

"You may take it from me that there is. Oh, Lenore, this is the last thing I wanted to happen. I've worried a lot about you. Since Philip's death you have been lonely."

"Lonely! With you and Katie and the Countess and Cassie?"

"I mean missing your husband."

"I miss him, of course."

"And this Gaston de la Tour . . . he seems to have made an impression on you."

"He is quite an impressive person."

"You are bemused by his title and his possessions . . . his power . . ."

"I suppose they are very much a part of him."

"You saw a great deal of him?"

"We were together every day in Paris. He took me to so many

places and he is so knowledgeable about art, history and architecture that he made me see things differently."

"Oh, Lenore . . . don't you see . . . ?"

"Look, Grand'mère, you are worrying unnecessarily. I came back to London, didn't I? I could have stayed in Paris. He was there."

"I know that he is attractive and that he has a way with women. His attitude towards them is quite lighthearted. He is not good for you, Lenore. I know the family well. They have lorded it over the neighbourhood for generations. They thought they had rights to any woman they fancied. That was how they lived in the old days and Carsonne has not moved with the times."

"I understand that, Grand'mère. I was aware of it all the time, but I did enjoy meeting him. He was so . . . alive . . . so amusing . . . and different from any man I have ever known. As you say, I have been a little dull perhaps since Philip died. I enjoyed our meetings but I never lost sight of what our friendship meant to him and what his ultimate aim was. I was as determined that he should not reach it as he was determined to. It needs two people to come to a decision like that, Grand'mère, and we were not in agreement on it. I know what is in your mind so I will assure you that I am still a chaste widow."

"There would be heartbreak with that one. I am sorry you met him."

"Don't be, Grand'mère. It was an experience . . . and I am none the worse for it."

She sighed with relief. "Thank God you are home."

"Katie admired him," I told her. "He was charming to her."

"But of course he would be. He saw his way through her to you. *Mon Dieu,* I should have been worried if I had known it had gone so far."

"I was always aware of the sort of man he is."

"But I can see that you were not unaffected."

"Well frankly, it would have been difficult not to be. When I was there I heard about René's daughter, Heloïse. She killed herself because of an unfaithful lover. It is generally believed that the Comte was the man in the case. He would take a delight in seducing a St. Allengère. That feud has been going on for a long time. That sort of thing is so senseless. I believe my grandfather is not the saint he makes himself out to be."

"You are right. A bigger hypocrite was never born."

"So I gathered. Passions run high in your native land, Grand'mère. Knowing all this I am not likely to want to get involved, am I?"

"That's true enough. I often think of how pleased I was when you and Philip were married. Such a good man he was. I thought you were settled for life. I was so content."

"But one never knows what is going to happen, Grand'mère."

"Alas, that is true. To think that it went wrong . . . Then I wanted you and that Drake Aldringham . . . Now there was a man one could trust. I never cease to regret that went wrong."

"You can't make life work out just as you want it to."

She nodded. I asked her about the business and what had been happening during my absence; and I began to think of Drake. His image had dimmed considerably since my meeting with Gaston de la Tour.

* * *

Cassie was delighted to see us back. She told me how much she had missed Katie and me.

"Sometimes I wish we were all together as we were in the beginning," she said. "The Paris salon has split us up."

"You should go over to Paris, Cassie. You would enjoy it."

She shook her head. "I'm better here."

It was true she was invaluable to the London salon. She had become an excellent business woman; she was determined to make the best of life, to forget her disabilities and concentrate on her assets. She and Grand'mère had become very close and worked well together.

After she had shown me what was going on in the workroom—her special domain for she had an aversion to dealing with clients—she told me how worried she was about Julia.

"She is drinking more heavily than ever. People are talking about it. They are saying that Drake made the biggest mistake of his life. He married her to further his career and she is turning out to be an impediment. I visit her. Drake isn't there much. Julia is unhappy. I think she cares for him quite a lot . . . but he can't return her affection. He stays away and is in that country place most of the time. I don't think it is helping his career. I have seen them together now and then . . . and I think he has come near to hating her."

"How very sad."

"You must come and see her sometimes. She probably knows that you are back and will be hurt if you don't."

"But I don't think she wants to see me."

"She does. She is always talking about you."

"I'll come one day then."

So I went with Cassie to Julia's house which was now Drake's London headquarters.

When we were ushered into the drawing room I was amazed to see the change in Julia. She had grown very fat; her colour was deeper and tinged with purple; her eyes were a little glazed.

I was greeted effusively.

"Lenore . . . recently come from Paris! You look it, my dear, doesn't she, Cassie? So elegant! How do you keep so *thin?* I'm overflowing everywhere . . . even my maid sees that it is useless to force myself into my corsets. There comes a time when you give up trying to look what you are not. Have some sherry. Cassie, ring the bell. Tell them to bring some of those wine biscuits."

Cassie obeyed and Julia poured out the sherry—an ample one for herself, I noticed.

"Well, this *is* fun!" she said, lifting her glass. "Like old times. Do you remember . . . at The Silk House. Quite a lot has happened since then. Poor Philip gone . . . and you a widow, Lenore. Did you ever think of marrying again?" Was there something sour in her look? Was she implying that she remembered how it was once between Drake and me?

"I've remained a widow," I said.

"Poor Lenore! It must be from choice."

I did not answer. She refilled her glass and drank quickly.

"Being a political wife is not all that much fun, you know," she said. "I sometimes think I should have been like you, Lenore, and remained a widow." She shrugged her shoulders. "Well, as long as one knows how to enjoy oneself."

Cassie looked uneasy and I was wondering how soon we could take our leave when Drake came in.

Julia was suddenly alert; she set down her glass; and I wondered whether she had arranged our meeting for a time when he would be there. She was watching Drake intently. He could not hide his surprise . . . and pleasure . . . at seeing me.

"Why, Lenore," he said, advancing and taking my hands.

"It is nice to see you, Drake," I said.

"I heard you were in Paris."

"I have not been back so very long."

"Have a glass of sherry, darling," said Julia.

"No thank you."

She pouted. "I suppose you think I have had too much."

"I did not mention the fact."

"No, but you looked it. When you marry, Lenore, make sure you don't get a critical husband. They are such a bore."

Drake did not answer. He turned to me. "I hope all is going well with the Paris branch."

"Very well indeed. The Countess is a wonderful business woman."

"I suppose you all are. Cassie tells us things are working out well."

There was silence.

"You should have gone in for that line of business, Drake, instead of politics," said Julia. "It might not have kept you away from home so much . . . if that is what keeps you away."

The colour in her face had deepened. I wondered how much she had drunk before we arrived. She turned to us. "He is so rarely at home . . . only flying visits when it is essential for him to be in Town. He longs to be back in the country, don't you, Drake? All that nursing of the silly old constituency. It's not very grateful, is it? Last time he scraped in with a minute majority."

Drake tried to infuse a note of conventionality into the conversation.

"That is how elections go," he said.

"Of course he was hoping for a government post. But you never know where you are in politics. The party is out and you are out. No one with any sense goes into it."

Drake laughed apologetically. "I daresay you are right," he said.

"I think it is an exciting profession," I said. "Of course there is a great deal of luck needed, and so much depends on what party is in power, but guiding the way the country goes must be fascinating."

"More sherry?" asked Julia.

Cassie and I declined and she helped herself to another glassful.

Drake frowned and said: "Julia, do you think you ought?"

She laughed. "Do I think I ought, he says! That's because you two are here. He doesn't care how much I drink. He's hoping I'll drink myself to death."

Suddenly she began to cry. It was most embarrassing. I knew she was intoxicated. Drake went to her and laid a hand on her shoulder. "Julia is not very well," he said. He took out a handkerchief and wiped her eyes and then gently took the glass from her.

She clung to him passionately.

Cassie rose and said, "Well, we'll be going. We'll see you soon, Julia."

Julia nodded.

Drake came with us to the door. He took my hand and said: "Lenore, I must see you. Could we meet in the park . . . where we used to . . . near the ducks?"

I nodded.

As we left the house Cassie said: "That was most unfortunate. She is in a sad way. You can see how she is drinking. She is very unhappy really. She loves Drake passionately . . . and he doesn't love her. He is very good really. He tries to pretend but it shows, doesn't it? She's not usually as bad as that. I think it was because you were there. She's always been jealous of you, Lenore. I often feel that if Drake could fall in love with her, it might save her."

"He is her husband."

"That doesn't make any difference. He has never really loved her. He married her to help his career, people say."

"I don't think that was quite the case."

"At one time we thought he was in love with you."

I did not answer.

"But he married Julia. I think it was because she was rich. It is a mistake to marry for that reason. He soon found that out."

"I think perhaps you misjudge him. One can never really know why people do certain things."

"You're right, of course, and I am so desperately sorry for them both. He must have thought it was going to be so different when he married her . . . and so did she. It's all gone wrong for them."

I was certainly depressed by what I had seen that morning.

* * *

I was uneasy as I prepared for my rendez-vous with Drake. It seemed so strange to be meeting him in the park where we had met so many times in the past. He was waiting for me on the seat where we used to sit.

When I reached him he took both my hands and looked searchingly into my face.

"It is so good of you to come, Lenore," he said.

"It is like old times," I replied.

He sighed. "How I wish I could go back. I'd do it all so differently."

"That's what we all feel at some time."

"I had to talk to you. I had to tell you what was really happening. Life is quite intolerable at times . . . and when I think how it might have been . . . Lenore, I wonder how I can go on."

"You have your career," I said.

"Thank God. I am kept busy, but working here is difficult. I am in Swaddingham as much as I can be, but I am baulked at every turn."

"Poor Drake! I am so sorry."

"It is wonderful that you are back in London. I've missed you so much. Lenore, if only things had gone differently. Please don't go away again."

I said: "I daresay I shall be here for a while."

"You understand . . . about Julia. I realized very quickly that there was not to be a child. She tricked me. God forgive me, I hate her for it. I try not to. She is pathetic sometimes. You saw something of what she was like when you were with her, but you have no idea how violent she can be. And partly it is my fault. She has an obsession for me. If I could only return her feeling . . . if only I could convince her . . . but I can't, Lenore. It's all so false. I can't pretend to that extent. She knows I never loved her. She knows I married her because I was tricked. She hates herself for tricking me. Poor Julia, I want to help her. I want to cure her of this drinking . . . but it is beyond me and sometimes I show the repulsion I feel. I think of you constantly. Always I say, If only . . . I must see you sometimes, Lenore. Please, let us meet."

"In the circumstances, Drake, I think it would be unwise for us to meet," I said.

"I was sure you felt something for me. I wanted to ask you to marry me. I hesitated. I thought a great deal about your first husband. I know you cared for him. I was always saying to myself, I must wait . . . wait until the time is ripe . . . wait until she has completely broken away from the past. But I waited too long . . . and this has happened."

I felt numb. It was a fact that had he asked me I should have said Yes. I was sure that I loved him then; he was a part of my past: the gallant man who had rescued me from the mausoleum, who had come again into my life to take me away from that lost past with Philip, just as he had from the fear of that dark place. I would have gone to him gratefully. I believed that I should have been happy with him . . . in a quiet, safe way . . . the way Grand'mère wished for me. We would have raised a family in that delightful country house; there would have been visits to London. I should have kept my interest in the salon. Yes, I could see that it could have been a happy way of life.

But I had been disturbed. Should I have been completely happy? I kept seeing the ironic, amused and sardonic eyes of the Comte—the dark, rather saturnine good looks, the magnetic charm, the exciting personality. I could never now settle into the quiet way of life without thinking of him and what my conventional upbringing had forced me to miss.

His coming into my life had changed everything. I was foolish to think of him. He was as forbidden to me as Drake was.

I said: "It is all in the past, Drake. No good comes of thinking of what might have been."

"I could find it more tolerable if I knew that you loved me. If I had asked you, would you have married me?"

I nodded.

"Lenore, that has made me very happy."

"We should not talk of these things."

"What you have said makes me feel that I can tolerate life here in London the more easily . . . thinking of you. We must meet again here."

"I can't believe that would be a wise thing to do."

"We could meet . . . by chance . . . by the pond. If I could just see you from time to time . . ."

I shook my head.

"Please," he said. "It would help me so much."

"We should not make a habit of it."

His face lightened. "I want to talk to you about so many things . . . politics . . . the constituency . . . I've often looked up at the gallery and imagined you were there. You would have come to see me at the House, wouldn't you? You would have done so much to help me. Julia, I think, hates my work. I feel so much better now that you are back."

He seemed so vulnerable, which was strange for Drake. From the moment he had visited The Silk House he had seemed the strong one. Julia was ruining her life with drink. I was sorry for her but I could see that Drake was almost as helpless.

Surely there could be no harm in an occasional meeting in the park?

* * *

My father had gone back to France and I turned once more to work which had been such a solace to me on other occasions. There was plenty to occupy me. I tried not to think of the Comte. Grand'mère was right about him. To him I was just another woman whom it pleased him to pursue for a time. I imagined that since the hunt had not been productive he had decided to turn his attention elsewhere. I was depressed hoping that he would come to London and prove to Grand'mère that she had misjudged him.

Drake was a more immediate concern. He called at the salon. There was a certain recklessness about him. Grand'mère was very fond of him, but she did not wish me to be caught up with a man who had a wife. That would be even more undesirable than my friendship with the Comte.

I had told Drake several times that we should not see each other, but he was so sad when I did. "To see you . . . to talk to you . . . I cannot explain what it means to me. Sometimes I am afraid of what I will do if I don't break away."

"You have always been so calm," I told him. "So very able to deal with any situation."

"I have never been faced with such a situation before and to realize I have brought it on myself does not make it any more acceptable. There are times when I can hardly trust myself not to do her some injury."

"For Heaven's sake, don't talk like that."

"I can understand how some people are goaded too far. I want you to know my feelings, Lenore. These meetings with you do so much for me. I must see you."

I was really afraid for him. I was very fond of him. I did see in him all the sterling qualities Grand'mère had pointed out to me. After all, he was in this position because of his honourable nature. He had married Julia because he had thought it was the only right thing to do. How could he have guessed that she had tricked him.

I was desperately sorry for him—and in a way for Julia too. I knew from Cassie what the situation was for when she was in a state of intoxication, Julia could be very frank.

I could see it all so clearly: Julia passionately in love with a husband who hated her. I think she had loved Drake . . . idolized him . . . from the time he had come to The Silk House as a handsome boy, head of the school, the hero, looked up to by Charles who had considered it such an honour when Drake consented to spend his holidays with him. I remembered her wrath against me when he had gone. Julia had wanted Drake from the moment she had set eyes on him. She had contrived to get him—but in trapping him, she had lost him.

Poor Julia! I could imagine those tormented nights when he was in the house . . . sleeping in another room. She had told Cassie how she paced her room, railing against his indifference, turning to the bottle which was always beside her wherever she was. She told me of the quarrels between them, how she was always upbraiding him because he did not care for her enough, how he would not indulge in quarrels. "Escape! He always wants to escape," Julia had cried. "He always wants to get away from me but I will never let him do that. He is mine for as long as we live. If I can't have him, no one else shall."

I thought a great deal about them. It stopped my thinking solely of the Comte and wondering what he was doing now. I imagined he had returned to Carsonne. I wondered if he ever thought of me. Perhaps now and then as the frigid woman who had refused to be seduced . . . and on whom he had wasted too much time.

And so I continued to see Drake. It was unavoidable. When I went out he would be waiting for me. It was no use remonstrating with him. I could see how much he needed companionship. We talked of the state of the government and what Salisbury was doing and what Gladstone would have done, but somehow we always got back to Julia.

There was a little tea shop just off Piccadilly conveniently near. It was a pleasant place with tables in alcoves where one could talk in peace. They sold delicious maids-of-honour and madeleines. Katie considered it a special treat to be brought there to tea.

One day we went there. We sat and talked. I wanted to hear how things were going. I was always trying to make him forget his unsatisfactory marriage which I hoped he would do by his complete absorption in politics.

He brightened considerably when he discussed his aims and achievements. He confided in me his concern about the health of Gladstone which was fast failing.

"Rosebery is not his equal," he said. "But then, who is?"

"Gladstone could not always hold the party together, and he is now an old man."

"There are many people jostling for power . . . ready to do anything however discreditable to take a step up the ladder."

"But you are not like that, Drake."

"Perhaps that is a lack in me."

"Never," I assured him.

"Oh, Lenore, how different it might have been. When I think of that I feel mad with rage. So easily it could have happened and somehow it slipped away from me."

"There's no going back, Drake."

"I have loved you ever since I brought you out of that mausoleum. You were so small and frightened. Then I didn't see you for years . . . but I felt the same when I did. Why did she have to be there? If I were free, you would marry me."

I was silent.

"You would, wouldn't you, Lenore?" he said earnestly. "You do love me?"

It was almost as though the Comte was sitting opposite me, laughing. Do you feel excited with him? Do you feel that sense of adventure? Do you feel that you want to be with him more than anyone else on earth? That is how you feel about *me,* Madame Sallonger. Do you feel the same for this man? Tell the truth now.

I said: "I'm so fond of you, Drake. I love you, but being in love is different, isn't it?"

He looked at me steadily. "You mean you are fond of me but not in love with me?"

"I was in love with Philip and I thought it would be forever. And, Drake, it is unwise to talk in this way."

"I could make you happy, Lenore, if . . ."

"It cannot be," I said.

He was silent and so was I. I wished I could rid my mind of the image of that dark sceptical face. But I felt I never would forget it and it was going to make all the difference to my feelings for anyone else.

He put his hand across the table and held mine.

Then I heard my own name. "Lenore! How wonderful to see you!" Charles was standing by our table. Embarrassed, I hastily removed my hand.

"Lenore . . . and my respected brother-in-law! How are you, Lenore? You look well."

I was blushing, for being so discovered by him.

He was not alone. There was a woman with him and her face was vaguely familiar.

"This," he said, "is Signorina de' Pucci."

She smiled and bowed her head. She was outstandingly beautiful; her almost coal black hair was visible under the jaunty white straw hat with its black and white ribbons; her costume was black with white stripes, and the frilly silk blouse she wore was white. She was a very elegant woman.

"This is Madame Lenore of the Lenore Salon of which, dear Signorina, you will be aware if you spend much time in London. Lenore is a very clever business woman; and this is my brother-in-law, Drake Aldringham."

She said she was charmed. She had a faint accent which like everything else about her was charming. Her name was familiar as was her face . . . although it was many years since I had seen her.

I said: "I remember now. You had an accident and came to The Silk House."

Her face lit up. "So you remember."

"It was hardly the sort of thing one forgets."

"You were the new bride. Oh, I recall it so well . . . such a charming couple. And your husband . . . ?" She looked at Drake in puzzlement.

"Yes," I said, "Philip Sallonger. He died soon after."

"Oh . . . how sad."

Charles was giving me that speculative look which I remembered so well.

"We have just had tea," he said. "Those maids-of-honour are delicious. I was determined to introduce Signorina de' Pucci to them while she is in London."

I said: "It all comes back to me so vividly. You left us suddenly."

"I did not think it was sudden. My brother sent for me . . . and I went."

"I was furious, wasn't I, Lenore?" said Charles.

"Yes, you were."

"But why?" she asked. "Why should you be furious?"

"Because you had left us. I wanted us to get more and more acquainted. We were making good progress."

"Has Julia met the Signorina?" I asked.

Charles shook his head. "She will, though. She will be interested. We all remember your visit so well."

"I trust there were no ill effects from the injury?"

"Injury?" she murmured.

"Didn't you hurt your ankle in the carriage upset?"

"Yes . . . so I did. It soon healed." She smiled charmingly at Drake. "I do not know what would have become of me but for these good friends."

"We were glad to do what we could," said Charles. "By great good fortune I ran into the Signorina close to the house. We stared at each other. I'm afraid I was rather rude."

"No . . . no," she protested.

"I was so delighted," said Charles.

"And how long will you be in England this time?" I asked.

"It depends on my brother. He does much business. He is in your Midlands. When he comes I go back with him."

"I remember your maid . . . Maria. Is she still with you?"

"Maria is with me."

"Well, I hope you enjoy your stay."

"I shall see that she does," promised Charles. "Well . . . I did enjoy seeing you both." He looked from one to the other of us significantly. "I daresay we shall see you again. I am taking the Signorina to see Julia now. *Au revoir.*"

I watched them go. Then I said: "That was most unfortunate. I mean . . . Charles's seeing us together here."

Drake lifted his shoulders. I thought then that he was so desperately immersed in his own unfortunate situation that he refused to see the danger. But I did not like the manner in which Charles had looked at us; nor did I like the implication of his words.

I told Drake what had happened, how the Italian had had her accident outside The Silk House and had stayed there for a few days, and how she had left to join her brother and there were only letters of thanks sent from a London hotel, so that she had completely disappeared from our lives.

"It was soon after that that Philip died," I said. "I forgot all about the incident. In fact at first I could not recall who she was, although she seemed familiar."

"It's interesting that Charles should have met her . . . just by chance."

"It seems to me that almost everything happens just by chance."

After I was back in the salon I could not help thinking about that meeting in the tea shop, and I felt rather uneasy because Charles had discovered Drake and me there together, and of the construction which I was afraid a man of his nature might put upon it.

* * *

It was Cassie who told me about Charles and Madalenna de' Pucci.

"She is staying in a hotel with her maid while she is waiting for her brother to join her."

"Yes. She mentioned that when I met her." I had told Cassie about seeing her in the tea shop where Drake and I had decided to have some tea.

Cassie looked a little subdued. She knew about my friendship with Drake. In fact she knew a good deal. Cassie was inclined to live vicariously. She was very interested in what happened to other people. She was kindly and deeply understanding and I had always thought that this was due to her interest in people. She knew them so well that she understood their motives and that made her sympathetic towards them.

"Charles," she told me, "is very taken with her. Of course she is very beautiful . . . exceptionally so and I suppose being foreign makes her look more so. It is very sad about Charles and Helen." Helen was his wife. "He has never been a faithful husband. I think she has long accepted that. But in this case he seems to be deeply involved."

I said: "He was attracted to her when she came to the house before. I remember how angry he was when she went away without letting him know where."

"It is very distressing. When I think of that marriage . . . and

Julia and Drake . . . I come to the conclusion that one is often better off single."

"It makes life less complicated," I agreed. "One is on an even keel. There are lots of ups and downs in most relationships."

"I should hate to be Helen with an unfaithful husband . . . or Julia to love so intensely and be rejected. It was different with you and Philip. That was wonderful but he died."

I nodded.

"I'm sorry," went on Cassie. "I should not have mentioned it and reminded you. Oh dear, you ought to have married Drake. It is clear that he loves you. It was what your grandmother wanted."

"Things don't always turn out as people want them to."

"I do wish Julia could be happy. But I don't think she ever will be. I am afraid she is getting worse. She is drinking all the time . . . far more than we see. She was lying down when I last called and I went to her bedroom. I was sure she was intoxicated. I went to the wardrobe to get her a wrap and I saw several bottles there. She drinks in secret as well as in front of everybody. How did she get like that, Lenore? Was it unhappiness?"

"Her first husband was a great drinker. She may have learned the habit from him. I expect she found it to her liking and now it seems to be a solace. She is ruining her health and her life and her chance of happiness."

"It is a tragedy. I often think of those days when she was coming out. Do you remember how excited she was? Then the Countess came . . . and how frightened she grew. Poor Julia. She used to eat too much then and now it is drink. She was so sure of herself at one moment and so unsure the next. And how awful it was for her during that first season when she didn't come up to expectations!"

"I remember it well."

"Then she married that old man and he left her rich. I think if she had found someone younger before she got the feeling that she was not as attractive as some girls . . . she might have been different. I feel a sort of protectiveness towards Julia."

"I think you do towards us all."

"I do want you to come with me when I go to see her. Do, Lenore. I am sure she wants to see you, too."

"I am not sure of that."

"But she does. She is always talking about you. Do understand, Lenore, she is very unhappy."

I did go to see her. She made me very welcome. She looked much brighter. I wondered if she realized what harm she was doing to herself and was trying to reform.

She was excited. She was going to give a party. It was the fashion now to engage a pianist to give a performance. She thought that would be a wonderful idea. A number of Drake's colleagues would be invited. "A piano performance and then a buffet supper afterwards," she cried. "Don't you think that would be a good idea?"

Cassie was so glad to see her interested that she was enthusiastic.

"You will come," she said to me, and I agreed to go.

Grand'mère was rather subdued these days. She knew that I was meeting Drake and this worried her. She was very anxious. I believed she was thinking I had been celibate too long. I was young and I had tasted the joys of married life briefly. Grand'mère would like to see me respectably married to a good man. I think that was her great desire. Drake would have been ideal in her eyes if he had not been married already.

I sensed then that she had a fear that I might be carried away by my emotions. I wanted to explain to her that my feelings for Drake had never been such as to drive me into reckless action. I was fond of him in an enduring and steady way. I knew how differently one could feel about people . . . now.

Cassie and I went to the party. Cassie was pleased for she said this was exactly what Julia should be doing. "It gives her an interest," she said. "It is exactly what she needs."

Julia and Drake, side by side, received us. I was a little dismayed to see that Julia was unnaturally flushed and there was a purplish tinge in her cheeks; her eyes were bright with excitement.

"Dear Cassie! And Lenore! You look lovely. So elegant, doesn't she, Drake?"

Drake smiled at me sadly.

I said I was looking forward to the evening and hearing the pianist. Then we passed on while they greeted other guests.

As we moved away I saw Charles. Madalenna de' Pucci was with him. She looked arrestingly beautiful in a gown of red velvet which accentuated her dark Italianate looks.

Charles greeted us effusively.

"How nice to see you here. I am sure Julia is delighted to have you." He smiled slyly. "Drake, too. Quite a gathering, isn't it? Some of our most famous . . . or should I say notorious politicians are here. All for Drake's benefit." He turned to his companion. "My dear, this is a section of English society. Those who make the rules and those who obey them. I must say Drake looks very pleased with himself . . . and the company."

Again he was giving me that significant look. I was more than a little afraid of Charles.

He stayed with us, which made me uncomfortable. He had a proprietorial air as regards Madalenna, but the manner in which he kept glancing at me disturbed me.

In due course Julia came over to us.

"It's fun, isn't it? I've got a man coming to take pictures. I want it done soon . . . at the beginning . . . before people start to droop. After that we'll have Signore Pontelli to play for us, and when that is over the buffet and dancing. It's been fun arranging it all with the caterers."

"You've done wonderfully," I told her.

She smiled at me warmly. "I'm so glad you think so."

"I was just saying how pleased Drake must be."

"I hope so . . . oh, I do hope so. Oh look, there's the man for the pictures. I'll go and get him. Stay where you are. I'll get one or two more and you can be in one group."

So I was with Charles and Madalenna when the pictures were taken. There was a good deal of fuss while we were placed in position; the photographer told us to smile and we stood there with our lips drawn back affecting great pleasure while he hummed and hawed and the grins froze on our faces.

At length it was over.

The pianist arrived and played with great efficiency and expression —mostly Chopin—and he deserved more attention from the audience than he received.

When it was over he was quietly applauded and the musician played for dancing and after a while we went into supper. I was with Cassie and Drake joined us with a political friend. An interesting conversation ensued while we ate cold salmon washed down with champagne. I enjoyed the talk until I saw Julia at a table watching us intently. I noticed that whenever I looked her way she had a glass in her hand.

After supper there was dancing. Julia had cleverly turned one of the rooms into a ballroom; it looked very elegant with potted plants brought into the house for this evening. There was a small orchestra to play for the dancing.

I knew that Drake would seize the opportunity to dance with me. There was a recklessness about him which I thought was alien to his nature. I think he had had so much to endure that he was becoming indifferent to convention. He must have known that Julia was jealous of his feeling for me. I was sure that in one of her drunken rages she had made that clear. There were times when I thought he did not care —in fact that he was trying to bring their marriage to some sort of climax.

The dance was the waltz which had originally shocked people when it had first come into fashion. They thought it was rather bold.

Drake swept me round the floor.

"It is wonderful that you are here," he said.

"Julia has arranged a very successful occasion."

"It is successful . . . now. What do you think about Jameson's views?"

He was referring to our suppertime conversation.

"Interesting," I said.

"I think he is leaning towards Salisbury."

"But he is one of your Liberals."

"There are a lot of waverers."

We were silent for a while, then he said: "This is bliss . . . holding you like this."

"Drake," I begged, "please be careful."

"There are times when I can't be . . . when I don't seem to care. Something has to happen soon. Why don't we go away together?"

"You can't mean that."

"I don't know. I think a lot about it. I plan . . . and sometimes it seems the only way."

"Think of your career."

"We could go right away . . . start afresh."

"No. It would be wrong. Besides . . ." He looked so wretched that I could not tell him I was not sure if he were free and asked me to marry him that I would. I was so sorry for him. I was so fond of him.

I did not want to hurt him more than he had been already by telling him that I was not in love with him.

He said: "I feel so frustrated at times. Julia is . . . intolerable. It becomes more difficult every day. Sometimes I feel I would do anything . . . just anything to end it all. Now that you are here it is even harder to bear."

"Perhaps I should go to Paris for a while. That could be easily arranged."

"No . . . no." He held me closer. "Don't go."

I was aware that Julia was watching. She was not dancing. She was standing with her hands gripping one of the chairs as though to support her. The inevitable glass was in her hand and I noticed that she was swaying dangerously and some of the champagne had slopped over onto her dress.

Then suddenly she cried out: "Listen everyone. I have something to say."

She stood on the chair. I thought she was going to topple over at any moment. There was a stunned silence. The music stopped. She pointed at Drake. "That," she said, "is my husband, Drake Aldringham, an ambitious politician." Her words were slurred and to my horror I realized that she was completely intoxicated. "He doesn't want me. That's the one he wants . . . that one he is dancing with . . . holding her tightly . . . whispering to her . . . telling her what a terrible time he has with me. He wants her, the dressmaker, Lenore the bastard. No, he doesn't want me. I'm only his wife. She is his mistress. She's taken him away from me."

There was a deep silence. I could feel the furtive glances which were coming our way.

Drake went to her and said in a voice of disgust: "Julia, you are drunk."

She began to laugh wildly. She would have fallen if Drake had not caught her. Then she slid gently from his arms and lay prone on the floor, her eyes wide, staring at nothing.

I saw Charles making his way towards her.

"Better get her upstairs," he said and it seemed to me that he could not quite hide his amusement.

Cassie was beside me. "We ought to go home," she said.

And so . . . the party was over.

* * *

I cannot think clearly even now what happened after Julia's out-burst. I felt stunned. I was aware of people about me, avoiding looking at me.

Cassie was strong and practical in a crisis. She had taken my arm and I found myself outside the house. The carriage was to have come for us much later so there was no conveyance to take us home.

Cassie said: "Let's walk."

So we walked through the streets, she holding my arm, saying nothing. I was glad of that.

As we entered the house Grand'mère came down to see what had happened and we went into her room to talk about it. She listened horrified.

"Poor Julia!" said Cassie. "She was quite unaware of what she was doing . . . what she was saying."

"It must have been in her mind," I said. "How could she make such false accusations before all those people!"

"They will all know that she was drunk."

"That was obvious. But what she said! People will believe the worst."

"My dear child," said Grand'mère, "try to be calm. We'll find some way out of this. Perhaps you could go away. You could go back to Paris." She stopped, frowning. I knew what she was thinking; go back where I might possibly fall into the hands of the Comte. I could sense her weighing up the situation and deciding that in spite of the scandal and the difficult times ahead I was safer here.

"That would seem like running away," I said.

She nodded. "I'll tell you what. I'm going to make us a nice sooth-ing drink. We'll take it and get a good night's sleep. We'll all feel better in the morning."

In spite of the drink I could not sleep. I did doze a little at dawn only to wake with a feeling of deep depression as the memory of that disastrous night came flooding back to me.

Could I leave? I wondered. I wished the Countess were here. With her worldly wisdom she would have summed up the position more clearly than the rest of us could. Suppose the Comte was still in Paris. He would think I had come back to be near him. He would continue his pursuit. I wondered whether I should find it irresistible.

I felt that I wanted to look at the situation more clearly than I had on the previous night. Of one thing I was certain: those who had been present would already be telling their friends of that scene last night. For a woman to accuse her husband of adultery with someone there, had surely never happened before. Those who had witnessed this scene would want to take advantage of having been eye witnesses.

I wondered what would happen now. Would credence be given to the story that I was Drake's mistress? I was sure it would.

Perhaps I should get away after all.

I thought of being in Paris . . . of the possibility of seeing him, putting all this unpleasantness behind me. They would be sure I was running away—and so I should be!

A day passed. We were very busy. Far from custom falling off, there were many who could not curb their curiosity and came on the pretext of buying something. I stayed out of sight.

Two days later to my amazement Julia came to the salon.

Cassie came to tell me that she wanted to see me.

"I can't see her," I said. "I think it better that I should not."

"She is very distressed," said Cassie. "She's crying. She must see you, she says. She can't rest until she does."

I hesitated but Cassie was looking at me pleadingly. Cassie had become very motherly over the years and she seemed to feel that her mission in life was to protect us all.

"Do see her," begged Cassie. "I hate these quarrels in families."

So I agreed.

Julia came in. She was rather pale and the receding colour made the tiny veins in her cheeks more visible. She looked older and pathetic.

We regarded each other in silence for a moment, then she burst out: "Oh, Lenore, I am so terribly sorry. I didn't know what I was doing . . . what I was saying. I don't remember much about it. I was standing on a chair . . . and I don't know how I got up there."

"You shouted a terrible accusation about Drake and me."

"I didn't mean to."

"How could you think such things?" I demanded. "They must have been in your mind."

"I'm so unhappy, Lenore. I think I've always been jealous of you. Drake liked you from the first . . . better than he ever liked me."

"He's married to you, Julia."

"I know, but that doesn't mean everything, does it? He doesn't love me. Sometimes I'm frantic. I was afraid that he'd marry you. That's why I tried to stop it . . . like I did when we were at Swaddingham and I forced my maid to pretend she was the ghost up in that gallery . . . the ghost that appears to warn them about marrying . . ."

I was puzzled then I remembered.

"Oh Julia," I said, "how could you be so . . . so foolish. Your implications are untrue."

"I'm so sorry, Lenore."

"The harm is done now. What are people thinking? They are believing you, of course."

"I will tell them all that I did not know what I was saying. Sometimes I think Drake hates me. It maddens me . . . makes me frantic." I could see that she was beginning to get hysterical again and I had to calm her.

"All right, Julia," I said. "Let's try to forget it."

"Do you mean that?"

"Yes, I do. Let me tell you that I am not and never have been Drake's mistress."

"But he was on the point of marrying you once."

"He did not ask me to, Julia. Forget it. He has married you."

"Yes," she said. "He did that, didn't he?" She was smiling a little slyly remembering I supposed how she had tricked him.

In spite of everything I was sorry for her. She was a poor hysterical woman. She might be rich but life had not gone very well for her. She had been obsessed with Drake from the moment she had seen him and would clearly use any means, however dishonest, to get him.

"Do let's try to forget it," she said with a smile.

I thought; With London society aware of it? What harm was this going to do to Drake's career? A politician with an unstable wife could not hope for advancement. Perhaps even now the damage done was irrevocable.

I had not seen Drake since the outburst and I did not really want to. I feared what he might have to say for I believed he would be more eager to get away from Julia than ever. His career was in jeopardy. It might, even now, be impossible to save it.

But Julia was here before me. She was truly contrite. I was sure her remorse was genuine. It was true that she had been intoxicated and had not realized what she had said. What was the use of railing against her? I must try hard to remember that when she had drunk too much she did not know what she was saying. She was pitiful.

"I am going to try to give up drinking," she said. "I am sure I can if I try hard enough. It helps me, you see, Lenore. It helps me to forget. I wanted so much to help Drake, and then I did what I did the other night. It was seeing you dancing with him . . . and he looked so happy. I said to myself: Why is he not like that with me and before I knew what I was doing . . ."

"Please, Julia, do understand that he is just a good friend of mine. He married you . . ."

"Yes, he married me. So we are friends again, aren't we, Lenore?" Cassie was looking at me pleadingly.

"Yes," I said, "we are friends."

* * *

Before the week was out a tragedy occurred which sent our little scandal to the back of people's minds.

Charles's house was burned down.

He had been alone in the upper part of the house. The servants were all in the basement. Charles had had a guest to dinner and had ordered that he was not to be disturbed. The guest must have departed for there was no sign of her. Charles had had a lucky escape. His valet, who had had the night off, had returned earlier than expected. Fortunately he had smelt the smoke coming from Charles's room. When he opened the door the flames shot out. He called to Charles, and there was no answer but he was convinced that Charles was in that room. Wrapping a damp towel about his face he investigated. Charles was sprawled across the bed, presumably overcome by fumes. He was unconscious but the valet, a very resourceful man, dragged him to safety. He gave Charles artificial respiration and by doing so saved his life.

Charles had indeed been fortunate. He could so easily have died in the fire and would certainly have done so but for the prompt action of his valet.

Julia cast aside her depression and became quite energetic. Charles's wife, Helen, was away in the north of England. There was no need for her to be disturbed, said Julia. Charles should come and live with her until something could be sorted out.

* * *

Katie was too observant not to have noticed that something was wrong.

"What did Aunt Julia *do?*" she asked.

I pretended to look puzzled.

"It *was* something," she went on. "People's mouths go straight when they talk about it as though they think it was wrong and are rather pleased about it."

"Oh . . . she is not very well."

"She seems well. She has such red cheeks. They are purple too."

I said to her on impulse: "How would you like to go to Paris?"

"When are we going?"

"I didn't say that I would. I wondered if you would like to go and stay with the Countess."

"And leave you here?" She was dismayed.

"I . . . I thought you might like it."

"Why can't you come?"

"Well, there are things to keep me here and I thought you might like to go."

"I could see Raoul and the Comte. I'd like that but I'd want you to be there, too. Besides, the Comte wouldn't come to see *me,* would he? He comes to see *you.*"

I was surprised at how much she knew. Children are far more aware than one sometimes realizes. I wondered how much she knew about the Comte's pursuit of me and my involvement with Julia and Drake.

Grand'mère came in. "Grand'mère," said Katie, "Mama thinks I might go to Paris."

Grand'mère looked at me and I said hastily: "I thought Katie might like to go there for a while and stay with the Countess."

"Without you?" asked Grand'mère.

"Somehow I feel I ought to be here."

Grand'mère nodded.

"I wouldn't want to go without Mama," said Katie.

"I think you should both stay here for a while," added Grand'mère.

Afterwards she said: "You wouldn't want the child to go without you."

"It was just that I was thinking she might see more than we realize. She is aware that something is happening. She might have heard scraps of gossip. Children do. I thought it might be a good idea for her to get away for a while."

Grand'mère shook her head slowly. "No . . . no, better that you should be together."

* * *

I was disturbed when Charles came to see me. He looked very jaunty in spite of his recent experience.

It was afternoon. Cassie had gone to the park with Katie. Grand'mère was resting and I was alone, working on some accounts. Since the scandal I did not dare to meet people.

One of the maids came in to say that Mr. Sallonger had called to see me.

I was on the point of telling her to say that I was out when he appeared at the door. That was typical of Charles. Anticipating my desire not to see him, he was determined to flout it.

"Lenore, how marvellous to see you!"

He came forward. The maid shut the door and we were alone.

"Well," he said, "congratulate me. Did you realize I have been snatched from the jaws of death?"

I said: "Congratulations."

"Jedder is a good fellow. It would have been kingdom come for me but for him."

"You must be very grateful."

"Oh, I am. I have no desire to slip off this mortal coil just yet. And Lenore, as always, you look enchanting. I've brought something for you."

He produced a picture.

"A memento of a memorable night," he said.

It was the photograph which had been taken at Julia's party. It was very clear and we were all recognizable: Charles, Cassie, Madalenna, two other men and myself.

"Very good, do you not think so?"

I wanted no memento of that night. It was one which I was trying hard to forget.

"It is very clear of us all," I said.

I put it into a drawer. I could not bear to look at it.

"I thought you might like to have it," he said mockingly.

"It is a night I prefer to forget."

"Oh, you are thinking of Julia's outburst." He laughed. "Poor Julia! Very far gone, I'm afraid. I was, too, on that night of the fire, you know. It must run in the family. I was entertaining a lady *diner à deux* . . . and I don't remember a thing. Well, Julia certainly let herself go. She's being a good sister to me now. Do you know, there is very little left. My Chippendale bureau is gone . . . burned to a cinder . . . also some of my Hepplewhite pieces. I really had some good stuff in that house."

"I thought you might have gone down to The Silk House for a while."

"Oh, there is too much to do in London."

"And is Helen coming back?"

"There doesn't seem to be any reason for her to hurry. We get along because we don't see very much of one another. It's a good recipe for marriage."

"You are quite cynical."

"Realism. That's what I call it. Julia is playing the good Samaritan and Drake has no objections so I might as well stay at their place till I find a new nest in London. But I haven't come to talk about all that."

I raised my eyebrows, and he smiled at me coming towards the table at which I was standing. I had not sat down nor had I invited him to do so since he had come in.

"What *did* I come to talk about? you are asking. Well, I will tell you. I came to talk about *us.*"

"Us?"

"Yes . . . you and myself."

"What have you to say about us?"

"That we should be better friends. I'm a little jealous . . . of Drake. You seem to be so fond of him . . . and really you shouldn't be. After all, he is Julia's husband and it's in the family . . . more or less. I get really angry when I think about you and Drake, and how you are leaving me out in the cold."

"You are talking nonsense."

"I don't think that would be the general opinion after . . ."

"I don't think there is anything to say."

"There is a great deal to say. I am rather obsessed with you, Lenore. I can't get you out of my mind. You flout me. You are so virtuous . . . on the surface. Such an innocent child, weren't you when you captured Philip. But tell me, why did Philip kill himself?"

"I am not sure that he did."

"Oh, come now. Do you think I murdered him? Out of jealousy perhaps, because he had the prize I coveted. No, my dear, that is not so. I believe he discovered something about you. He had a rather austere outlook on life, did Philip. He was the knight in shining armour. Anything less than perfection would have shocked him deeply. What did he discover about you, Lenore?"

"You are being ridiculous."

"Such a dark horse you can be. Just think of it. Illegitimate daughter of the house of St. Allengère. Papa turns up just in time to help with the business. The little waif who marries one of the Sallonger heirs. Very romantic—melodramatic, in fact, particularly when the husband commits suicide. You'd think that would be enough but oh no, not for Lenore. She has to fascinate poor Julia's husband. Ambitious politician. Then there is the problem for the poor man. All the world well lost for love?"

"I do not want to listen to any more."

"I am afraid you will have to. Did you know I am not a very nice man?"

"That is one thing on which we can agree."

He caught my arm. "But people who are not so nice can be attractive, you know."

"You, however, are not so to me."

"Be careful. I should warn you that I can also be a vindictive fellow. Remember the mausoleum?"

"I shall never forget it."

"And how kind and noble Drake rescued you, and not content with that he had to show his knightly qualities by throwing me in the lake. I don't forget that either. There are old scores to settle there."

"Charles, I wish you would go."

I wrenched my arm free, but he came close to me so that his face was almost touching mine. His eyes were mocking, lustful. I felt very much afraid of him.

"But I wish to stay."

I said: "Has the most beautiful Madalenna departed?"

"She is with us still."

"I thought you were pursuing her."

"My appetite is voracious. Madalenna is luscious, beautiful but oddly enough I still hanker after you."

"Then stop it, for you are wasting your time."

"No . . . no. It is going to be time well spent."

"Listen to me, Charles, after this I never want to see you again."

"I shall make you change your mind."

"I am able to make my own decisions."

"Lenore, I've had enough of this banter. I am serious. If you continue to flout me, it will be the worse for you . . . and for Drake Aldringham. What if Julia decided to divorce him and cite you as the lady in the case?"

I went cold with fear. I knew that he was not talking idly.

I said quickly: "It would be obviously false."

"Would it? Meetings in the park. Julia's outburst before so many. This could mean the end of Drake as a politician, and would betray you as a somewhat wanton lady."

"Julia has already done a lot of harm."

"He could be saved . . . so could you . . . if you would be sensible."

"How?"

He leered at me. "You know the answer to that question. By my friendship, of course."

"By which you mean . . ."

"Suppose you became my very dear friend."

I laughed. "You're crazy, I think."

He shrugged his shoulders.

"It's a sort of blackmail," I said.

"Often an effective weapon."

"You are so melodramatic."

"Rather intriguing, eh?"

"Far from it. Rather absurd and quite meaningless."

"My very dear sister-in-law, with the rather disreputable origins, the clever girl who in spite of being brought into the Sallonger fold as an underling, her grandmother one of our workers, somehow managed to entrap one of the Sallonger heirs into marriage."

"How dare you tell such lies!"

"Lies? Did you not marry my brother? Was he not one of the heirs to our father's estate? Were you not raised from a menial position in the household to become one of us?"

"I did not trap Philip into marriage."

"With your wiles and your pretty ways you did. He was always your slave. You saw he was a better proposition than I. Poor Charles was scorned. Then he dies and in mysterious circumstances. Suicide they say. But was it? Be careful, Lenore. You are not in a very secure position. I have great influence with Julia. I might decide to advise her on a divorce. She would listen to me. I am her adviser now."

"She would not do it. She has already harmed Drake considerably and I believe she is contrite about that."

"Contrite? Perhaps for a while. Then she will be ragingly jealous. It depends on the bottle. I have seen her in the many moods it inspires. Maudlin, sentimental, becoming jealous . . . venomously so. It would not be difficult for me. Pity, for they say that, given a chance, Drake could become a brilliant politician. A divorce would finish him. And you, too, my dear. Think of your position. Old scandals revived. The woman whose husband killed himself a few weeks after marriage. That would not sound very pleasant, would it, in a court of law?"

"You would not do this."

"Would I not? I think you have a great deal to learn about me. It would be the story of the mausoleum all over again. You flouted me then. If it had not been for Drake how long would you have remained in that cold dank place with the remains of long dead Sallongers?"

"Nothing on Earth would induce me to become, as you call it, your dear friend."

"We shall see, Lenore my darling. We shall see."

"Will you go now?"

He bowed his head. "But," he said, "I shall be back. I think when you consider this matter and all it entails you may change your mind."

"I never shall," I told him.

"*Au revoir*, sweet Lenore," he said.

When he had gone I felt shaken and exhausted. I had always known he was a dangerous man; but I had not until that moment realized how dangerous.

* * *

I did not tell anyone of that interview with Charles. I could not bring myself to talk of it. I was in a state of great anxiety. One thing I knew was that Charles was not talking idly. He had always had a special feeling for me which fluctuated between desire and dislike. He wanted to humiliate me, to hurt me; he had sought opportunities, as in the case of the mausoleum; but this was a more serious matter.

I should have loved to take my troubles to Grand'mère but I did not want to worry her. I had brought her a great deal of anxiety through my relationships both with the Comte and with Drake. She took these things too much to heart. I could not burden her with this new and frightening development.

Then I had a letter from Drake.

"I must see you," he wrote, "but after Julia's outburst it would be unwise for us to be seen together. I have an idea. My old nanny has a house in Kensington. I have always visited her over the years. Could we meet there? She would be very discreet and do anything for me. She has always been like a mother to me. She is Miss Brownlee of 12 Parsons Road. Do come there. Could it be tomorrow afternoon. I shall go there then. Say two thirty. I must talk to you, Lenore. Please come."

I could not ignore the plea and I did feel that I had a great deal to say to Drake. I also realized how unwise it would be for us to be seen together particularly after Charles's threats.

I did not say where I was going. I took a cab. The journey was quicker than I had anticipated, and I arrived at the house quite ten minutes early. There were very few people about. A cab did just draw up as I was getting out of mine. That was all. The house was small with discreet lace curtains and a highly polished knocker.

It was opened by a pleasant-faced woman of about sixty with rosy cheeks, white hair and bright blue eyes. She smiled at me warmly. "You must be Mrs. Sallonger," she said.

I said that I was. "And you are Miss Brownlee."

"That's right. Master Drake has told me you were coming. He will be here shortly. He is always punctual. Come into my little parlour."

The parlour was a cluttered little room with windows which looked out onto the street, but the view was discreetly hidden by the lace curtains. There was a settee, several chairs, and in the fireplace a bunch of roses. A big ormolu clock stood on the mantelshelf in between two large vases with angels clinging to them as though supporting them. In one corner of the room was a what-not with innumerable little ornaments on it and in another a corner cupboard with glass doors displaying more ornaments.

Miss Brownlee bade me sit down.

She said: "It's a pretty little house, isn't it? I'm proud of it. He bought it for me . . . you know, Master Drake."

"Oh, did he?"

She smiled. "My wonderful boy. Of all my children, he was the best."

"I know you were his nurse."

"Nanny Brownlee . . . that was me. I had some little cherubs in my time, but there wasn't one that could touch Drake. I used to say to him, 'You're going to forget all about me when you go to school and get your grand friends.' 'I never will, Nanny Brownlee,' he said. And he was right, God bless him. Always he remembered . . . birthdays . . . Christmas . . . and then when I'd done with working he bought me this little house. And he comes to see me. He'll talk to me too . . . Tell me his troubles. I want to see him Prime Minister one day. If they had any sense they'd make him one right away."

"It is clear that he has an ardent supporter in you."

"Well, I know him. He'll be here soon. Right on time. I taught him that. I said, 'You must be punctual, Master Drake. It's bad manners to be late. Like saying you don't want to come much and what could be ruder than that.' He remembered. He always remembered. I like to think I helped to make him the man he is today." She looked at me quizzically, her bright blue eyes penetrating and alert. I wondered how much she knew about my relationship with Drake. A good deal, I imagined, for he would have confided in her.

"He's very sad just now, and has been for a long time. It was a terrible thing that happened to him. I pray that it will all come right and he'll get what he deserves . . . and that's the best."

The doorbell rang. She glanced triumphantly at the clock.

"Right on time," she said. "I knew it."

She left me sitting there while she went to the door. I heard her say: "She's here."

She brought him into the little room.

"Lenore," he said, "so you came."

I smiled at him. He looked tired and drawn.

Miss Brownlee said: "Well, I'm going to leave you two to have a talk. A nice cup of tea say just before four? How will that be?"

"Thank you, Nanny," said Drake.

She looked at him with such love and pride that I was deeply touched.

When the door shut Drake turned to me. "I had to do it this way," he said. "I felt that in view of everything we could not meet where we might be seen."

"I understand. I was glad to meet Miss Brownlee. She is so devoted to you."

"She has always been like a mother to me. I suppose I felt closer to her than to anyone for years. The other night . . . It was monstrous . . ."

"I know."

"You understand what I have to endure?"

I nodded.

"She is unpredictable, Lenore. There is no escape from her. I spend as much time at Swaddingham as I can but she will come there. Ever since that night I have been thinking. Something must be done. What a fool I was to get myself into this."

"You did what you thought was right. You felt you had to marry her."

"She tricked me, Lenore."

"I know. I know."

"It was when I thought that your father was your lover . . . How stupid I was! I can't tell you how I felt. I was hurt and humiliated and enraged. I should never have doubted you but it seemed to fit and she did it so subtly. And then I was weak. I didn't care what happened. I stayed that night in her house. You know the rest."

"It's no use going over it, Drake. It's past and we are in this situation."

"She pretended to care for me and she is trying to ruin me."

"She is a jealous woman and when she is drinking she is capable of anything. That night was an example of that. We have to be careful, Drake."

He nodded. "I have thought and thought. I have come to the conclusion that I have to make an end of it. I am going to leave her."

"There would be scandal."

"There already has been."

"You could perhaps live that down."

"Do you think so?"

"Perhaps. If you are discreet. If you and I do not meet. I could go to Paris for a long time. Things would settle down."

"That's the last thing I want. I shall give up politics. I can see that I shall have to do that eventually . . . even if I remained with Julia. She will not be accepted and she grows worse."

"Perhaps she will reform. I think she might if she thought you cared for her."

"I don't," he said. "And I can't pretend."

"Some scandals can be lived down. Think of Lord Melbourne."

"He is always cited on these occasions, but I think he had special qualities. He was a natural survivor. I don't want to live this down. I'm ready to give it up. Lenore, let's go away together."

"No, Drake, that isn't the way."

"There was a time when I thought you loved me."

"I do love you, Drake. You are my very dear friend."

"You mean you do not love me enough."

"I mean that I do not love you in the way I should have to. People who give up all for each other have to love in a very special way. I am so fond of you. I have always admired you, but . . ."

"You've changed, Lenore. There is someone else."

I was silent.

"I felt it was so," he said. "I understand."

"No, no, you don't. It is true that I did meet someone. He just had a strange effect on me."

"You are in love with him."

I shook my head. "I don't know. It would be foolish of me if I were. No, I am not in love with him. But I feel stimulated and excited to be with him and I think of him a great deal. Perhaps it is ridiculous. I daresay it is. He is not serious. But it is just that if I could feel like that about another person, I shouldn't think of being in love with someone else."

Drake looked puzzled.

"I can't explain further," I went on. "It was just an . . . encounter, but it made a deep impression on me. No, there was no real relationship between us. He would have had one . . . and then passed on. He is that sort of man. I could not accept that and yet . . . I am being frank with you, Drake. I think of him still and that makes me feel that you should not make any sacrifices for someone as unsure as I am."

"I have always felt that you and I were meant for each other."

"I have felt that, too, at times. Grand'mère thinks it. She was terribly upset when you married Julia."

"She is a very wise woman."

"Her thoughts are all for me. Your Miss Brownlee reminds me of her. She loves you very dearly."

"I know."

"And you have looked after her. She is so grateful."

"It is I who should be grateful to her."

"Drake," I said, "what are you going to do? Julia may well bring divorce proceedings against you."

"I should welcome them."

"Charles has suggested that he may persuade her to do so and . . . cite me."

He gripped my hand.

"It would be our way out," he said. "I would welcome any way to end this. Sometimes I think I could be capable of anything."

"Please, Drake, don't talk like that. Think what this would mean. It would be the end of your career."

"But I have already decided to give that up."

"You think that now but what would you feel in five or ten years' time? Politics are in your blood. That is your life, Drake. You would always feel that you have missed something."

"I could be happy if you were with me. You would forget that man. I would forget politics. We could be happy together. I know it."

"Let us not be rash, Drake. Perhaps something will happen."

So we talked and talked round the subject and always we came back to the same point. My uncertainty . . . Drake's determination that he could not go on and something was going to happen, for if it did not he would soon have to make it.

I was on the point of telling him all about Charles and stopped myself in time. I did not want to add to his anxieties and I did not know what action he would take. All those years ago he had thrown Charles in the lake and so had started festering this resentment against us both. I did not want more trouble so I remained silent.

In due course Miss Brownlee came in with the tea in a big brown tea pot with scones and fairy cakes.

"He always did like my scones," she told me, "didn't you, Drake? And fairy cakes were a special treat. Do you remember?"

He assured her that he did. And there in that little room with this woman whose love for him was so evident, I thought what a good man he was and what a tragedy it was that he should be caught up in such a situation. Perhaps if I had married him we should have been very happy together.

We left separately. That seemed wise. Drake had ordered a cab to come and take me home. I left him there. It would return for him later.

I said goodbye to Nanny Brownlee and she assured me that she would be pleased to see me at any time; and I went out to the cab.

A man was walking slowly past the house as I was driven off. I did not think there was anything unusual about that at the time.

* * *

I was in a perpetual state of anxiety and the attempt to appear normal was a strain. My main thought was for Katie. She was becoming very knowledgeable and was particularly observant. Sometimes I found her watching me intently. I guessed she knew something was afoot. She was very fond of Drake, but she was fond of many; she had had a great admiration for the Comte. Katie was ready to love anyone in the belief that their intentions were what hers would be. In spite of being fatherless she had been surrounded by love all her life and she could not imagine anything different. I could not bear to think of her being brought face to face with unpleasant realities—particularly those in which her mother could be involved.

We went to the park to feed the ducks—a regular occupation of hers and on this particular day, as we were by the water, Charles appeared. I think he must have followed us.

He swept off his hat. "Good morning, Lenore. Good morning, Katie."

"Good morning, Uncle Charles," cried Katie beaming at him. "We are going to feed the ducks."

"Such angels of mercy," said Charles casting his eyes up to the skies.

Katie thought that was very funny.

"Some of them are rather greedy," she said.

"A common failing in most living creatures," commented Charles.

"There is one who is especially greedy. He tries to get everything . . . everyone else's share as well as his own. I try to stop him. It's great fun."

"I must stay to watch the fun," said Charles.

"I am sure you will find it rather boring," I said.

"By no means. I find such good deeds inspiring. Casting your bread upon the waters."

"It's only stale bread," put in Katie, adding: "That's in the Bible."

"I was hoping you would think it was original."

"Stale bread and crusts," said Katie.

"But very acceptable to those greedy creatures obviously."

"Would you like some, Uncle Charles? But don't let that greedy one get it."

"I am going to leave the feeding to you, dear Katie. I know that in this matter of feeding the ducks you have the wisdom of Solomon."

Katie thought his conversation very funny.

"I have an idea," he went on. "Your mother and I will sit on that seat and watch justice being meted out."

He drew me back to the seat and I had no alternative but to sit down beside him.

"An enchanting child, your daughter," he said.

I was silent.

"She is very bright," he added. "I wonder what she will make of this horrid scandal when it breaks upon the world."

With an almost uncanny precision he had interpreted exactly what was in my mind.

"But of course," he went on soothingly, "she will never hear of it for you are going to be sensible."

"Charles, I wish you would go."

"But I am enjoying this so much. Katie is a charmer. I am proud of my little niece. It would really hurt me to have her thrust into a welter of unpleasantness."

"But nevertheless you would take a delight in it if it came to pass."

"But it need not—though you have to make up your mind quickly. I have spoken to Julia. She is wavering at the moment. She fluctuates according to her liquid intake. But now that I have the evidence, I think she will need little persuasion."

"What evidence?"

"Of the little love nest."

"What are you talking about?"

"Number 12 Parsons Road."

I was numb with shock.

"I see my revelations have upset you. I have had you watched, dear Lenore. For some time I have been doing this and now vigilance has borne fruit. You and Drake were seen to arrive separately at Number 12 Parsons Road and after a sojourn of about two and a half hours you were seen to depart separately and in a most discreet manner. It is all recorded."

I felt sick with horror. I remembered now the man who had alighted from his cab just as I had from mine. He must have followed me to Parsons Road, and he had stood about waiting while I was there. He would have seen Drake arrive and have witnessed our departure. I could imagine the construction which Charles intended should be put on this.

He was watching me closely. "There is an easy way out," he said.

"You are absolutely wrong."

He raised his shoulders. "You are not going to deny that you were there together."

"You who are so knowledgeable must be aware that it is the home of Drake Aldringham's nurse."

"Old nurses can be very accommodating and are well known for indulging their charges' whims."

"Are they?"

"Oh yes . . . particularly when the charges are such little angels as Drake must have been."

Katie ran to me. "There's no more bread," she said.

"We must go home," I told her.

"So soon, Mama?"

"Yes, we must. I have certain things to do."

"I shall escort you," said Charles.

Katie prattled all the way home and Charles responded in a light-hearted manner. But I sensed that was no reflection of his mood. He was deadly serious.

I was very quiet. In fact I was overcome by apprehension.

* * *

What could I do? I did not want to worry Grand'mère. Already she was very uneasy; even though she did not know how far this matter had gone.

It occurred to me that if I could see Julia I might make her understand that in harming Drake and me she was hurting herself. If she were in a reasonable mood, if she really loved Drake—as I thought she did—surely she would not want to lose him.

I chose an afternoon. Perhaps she would be resting, but it was a quiet time of the day and I wanted as few people to know of our meeting as possible. She might refuse to see me but if she did I might get a chance to talk to her and if she were in a mellow mood perhaps I could make some progress. I might hint at Charles's motives. So much would depend on how I found her.

I felt great trepidation as I rang the bell and I was ushered in by a parlourmaid. Mrs. Aldringham, I was told, was in her room. The maid would see if she were sleeping or if she could receive me.

After a few moments I was taken to Julia's bedroom. She was sitting on a chair by the window and she smiled when she saw me.

"Do come in, Lenore."

"I hope you are not resting."

She shook her head. "I was going to lie down . . . but it doesn't matter."

She was in a peignoir of her favourite violet which matched the colour in her cheeks. She may have been drinking but she was by no means drunk.

I saw the inevitable decanter and a used glass on the table near her bed.

"I'm glad you came," she said. "I wanted to talk to you. I have been so worried about you . . . and Drake."

"Julia, there is nothing to be worried about. Drake and I are good friends . . . that's all."

She shook her head. "He thinks a lot of you, I know."

"He's married to you, Julia. If only you . . ."

"Yes," she said, "what?"

My eyes had strayed to the decanter.

"I know what you mean," she cried. "Stop drinking. I try. I do . . . for a time and then I have to go back to it. I can't help it. I just have to."

"If only you could . . ."

"Do you think that would make any difference?"

"I think it would make all the difference."

"How can it when he is in love with you?"

"You're his wife, Julia. That's important."

"No. It was always you . . . even when we were children it was you he liked."

"But he married you. It was what you wanted. You ought to be happy. If you would only try . . . stop drinking . . . do all you could to help him in his career instead of . . ."

She began to cry. "I know. It was a terrible thing I did. He will never forgive me. You won't either."

"I do understand your distress, Julia, but if you would only be reasonable . . . try to understand him . . . He's ambitious. He could go far. Everyone seems to think so . . . and all this is spoiling his chances."

"Charles says I should divorce him."

"If you did that you would lose him."

"I know."

"Surely that's the last thing you want."

She hesitated. "I don't know. Sometimes I get angry and it all seems different. I hate him then. I want to hurt him . . . as I've been hurt. Charles says I should be happier if I did."

"It's for you to decide what you want . . . not Charles."

"Charles has always influenced me. I've admired Charles. Philip was so gentle. But Charles was the man of the world. He married Helen. They are not even good friends but he doesn't care in the least. He's quite happy with the arrangement. He is blatantly unfaithful to her and yet he seems to enjoy life. I wish I were like Charles . . . not caring."

"You wouldn't want to be like that."

"Oh, I should. I couldn't care then whether Drake loved me or not . . . I'd be like Charles. I'd take lovers. He doesn't care in the least. He's having a love affair with that Italian woman now."

"Do you mean Madalenna de' Pucci?"

"Yes, that's her. He sees a great deal of her. She's always in and out of this house. And she's in his rooms. I believe he has given her a key so that she can come in when she pleases."

"Really . . . but it's your house."

"It's Charles's home when he's living here. Oh, he's deeply involved with her. Charles is so sophisticated. He'd never get hurt like this. I wish I were like him."

"You must not let him influence you, Julia. Your life is in your own hands."

"Sometimes I think Charles is right. Then sometimes I don't. Sometimes I think I don't care. I just want to hurt Drake as he has hurt me . . . and then at others it all seems different."

I said: "You would ruin his career and your life at the same time."

"I know . . . I know. I say I mustn't and then I say I will. I'm wretched so everyone else shall be too."

"Oh, Julia, I wish you'd drink less and be like you used to be."

"It's so comforting. You're miserable and then you feel you don't care . . . and after you feel quite merry and that nothing matters. But sometimes you feel so wretched you could end it all . . . not only for yourself but for everyone else."

"Julia, it's not too late . . ."

"Isn't it?" she asked eagerly. "Isn't it?"

"Really, Julia, it isn't."

"I'll talk to Charles tonight. I'll tell him I'm going to try. I'll be a good wife to Drake. I'll help him. That's what I always wanted to do. Yes, I'll tell Charles tonight. I'll tell him I've made up my mind. I'm going to be different. I'm not going to drink . . . so much. I'll wean myself from it. You can't do it quickly . . . not when you're as involved as I am with it. Yes, I shall talk to him tonight."

"Always remember, Julia, I want to be your friend."

"Oh, I know. I know, Lenore." She was near to tears. "I'm going to be different. I'm going to tell Charles tonight that I won't do what he suggests. I'm going to try and be a better wife to Drake. I'm going to make him love me . . ."

I rose to go. I went to her and kissed her. I said: "Don't get up. I'll let myself out."

As I came into the street I told myself that the meeting had not been in vain.

But by the next morning Julia was dead.

* * *

The days which followed are like a grotesque nightmare in my memory. I kept telling myself that I must wake up and find that I was dreaming.

The cause of Julia's death was established. She was found in Charles's sitting room. He had had his own little suite of rooms in the house since the fire; they comprised a bedroom, a dressing room and a sitting room, and although they were part of the main house and were situated at the end of the first floor corridor, there was a back staircase which led only to them. Because of this they were especially private.

Julia had given them to Charles so that he could feel a little apart until he was able to make arrangements as to where he would live.

The valet—who had saved him at the time of the fire—had told Julia that Charles had said he would be home round about seven o'clock.

Julia had gone to his sitting room as she wished to talk to him without delay. There she intended to wait for him. She must have seen the decanter and found it irresistible. Julia's passion for drink had killed her. Her death had been instantaneous. When Charles had come in, he had found her dead. It seemed that she had drunk poisoned sherry which must have been meant for Charles.

When I heard the news I was overcome with shock. I had to get away from everyone to think clearly what this could mean. Someone had tried to poison Charles and Julia had died instead.

Grand'mère came to talk to me alone.

"My dear child," she said, "what does all this mean?"

"They meant to kill Charles," I whispered. "They did not mean to kill Julia."

"Why should anyone want to kill Charles?"

"He must have had many enemies. He is not a good man. He is wicked . . . mischievous . . . He likes to make trouble."

Grand'mère was looking at me intently. "Tell me everything, Lenore," she begged. "Don't keep me in the dark."

So I told her how he had pursued me, how he had had me followed to Parsons Road, how he had tried to persuade Julia to divorce Drake and cite me as the reason.

"Mon Dieu," she murmured. "Oh . . . *mon Dieu."*

"Grand'mère, you don't think . . . I wouldn't know how . . . even if . . . I have never been in his rooms."

"There will be an inquest," she said. "Questions will be asked. You saw her the day she died. You must have been one of the last to see her alive."

"I talked to her, told her how unwise she would be to divorce Drake. She said she was going to talk to Charles. That must have been why she was in his rooms."

"When this sort of thing happens there are many questions, there is much probing."

"Grand'mère," I said. "I am frightened. I am thinking of Katie."

"Katie must go to Paris."

"I can't go, Grand'mère. It would look like running away. I suppose I might not be allowed to go. Perhaps you could take her."

Grand'mère shook her head. "My place is here with you. Cassie could take her . . . and the two governesses with her. That's the best way. It is wise with something like this to take one step at a time . . . and make sure that it is the right one. Our first plan then is to get Katie away."

I knew she was right.

Cassie was greatly upset. She had been fond of Julia and was completely stunned by what had happened.

"I keep thinking of her when we were little," she said. "All the little things she did. That this should happen! I'm glad Mama is not alive to see it."

I wondered how Lady Sallonger would have taken the news. Calmly, I should imagine. She had never allowed herself to be much affected by others and Julia would have ceased to play a part in her ladyship's life.

"Cassie," I said, "we have to do something quickly."

I had to explain certain things to her. She was horrified to learn of the part Charles had played but she was not greatly surprised. She knew her brother. In their childhood he had taken a delight in teasing his sisters and had often reduced them to tears. There was—and always had been—a sadistic streak in Charles.

Cassie had grown quite worldly wise when she had left The Silk House. She saw at once the need to get Katie out of London and would make her preparations to leave at once.

Katie was full of questions. "Why can't you come with us, Mama?"

"I have things to do here. I can come later."

"Why don't we wait for you?"

"It's better for you to go now. You'll have Aunt Cassie and Mademoiselle and Miss . . ."

"I'd rather you came, Mama."

"I know, but it isn't quite convenient yet."

"Then . . ."

But I silenced her with a kiss and said: "You know how you love Paris . . . and it won't be long."

"Shall we go to Grandpapa's vineyard?"

"I expect so . . . one day."

"Will he be in Paris?"

"I don't know."

"I hope I go to the vineyard. I want to see Raoul."

She prattled on and there was a certain speculation in her eyes. I could see that it would have been very difficult to keep the news from her.

I had to attend the inquest. It was an ordeal. Drake was looking pale and strained and the fact that Julia was the wife of a politician who was becoming known to the public meant that there was full press coverage.

Some searching questions were asked of Drake. He knew of no reason why anyone should wish to kill his brother-in-law. He knew very little of him really. His rooms in the house were tantamount to a separate apartment and as they were both busy men they saw little of each other. He was so calm and dignified that I could see he was making a good impression.

I was asked about my last meeting with Julia and why I had gone to see her on that day. I said we had been brought up together and saw each other frequently. Had we discussed her brother and why anyone should seek to kill him? I said he had been mentioned and she had told me that he was out and she looked forward to having a chat with him when he came home that evening.

I was relieved when it was over.

Charles was the main witness for he had been the one to find her. He explained quietly and with great sadness how he had been living in the house of his sister and brother-in-law since a fire had destroyed his home. He had been out all the afternoon and when he had returned it was to find her dead in his room.

In due course a verdict was reached. It was: Murder by a person or persons unknown.

Now the investigation would begin in earnest.

The Reason Why

 I did not see Drake. Grand'mère said it would be dangerous and that if he should be unwise enough to call she would not allow him to see me.

Charles came though. He was above suspicion for the attempt had been made on his life.

Grand'mère came to my room to tell me that he was below.

"I'll have to see him," I said.

"Is it necessary?"

"I think so. I have to know what is in his mind."

So I saw him. We faced each other in the little room where we took clients for discussions. He was subdued, so even he was affected.

When we were alone, he said: "So you thought you could be rid of me. You are indeed a vixen under that calm exterior."

"I have never been in your rooms."

"You had the motive. There was nothing you wanted more than to be rid of me. You were with Julia that afternoon. Nobody saw you leave. You know the house. You could have gone into my rooms after leaving Julia. You could have slipped down by means of that back staircase. You must have known it was my custom to take a glass of sherry while dressing."

"I know no such thing."

"Servants talk. Or you would have guessed I should be at that decanter some time. My dear Lenore, no one had a greater motive than you. I was going to make trouble for you and your lover. It was a clumsy attempt, my dear. And what he wanted more than anything was to be rid of Julia. I believe he even wanted a divorce. It could have worked, you know. But Julia came there and saw the decanter . . . something she could never resist. You should have been more subtle, though. Fancy using a poison which could be detected immediately. How did you expect to get away with that?"

"You talk as if . . ."

"That is how they will talk to you, Lenore. You will be suspected, you know, once the real investigation begins. You wanted to be rid of me, didn't you?"

"You are talking arrant nonsense."

"It seems to fit the case. Who wanted me out of the way? You! Who wanted Julia out of the way? Drake and you. Looking forward, both of you, I suppose, to the days when there would be no need for secret meetings in Parsons Road. You can be together under the cloak of respectability, and perhaps no one will ever know what you had to do to reach that happy state."

"How dare you say such things?"

"I merely state the obvious."

"Charles, go away. I shall tell the truth when I am asked. I visited Julia. I went straight in and came straight out by way of the main staircase. I have never been to your rooms and I have no knowledge of poisons."

"No? Perhaps that is why you were so clumsy. Where did you get it? A little arsenic . . . They say you get it from fly papers. I believe there is a weed killer which can be very effective."

"Please go away."

"In my own time. Was that what you were planning in Number 12 Parsons Road? Did Nanny give her darling a few hints? Perhaps she provided the fly papers . . . or the weed killer? Nannies are so full of unexpected wisdom."

"Go away! Go away!" I cried.

"You are not being your usual clever self. Think what I know. I could put a rope round your neck, my sweet Lenore . . . and perhaps one day your lover's too."

"I will listen to no more of this wicked talk."

"Well, I will say *au revoir*. I will thank you for your warm welcome and your lavish hospitality. I shall be back to see you, Lenore. Who knows, we may be able to work something out together."

Trembling with apprehension, I shut the door after him and sank down, covering my face with my hands. I wanted to shut out all thought of him. I wanted to forget this shocking tragedy which threatened Drake and me . . . and everyone connected with us.

I did not trust Charles. There were secrets in his eyes. I knew that he would have no compunction in destroying me.

* * *

I awoke in the morning to a feeling of dread. I was so pleased Katie was now in Paris. At least I did not have to worry about her.

I knew that questions would be asked. I knew, too, that there was a great deal of gossip. The servants looked at me almost furtively, as though they were summing up the situation and finding me the centre of the storm.

There is little our servants do not know about us. They are like private detectives . . . aware of every movement we make, ears strained for revealing conversations; and there is communication between the houses of friends whose servants are acquainted with each other.

It was well known that Drake and Julia had not got on well together. Many an outburst must have been overheard; and since the musical evening everyone was aware of my friendship with Drake.

The most sensational inferences were always put on these matters. I could sense that between them all, they had come to the conclusion that Drake and I were lovers whose aim it was to get rid of Julia. So Julia had died. True, she had taken drink which was meant for her brother, but nevertheless she had died and that was exactly what they believed Drake and I wanted.

The inevitable questions were asked. A man in a dark grey suit came to the house with another. They were police officers.

I was asked a great many questions. I had seen Julia on the day of her death. I had called in unexpectedly. I had spent a little time with her. How had she been? Very much as she usually was, I told them. She had not been drinking on that occasion? Not enough to make her intoxicated. We had spoken together quite rationally. What was the subject of our discourse? I knew I must be truthful. I said: "She was considering divorcing her husband. I had suggested that she should make an effort to save her marriage."

"You were very good friends with both Mr. and Mrs. Aldringham?"

"Yes. She and I were brought up together, and we had both known Mr. Aldringham during our childhood."

"I see, I see," said the man, smiling discreetly. "And you were equally friendly with both of them?"

"I . . . I was friendly with both of them."

"Had you at any time been engaged to Mr. Aldringham?"

"No."

"Had there been any understanding between you?"

I hesitated.

"There was," he said. "Yet he married this lady who has met this untimely and unfortunate death. It was a surprise to you that he should do so?"

"I knew that they were friends."

He nodded.

"I don't think there is anything more we have to say to you just now, Mrs. Sallonger. I have no doubt we shall be calling back."

When they had gone Grand'mère insisted that I should lie down. She made me drink one of her cordials, and she sat by my bed. "Just till you sleep," she said coaxingly.

As if I could sleep!

* * *

I was trying to rest when I heard the sound of raised voices coming from below. I lay listening for a moment and then got up and went to the door. They were coming from the reception room. The door must be open.

I hurried down and went in. I thought I was dreaming. Grand'mère was standing there, dismayed and defiant, two angry red spots of colour on her cheeks and her eyes blazing with fury. But it was not Grand'mère who startled me—for her companion was the Comte.

There was silence as I entered. He came towards me, smiling almost suavely as though it were the most natural thing in the world that he should be there.

"The Comte de Carsonne!" I cried. "What are you doing in London?"

"Please not so formal, Lenore," he replied. "And I am in London to see you." His eyes went to Grand'mère briefly as he added: "And I was determined to."

He took my hands and I felt faint with relief and a ridiculous lightheartedness. For one glorious moment my fears and uncertainties seemed to vanish. There was only one thing I could think of: He was here and he had come to see me.

"You are well," he said holding my hand and looking into my face anxiously.

"We have had some trouble here."

"That is what I have been saying," said Grand'mère tersely. "And we do not want to add to it." She went on defiantly. "I have been telling Monsieur le Comte de Carsonne that you have no time just now to receive acquaintances."

"Yes," said the Comte sadly, "Madame has been telling me that I shall not be welcome here."

"We have enough trouble," said Grand'mère. "My granddaughter should be resting." She turned to me. "You have a great deal on your mind. That is why I am telling Monsieur le Comte that you could not see him."

"So," he put in lightly, "you came down in the nick of time to prevent my being ordered to leave."

"Grand'mère," I said. "I wish to speak to the Comte."

She was silent and I felt very sad to go against her wishes which I knew so well were all for my good. I knew how she cared for me and how she feared this man was going to do me some harm. But I had to talk to him . . . alone. I had a feeling that he could help me in some way. I did not know how. But he emanated strength and just to be with him gave me comfort.

"Please, Grand'mère . . . I shall be all right. I promise you."

She looked at me helplessly and shrugged her shoulders. Then she turned and threw a venomous look at the Comte.

"Don't be long," she said pleadingly.

"I won't," I said.

The Comte bowed to her as she went out.

"She does not like me," he said ruefully.

"She has heard stories of you."

"Of me? I was a child when she went away from the place."

"She has heard stories of your family and she thinks you are like them."

"The sins of the fathers," he murmured. "But here I am. I have defeated the dragon . . . temporarily . . . and reached you."

"How long have you been in London?"

"One hour."

"So you came straight to me." It was absurd to feel so happy. Nothing had changed . . . only the fact that *he* was here.

I had not realized until that moment how deeply he affected me.

"I left Paris soon after you did. I had to return to Carsonne. Raoul had an accident. He fell off his horse."

"Raoul! Is he all right?"

"It turned out to be not so serious as they thought. He is recovering. I came back to see you and Mademoiselle Cassandra had much to tell me."

"I see. So you know . . ."

"I read in the press. This politician's wife—she is related to you."

"We were brought up together. You know the story of the Sallongers and the St. Allengères."

"There is much I wish to know. I am going to help you."

"What can you do?"

"I shall find some way. What has happened so far?"

"They are looking for Julia's murderer."

"And they suspect . . . ?"

"I was one of the last to see her alive. It was her brother who found her. He came to his room and she was dead having drunk the sherry which had been intended for him."

"And he has his enemies?"

"Apparently."

"And you were one of these?"

"He accused me of being Julia's husband's mistress."

He raised his eyebrows. "And were you?"

"Of course not."

"I am glad of that. I should have been very angry with you if it had been true."

"Please don't be flippant. I cannot endure that. I feel far from flippant."

"This Charles," he said, "he was what you call the great lover?"

"You mean, did he have many love affairs? I think he had something of a reputation for that. He and his wife saw each other rarely. He married her for her money and they agreed to live separate lives."

"Perhaps this was a *crime passionnel*. Do you know any of his mistresses?"

"I know little of his private life. But there was a woman . . ."

"Ah, one you know."

"I heard she visited him. Her name was Madalenna de' Pucci. I have a picture of her. We were taken together at a function."

"I should like to see it. Perhaps *she* knows something of this little matter. It would be worth while finding out and asking."

"I don't think we should find her. She was here . . . some time ago. She may have gone back to Italy."

"So she is Italian. They are a very passionate people. Where is the picture? Shall we see it?"

"Stay here. I will get it."

I was astounded at the effect the picture had on him.

"Madalenna de' Pucci!" he said. "What an outstandingly beautiful woman."

I felt angry. I took the picture from him but he took it back and continued to gaze at it.

"You are clearly impressed by her," I said coldly.

"Yes . . . impressed. Madalenna de' Pucci. I think I may have met her in France."

"I daresay she is a much travelled woman. She was here with her brother . . . on business."

"Did you meet the brother?"

"No . . . no. He was travelling . . . in the Midlands, I think. She was waiting for him in London."

"Tell me more of Madalenna de' Pucci."

"Do you really find her so interesting?"

"Immensely so."

"I first met her when there was an accident outside The Silk House. Her carriage was overturned and she sprained her ankle. She came to the house and stayed a few days."

"When was that?"

"It was just after I was married."

"So your husband was alive then?"

"He died soon after."

"You say she stayed in the house with you?"

"Yes, for a few days. She made a great impression on Charles . . . as she obviously has on you."

"She is one to make an impression. Go on."

"Well, Charles was very taken with her. I remember he, with my husband, went to London for the day on business and during that day her brother sent the carriage for her. She was to go back to London as they were leaving for Italy immediately."

"And you say your husband died soon after that?"

"Very shortly after. I forgot all about Madalenna de' Pucci then."

"Naturally. And your husband was found shot, you say."

"In the forest, yes."

"With his own gun?"

"Well, with one of the guns from the gun room."

"And then she returned to London . . . not long ago."

"Yes, Charles met her in the street by chance."

"Fortuitous, eh?"

"He was delighted."

"I can understand that, cannot you?"

"He was attracted by her as you obviously are."

He smiled as though well pleased. He could not keep his eyes from the picture.

"How far did this affair between Charles and the beautiful lady go?"

"I don't know. Julia did mention that she had been at the house to visit him. His rooms could be reached by a rather private staircase . . . a back staircase which led only to them."

"So there were two ways to the rooms?"

"Exactly. The rooms were at the end of the first floor corridor. There was a door, I believe, which opened into the sitting room and the back staircase stopped at the dressing room door. I had never been on the staircase but Julia told me about it when Charles went there after his house was burned. She was saying how private he could be."

"So his house was burned down?"

"Oh yes. He had a narrow escape. He would have been burned to death if his valet had not come back unexpectedly early. He had been drinking heavily, I think . . . and that was probably why he was trapped."

"How dramatic! And this poisoned wine . . . that was intended for him. Does it not seem strange that he should have been almost burned to death and then shortly after there should be this attempt to poison him?"

"You think the burning of the house was deliberately planned?"

He looked steadily at me and lifted his shoulders.

I said slowly: "It is like a pattern. There was my husband. I never really believed he killed himself. There was no reason. It was very strange because there was a man . . . and that was in Italy . . ."

"Tell me."

I reminded him about Lorenzo who had gone into the streets of Florence wearing my husband's opera cloak and hat and had been stabbed to death. "And then . . . when we came home Philip died."

The Comte was thoughtful. "This is interesting. This Lorenzo could have been mistaken for your husband. Then soon after he is shot. This Charles . . . he is nearly burned to death and saved by his valet. Then he could have been poisoned and is saved by his sister who is killed instead of him. Does it not strike you as strange, Lenore?"

"It is very mysterious."

"Now what I want to hear is about your politician."

I told him about our childhood meeting and how we later became good friends.

"How good friends?"

"Rather special good friends."

"And he was in love with you?"

I nodded.

"And you?"

"I thought it would be good for me . . . and for Katie . . . not to be alone."

"My poor Lenore, so you were lonely."

"No . . . no. I had my grandmother. I had my daughter. I had good friends but . . ."

"And the thriving business. Yes, you had much. But you thought this Drake could make you happier. But he married Julia . . . and you were hurt and then you came to France with your father . . . and I found you. It is all becoming very clear to me. I am a little jealous of this Drake."

"Please, this is too serious a matter for meaningless gallantry."

"Is that how you regard me . . . as a flippant gallant?"

"Where are you staying?" I asked.

"At the Park Hotel."

"And you are . . . comfortable?"

"I do not know yet. I took my room . . . I leave my bags and I come at once to you."

"It was good of you."

"I will go now. I will see you soon. Do not fret. This will pass. The truth will be discovered."

"I appreciate your coming," I said.

"But of course I came."

He took my hand and kissed it.

When he had gone I realized that he had taken the photograph with him, and that took away the pleasure I had had in seeing him again.

Depression descended on me once more.

* * *

How long the days were! I seemed to be walking about in a dream. I was deeply apprehensive.

I had visitors—steely-eyed men who hid their suspicion under cool politeness. The endless questions began again. I could see that they were trying to trap me into betraying something which would assure them of my guilt.

I wondered how long it would be before they came to a definite conclusion.

I believed Drake was undergoing the same sort of interrogation. The papers announced that the police were continuing with their enquiries. There was an account of Drake's career, of his marriage to Julia, one of the Sallongers, it was stated, a member of the silk manufacturing family; Mr. Charles Sallonger was the one who had revolutionized the silk industry by putting on the market one of the finest silks ever known. There were accounts of how I had married Philip Sallonger who had shot himself shortly after the marriage. They had cast me in a very dramatic role—a woman whose husband had killed himself almost immediately after the marriage must be a *femme fatale*.

People paused to look at the salon as they passed. I did not go out during the day. It was too embarrassing to do so.

It was comforting to know that Katie was not here. She would be completely ignorant of what was going on and that was how I wanted it to be.

I did not know what would become of me, but I had been made to feel that I was under suspicion. I thanked God for Grand'mère as I had so many times in my life. If anything should happen to me she would look after Katie as well as could be possible in the circumstances. So would Cassie and the Countess. I wished they were both with us now, but I must rejoice that Katie was in their care.

Sometimes I found myself thinking of the Comte. I kept going over in my mind that moment when he had entered the room. What joy that had brought me! I had let my feelings for him go too far. I had pretended that this was not so—but of course I was wrong. I had betrayed myself to myself in those few moments.

I wished I had stayed in France. I wished I had had the courage to continue to see him. Then I should not have been here when this frightening thing had happened. But when I had seen him and learned that he had come to England to see me—in spite of Grand'mère's disapproval of him—that wild joy had temporarily obliterated everything else and really explained my feelings towards him—and there was no point in denying them.

But he had disappointed me, as I should have known he always would. He could not be faithful even for a short while. While he was saying he had come to see me, he was so taken with the picture of the beautiful Italian that he had forgotten me and my predicament in his admiration for her.

And he had taken the picture.

It was a strange coincidence that he should have known her, but then he was a much travelled man and he had lived on the borders of Italy and would doubtless have been in that country often. They must have met at some gathering for he had recognized her at once—and from that moment it had seemed that the picture obsessed him.

That was how it would always be with him. I had been a fool to let myself dream dreams which had no foundation in reality.

Grand'mère was right. What would it mean with him? A few weeks of happiness . . . and then he would make the excuses . . . oh, very gallantly, of course, very suavely—and then off on the next pursuit.

I had not seen him for four days. Why did he not call? He had said he would come and see me . . . and he had been near.

I must forget him. But how could I?

I felt a kind of obsession. I had to see him. I had to tell him that I was hurt because he had not come to see me as he had promised. It was a humiliating thing to do, but I couldn't help it. I had to know.

It was dusk. I put on my outdoors clothes and went out. It was not far to the Park Hotel. I slipped in through the swing doors and approached the desk.

"Yes, Madam?" said the clerk.

"I wanted to know if the Comte de Carsonne is in?"

The man looked at me in surprise. "Madam, the Comte left some days ago."

"Oh," I said faintly. "I see."

He consulted the book. "Yes, he left on the afternoon of the 14th."

It was the day after I had seen him. He had taken the picture and gone back . . . without even telling me that he was going. He must have gone straight back to the hotel after leaving me and made plans for departure.

I felt desperately unhappy.

It is typical of him! I told myself angrily. But anger did not help me. I felt lost, bewildered, and the clouds of apprehension which had been hanging over me so long seemed heavier and closer than ever. I had never felt so wretched in my life.

* * *

Tension was mounting. I endured more visits and more questions. I felt they were closing in on me. I wondered what Drake was feeling.

There was speculation in the press. It was thought that the police would soon be making an announcement. That, I presumed, meant an arrest. Would it be Drake, the husband? Husbands are always suspects on such occasions. Could it be Lenore Sallonger—the "mysterious widow," they were calling me—the famous dressmaker whose husband had committed suicide? I was tired of it . . . tired of it all.

And so it went on.

Grand'mère and I would sit together in the evenings, not bothering to light the gas. We sat in the dark, holding hands sometimes. She, too, had never been so frightened and wretched in her life.

We did not speak of the trouble. Neither of us had anything more to say. She would dwell on the past and tell me little incidents from my childhood, and then suddenly her voice would break and she would be unable to go on.

I used to let my mind wander back to those days in France. I thought of the *château* and wondered what he was doing now and whether he had been successful in his search for Madalenna. I tried to tell myself that it was for the best that I should learn how he was before I made a fool of myself. Thinking of him was painful so I tried to think of Drake.

Grand'mère, as she often did, seemed to read my thoughts.

"When this is all over," she said, adding firmly: "as it will be . . . Drake will be free. In time . . ."

"I don't want to think of that, Grand'mère."

"When the present is hard to bear it is well to look ahead. Trouble doesn't last forever. This time next year . . . He is a good man, Lenore, and good men are scarce. He loves you. I know he does. He was rash. He should have spoken about his suspicions of your father. It was foolish of him but we all do foolish things at times. *Mon Dieu,* poor man, he has paid for his folly. But the days will come when he is free . . . and then . . ."

"Grand'mère, please don't talk of it. I could not marry Drake."

"That's nonsense, child. He loves you. He would be the best of husbands. You have suffered a great deal. Philip was good . . . you could have been so happy with him. You must think no more of the Comte. He is no good to you and no good to any woman."

"I am not sure of anything, Grand'mère."

"Of course you are not. This is too close. But when it is over, Drake will be waiting . . . and this will seem like a nightmare."

I did not answer. It was no use trying to explain my feelings to Grand'mère. I was not even sure of them myself.

* * *

Then the miracle happened.

"New developments in the Aldringham case," said the headlines. "The police are anxious to meet a woman who visited the house on several occasions. They believe she could help them with their enquiries."

Two weeks passed, during which there was no mention of the case.

I was not now troubled by callers who wanted me to answer questions. It almost seemed as though the case had been set aside.

Then came that wonderful day when the Comte returned to London. He came to the salon and said he wished to see me . . . alone.

He managed to evade Grand'mère and when I heard that he was waiting in the reception room I wanted to refuse to see him. How dared he return casually like this after he had left so abruptly! Grand'mère was right. I should not see him. But of course I went down.

There he was suave as ever, smiling, taking my hand, kissing it in the courtly way which I had always found so enchanting.

I said: "So you are back in London?"

"It would appear so," he said, his eyes mocking—just as they always had during our meetings in France; no one would have thought that I was a woman with a possible charge of murder hanging over me.

"I trust you have had a good stay in France."

"Most profitable."

"And you were successful in your search for Madalenna de' Pucci?"

"Very successful. I could not have guessed how pleasing it would be."

"Congratulations."

"Enough," he said. "I have something to tell you which will be of great interest to you."

"Regarding you and this lady?"

"Indeed it concerns her . . ."

I thought: Oh no. He is just being cruel. He knows my feelings. I have betrayed them. He knows a great deal about women. He just wants to torment me. Charles first . . . now him.

"It also concerns you . . . deeply," he went on. "Shall we be serious? This is a very serious matter."

"About you and Madalenna de' Pucci. I don't . . ."

"It concerns you, too. Come, sit down, so that I can see you. I have been working hard on your behalf. It saddened me to see you as you were . . . and as you are now. So I determined to make you as you were before. So I went to work. First let us take the beautiful Italian. I told you I had met her before."

"Yes, you did mention that. You took the picture of her."

"It was also a picture of you, was it not? Now listen to me. I was greatly interested to see the lady because I knew her . . . but not as Madalenna de' Pucci. That, I have proved now, was not her real name."

"Who is she then?"

"She is, in a manner of speaking, a connection of yours. Her name is Adèle St. Allengère."

I stared at him in astonishment.

"You see it was too fortuitous. People are never careful enough.

There are these little slip-ups and these result in the big scheme falling to the ground. You have seen something of life in Villers-Mûre and in Carsonne. We are a fiery people. You know of the feud between my house and that of St. Allengère. Vendetta. It is a common word on the border because of our volatile neighbours. We love and hate . . . vehemently. There is much to tell you. I began to piece things together when you told me so much, and because I did not wish to see you unhappy living under a cloud of suspicion as you would have done perhaps all your life, I determined to unravel the mystery. Also, it intrigued me. I have put the confession in the hands of the French police who are now in touch with those in this country. Soon the mystery will be revealed but I wished to tell you first."

"You are keeping me in suspense."

"You deserve it for thinking I had left you to go in search of the beautiful Italian. You did believe that, did you not? And it was true. But not for the reason you had decided on. You were most displeased."

"Please tell me what all this is about?"

"It is all about Vendetta and a wicked old man who is now considerably chastened. You were right. I had gone back to France to look for Adèle St. Allengère. I was determined to have the whole story from her. It is not difficult for me. I have many people working for me. I told you we were feudal in our part of the world. My word is law and if I say 'Find Adèle St. Allengère,' she will be found."

"I still can't understand what all this is about."

"I am telling it badly. I will begin at the beginning. Two brothers went to France when their father was alive. They were Charles the elder, and Philip, who was to become your husband. Charles was the lover of pleasure. Philip was seriously interested in the business of producing silk. They visited Villers-Mûre where they were accepted as distant connections of the family . . . the Huguenot branch. The old man—stern bigot that he was—was not pleased about this, and the displeasure of the Catholic St. Allengères towards the Huguenots has lasted for three hundred years. But they were members of the family; moreover he wanted to know how the silk industry was progressing in England. So they were accepted into the house. He saw that Philip was the one who cared about the business. Charles he had dismissed as no good.

"Now, he had had a group of men working for some time on a

special kind of silk which was to be different from any other kind which had ever been produced. It was very secret. The old man's granddaughter Heloïse was being courted by one of the men who was working on this project so that she was aware of what was going on and he gave her access to the particular section where the research work was in progress. This would have been forbidden had it been known. Charles Sallonger was a very plausible young man, handsome too, apparently; he was different from anyone Heloïse had ever known before. She fell in love with him. She must have talked to him about the secret work which was being done and he prevailed on her to show him the formula. This, poor lovesick girl, she did. Then . . . the brothers departed. Heloïse realized that she had—as they say—given herself to a philanderer. More than that she had betrayed her family's secret to him. When it was learned that the English had put this special silk on the market and claimed credit for having discovered the method of producing it, the St. Allengère household was in turmoil. Unable to bear the shame of having betrayed her family to a false lover, Heloïse drowned herself in the river which wound its way through the grounds of the house. She left a note, however, in which she explained what she had done, but she omitted to mention her lover's name. As Charles had appeared to be indifferent to business, it was naturally concluded that Philip was the thief and the false lover. You now know something of what the old man is like. He demanded vengeance and set out to get it."

"So Philip was to have been murdered . . ."

"Yes. The first attempt went wrong—in the case of the Italian Lorenzo. The overturned carriage was a way of getting into the house and when she was there Adèle with her servant stole the gun from the gun room. They took it with them when they left. Then one of Alphonse's hired killers was commanded to lure Philip into the forest and shoot him. This is what he did making it appear suicide."

"It is all becoming horribly clear."

"Then, recently, the fact that Charles was the culprit was revealed."

"I know," I cried, "I told René in the graveyard."

"So it was decided that Charles should pay the full penalty. Adèle was despatched to England once more. She had ill luck from her point of view because the fire she started did not have the desired effect on account of the valet's returning early. Adèle had to try again."

"So she poisoned the wine. How can you be sure of this?"

"I had it from Adèle's own lips."

"Why did she tell you?"

"When I saw the picture I recognized her immediately. I guessed she was up to some mischief here. I was intrigued by the story of the unfortunate Lorenzo and the fact that shortly after Adèle's visit, your husband died. Then, of course, Charles's life was in danger twice after her visits. I know the way the St. Allengères work. I knew she was up to no good."

"Then you have no proof."

"But I have. I have Adèle's written confession."

"Do you mean she gave it to you?"

"I am very determined when I decide on a certain action. I was sure that the St. Allengères had had a hand in this. It is just the way the old man would work. I will not be over modest. We de la Tours have ruled our neighbourhood for years. In the old days we were all powerful. Times have changed but customs cling. I wanted Adèle brought to me and my wishes were obeyed."

"You mean you held her prisoner?"

"I did. I demanded the truth. I let her think that I knew a great deal more than I did. And while I had her there in my castle I went to see the old man." His eyes glistened. "It was a great occasion for me. Face to face with the old villain himself. We were two titans . . . though you will doubtless think me immodest for saying it. I come from a long line of ruling Comtes and he was the head of the St. Allengères who hold the none-less-kinglike sway in their little terrain. Villers-Mûre is like a little state within the bigger state of Carsonne; but it is independent of Carsonne . . . like Burgundy and France of old. That is one of the reasons why he hates my family. We have always been determined that he shall not encroach further."

"So you revelled in the confrontation."

"I did. He was speechless with rage. I accused him of murder. I told him he had broken one of the commandments . . . the most important of them all. He had sold his soul for Vendetta. I explained the innocence of Philip whom he had killed, for his was the ultimate responsibility and those who had performed the deed were acting only on his orders. He was the one who would have to face his Maker. He shouted that these men had come to his house as guests and one of them had replied to his hospitality by stealing an important formula and seducing his granddaughter. The righteous God would call that justice. The French had done all the work on an important project and the perfidious English had stolen the secret when it was on the point of perfection, seducing a daughter of the house of St. Allengère in order to steal it. The punishment was deserved. I had to agree with what he said. It was the kind of action the Comtes of Carsonne would have taken.

" 'But,' I pointed out, 'you killed an innocent man, and for that you will have to answer in Heaven.' He wouldn't believe it until I told him that Adèle had confessed all to me. He shouted at me, abusing me, accusing me of seducing Adèle. It was very strange that a man incapable of love will look for it in everything that happens. I left him raging, but he was frightened. I had seen his face grow ashen at the thought of Heaven's revenge. He sees himself burning in Hell in spite of what he would call his good life and all because he has committed the one great sin of murder."

He paused and I could see how he had relished that interview.

"That night," he went on, "he was taken ill. He had a stroke. He had never been so shocked in his life. He lived according to his own rules and he would tell you he was a just man. Sin had to be paid for and he was the judge of us all—a sort of Commissioner under God, but only just. He had pictured his God of vengeance with the heavenly choir singing praises of the virtuous Alphonse St. Allengère—and hell fire for the rest of us. And now he had committed a mortal sin. He had caused an innocent man to be murdered. There would be no compromise. In spite of a life of impeccable virtue which had brought misery to thousands, he himself was among the sinners. It had been too much for him. He might have died with his sin upon him. Now he was fighting desperately to regain his old standing with the Almighty. I have hinted that we shall expect him to expiate his sin. The change in him was a miracle in itself."

"You are gloating over him."

"Of course. This is the justice in which he has always believed. We shall use his fears to good advantage. He is to take full responsibility for what has happened . . . for the death of your husband . . . for the death of Julia Aldringham. He is responsible. Those who committed the crime are merely his puppets."

"Will that exonerate them?"

"Not entirely. But mercy will be shown to them, I am sure. I do not know what will happen . . . whether Adèle will be brought to England to stand trial or not. Perhaps so. Whether they will insist on the old man's revealing the name of the man who shot your husband . . . that I cannot tell. All I know at the moment is that that is the story and that you are no longer under suspicion . . . nor is Mr. Drake Aldringham. Your police know of this. Perhaps the whole story will be disclosed . . . perhaps not. It may be that they will just allow the details to be told which seem right to them. As for Monsieur Charles, I think he may be in trouble. There could well be a case brought by the House of St. Allengère concerning the theft of the silk formula . . . which could plunge him into financial disaster . . . heavy damages and so on. Who can say at this stage. But it will be no more than he deserves for it was his action which started this murderous train of events. But that is not our concern. Have I made you happy now?"

"Just now I am bewildered. I do not know what to believe."

"Do you mean that you doubt my words?"

"Of course not, but it is bewildering to learn so much in such a short time."

"It took little time to tell but a long time to act out. So you are very grateful to me, eh?"

"If . . . this is all true . . ."

"Have I not told you?"

"Yes . . . yes . . . but . . ."

"Well?"

"I don't know how to express my thanks for all the trouble you have taken."

"I will tell you how."

I looked at him questioningly.

"Very soon," he went on, "I shall show you."

I thought of Grand'mère and her warning against this man.

I said: "I want to tell my grandmother what you have told me. She has suffered a great deal of anxiety. I must tell her at once."

"Yes, you must tell the good dragon. Tell her what I have discovered. She breathes fire every time my name is mentioned, I know. It would be pleasant if she did not regard me with such animosity. Please tell her what I have told you. Make her see that the trouble is past."

"I must go to her at once."

"That is what you wish, so be it. Tomorrow some of what I have told you will be confirmed and I shall come and see you again. I can see the headlines . . . 'The Silk Vendetta' . . . what a story for them. *Au revoir* then, Madame Sallonger, till tomorrow."

* * *

Grand'mère was incredulous.

"Do you believe this?" she asked.

"He assured me it is true. He has Adèle's confession. It fits in with everything."

"It may be that he tells this story to delude you."

"Why should he?"

"Don't forget I was brought up in the shadow of his family. I know the de la Tours . . . all of them. In the old days they were often at war with the kings of France. They ruled their land as despotically as ever the kings did theirs. They want something and they think it is their right to take it. And your grandfather is such another. Ruthless, demanding vengeance and turning others into murderers to suit his own ends. If it is true what you tell me . . ."

"Grand'mère, I feel it must be true."

"Then you and Drake are free. He . . . the Comte knows that. Why should he do this? He knows about you and Drake, doesn't he?"

"He wants to see justice done."

"The de la Tours always had one motive—to serve themselves. He must be very interested in you."

"I think he was intrigued when he saw the picture of Adèle and wanted to find out why she was posing as someone else."

She looked at me shrewdly. "Drake Aldringham is the one for you," she said firmly.

"After all this I feel we could not be together. He might feel the same."

"No, no. He loves you. He will give you everything to make you happy. He is a good man—a man you can trust. You would always be sure of him. The best thing in life is peace of mind. He would give you that."

Would he? I wondered. If I married Drake I would always feel that some part of me was at Carsonne. That man had laid a spell on me and nothing would ever be the same again.

"I know you are right in a way . . ." I said.

"Then be sensible."

"It wouldn't be fair to Drake."

"Tell me the truth. Surely you have always been able to do that with me. You are bemused by Gaston de la Tour. He seems to you a figure of power and strength; and he offers excitement . . . romance, I suppose. I know his reputation. It is the same as that of his forebears. They were never faithful husbands. But he would never marry you. The de la Tours have always married those of their own kind. He would tire of you quickly. It is their way of life. For centuries they have lived like feudal kings . . . petty monarchs even when there were no longer kings of France. Come out of your day dream. Drake is waiting for you. I know a good man when I see one and Drake Aldringham is one."

I did not answer. Common sense told me that she was right.

* * *

Later that day the news was out. The mystery was solved. "The Silk Vendetta" proclaimed the headlines. "The long standing feud between two branches of the same family. The story of Sallon Silk which should have been St. Allengère Silk."

There was speculation everywhere. Sallongers would be in trouble. This would ruin them. The French firm would demand crippling damages; but the main interest was in the solution of the mystery.

Drake came to see me. I was dreading the meeting.

He took both my hands and looked earnestly at me. He was like a man who has suddenly cast off a crippling burden.

"I feel free, Lenore," he said. "I can't get used to it."

But I was not free. I was caught up in a web from which I could not escape—a web which Gaston de la Tour had woven round me. I knew that I was foolish. I knew that a peaceful dignified life could lie ahead of me with Drake—but always my thoughts would be in Carsonne.

Drake went on: "This means so much to us, Lenore."

I was silent. I could not meet his eyes.

He said: "You don't want to marry me, do you? Is it this Comte? He went to a great deal of trouble. Are you going to marry him?"

"Marry him! He has never suggested such a thing. Drake, I'm sorry. I'm so fond of you, but I have a feeling that it would not be right. You made one mistake. You must not make another."

"With you, Lenore, I feel I could face anything. It won't be easy after all this. Even though one is shown not to be guilty it is never wholly accepted. Perhaps you will change your mind."

"Drake, please understand."

"I do understand. I know we should have a good life together."

"People would always remember that we had been suspected of being lovers while Julia was alive. They would always believe it of us. It would harm your career."

"We could live that down. We could fight together. I would get back everything I have lost . . . if only we were together."

I nodded. I thought perhaps I might.

* * *

The next day the Comte called. He took my hand and kissed it looking at me with that half mocking expression which I knew so well.

"So," he said, "the news is out. It made exciting reading. The whole of London is reading of the Silk Vendetta. How does it feel to be one of the central figures in such a story?"

"Embarrassing."

"Believe me, it will be forgotten in a few weeks. Something else will turn up and lo! . . . Who are these Sallongers? It will not be over for Monsieur Charles, of course. He will have to pay rather highly for his sins, I do believe. But why should we concern ourselves with that gentleman? I have come to tell you that I have decided to marry. I thought you should be the first to know."

I hoped I did not show my feelings. I was suddenly so wretched. I should have guessed, of course. It would be some member of the old French aristocracy . . . someone whose family had survived the holocaust of the Revolution as his had done.

"Yes," he went on. "Raoul has been very ill. He nearly died in that fall. It set me thinking. I used to feel I had done my duty by providing the heir. But the family needs more than one heir . . . life being so precarious."

"I see. So you have decided to marry again?"

He nodded. "We have always had marriages of convenience in our family. It was considered a duty. *Noblesse oblige* and that kind of thing. And now the time has come for me to contract such a marriage. I must first of all consult you."

"Why?"

"Because it concerns you, of course."

He put his arm about me and held me tightly against him. "What suits my convenience has always been my chief concern . . . and this would suit me very well. What do you say? Could you give up your great business interests to become the Comtesse de Carsonne? Could you change your modish style of life for one of feudal customs? It is no use saying No. I warn you in advance. I have promised Raoul that he shall have the company of the delectable Mademoiselle Katie each day. What do you say?"

"You are asking *me* . . ."

"Who else could possibly suit my convenience but the one who inspires me with emotions which I have never felt before? It is love, I suppose."

Waves of great joy swept over me. I felt so happy. But I thought: This can't be true.

"My dear one," he said, "you do not look overjoyed."

"I am too overjoyed to feel anything but shock."

"So I have your agreement?"

"You . . . you have made up your mind."

"How well you know me! You would not have been allowed to refuse. It is well to understand the man you are going to marry."

I laid my head against him and let myself become suffused with happiness.

"The good Grand'mère must be told," he said. "The *château* is vast. There will be room for her. She must be with you for I know what she means to you. Besides, with her I am not the chosen one. I look forward to skirmishes with that redoubtable lady. We have only one thing in common, she and I, but that is the most important thing in the world to us—our sweet Lenore. She will do her best to dissuade you, you know."

"I know."

"She will tell you that you are making a big mistake. You should take the virtuous Drake. You are going to a life which is different from anything you have known, with a man who is not of her choice. What shall you say, Lenore?"

"I shall say that is where I want to go . . . and what I will find will be what I could never have borne to miss."

"That is what I hoped to hear," he said. "Now let us go together and face the dragon."